Fog of War

Gold 1 Book 1

Forest Wells

This is a work of Fiction. Similarities to real people, places, or events are entirely coincidental.

Fog of War

Copyright © 2023 Forest Wells

Editors
Charlie Knight http://cknightwrites.com/
Edge of the World Editing https://www.fiverr.com/share/yp8yE0

Cover art by
Ilya Royz https://www.artstation.com/ilyar

Cover and Interior design by
Éric Desmarais http://www.EricDesmarais.ca

First Edition

Paperback: 978-1-7337124-4-6

Hardcover: 978-1-7337124-5-3

E-book: 978-1-7337124-6-0

To my father, mother, and brothers,
Your support keeps me sane through everything.

And to the victims of 9/11,
Without whom this book, and this author, would not exist.

Books by Forest Wells:

Luna's Journey
"Luna, The Lone Wolf"
"Blood of an Alpha"

Gold 1 series
"Fog of War"

Contents

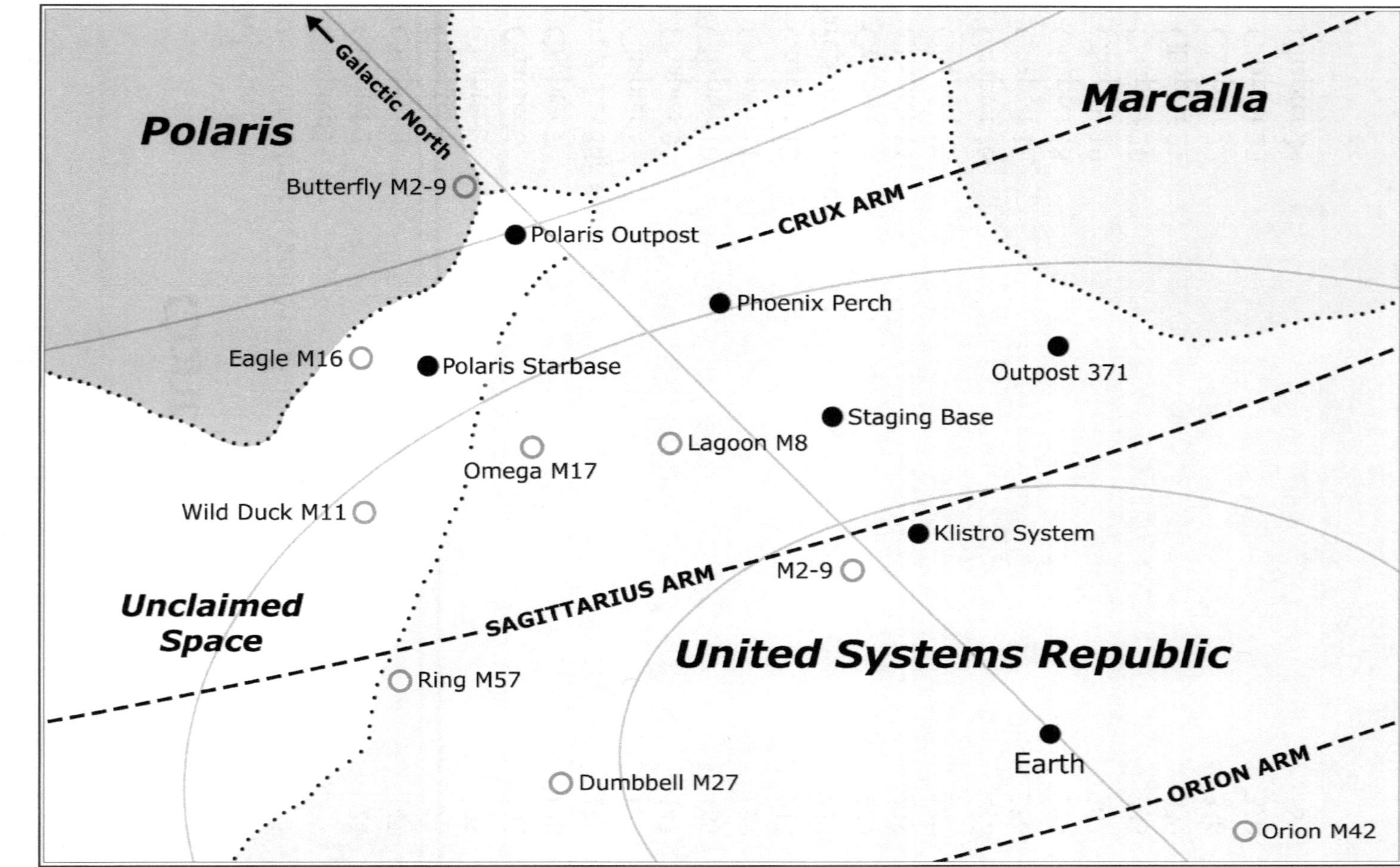

Polaris
Marcalla
Galactic North
Butterfly M2-9
Polaris Outpost
CRUX ARM
Phoenix Perch
Eagle M16
Polaris Starbase
Outpost 371
Staging Base
Omega M17
Lagoon M8
Wild Duck M11
Klistro System
SAGITTARIUS ARM
M2-9
Unclaimed Space
United Systems Republic
Ring M57
Earth
ORION ARM
Dumbbell M27
Orion M42

A Warning to my Readers:

Some elements within the story are graphic, and may be triggering to some people with emotional scars.

"War is the realm of uncertainty; three quarters of the factors on which action in war is based are wrapped in a fog of greater or lesser uncertainty. A sensitive and discriminating judgment is called for; a skilled intelligence to scent out the truth."

— Carl von Clausewitz

Prologue

More than likely.

Admiral Solez knew he should have pulled that asset sooner. Young Talbert's assertiveness had seen him quickly rise through the ranks of the enemy fleet, but the more Interstar rewarded him, the more eager he got. Some reports suggested he had begun to risk his cover. Now it would appear those efforts had gotten him killed. A waste of an asset, but perhaps it was just as well. At least that was one less thing to worry about.

He had enough on his plate.

Fifteen years of planning, building, and training for this moment were finally coming together. Soon, the Confederation of Polaris would be ready to rise from the false ashes of its assumed demise. Solez read the rest of the report one more time to reassure himself that things were indeed going well despite the one problem. There was more than the lost asset, but a quick skim suggested it was all trivial. Nothing worth the grand marshal's time.

Unfortunately, Admiral Solez didn't seem to be worth his time either. Whenever he asked the aide for an update, she could only check her screen and confirm that the grand marshal was still in conference.

That left the admiral with nothing to do but stare at the grey walls of the outer office, empty save for a large banner with the Polaris insignia; a dark-navy bear silhouette outlining the full constellation of Ursa Major with a bright star above the bear. To the side of that banner, a thin window allowed Admiral Solez to get a glimpse of the city far outside the base.

He had to shake himself to keep his emotions from taking over. He only allowed a moment to rub his wedding band. She'd told him to always remember, and he always had.

She had been among the volunteers. The brave men and women who gave their lives to protect those left behind. He hadn't been able to talk her out of it, but he could do his best to see that she, and they, would be able to rest in peace at last.

Assuming he ever got the chance to actually move things along.

The grand marshal had demanded an instant report, yet he'd spent the last half hour locked in the inner office arguing with... Solez didn't even know who. Some man he knew only as 'Multi-Step.' Being kept in the dark sent Solez past irritated headed for pissed off. Half of him wanted to barge in, deliver the report, and then leave so he could get on with the operation.

Yet he would have to bite his tongue now just like always. Technically, the grand marshal could see him killed for sneezing if he wanted. He never abused that power, but he had the right, which was enough for most men with any trace of intelligence. The rest, if they were lucky, found themselves stuck at low ranks with the worst jobs on the docket. The admiral had neither, so if he had to bite his tongue to keep his rank and position, he would.

At last, the doors to the main office opened. The grand marshal stormed out, only to stop with a hand on his hip when he saw Admiral Solez. The marshal wore a simple, clean, black suit and a blood-red tie with black lines. Every hair on his head was straight and blond – no grey allowed – but the man did have a slight belly bulge.

"This better be good news, Admiral," the marshal said.

So, it happened again. Admiral Solez knew better than to touch it. "It is, sir. Our agents report Operation Juno is progressing well. The Gold Group will be primed and ready for us."

"Gold Group? We got that lucky?"

"We did, sir."

"Even better. Though we may want to send some help along. Major Harlem shouldn't be underestimated."

"Covered, sir. I sent two of our best non-frigates with additional troops for the intercept."

Admiral Solez always had to swallow that one. Once they came out, it would be hard to hide who all the 'non-ships' really belonged to. The whole thing was a propaganda move, really. "Oh, we don't condone piracy." *Bullshit!* Solez started on those "non-ships" long before Polaris had to fake being destroyed by Marcalla. Their activities were more than condoned, they were ordered.

The grand marshal hummed with a devious smile. "Good. At least someone out there has some courtesy. Unlike a certain admiral I know."

This time, Admiral Solez couldn't leave it. Whoever this other admiral was, he wasn't a member of their own forces. The Polaris leadership had made a point of making sure all their assets went through him. That meant this other admiral was an outsider. Forget pissed off, the idea of someone separated from Polaris being so intimately involved, and thus out of their control, sent Solez's stomach into a knot.

"Who is this admiral, sir?" he asked without hesitation. "Why is he so important that you put up with him brushing you off like that?"

The grand marshal's body bounced in silent laughter while he thumped his hand on the admiral's shoulder. "He's a means to an end, Admiral. Too bad he knows it as well as we do. Still, even he doesn't know our real plan."

"But who *is* he, sir? Someone within Interstar?"

Now the marshal laughed loud enough to echo in the outer office. "Hardly. Let's just say he's a non-human that has been directly involved with Gold 1 on more than one occasion, sometimes without them knowing it."

Admiral Solez went blank while his mind decoded the message. The reference to a 'non-human' was an obvious clue. It didn't take long for him to whittle down the list to just one that would even consider taking part in their plan.

After that, Admiral Solez knew he wouldn't be sleeping well for a long time.

"You can't be serious," he said, not trying to hide his shock. "With respect, how can you work with the very people who destroyed our original colonies? To say nothing of dealing with the man who *led* those attacks."

"As I said, he is a means to an end. He'll accomplish what no one has before, and we'll help him. Then he'll help us get Marcalla and the United Systems Republic right where we want them."

"And then he'll stab us in the back."

"Of course he will. He's a fanatic who believes some nonsense about jantans being the supreme race in the galaxy. But that same belief will sow the seeds of his own demise."

Assuming he doesn't kill us in the process. Admiral Solez felt his military pride silence the comment, which he used to draw himself up in a show of confidence to his leader. *Kill us? Ha! Not a chance.* They were too well prepared now. Polaris wouldn't need to fake their destruction this time; they would be the aggressors. He would see Polaris make good on their promise to find justice for the fallen. For them, for her, and for the son who may yet see a nation safe at last, Admiral Solez would not allow them to fail.

The admiral rubbed his wedding band again while the grand marshal checked an ancient pocket watch. "From one brick wall to another," the grand marshal said. "I'll be out of touch for a while, Admiral. I expect you to handle things from here on out."

Admiral Solez offered a soft salute. "Yes, sir. I won't let you down, sir."

The Grand Marshal returned the salute then headed for the outer doors. Admiral Solez turned to catch him there. "If I may ask, sir, where will you be?"

"In conference with our dear command council."

"I thought President Markus was on his war tour."

"Wrong council, Admiral. I'm talking about the one that *doesn't* know what's going on."

Admiral Solez nodded with a devious smile all his own. Then he watched the most successful asset in Polaris' history walk out the door.

Part 1: Of Admirals and Marshals

Chapter 1

Foolish Orders

Major Jason Harlem could almost feel the heat from the PMM14, or P-mag, on his hip. Hours of shooting holograms had done little to cool his insides. So, he found himself in the mess hall trying a cup of Earl Grey tea. It was as much a joke as a drink choice, but it still failed. Much like his efforts with his superiors.

He'd spent his time on long range comms with Earth trying to convince them to send someone else. The lines had been silent for months, but that was more than enough time for the jantans to gather a force for their next assault. Based on recent deep scans, that's exactly what they were doing too. Sooner or later, this little outpost would be on the front lines of the latest 'Jantan War.' Yet, command seemed to be looking at recent events rather than their own intelligence. *A few months of silence, and suddenly command thinks Marcalla has given up? Yeah, right.*

It's not like he relished combat. Jason had buried a lot of friends and group members over the years. But that was also what had his chest hotter than the tea he now drank. The only way to put an end to it was to remain vigilant and ready for the next offensive. Interstar needed to have the best on the front lines to ensure civilian and soldier alike lived to see tomorrow. His group had proven their ability to do just that more times than he could count. Though not everyone had come back from those missions.

So where was his highly decorated group being sent now? Back to the inner worlds, to cover freighters traveling from one colony to another. A task so simple that a corvette would be enough. Okay two, but it's not like they got to shine on their own very often. Having his front-line group sent to do a job two such ships could handle in their sleep made the whole thing even more insulting.

Worse than that, a civilian councilman, a 'suit,' had written the orders. He didn't technically know that's what had happened, but the signs were all there. Signs purposely dropped by his superior to express his own displeasure at the source.

Suits couldn't give orders to the military officially, but General Carson had gotten his hands on the request, and it didn't take a genius to connect the dots. It had read, in part, 'specific protection should be arranged for a high-value civilian convoy to ensure the safe and efficient delivery of necessary civilian materials and personnel for necessary civilian endeavors.'

In other words, a suit has some pet project, good or bad being irrelevant, that needed protection, and they want the military to make a *show* of protecting it as a 'symbol to the civilians' and so on. It didn't matter what was really needed. Only that the flag be shown in strength.

It was a waste, it was foolish, it was nearly criminal, and it was beyond his control. He had his orders. He could only hope the lines would hold long enough for him to get there before the jantans broke through and threatened any more colonies.

Jason rubbed a heavy hand across his face. He gave a soft chuckle when he thought about the many who thought he was too thin to be a soldier. Even his mom, God rest her soul, used to joke about his face looking squished in on the sides. Some said his dark brown hair and eyes, along with his smooth features, helped balance that a bit. All he cared was that he had barely changed since the academy, at least physically. *Small favors.*

Those favors soured when the years caught up with him. His deep-blue uniform with silver sash made of three beveled lines had been soaked in blood more often than he cared to consider. The navy-colored rank tab on his shoulders and sleeves had two silver falcon wings with two mini suns in between them. The wings of command and the suns he defended, or so said the ethos. In practice, it reminded him of how much blood he'd seen over the years. Three shooting stars in front of a star-field background lay over his heart, the 'shield' of Interstar, though it may well have been a shield in one case, with his rank, name and pilot's wings above it. On his arm lay the only insignia he really drew pride in: a tricorn design of gold and black with a three-bar pyramid of gold in the middle. The design also held the group motto: First called, final star, we hold the line.

Jason's sigh was almost a growl as he held the back of his head. *'First called.' Yeah, to blasted corvette duty.* One hand went for the hilt of the combat knife in the middle of his back. He liked to keep it there so either hand could reach it at any given time, though right now, all he wanted to do was bash it on the table. It was better than thinking about the idiocy of his orders or the two times he'd used his officer blades for more than training and ceremonies.

He stared at his mug for a moment while the urge subsided, then downed the last of his tea before heading out. He dropped most of his thoughts as he passed through the door like discarding a jacket he no longer needed. Something he'd gotten too good at doing over the years.

Jason marched down the corridors as if in a hurry. In truth, he was trying to walk off the anger that killing holograms and drinking joke tea hadn't cured. About all he managed was to make his step barely audible on the metal floor. It and the walls were soft blue, though the walls were more a tint than a full color. It seemed the designers of Interstar bases, uniforms, and most ships had a love affair with the color. Didn't keep the place from feeling military, despite the oval shape of the corridors.

Jason tried using these thoughts to distract himself from his anger. When that didn't work, he tried clenching and relaxing his fists in a vain attempt to drop his emotions like he had his thoughts. It didn't help that he clipped his shoulder on one of the many support beams while trying to dodge an equipment trolley. The crewman tried to apologize, but Jason kept marching while he tried not to dig his fingernails into his palm.

He held the shoulder till it stopped throbbing during the lift ride to his quarters. He softly laughed when he thought about what he'd like to do if he were in the same room as his superiors. *Wonder how many would hit the deck if I pulled my P-mag on 'em.* He knew one wouldn't, but the others... *Might almost be worth it to see the looks on their faces. Almost.* At least the fantasy put the first dent in his frustration.

A dent was all it felt like as he marched down the corridor to his quarters. The main room was furnished with simple, violet chairs and a short couch crammed around a glass table all looking out a window with a blue-green planet just below. Not Earth, but the glow felt enough like it to help it feel like home. A tiny table with a food dispenser in the corner was currently dark like some forbidden land no one dared enter, much like his work desk nearby. Doors on the opposite side led to the bed he'd really like to drop into, assuming his emotions would let him. Since they currently wouldn't, he would have to settle for the large space his position afforded him. The quarters would normally be his alone, but he shared his with company that was welcome and requested by all parties involved. Once they were assigned to the same fighter, getting permission to share a room had been the easy part. Satisfying Interstar's regulations had not been.

One co-habitant, his comrade Sundale, sat just to the side of the door. He was biting an itch beneath his dark, sandy-gold fur that held the same color throughout. The only break in the gold was a white underside that extended up his front to the top of his muzzle, just touching his cheeks. The fox-looking holdren had all three tails sticking straight out in response to the itch. The rust-red tail tips, with matching bands below, would have made perfect warning beacons were they glowing. He sat on four legs and just a little taller than the largest of Great Danes. Despite knowing better, Jason couldn't help seeing the animal first. It made Sundale feel more pet than companion sometimes, which made yet another dent in his anger.

The dent grew into a real mood change as the doors closed behind him. The anger faded into simple frustration as Sundale stopped his biting to see who had entered. He ruffed, shook his head, then shifted to sit facing the newcomer.

"Who won this time?" Sundale asked. His voice was not so much nasal as it held just a touch of a higher pitch. Something apparently unique to him rather than the norm among holdrens.

Jason wished he could growl as he unbuckled his weapon belt. "I think the holograms did. That or command. I'm not sure which."

"Couldn't change their minds?"

"Nope. Worse yet is the orders came, unofficially of course, from a councilman. Not sure how Rickey found out, but I appreciate him telling me. At least I know it's beyond his control too. Unfortunately, that still means we're stuck on corvette duty."

Sundale only flicked an ear and returned to his itch. Jason, meanwhile, nearly ripped his knife harness out of the buckles. He tossed it and the weapon belt onto the couch, again wishing for the chance to vent on someone real.

He flinched when a sharp yip came from the couch. His weapons clattered to the floor as the dull orange shoulders, back, and neck of the other holdren rose above the top of the couch.

Much like Sundale, the rest of his mother's fur was sandy-gold with a white underside, although her white covered her entire face up to between her ears. Grey covered the tip of her muzzle and chin, though it just barely touched her whiskers and didn't touch the top of her muzzle at all. Then the grey changed into a thick pattern of darker grey flecks that covered her face and throat which enhanced the glare she was casting at him. It was only then Jason noticed three red tail tips, void of the red bands only males had, hanging off the side of the couch.

"Sorry, Yarain," he said. "You all right?"

"I'm fine," she said in an even tone that betrayed no emotion. Not robotic, just level and always soft, gentle, and smooth in a way that left Jason looking for a British accent she didn't have. She also didn't expand on her answer which, as Jason had learned, *was* a norm among holdrens.

Combined with her glare, it forced him to be sure he had all the info he needed. "You sure? That yip didn't sound fine."

"I *was* sleeping."

"And now I feel worse."

Yarain gave a set of short, repeated ruffs that were the Holdren form of laughter. A sound Jason had yet to find degrees in. He knew panting was sometimes also laughing, but he still didn't know the difference between a chuckle and busting a gut. If only holdrens smiled. At least then he'd have something to work from.

"Don't worry, Jason," she said. "I don't bite unless threatened."

"But she can kill whole herds with one glare," Sundale said.

They may not smile, but they can't keep it from slipping into their voices. Despite the lack of facial expressions, Jason could hear the matching emotion in both of them. Their joy put him at ease at last. He did some laughing of his own when Yarain curled her lips in what even he could tell was a teasing snarl. Sundale countered by giving an equally fake cower and a pathetic whimper that sounded more like a pained meow.

Jason laughed as the holdrens continued an energetic fake duel. Times like these made it hard to see them as anything more than foxes, which had almost been a problem. They themselves said they were wild animals first. Wild animals usually run on instinct. Something that could be a problem for a mother and son fighting on the same battlefield. Regulations written in desperate times meant it could still be done, but many joked that a cadet had an easier time getting a private dinner with a marshal. Thankfully, they had managed to convince every superior they needed to. Over the years, they proved multiple times they were more than capable of maintaining composure when shit hit the fan.

Though right now, Jason failed to keep his as the snarls and whimpers got sadder by the second. Each one put another dent in his frustration, and a chuckle in his gut. It was a good thing too since his wrist computer, or wrist-com, beeped to announce the arrival of a new message. He expected some dry conversation with who-knows-who. Instead, he saw it was from the Personal Artificial Intelligence Combat Computer Assistant, PAICCA. He tapped the button to receive, and the computer program spoke in a non-robotic, male voice, "Major, the updated mission profile has been received."

Jason grumbled as Yarain dove at Sundale so they could trade more pathetic paw swipes and weak bites at each other. "Why am I getting it?"

"It defaulted to you because it's marked important, but Captain Yarain has not yet responded to its arrival. I suspect she has her wrist-com off while she's off duty."

Why didn't I think of that? "I don't suppose you could just deep-six the whole thing?"

"I could, but it wouldn't help. You'd still have to deal with it later."

Jason grumbled again. Darn thing sounded like a true AI, but it really wasn't. More like a *very* adaptive program. Trouble was it had a knack for being right. He knew that now was the time to dig into messages he didn't want to read. At least he didn't want to kill anyone anymore.

He dragged himself to his desk as the fake holdren fight faded into affectionate rubbing. "Send it to my computer, PAICCA. Might as well get this over with."

"Confirmed, Major. I'll be sure to put the range on stand-by."

We sure that thing isn't a true AI?

Either way, the joke helped add another dent as the computer blinked on.

Just as PAICCA opened the mission profile for him, Sundale pushed his head under Jason's arm into his lap. There he stayed with a rolling trill Jason swore he'd learned because it sounded like a purr. It was a sound Sundale never made for anyone else, ever.

"Can I help you?" Jason asked as he would a pet.

"I just wanted to know what our mission is," Sundale said innocently.

"I thought you could read."

Sundale half barked the first words, the closest thing holdrens had to an accent. "*I CAN*. I just choose not to."

Jason put one hand on his hip with a glare of his own. Sundale replied with a 'pet me' look along with his purr. Jason laughed again while pushing Sundale off his lap.

"Get out of here you crazy fox."

Sundale jumped back, got low on his forelegs, and yipped excitement while his tails swished playfully behind him. "Come now, Jason. You know I'm not really a fox."

Jason turned his chair around and folded his arms. "Close enough, as you yourself have said on more than one occasion."

"You still should know better." He ruffed again, his tails still swishing as they only did when playing.

Jason shook his head, trying very hard not to feel better. He'd already failed. The pointless argument had triggered a laugh he couldn't stop. Before he knew it, most of his rage was long gone.

"Sun," he said through his grin, "sometimes I don't know what to do with you. Thanks."

Sundale dropped his display, but not the joy in his voice. "Think nothing of it. I hate seeing you in such a rotten mood."

"As do I," Yarain said. "However, I would like to know our mission."

"You could read it yourself, you know," Jason said. "As third seat, mission profiles go to you first. PAICCA just sent it to me because you don't have your wrist-com on right now."

"I'd have to forward it to you anyway. No reason to avoid the hunt you know is coming."

Jason huffed at her perspective as he returned to his computer. Despite what he'd said, as group leader, it wasn't uncommon for Jason be the one to read over mission profiles first, even though most of the briefing prep was still Yarain's responsibility. Add in the sharing of quarters, and it was a fifty-fifty split as to who got to tell whom about the next mission.

A few more taps found his rotten mood returning with a slump of his shoulders. His summary came out almost robotic to match his contempt.

"Five transports. General cargo, ground vehicles, building supplies, equipment, and materials to build a star port, a smattering of specialists to help them build it, all being escorted through quite possibly the safest portions of United Systems Territory."

"A sleeper escort," Sundale growled.

Jason wished he could do the same. *What a waste.* The Gold Group, considered by many to be the best in the fleet, comes off the line to nap their way between inner systems? *The jants must be getting a kick out of this.*

"Are there *any* interesting people on the transports?" Yarain asked.

Jason skimmed the mission profile in the hopes of finding something, anything, to salvage the mission. He didn't get far before he rubbed his eyebrows as if he might wipe his frustration away. "We're not that lucky. Although command does want us to stop by the Klistro Seven to test the new sensor pods they're installing. See if they pick up anything new."

"I can barely contain myself."

Jason nodded silent agreement. It was something, but no one liked sleeper escorts.

With little else to do for the night, the pilot rose to find something to wind down with. He couldn't take a step in any direction as each option was rejected. Reading? Too angry. Sleep? Wouldn't happen. Old TV shows? Wrong mood. Not even the antics of some 20th century "sci-fi" characters would be enough. He had too much on his mind. That, and deep down, he still wanted to kill someone real. Especially if they were a suit.

His mind soon settled on an old cure for a busy mind he'd learned from a fellow pilot years back. "When all else fails," he used to say, "wear yourself out while focusing on any single task. Especially if it's monotonous, tiring, or simple."

Jason knew of only one such task, and it met all three criteria. He thanked the advice of his late father for making it available.

He went to the couch to retrieve his knife, which he tossed onto his back with all the frustration still steaming inside.

Sundale's ears perked, curious. "Where are you going?"

Jason slammed his P-mag into its holster with equal frustration. "Down to the hanger. Between my fight with command and the strange movements from the jantans, I need to find some mental unity if I expect to sleep. Best way I can think of to do that is to help install the new sensor pods."

Sundale rose to his paws, stretching as he did. "I'll join you."

"Thanks, Sun, but I can handle this alone."

"I want to look at the turrets."

Jason's hand went to his hip again. "Oh? May I ask why? Remember, I need details."

Sundale ruffed annoyance, but that's as far as it went. "We're overdue for a maintenance check. There's nothing more than that."

Second Seats are always so fussy about their ships. "You call two weeks overdue? Never mind. I won't turn down company. Come on. You joining us, Yarain?"

A backward tick in her ears replaced what would be a shake of the head for a human. Sundale knew it without effort. Jason almost missed it.

"*NO*," she said, more ruffing the word instead of saying it. After a second, she added, "Thank you, Jason."

Jason shrugged a silent "okay," then headed out. He stopped as the doors opened when he saw Sundale approach the desk. Before Jason could ask what he was up to, he got a reminder of how unique holdrens were.

Sundale's body gave a shimmer as he pushed off on his forelegs to stand upright. As he did, his hind legs grew larger, and his front paws became hands that remained largely paw-like, including pads and claws. His head tilted down to face forward as he took a step back to maintain his balance. His muzzle now stood just above Jason's not-quite six-foot forehead. Sundale's tails gave a single, adjusting wave as he completed his shift into his "finesse form," as the holdrens called it.

Like Yarain forcing the polite response a moment ago, Jason had gotten used to the differences. Mostly because there really wasn't much of a difference between this and their four-legged "primal form." The most striking was only because now that Sundale was on two legs, the small pouch that covered his genitals was more apparent. Being near the change, however, sent a chill down Jason's spine that he had to shake his head and shoulders to silence. He shook his head again as Sundale went for his custom uniform on the desk. *Right. Of course.*

While the core design was the same, Sundale had to slip his tails through inch long socks in the back as he stepped into it. It was also a one-piece suit that zipped up the front from the sash, and the sleeves and pants stopped at the first joint.

It was a compromise that command had surprisingly agreed to. Since even the most form fitting of clothing was shown to reduce a holdren's speed and agility to a small degree, they were allowed to go bare-paw unless there was risk of something that could damage their paws. A pretty small margin really, but both holdrens had shown its value more than enough times to earn the right.

That said, decompression and other hazards meant they couldn't always go without. Gloves and full length pants with shoes were still there, they were just tucked up against the end of the sleeves and pant legs so tightly you could barely notice them. In much the same way, the tails had full length socks of their own tucked at the base of each tail, and a hood sat on the back of the neck just like Jason's.

While Sundale worked into his uniform, Jason couldn't help a chuckle born of memories. "Eleven years," Jason said. "You'd think I'd get used to that."

"Better than the first time," Sundale said.

Jason threw his hands up in mock defensiveness. "Hey, I didn't shoot. I only drew. You can't blame a young soldier for being careful."

Sundale ruffed amusement while slipping his arms through and zipping it up the front. "I didn't."

"Good thing you didn't shoot either."

"If you hadn't relaxed as fast as you did, I might have."

"Not that it would have mattered. You missed the first time. I can't imagine the second being much better."

Sundale gave a playful growl to match his look while he slipped his wrist-com onto his right arm. Jason double checked to be sure he had his own before they left for the nearest lift. They took it to near the bottom of the starbase where an empty hallway suggested the hangers would be dormant.

Jason knew better.

They marched through the heavy doors into exactly what he'd expected. First came the strong stench of welded metal and fused wiring. A nice fit for the industrial yet polished walls, as well as the flood lighting that sometimes didn't feel as bright as it really was. Then came the chatter. A little on the quiet side but no less busy as techs worked all over the various craft on the hanger floor. Most of them G-21 Scorn heavy fighters. A patrol must have just come in or left since the bay doors at the end of the hanger were closing. All in all, a normal day during an upgrade.

Sundale went toward the storage cabinets on the back wall while Jason walked through the fighters looking for his ship. He offered salutes as needed to engineers on the way, wondering how much they knew about his orders and how he'd reacted to them. He got so lost in his thoughts, he almost killed his eye on the wing of his fighter.

She was a fair little ship that Jason had grown fond of. The cockpit started at a rounded nose that stuck out the middle of the central block and created a rounded bevel as it ran the length of the fighter. The ship's main weapons and systems occupied the rest of the block between twin-engine nacelles. Each nacelle had a cone recessed a few centimeters into the front that held most of her sensors. A twin-gatling plasmoid turret sat on top of each nacelle just behind the cones on each side. Her wings weren't wide, but still large enough to add to her profile and thick enough to hold spare components for in-field repairs, as well as the ship's main heat sinks. On rare occasions, they could hold some small cargo too. Her hull was a dark red, except for the Interstar and wing insignias painted on her sides.

While waiting for Sundale, Jason found himself running his hand over the "X1" painted beside the group logo. A lot of history there for him. Much of it bloody. To think the fools at headquarters were casting it off like it never happened. They were putting the whole of the alliance in jeopardy. If only he could do something besides yell.

"Saying hello again, Jason?" Sundale said, carrying a tool belt for each of them.

"That," Jason said, "and more. None of it important right now. I can't change the future. As much as I'd like to."

"Don't try. When the danger comes, we'll face it, lick our wounds, have a few cubs, then return again the next day. Only thing you need to worry about right now is yourself and the state of your pack. Your pack is fine. Trust yourself enough to believe that you are as well. I know I do."

"No cowering behind the seats, eh, Sun? I guess you're right. At least I'll be out there in a position to make a difference."

Sundale gave a very real, though short, growl. His ears didn't perk, which Jason knew meant the growl was only minor annoyance, or to get his attention.

"**WE** will be out there," Sundale said, ruffing the first word. "Don't forget us, Jason. You need us as much as we need you."

Jason nodded understanding while accepting a tool belt. "Point taken. Thanks."

Sundale gave a trio of quiet, trilling barks. Among Holdrens, it could mean any number of things. Sundale had adopted this exact call as an expression of the bond between them. Jason regretted not being able to return anything beyond a smile and a nod. The one time he'd tried to repeat the call, he sounded more like a sick hound dog. After that, Sundale had made it clear the smile was enough.

Jason strapped on the tool belt just as a tan-colored, hairless head with broad, engine-soiled shoulders appeared above them. His blue and silver jumpsuit wasn't much cleaner, yet it somehow didn't touch the rank on his arms. It was marked by three thin chevron lines above three bars with a hollow diamond in between. Like Jason, at the bottom of his rank tab sat a tiny, winged ship with a sun on each side of its nose. The insignia of the Precision Strike Command or PSC, their branch of Interstar.

"Excuse me, sirs," First Sergeant Tillman said, "but are ya'all going to talk all night or do you plan on actually doin' something?"

His tone said teasing, but Jason was still reminded why he was there. He pushed other thoughts as far back as they would go while climbing a ladder to the top of the fighter. Tillman and a tech were kneeling beside the rear half of the starboard engine nacelle with tools in hand. Jason looked back to offer Sundale a hand, only to find him heading off after an equipment trolley.

"Glad you decided ta join us," Sergeant Tillman said with a grin.

"Sorry," Jason said, trying to sound lighter than he felt. "I've got a lot on my mind lately."

"You an' every other pilot on this base, sir. It's like ev'ry one of 'em is expecting trouble. You ask me, the lot of you need a vacation...sir."

Jason waved him down before he had a chance to worry. "Relax, Sergeant. I agree. I just don't see it happening any time soon. Anyway, I'm not here to debate the mental state of the group. I'm here to work on those sensor pods."

The tech beside Tillman froze while the engineer himself tried not to look insulted. "May I ask why, sir? I didn' 'dink my abilities were in question. Unless this is an inspection in which case, I must admit, sir, I 'in no mood for it."

Jason might have slapped him down for such a comment, except that during his posting to the base, they'd gotten acquainted well enough to know where the line was with each other. Sergeant Tillman just walked closer to that line than Jason did. As such, he let the comment pass with only a slight edge creeping into his voice.

"I never said I doubt your skill, Sergeant. Nor is this an inspection."

First Sergeant Tillman's eyes darted back and forth for a second. "Then, if I may ask, sir, what is this?"

"A sleeping pill," Sundale said. He'd just returned with a diagnostic pack slung over his shoulder.

Both engineers looked around to stare at Sundale while Jason stifled a laugh.

"He's not far off," Jason said. "As I said, I have a lot on my mind. Can't sleep through it, so I came down here to get my thoughts centralized on something besides how many different ways there are to kill my superiors."

Sergeant Tillman laughed while his young assistant shook his head in disbelief. The latter probably thought he was crazy. Jason decided to let him. After all, he wasn't all that wrong, and not just because Jason had chosen to be one of those rare pilots who actually knew how to fix his own ship.

While technically in-mission repairs would fall to Sundale as the Active Engagement Systems Officer, or 'AESO,' Jason's father had told him there was a lot more value to the skills than just redundancy. *The more you know about your ship, the more you know what you can get out of it.* There were no regs that said he couldn't learn, and it gave him an additional way to get his mind off things. Plus, he liked the idea of not being dependant on one individual to put his ship back together should they get shot down. Most didn't mind him helping out either, so long as he didn't get in the way. Something he made an effort to avoid as much as possible.

Sergeant Tillman motioned Jason closer, still shaking off the laugh. Jason knelt beside him while Sundale went to perform his promised check on the turrets. Jason shook his head at him. *Darn fox is stubborn when he wants to be.* So be it. At least the turrets would be in perfect condition.

The tech opened the maintenance panel for the starboard nacelle. The armored hull lifted up first, then another layer of components and armored plating opened to reveal the starboard power core. Four, long, sea-blue crystals ran a fourth the length of the nacelle just ahead of the aft engine assembly. They were connected to each other around a central hub that regulated and distributed the power stored in the crystals. It also served as a surge protector and, if need be, launching platform should the core need to be ejected. They were glowing just enough to cast a ghost light on the first of the foot-long Vilon missiles stored in the starboard magazine.

"You disarmed them warheads, didn't you, Marn?" Tillman asked his assistant.

"Yes, sir," he said. "All systems are in standby mode."

"Good. Pard'n me, Major, but I assume you didn't get the instructions on these things yet."

"Use only," Jason said. "I hadn't gotten to the more technical stuff yet."

"I don't blame you. It's dry stuff, it is. These new pods need more power than the old, so to start, we're gon'a need newer connections that can handle the drain."

Jason nodded understanding with a look where they'd be working. "I was wondering why you were starting back here. Shouldn't be a problem."

"Give me a second though," Sundale said. "I want to do a quick power test. Hands off the core."

All three raised their hands to make sure they weren't touching anything live. A soft hum rose from the core, held for a minute, then faded.

Just as it did, Jason saw a spark so soft it was more a tick. "Did you see that?"

"I'm not sure," Sergeant Tillman said. "Excuse me, Cap'n. Could you run your test again please? Hold the power level for longer if you could."

"*SURE*," Sundale yipped.

Just like before, the core softly hummed and held for a minute. The spark struck again just before the hum faded.

"Cut the power," Jason said. "We may have a problem here."

The two workers disconnected all systems from the core, then Jason reached in to remove a black box from the end of one of the crystals. Sergeant Tillman watched as Jason turned it over in his hands until he found scorch marks on the bottom.

"That's odd," Jason said. "I've never seen a junction box do that before."

"Me neither," Sergeant Tillman said. "With your permission, sir, let me take a look."

Jason handed the box over while Sundale came over to dig at the core some more. Tillman used his tools to pry the box open to show the power relays and other circuitry inside. He pulled at the wires so he could see the bottom of the box.

Jason watched with a mental alarm on the verge of sounding. "Sergeant, am I crazy, or is this thing missing some redundancy?"

"Yer not crazy, sir," Tillman said. "See this little tower here? 'Dere should be three of 'em. It's also not hardened enough. Good 'ting we found 'dis. One wrong nebula at combat power likely would have fried it. Without the redundancies, there we be no recovering from it. You'd be down an entire crystal for a while if not permanently."

"It gets worse," Sundale said. He lifted another such disassembled box to the others. A quick inspection showed it to be just as flawed as the other.

Sergeant Tillman nearly growled himself. "I don' like it. This is my h'nger. No work should'a been done at all without prior notification. Least of all work this shoddy. Someone's gon'a lose their head over this, they will."

"Perhaps literally," Jason said. He wasn't quite serious since beheading wasn't on anyone's punishment list anymore. Though when one considered what would happen, politically or career-wise, the effect might as well be the same.

His mind soon touched on a more terrifying prospect. If his fighter had this issue, what else had been hidden? And that was just his own ship. When he considered the rest of the group, and possibly every other ship on the base, his shoulders sank as he bid a fond farewell to any chance at a good night's sleep.

"Sergeant, you better call in some help. We've got a lot of work to do."

"I was thinking da same 'ding," Tillman said. "I just wanted to enjoy the lie of not having to for a moment."

I hear that. "Sun, contact base security. Have them restrict outgoing communications till we sort things out."

As Sundale and Sergeant Tillman climbed off the fighter to carry out their orders, Jason stared at the place where the junction boxes had been. The whole thing left him with an empty feeling born of the last time little things started adding up. Then, it was an officer brainwashed by a Jantan process that thankfully proved amazingly hard to maintain, even harder to find a receptive subject, and whose architect had not survived his last attempt. This time, who knew what it was. Perhaps they'd recreated the procedure despite losing the man and the tech that made it work. Or it could be as simple as a commando who had somehow slipped past security.

Of course, there was one possibility his mind wouldn't accept. A human working of his own free will. What could his motives be? Could someone at HQ hate him that much? He shuddered at the thought and prayed this was less than it seemed, all the while feeling certain his prayers would go unanswered.

Chapter 2

The Sleeper Escort

Transmission detected.
    Scale twelve encryption...stand by...
Encryption broken.
Monitors active.
Attempting trace...
From: COMEXTCOL
To: EXTCOL 2187
Classification: TOP SECRET Eyes Only
Message: Enact protocol 20 immediately.
Waypoint Friday compromised. Assets unresponsive. Proceed to Waypoint Friday with all speed. Investigate fate of NF-271 & NF-272. If intact, instruct to abort mission.
    Enact protocol 21 following mission completion at your discretion.
End message
Transmission complete.
Source...unknown
Destination...unknown
Carrier...unknown
Trace failed.
Forwarding reconnaissance report...

Sundale gave a soft growl while biting into the fur of his arm. It's not like he had much else to do. His sensor screen had little more than the convoy on it, his target data and ship status screens had nothing to offer, and his turret targeting display only showed empty space ahead of them. In other words, nothing had changed since they began the escort mission. Only the hum of the hyper-light engines and the slight changes in sensors provided any confirmation they were moving.

Not that it felt like it. Sundale's tails had more energy than he did, and they were floating back and forth through the space in his chair. A sigh from Yarain on the opposite side of the cockpit suggested she wasn't doing any better. Sundale glanced behind him to her station and found no more change in her group status screen. He stared at his turret controls, almost longing for a fight. Instead, all he could do was work his fur clean from the night before.

What a disaster. Jason's quest for mental unity had become a full-fledged hunt through the group's systems. As feared, every single junction box had been wrong. That left the techs with a long night of work, triple checking everything. It also meant Jason insisted on being there to assist until Sergeant Tillman and Sundale insisted that he sleep. On some level, Jason may have known better. His step had gotten heavier by the minute on their way back to their quarters. At one point, Sundale feared he might fall asleep in the corridor. How he found the energy to change out of his uniform was nothing short of a miracle.

At first, Jason had remained uneasy. Base security had turned up nothing, which led to a warning to the group at the briefing to be ready for anything. Except nothing ever happened. Two days to reach the rendezvous point, two days more flying escort, and the only thing they encountered was an abundance of boredom. The longer that lasted, the weaker the stench of tension hovering over Jason became. By the time he woke from his sleep rotation that morning, it had faded to almost nothing.

Something Sundale felt thankful for. Sensing the tension in his CO made the boredom that much worse. Time passed more slowly because his instincts kept looking for a predator his mind said wasn't there. Now at last, he could focus on his duties in a way that would pass the time without neglecting them.

Though it would seem Jason had gone further than his scent suggested. When a hum drew Sundale's attention to the front of the cockpit, his ears ticked forward in approval. While the view out the forward windows hadn't changed, one of Jason's screens had. It showed the familiar chess board with icons standing in for the pieces. He was playing yet another game with Carter Gomez, the energetic pilot of Gold 2 and one of Jason's closest friends.

It was a rare moment. One that said more than anything how pointless their orders were. Major Jason Harlem, a man regarded as one of the most dedicated and disciplined pilots in the fleet, was playing chess with one of his group mates during a mission. Sundale couldn't blame him. After so much time worrying about something that apparently wasn't going to happen, he deserved to relax a little. Besides, if something actually came up, Jason would be ready and alert in a fraction of a second.

Sundale growled again. *We could only be so lucky.* The entire mission felt more like a test of their professionalism than true protection. Worse still was the transports had a standard hyper-light cruising speed of only factor five. Any faster, and their coils would eventually run the risk of tearing themselves and their ship apart due to overheating. Of course, 'eventually' meant holding such speeds for about a week non-stop, but there was no need to rush the trip, so factor five it was. The problem lay in the fact that for people used to traveling anywhere from HL nine to fourteen, sometimes fifteen when pushing the engines to their limit, factor five was downright crawling.

Sundale ran yet another intensive scan of the area and rechecked the status of the fighter. Still no change. Thirty-five Scorns in formation around five large, rectangular transports, all traveling through an area of space devoid of anything beyond general interstellar material. Gold 1 herself was running in perfect condition, no signs of any problems. The very definition of a sleeper escort. If only Sundale could run it instead of flying. At least then he'd get some exercise as well as the comfort of the wind running through his fur. He wouldn't mind flying it himself, but even with wings, he'd be trapped inside the grey hull of the heavy fighter.

The only saving grace was Scorns had a comparatively spacious cock-pit. Sundale's flight instructor used to say that pilots of the Phantoms he started on "wore" their cockpits. A phrase that wasn't far off, which made the Scorn feel like a luxury. While the space between him and Yarain was barely big enough for a person to stand in, a Phantom didn't have any at all. The Scorn had just enough space on one side for two emergency fold-out seats. A toilet, often called the bucket, lay beside the food processor in the opposite corner, with a narrow access way splitting the middle to the rear hatch. The extra space left Sundale feel-ing far less caged than the Phantoms ever had. There also weren't as many memories attached to it that Sundale would like to forget. While holdrens didn't dwell on the past as much as humans did, he always had a harder time letting go of it than Yarain seemed to.

Then Carter's voice came over the comms. "Checkmate, Jason."

Sundale's ears turned toward the front of the cockpit. He heard a grumble close to a growl from Jason as the board vanished from his screen.

"I don't get it," Jason said. "You'd think by the law of averages I'd win one of these games."

Sundale heard a boisterous laugh from Carter. "Face it, Jason. You'll never be a match for the chess master."

A smile crept into Jason's voice. "Chess master huh? This from the man who got beaten by his eight-year-old niece last month."

"I let her win."

"And General Carson?"

"One way to get promoted."

"You're hopeless."

"Sure am, and damn proud too!"

Sundale gave a quiet ruff of amusement while Jason huffed his own. *That's Major Gomez for you.* One crazy half-Mexican, as he often described himself, whose only competition for the biggest nut of the group was Jason. Though in that regard, Carter didn't have a prayer.

One thing Carter could do was manage to calm Jason down. For the first time since they left the star base, Sundale found no trace of tension or alertness from him. Be it through amusement or forgetfulness, Jason had finally begun to relax.

When Jason and Carter fell into pointless banter, Sundale dropped his attention in favor of his station. As was his duty, he had more active sensor sweeps to go along with Yarain's passive screen. Another set of identical readings left him almost missing the times where each day brought another dangerous mission. That longing quickly died when he remembered the things they experienced during those days. After that, the endless hours of nothing seemed more blessing than curse... mostly.

A blessing that ended when the fighter shuddered, and Sundale's console beeped to life, as did Jason's and Yarain's. The sensors had caught a glimpse of something, but with range and interference working against them, they couldn't tell him what it was. So far, all he knew was the convoy had been forced out of hyper-light. The warp coils were suddenly very hot, yet his status screen showed no sign of damage or malfunction. Outside, a thin veil of red-orange stellar material tinted the stars like a fog. The rest was a jumble of incomplete sensor data he was already trying to sift through.

"What the?" Jason muttered from his seat. A second later, Sundale saw a channel open to the group. "Everyone, stay alert. No one do anything until ordered. Yarain, check with the group and transports for damage and answers. Sundale, can you tell me if it's a technical problem?"

"I don't think so," Sundale said.

"So, what is it? Why were we forced out of hyper-light?"

"Give me a moment."

With his ship diagnostic not offering much, Sundale tapped at his controls to retune the sensors in the hopes of cutting through the interference. His tails ticked with his heartbeat, both hoping to find something, anything, worth noting. There weren't many things that could collapse warp fields without causing damage, and most of them were artificial. They might get their chance at danger after all.

Then again, maybe not. When he noticed a recurring, though random, fluctuation in the warp field generators, it suggested a culprit neither artificial nor violent. A simple tick of the sensors into frequencies higher than normal confirmed his suspicion.

"Just a magnetic storm," he said. "P-7 rating. Probably the remnants of a supernova or a very big coronal mass ejection."

Jason grumbled. "A.K.A., an interstellar speed bump you can't see coming. No reports of it, Yarain? Those things aren't exactly small."

"None that I got," she said. "Forwarding a report of it now."

"Someone must have gotten lazy. You sure we're good, Sun?"

"*YES*," Sundale barked.

"Come on, Captain. I know you hate it, but I need a full report."

Sundale couldn't stop a growl. Humans. They were so detail oriented it hurt. What did it matter why they were good? Jason knew the answers anyway. But military protocol required he get a report like he was an idiot. *Whoever wrote the rule must have been one.*

"The storm is strong enough to create a short in energized coils, nothing more. The hull will protect the rest. We'll need to stay at sub-light until we clear it, but aside from heating the hyper-coils, emergency systems prevented any damage."

"Too bad," Yarain said. "I was hoping for at least a prankster we could bark at."

"Not me," Jason said. "I'll take bad weather over a warship any day."

While Jason told the group what they already knew, Sundale ran an intensive scan of the area so Yarain could plot the shortest course out of the storm's influence.

One of his sweeps caught a distortion that didn't match the storm. It wasn't far from them, but the same storm that was messing with the hyper-coils was also making a detailed scan difficult. He couldn't get enough to really see it, which got his ears up and his clawed-fingers moving on the controls. Were it not for his years of experience, he might have gotten lost in this new hunt using sensors.

Which meant he didn't miss Jason catching him doing it.

"Sun? What is it? What'cha got?"

"A scent," Sundale said.

Jason sighed, and Sundale swallowed one of his own. "I need more than that, Captain. You know that. So can we skip the process for a change?"

If we must. Though Sundale waited for an intensive scan that gave him more to work with. "I'm not sure what I have. It looks like a distorted ripple in the magnetic field. The only thing I know of that generates this effect is our own cloaking technology. There was also a brief high energy distortion consistent with a hyper-light engine, but I can't be sure through this storm."

Yarain ruffed, more like chirped, in holdren curiosity. "Why would one of our own be cloaked this deep in United Systems Territory?"

"They wouldn't," Jason said. "But if you recall, we're not the only ones that use it. First squad, form up!"

Before Jason finished, Sundale knew Jason's hackles were up, or would be if he had them. He could hear it in his voice. His words filled in the blanks Sundale had missed.

Years ago, when Jason was still a rookie, Marcalla had captured and brainwashed an Interstar pilot into thinking he was one of them. It was a process that took technology and repeated treatments to maintain. They'd kept it up long enough to get a hold of Interstar's cloaking technology. Jason rescued the pilot during his own escape and put a permanent end to those who had developed the technique.

That pilot, very intentionally, now flew Gold 2.

But Marcalla had still gotten a hold of the technology. Since it was stolen instead of developed, they remained a few steps behind Interstar in its advancement. However, a few steps behind was still enough for the technology to hide some of their ships. If this was indeed a Marcallan vessel, they might have bigger problems than a simple magnetic storm.

Guided by the sensor reading, Jason called Gold Group's first squad to shadow him as he turned the fighter toward Sundale's "ripple." Yarain was already relaying orders to stand by at condition two – high chance of danger or combat. Weapons and defensive systems were activated, as were the fighter's turrets. Through his target screen, Sundale could see the hull of the fighter give a ripple of its own, but this was the particle shields being deployed along the hull. It created an almost invisible layer half a meter thick and ten times as strong. Jason wasn't taking any chances.

With Gold 8 through 11 on her wings, Gold 1 went looking for the phantom ship. It didn't take long to find a small section where the stars and stellar material appeared to move ever so slightly. It was as if they were looking at a carpet with some tiny hill or mouse rolling under it. The stars would roll up onto it, then roll back off at the end of it. But the difference at the edge of this hill was all you could see. Otherwise, you wouldn't know anything was there.

Gold 1 did know. Even without the visual queue, Sundale's scanners had a solid lock on them now. Jason wasted no time letting the culprit know he knew they were there. Without warning or hesitation, he fired. A quick burst from the main gatling-cannons sent a short stream of plasmoids streaking in front of the ripple. The stars stopped moving. Jason fired another shot, then decided to talk.

"This is the Interstar fighter Gold 1. Identify yourself and your intentions."

No response. Holdren tails began to wave.

"We sure they're still there?" Yarain asked.

"They're there," Sundale said.

"Because...? Keep it together, Sun." Jason pressed.

Sundale growled annoyance. *Humans and their details.* "Yes, sir. Sorry, sir. No pulse. Even without the storm, jumping to hyper-light gives a flare of energy no one can hide."

"Besides that," Jason said, "they're as grounded as we are. They go HL now; they'll be a fireball."

"What about sub-light?" Yarain said.

"No refraction. They haven't moved since we found them. Time that changed." Jason dropped two of the main gatling-cannons to training power, then fired a long burst right between the refractions. The rounds splashed against the hull of the ship. The cloak kept its identity hidden, but those inside would know full well what just happened.

"This is Major Jason Harlem, pilot of Gold 1. Drop your cloak and identify yourself. You will not get another warning."

More uneasy silence. Sundale waited for Jason to give them a full powered shot. The waiting wasn't helping the exhaustion that hit him out of nowhere. The fact that he'd used sir with Jason twice in quick succession spoke volumes of how tired he really was. He had to work to keep focus on his sensors and the enemy ship. He made a note to request a day off next chance they got. Sergeant Tillman was right; they needed one.

Before Jason lost his patience, the unknown ship dropped its cloak. Sundale tilted his head in confusion when instead of an enemy, the ship turned out to be a fellow Scorn fighter. Her transponder pinged her as Red 7, which made even less sense. Her group wasn't stationed anywhere near there.

"Any transmission?" Jason said carefully.

"Just her ID tag," Yarain said.

"Crew?"

"Human," Sundale said. "And alive."

"For once, I might almost prefer a jantan. Them, I can shoot." Jason reopened the channel while quick ruffs of amusement sounded behind him. "Gold 1 to Red 7. Report status, over." Nothing. "Red 7, report status. That's an order, pilot!" More silence. A great sigh from Jason's seat followed by a great renewal of concern from Sundale's. "Status of her defenses?"

"Inactive," Sundale said. "Shields, inhibitors, and scanners are all on stand-down."

"Life support?"

"Fully functional. Before you ask, I can't speak to their comms."

Another growl from Jason again had Sundale wondering how much animal blood was left in humans. To be fair, it was more a strained sigh, but Sundale's ears heard the same thing: stress, frustration, and a sense of 'I really hate this situation.' Sentiments the young holdren shared.

More so because of a sudden tingle in his back he couldn't explain. It was almost painful like when a limb fell asleep. He first tried to clear it by sending a ripple through his energy matrix, the portion of his physiology made entirely of energy that coursed through his body and was the source of his abilities. It required occasional voluntary and involuntary adjustments to prevent problems of varying sizes, such as the tingle in his back, from developing. The ripple he triggered cleared the tingle, though not the strain it seemed to be adding.

"Is their transit pad active?" Jason asked.

"Yes, sir. Pad and beacon are online," Sundale said.

"In that case, Sun, I need you to flash over there and get some answers. Get their status and their mission immediately. *Do not* take no for an answer, Captain. Yarain, pick one of the squad's AESO's to join him. Arrange transport for back-to-back arrival. Weapons drawn, weapons tight, but don't hesitate to engage."

Both holdrens acknowledged their orders.

Sundale unbuckled his restraints, paused next to his chair, then decided his teeth, tails, and P-mag would be enough should he find trouble. He took position in the middle of the fighter in preparation for transport. As Jason tried to raise Red 7 one more time, Yarain glanced around her chair with a concerned dip in her ears.

When she spoke, she used the subtle sounds and movements animals use to communicate. Otherwise called 'Holdren' or 'Fox' by the humans since holdrens had no term for it, the most humans heard were slight ruffs or growls, if anything at all. Some of these sounds were so faint most technology couldn't catch them, much less human ears.

"First Lieutenant Antwan from Gold 8 will join you," she said. *"Be careful. You know how jumpy humans can be."*

Sundale looked over at Jason to indicate him as his example. *"Intimately. I don't think I'll have that problem this time."*

"Never take the lack of scent as proof there is no danger. Keep your ears perked."

"I always do."

Her ears shifted back for a second before her focus returned to her station. Shortly after, Jason called back, "Ready, Sun?"

Sundale drew his P-mag with a soft growl. "Ready."

"Yarain, transit when ready."

After a second to sync his arrival with Gold 8's, Sundale's body sparkled for a second before a bright flash enveloped him. When the flash faded, he found himself inside a cockpit he didn't expect. Red 7's port side turret station was a charred mess. Several over-head lights were shorted out. Debris was scattered everywhere. The contents of the starboard side cabinet were also scattered, save for the armor vest which lay inside the bucket.

Before he ever noticed the crew, Sundale's nose screamed danger. The scents didn't match the scene. Charred circuitry, yes. Even a human could smell that just by looking around. But there wasn't enough smoke in the air. He found no blood or burned flesh which, no matter where anyone was, would come with what happened to the port turret station. At the very least, he should have found singed hair. Instead, all he got was sweat, and it wasn't even exercise sweat. Add the icky tang of hot P-mag to the list, and a lot was wrong about the ship he stood in.

Despite his internal alarms, Sundale kept static as he took in the scene. The pilot was kneeling just in front of the starboard side turret station with a burned-out circuit board in his hand.

"***CLEAR!***" Sundale yipped.

"Clear!" Lieutenant Antwan said, a man whose face was so smooth and clean you'd think him too young to drink much less serve. His rank tabs held only two falcon wings, yet the confidence Sundale felt from him would rival General Carson, their division commander, in all the right ways.

Sundale lowered his weapon and scanned the cockpit. The turret operators were in the walk space in the back of the fighter working on her systems. They seemed to ignore both new arrivals, while the pilot's broad shoulders heaved up and down as he stood to face the holdren.

His hand went up to his forehead in salute just below thin brown hair. "S-sir. Captain Gary Molsen. Pilot of Red 7."

Sundale returned his salute while his nose went searching. "Captain Sundale, AESO for Gold 1." The man stood straight as a nail. "As you were pilot."

The man dropped attention, but to say he relaxed would be an outright lie. Even a human could have seen the tension in his body. "Welcome aboard, sir. What can I do for you?"

Sundale's ears perked. *What can I do for you? The fighter's a mess, and he starts with that?* The scent of stress threatened to overpower the damage, and that was without the shaking fingers Sundale noticed. Point-for-point, his eyes weren't much better than humans beyond his nat-ural night vision. But when it came to movement, humans were almost blind. He could see every twitch and sway in Captain Molsen's body. Each one left his tails wanting to wave uneasiness. He kept them still, but not his senses.

"You can give me answers," Sundale said. "We've sent hails with no response."

"Apologies, sir," Captain Molsen said. "The storm overloaded our HL drive. Caused a cascade that fried—well, as you can see, sir, damn near everything. Our hyper light drive is offline, as are weapons and shields. Sensors are also badly damaged, leaving us almost blind."

He's trying to distract me with a damage report. It made it harder than ever to keep his tails from waving. The pilot more than his crew stank of heavy, icky fear. Sundale might have excused it, except this was the kind of fear he found in his prey, not a soldier who knew he was about to get in big trouble. With each second that passed and word the pilot spoke, the feeling of danger rose. *What are they up to?*

"How are you and your crew?" Lieutenant Antwan said.

Sundale thought he saw triumph in the pilot' eyes. Or was it relief? "We're fine, sir. We caught the cascade in time to avoid getting caught in the blast."

Sundale pointed at the port turret station and almost lost a word in a bark, "You avoided **THAT** without serious injury?"

"I have a fast-acting crew, sir."

Not much of a diversion.

"Any other damage?" Antwan asked.

"Nothing major, no," Captain Molsen said. "Thrusters are online, and we just got the sub-light engines back."

"What about communications?"

The smell of fear spiked. The turret operators paused their work for a moment. Sundale's tails began to wave back and forth, ready to strike as he felt danger breathing down his neck.

The pilot tried to act cool, but he couldn't hide from Sundale's nose or eyes. "A-also down. We didn't respond because we never received any signals."

Sundale stared him down while his ears kept watch in back. "You have wrist comms, Pilot."

"They never reacted, sir. Perhaps the storm blocked the signal."

Sundale wanted to call him out on that, but he knew it wouldn't get him anywhere. Captain Molsen clearly meant to keep something secret. Something that might be more important to him than his career. Sundale decided to test just how far he planned on taking his denial.

Sundale extended his free hand, pads up. "Let me see your wrist-com."

The pilot's eyes widened despite his best efforts to control them. "S-sir?"

"Give me your wrist-com. I want to see what's wrong with it."

The turret operators stopped working, and the smell changed. Sundale wasn't the predator anymore. He was the prey. He tried not to let the tensing of his muscles show while Captain Molsen searched for something to say.

"I... I'm sorry, sir," he said at last. "I can't do that. It contains classified information that I have orders not to reveal to anyone."

Too late for that line, soldier.

"Are you serious?" Lieutenant Antwan said.

Sundale added a touch of a growl to his voice. "I got this, Lieutenant. Relax, Captain. I'll only be looking at the mechanics to find the problem. I can't access the files without your codes anyway."

Captain Molsen retreated while covering his wrist-com. "I'm sorry, sir. I have my orders."

Sundale's ears perked forward while his hackles rose. "As do I. *Major* Jason Harlem has ordered me to get answers. Now hand it over."

The pilot hesitated, then shifted his eyes to his turret operators. His mistake. Even if Sundale's eyes hadn't caught the silent message, his ears would have heard a P-mag slip out of its holster behind him. Based on the echo, one of the turret ops was shielding the other from Antwan's view.

"**DROP** Lieutenant!"

Lieutenant Antwan fell to one knee and ducked lower. Sundale glanced back at the other soldiers and aimed his outside tails. Just as one soldier took aim from behind the other, Sundale expelled a portion of his energy matrix through the tips. The crystal-like fibers that looked and felt like red fur on his tail tips turned the energy into a specifically calibrated beam, which struck both men in their chests. As they crumpled unconscious to the floor, he aimed both outside tails and his P-mag at the dumbstruck pilot. The tips and the red bands continued to glow, the former ready to fire again, the latter reacting to the rush of energy.

Sundale let his growl fill the cockpit. "I suggest you offer some answers, *Captain*."

Captain Molsen's shock turned to anger as he glared at the holdren. He reached for his P-mag on his hip. He hit the floor with two beam burns in his uniform before he got anywhere near it.

"What the hell is going on here?" Lieutenant Antwan said.

"A very good question, Lieutenant." Sundale sighed with a growl before activating his own wrist-com. "Sundale to Gold 1. I think we've found something."

"What do you mean?" Jason asked.

Sundale for once remembered how detail needy humans were. "The crew said they received no signals at all. The cockpit shows signs of damage I don't believe. When I tried to get a look at one of their wrist-coms, they pulled their weapons on me." There was more shock than concern in Jason's voice when he replied. "They what? You all right?"

"I'm fine."

Jason breathed relief mixed with underlying stress. "So much for a simple sleeper escort. What'd you do with the crew?"

"Stunned them," Sundale said simply.

"Okay, scratch that problem. With the crew out cold, you'll need to fly that bird. Can you handle it?"

Sundale glared forward, then growled when he remembered Jason couldn't see him. *Did he forget the two years I spent as a pilot? Never mind the requirement that AESOs have to earn their wings.*

"Yes," he said.

Sundale settled into the pilot seat while Antwan took the POSN, or Passive Operation Systems Navigator station, more commonly referred to as 'third seat.' Sundale had to tuck his tails alongside him since these seats didn't have the slot for them. While only a touch better than putting them between his legs, it still made him wish more holdrens were in Interstar. Maybe then the modification would become standard.

Of course, for that to happen, they'd have to find his home world first. Only Karol Corzon, the Interstar pilot who found him all those years ago, knew where it was. He had never let her talk about it for reasons that now seemed quite stupid. By the time that changed, circumstances saw him left behind on some unknown world where he almost died alone and Karol was killed by the jantans trying to lure them away from him. As for his parents... well, they were *very* different back then, which meant they couldn't find their way home either. Something else that was at least partly his fault.

Like so many times before, Sundale tried to shake the thoughts from his mind before they took root. Now was not the time to dwell on such things. He had a job to do and pondering the past would only get in the way. Besides, holdrens didn't dwell on things that are done and cannot be changed. Or so Yarain kept telling him.

With his seat adjusted to his liking, Sundale signaled Gold 1 he was ready.

"All right," Jason said. "Fall in behind me. We'll be landing on the *Marco Polo* so we can take a closer look at that ship."

Sundale's ears perked while his stomach sank. "We? Can't the freighter crews handle it?"

Jason's voice showed no sign he shared the sentiment. "No offense to them, but I don't trust them. Or more correctly, I don't trust their training to cover the kinds of things we'll be looking for. Never mind the higher clearance we hold, there are some things civilians just don't know about. That, and I'd rather keep this in house until we can make more sense of it."

In that, Sundale had to agree. The last thing they needed was a bunch of civilians gossiping about a Scorn fighter going rouge. Such rumors could still get out, but at least this way, details would remain closed until they got answers.

That said, agreement did not get Sundale's stomach back in place.

He still had grit in his fur from their work *four days* ago. Now it seemed likely he was about to add to it. Repairs and weapon maintenance didn't bother him. These were common, required, and among the duties of being an AESO. But all this grunt work of simple checks and rechecks and exploratory checks were wearing thin. He almost preferred the sleeper escort. At least then he could stay clean.

Sundale again noted the need for some shore leave. While Earth wasn't home, parts of it were wild enough to have the same effect. He could run through a forest, dig into snow after a mole, or find a tree big enough to shade him while he slept far away from technology. He wanted the freedom of the wild, even if it wasn't *his* wild. More so because it would mean his father, Harmus, could be there as well. With no other holdrens around, he relished any time, however short, his pack could be together.

Sergeant Tillman was right, he was tired. More than he should be, come to think of it. True, he'd spent much of the night working on Scorns, but that was days ago. He'd gotten more than enough sleep since, and even if he hadn't, he'd done that before without feeling so drained. He also noted that the tingle in his back wasn't in his body, but in his energy matrix. The short bursts from his tails weren't enough to cause it, and the armor of the fighter kept him safe from the storm. Was it all strain?

He began to think so just as he flew in formation behind Gold 1. He couldn't remember the last time he really had a day to himself. His last kill was a mouse he'd found in the hanger. Humans often warned about over-working. Now he knew why. It seemed the long hours, endless reports, and lack of any real fun were beginning to take their toll.

Sadly, his day was far from done. Jason landed Gold 1 inside the hanger of the *Marco Polo*, and Sundale put Red 7 down beside her. Really, to call it a hanger was to up-sell the slot. It was more like a cargo bay with an outside door. Plenty big, though you couldn't get more than maybe six Scorns inside, and that was if you squeezed every inch you could out of the place. It reeked of dust from previous crates as well as a number of smells Sundale didn't want to explore. Just a quick sniff had him sneezing and tasting things he'd rather not know the owner of.

Red 7's crew were taken to the brig by Lieutenant Antwan and the transport's crew. Meanwhile, the officers of Gold 1 dealt with Red 7 itself.

Jason stared at it like it might stare back for a while. "Sounds stupid but I'll ask: are we sure it's really Red 7?"

"**YES**," Sundale barked.

Jason thankfully let that stand. "Okay, so the ship's real. You said something about the damage being fake?"

"The damage is real. How it got there isn't."

"What do you mean?"

"I think they took their own P-mags to the cockpit to make me think a cascade from the storm did it."

"Can you prove that?"

Sundale glared at the fighter and growled. *There goes any chance of staying clean.* "If I can, it will be in the damage and their weapons."

"Best get to it. Yarain, I had their wrist coms left behind. See if you can find anything in them or their transmission records."

"Aye, sir."

When Jason gave no orders for himself, Sundale's ears perked his way. "What will you be doing?"

"Probably beating my head against a wall," Jason said. "I'll be in Gold 1 when you find something."

Jason walked out before either holdren could get anything more from him.

Yarain turned to her cub with her ears shifting in thought. *"Was there an answer there?"*

"I didn't hear one," Sundale said.

"One of these days he's going to charge into battle without noticing we're not there."

"He'll notice. What he'll do when he does is another question."

Yarain ruffed, flicked an ear, then turned inside the fighter on her hunt for answers. Sundale found a toolkit so he could do his own work on the fighter's AESO station.

The P-mags were still warm from fresh firing, and a scan of the damage showed only carbon scoring consistent with small arms fire. Diagnostic records and an examination of the power relays further confirmed the fighter suffered no damage from the storm or Jason's warning shots. There was little to be gained from the fighter herself, so Sundale took a wrist-com in the hopes of finding answers there.

He found more mystery. While Yarain got constant 'access denied' messages from the POSN station, Sundale found absolutely nothing wrong with the pilot's wrist-com. Stranger still was what appeared to be a fragment of a transmission record, but it was too well deleted to be sure it wasn't just standard operational data. Then again, if it were, there would be no reason to delete it so thoroughly. Yet several minutes of data were missing.

On a hunch, Sundale dug under the POSN console so he could get at the main transceiver. Few soldiers, even Scorn crews, knew that the transceiver kept a record of its own. When messages were received from long range, it forwarded the data to a crew's station or wrist-coms since they often couldn't receive sub-space messages. It also stored that message temporarily to ensure the message arrived before it got cleansed. Though all encryptions would remain in place, there was a chance of at least seeing the message itself.

After some work with the connections, Sundale pulled himself out of the console.

"Yarain, try to access back-up module T dash two. Should show on your system now."

After a few taps on the console, one message popped up. It was severely encrypted, but that didn't keep Yarain's ears from perking. "This isn't Interstar code."

"Do you recognize it?" Sundale said.

"No."

"No luck elsewhere?"

"No."

Sundale gave a soft growl. *Jason's going to love this.* He thought about quite literally taking the fighter apart, but that idea died on the spot. He'd be getting into systems that were booby trapped. Considering how willing the crew was to risk engaging them, he didn't want to take any chances without more equipment and personnel to assist. Instead, he spent a few minutes working with the pilot's seat to make sure no one could fly her any time soon.

"Thoughts?" Sundale asked as he started doing the same with the third seat console.

"Tell Jason," Yarain said. "We can't hunt any harder without our first father."

Sundale flicked an ear at the term. Partly because many humans still used the term "alpha," which was different than the Holdren phrase "first father/mother" or "first parent" for the same position. Even Jason had to catch himself now and then. The rest was because it was always odd to think of Jason that way. He didn't begin the pack or add new blood to it. The only part of being a first parent he fit was priority in terms of keeping the pack alive. Perhaps that was all Sundale's instincts needed to form the connection, though that too often felt like an inaccurate explanation.

Despite how it felt, Sundale's thoughts on it lasted but a moment. He then ticked his ears forward to agree with Yarain. They'd done all they could. Anything more would need more permission, guidance, or resources they didn't have.

Yarain and Sundale headed for the other side of the hanger to give their report. Even before they rounded to the aft of the fighter, they could hear Jason making his own echo as usual when fed up.

"I don't think you understand, Sergeant; I'm not asking, I'm telling. Get... me... General... Carson."

A young man on a screen of Yarain's station shook his head before leaning over his desk. The screen changed to show the Interstar logo with the words "stand by" under it.

"Is General Carson giving you the cold shoulder?" Sundale asked.

Jason shook his head while bouncing a fist on the arm of the chair. "Just caught him at the wrong time. President Priolozi wants him for a briefing in an hour. You can fill in the rest."

Indeed, Sundale could. Any time you were requested at a meeting with the Command Council, you spent that hour constantly re-reading reports or briefings you already knew by heart to be sure you got it right. Priolozi was a bit of a perfectionist, which meant anyone dealing with him had to be as well. Made one wonder how the Command Council, the executive branch of the United Systems Republic, did anything other than prepare.

"I wish we had better news," Sundale said.

"No luck?" Jason said.

"None. But we can prove they caused the damage. In addition, we found unfamiliar encryptions."

"Marcallan?"

"No."

"Terrific. Did you get any—"

The screen flicked on to show the stern, dark tan face of General Rickey Carson. For a second, it made his hair look darker than the jet black it normally was, though it still looked slick despite a military cut. Sundale knew at once how easy this *wasn't* going to be.

"All right, Major," the general said. "What's so urgent you had to badger my assistant?"

Glad he has an open mind, Sundale thought with a flick of an ear.

Jason showed more control than the holdrens could sense. "A serious string of mysteries, sir."

"Care to explain that?"

Jason counted each item on his fingers. "First, sabotaged power junction boxes installed on every fighter in my group. Second, a cloaked Red 7 that refused to answer my hails in any way, shape, or form. Third—"

"If they were cloaked, how did you find them?"

Intentional or not, his tone was fast approaching mockery. Sundale took a deep breath to silence the growl forming in his throat. His mother did the same. Were Jason a holdren, he might have done so as well. Instead, he took on the statue glare he used when he wanted to show his anger without letting it get out of control. Something Sundale never enjoyed seeing, especially when it was directed at him.

"Sundale noticed the distortion, sir," he said. "We were forced out of hyper-light by a magnetic storm that wasn't reported. It caught them, too. I tried hailing, got no response. They didn't drop their cloak until I fired warning shots. Even then, they refused to respond."

General Carson's gaze turned more surprised without losing the fire of frustration. "You fired a warning shot? That's a little extreme, don't you think?"

"Not when I'm dealing with an unknown cloaked vessel deep in United Systems territory, no sir. And that's not the end of it."

General Carson's head lowered while his tone became accusing. "What else happened?"

Sundale couldn't catch his growl this time. *He isn't listening!* For whatever reason, it felt like General Carson wasn't taking them seriously. Superior or not, he had no right to take that kind of tone with them.

Before it could become a snarl, Jason glanced back with a hand up that told him to calm down. Sundale's ears flattened in submission while Jason faced the screen with a clenched fist.

"I did what I thought was best, sir. I sent Sundale and Lieutenant Antwan over to get answers the crew wasn't giving me. That too, didn't go well. Captain?"

Jason motioned for his AESO to give a report. To his credit, General Carson didn't interrupt Sundale as he explained, in forced detail, what happened on Red 7. He noted that they now knew for certain the damage was faked. He took careful care to include the words he used to ask for the pilot's wrist-com. When he mentioned the weapon being drawn, and how he handled it, General Carson's expression changed.

He leaned forward on his desk without a hint of anger. "They what? Are you all right, Captain?"

"Yes, sir," Sundale said.

"You sure about that? You said you used your tails, not your sidearm."

Finally, he listens. "A couple of quick bursts isn't anything to worry about, sir. It's when they see heavy use that it becomes a problem."

"That's a blessing. Still, that doesn't make sense. Their mission was sensitive but not so classified it warranted that kind of a response."

Yarain's head tilted. "And what, if I may ask sir, was that mission?"

General Carson went blank a moment as if his mind had run away to consult its advisors. Then, much like a robot, he turned and tapped at a console out of view. Three long, deep tones from the console announced their connection had just been encrypted and secured.

"You didn't hear this," General Carson said. Gold 1 voiced their understanding. "I don't know all the details, just this: a group was requested for a high-profile diplomatic escort. Only other thing I heard is something about them wanting an escort that could be discreet and diplomatic while ensuring they would live to tell about it."

"That's not Red group," Yarain said.

General Carson glared at Yarain, forcing her and Sundale to drop their ears in Holdren apology. It didn't matter which had made the error. Instinct forced them both to seek forgiveness.

The general's voice matched his glare, which only sent their ears lower. "I don't need you telling me who is or isn't fit for a mission, Captain. A group was requested, and Red group was the name that came up. I had no part in the decision."

Jason didn't miss a beat. "Which makes this all the more curious, sir. Red group is one of yours. You never could let it go after they promoted you out of it. Why would such a mission be given to one of your groups without your approval? And why are they way out here alone? Besides that, Yarain is right. Red group's last *three* diplomatic missions went bad. Their last one almost triggered a war with the Siltians. A recent track record like that, and they're the ones tapped for a sensitive diplomatic mission? Without consulting you? It doesn't add up."

General Caron's demeanor again softened. For the first time, Sundale felt like they were getting through to him. He kept those feelings hidden to avoid damaging the progress they'd made. This fight was Jason's, not his.

"You have a specific thought there, Major?" General Carson said.

Jason looked at the floor for a moment before giving a single shake of his head. "No, sir, I guess I don't. I *do* know I don't like any of it. It smells of something more sinister than Jantan misdirection. It could even be from outside both governments. I don't know about you, old friend, but that scares me more than anything else."

Sundale couldn't help a sense of victory after Jason's dig. Actually, dig was too harsh a word. More like reminder. Ricky Carson had been Jason's direct superior going all the way back to Jason's first day as a pilot of Red 5. Even when Carson went from lead pilot to commanding a division, Jason remained under his command by taking over the Red and Gold groups. So much time together had forged a strong relationship. One that allowed Jason to remind him of those years and the lessons they'd learned along the way with just two words.

General Carson dropped his shoulders with a sigh and a nod. "All right. You've made your point. I'll see what I can turn up. In the meantime, do me a favor and don't do anything drastic until you hear from me."

"I make no promises, sir," Jason said. "Just my best effort."

"That'll have to do. I'll get back to you soon. General Carson out."

The screen flicked off, and Jason took a deep breath. "Finally. It's about time we found some sense in all of this."

"It's a start," Yarain said. "What do we do now?"

"The only thing we can do: continue our mission and hope Ricky can get us some answers."

Sundale stared at Jason with ears erect in shock. "We can't just sit and wait to be hunted."

Jason stood and shrugged. "What do you suggest? We don't know where the enemy, where the predator, is or for that matter *who* he is. We can't fight random unknowns; we could injure a pack mate while leaving ourselves vulnerable to the very enemy we seek to fend off. No. We have to wait until we know more. Impatience walks with disaster, Sundale. And I for one don't like disaster very much."

"Nor do I," Sundale said with softening ears.

He wanted to say more. He wanted to argue against just sitting back and watching from the brush. He also knew better than to try. Jason's mind wasn't going to be changed. He also kept quiet because somewhere within, Sundale might even agree with him.

He just couldn't stop wondering where the line was between being impatient and being proactive.

Chapter 3

Whisky Tango Foxtrot

Jason couldn't help a contented sigh. Auto-pilot or not, his hands rested on the controls as if he might absorb peace through them. The stars through the fighter's windows were nice too. Much, much better than the last two hours.

They'd spent that time trying, or rather failing, to get more answers out of Red 7. Jason heard the "access denied" tone so many times, he wasn't sure if he was still hearing it. Bypasses didn't get them anywhere, and the crew refused to offer a single word when questioned.

They'd finally surrendered and rejoined the group in space. At least there, they had some control, though even then, the veteran pilot couldn't help seeing danger on the horizon. With no actual sign of it, his instincts alone drove him to keep the convoy at condition 2 just in case.

So far, all that came was the auto-pilot announcing they'd reached their destination. *At last, the only highlight on the trip.* Jason took the controls as the convoy dropped out of Hyper Light inside the Klistro system. Jason left the convoy under Carter's care while he led 1st squad in close to the seventh planet so they could do their work. The rest of the group scanned from a distance to test their pods as well. In the meantime, his eyes did their own scanning.

Pictures do not do this thing justice. Klistro Seven was a gas giant slightly larger than Jupiter. While it also had bands of clouds on its surface, that was where the similarities ended. Many of those bands were perpetually on fire, but not all the same color. Iridescent reds and oranges gave it a sparkle and shine with pinks and purples creating an odd glow as everything swirled, most often in places where the bands mixed to a small degree. Parts of it flashed now and then as pockets of hydrogen ignited, setting off natural fireworks of the same shining colors. Despite a few scientific discoveries, no one really knew for sure why things worked the way they did within the clouds.

Even in low orbit, the glow filled the cockpit like a campfire in the dead of night. The scanner's noises were close enough to crickets that Jason thought he had one on his lap for a second. He thought about hitting the food-processor in the back for a marshmallow just for the heck of it.

This is what I joined for. He was too young back then to understand the perils of adventure, but not too young to know the wonders he'd see. Though he'd seen far more blood in his day than beauty, sometimes the beauty made up for it.

"What I wouldn't give for a field of grass to lay on right now," Yarain said.

Jason nodded his agreement, near laughing. "I know what you mean. Add a couple of mice, and I bet you'd be in paradise."

"Close to it. Uh, Gold 8 and 9 have finished their scans."

"We're not far behind. Once the squad's done, we'll be back on our—"

Alarms and dim blue lighting replaced the white, and Sundale's barks shattered everything.

"***SHELLS! RIPPLE! RIPPLE!*** Bearing zero-by-zero. Impact: ten ticks."

Jason felt the preverbal switch flip in his head the moment things changed. By the time Sundale's call came, his emotions had already been pushed into a corner so he could react without them getting in the way.

He threw the fighter into max reverse beside the other four fighters as his head snapped forward to find the torpedoes in the stars. Even without the sensor overlay, he saw the familiar sight of long black cylinders with a glow behind them. They were coming in a volley large enough to impress a locust swarm. Some were heading for the convoy while others went straight for him and the others retreating beside him.

Shit! "Flak formation. Cover the convoy. 1st squad, drop chaff now."

Jason hit the same button as he turned his guns into the volley. Pods along the hull scattered tiny magnetic mines between them and the torpedoes. The rest of first squad were also spraying the volley with streams of plasmoids from their four main gatling cannons. Each turret added an additional pair of streams, but even with Sundale's warning, it was too late. With no time to react, and the natural evasion patterns of the torpedoes, barely half a dozen were stopped before they came in for the kill.

The five fighters caught alone could only float around in a circle in the vain hope of getting some of the torpedoes to run into each other. It was a desperate tactic that did work on rare occasions, just not this time. The group gathered near the transports didn't have enough additional time to fare any better. Despite their extensive barrage of fire, several warheads would land on target.

At the last second, Jason turned Gold 1's belly to the volley, spun his ship to spread the damage, clinched his teeth, and prayed his shields would hold against that many torpedoes.

He felt the thud of impact, but the blast never came. Instead, each hit engulfed the fighter in an odd electrical field that did little more than add static to his screens. The lack of true explosion caught him so off guard he barely felt the impact of the rest of the salvo.

You've gotta be kidding me. Someone wastes a perfectly executed surprise assault by using some weird kind of EMP charges? They'd have done better with real torps packing the usual explosive, shaped charge, shrapnel, and plasmoid burst warheads. While they wouldn't threaten a shielded capital ship, the shields of a Scorn were thin enough that a salvo that large could have done plenty of damage. *So why the EMP treatment?*

"Gold group, reform on the convoy," Jason said, still a little stunned. He eased his ship back toward the transports, wishing for a bucket of aspirin. "Sundale, damage report. Yarain, situation report right after."

"No damage," Sundale said. "The sensors and static will clear up in a minute. All systems are fine, no drain on the shields. Go, Yarain."

"No sign of enemy ships as yet," Yarain said. "Sensors are still resetting. Multiple strikes on the group, no hits on the transports, but fleet wide status remains unchanged."

"How many got hit?" Jason asked.

"All fighters report hits. None on the transports."

"Same warheads?"

"Yes."

"I wonder what the plan was," Sundale said. "The only way we'd have an issue is if we hadn't caught the sabotage."

Jason felt his stomach plummet as the pieces fell into place. They find power junction boxes, modified to be less hardened and missing redundancies, installed in all their fighters without authorization. A few days later, they're ambushed by enough torpedoes to ensure each ship is hit by a strong EM field at least once. *Too much coincidence. Someone planned this.*

He glanced back at Sundale while his heart rate doubled. "Sun, hypothetical: we left the bad junction boxes in place. What would the effect have been?"

Sundale's ears turned in nervous thought, though his tails remained still. "Nothing at first. We might detect a problem with the circuit paths but nothing we could make sense of without more digging."

"Wouldn't condition two have triggered a failure?"

"Not immediately on its own."

"*NEW* contact!" Yarain said. "One, make that two, raider frigates coming around the planet. They are on attack vector."

"Their weapons are at full power," Sundale added. "Shields are inactive at this time. Jason, I'm reading multiple empty munitions racks on their outer hull."

"Well, there's an answer or two," Jason said. "Sundale, would this change things in our hypothetical?"

Sundale's tails had begun to wave, as had Yarain's "Yes. The EM field would have exacerbated the damage and without redundancies, the added drain of combat would strain the junctions past breaking point."

"Connections fail, we lose power, and the raiders would have thirty-five floating targets to do with as they please."

Jason blew out his stress while watching the frigates on their approach.

They were little more than dots against the glow of the planet, but their profiles appeared on his sensor screen.They'd made some updates, but not enough to change the design. They were still built like large, bulging ovals with wings at the back in a T formation on each side. Wires and other 'utensils' they used for salvaging their captures hung underneath like twisted bug legs, currently tucked for flight. Their dark purple paint job and few markings didn't make them look like much, but he'd faced enough to know the shell masked a surprisingly decent, if barely armed, starship. Their crews also tended to wear a shared uniform. The two details were unique to these particular pirates which had earned them the honor of being called "raiders."

Still didn't make sense though. Two raider frigates weren't a match for a full group of Scorns. The EMP torpedoes might have knocked them out, but that still left them facing a five to two deficit. Transports weren't built for combat, but neither were raider frigates. For one thing, their ECM and ECCM systems were basically non-existent, which meant even basic combat ships could easily target them at long range. They were more like mobile salvagers and troop deployment platforms. In a fight like this, he'd still bet on the transports if only by a narrow margin. So why not send a much better armed cruiser to ensure victory? It didn't add up.

Faced with no time to digest things, Jason went with the first idea that came to his mind. No matter how nuts it sounded.

He opened a channel to his group only. He needed the transports to stay ignorant if this was going to work. "Gold 1 to all units, listen up! When I give the order, turn like you're going to engage, count eight, then power down all systems. Make it look like you've been disabled. If they fire on us, power up and engage. Otherwise, you are to take no action. No questions, people. Stay alert, and be ready for more orders."

Jason turned to each of his crew to prepare his own ship for the maneuver. "Yarain, I need you to keep an eye on things. Tell me what the raiders do, what the transports do, everything. Walk the line between feint and alertness. I don't want to miss a step here."

"Understood, sir."

"Sundale, you're on system control. On my order, count eight, then kill us. Don't forget the auto-protocols. After that, see if you can manage a pulse of the active sensors without giving away the gambit."

Sundale punched at his console without so much as a glance forward. "Yes, sir. I'll be ready."

Jason returned his focus to his window and screens while his heart thundered in his chest. The next few minutes promised to be some of the most interesting of his career. Just so long as they weren't the last of his career.

Yarain reported ready status from the group as the frigates cleared the outer rim of the planet. By now, even the most inattentive soldier would have seen them, visually or on sensors. Their shields rippled on while a host of defensive turrets turned toward the Scorns. While not a real threat to a group with their heads on straight, they couldn't be ignored either.

Pawn to king's rook four. It was their first step. Time to take his.

"Okay people. Let's do this. Fan out as if we were going to attack on multiple vectors. Begin your count... now!"

He turned toward the incoming ships, acting as if he didn't have a gambit in play. He didn't bother counting. He trusted Sundale too much to split his focus. He left the fox to set the trap while he charged in. His mind checked details and plans as if he really was going to attack. The group spread out around him, selling the act. He tensed on the controls. *Any second now... should be coming—*

The fighter gave a shudder as power to her engines vanished. The lights flickered, then everything but his primary sensor display and controls went out. Sundale fired the braking thrusters in place of the emergency system, bringing their forward momentum to a halt just as the last of the systems went offline. When it was over, they were drifting and completely dark.

"Nicely done, Captain," Jason said between breaths.

Jason heard pure focus in Yarain's voice. "We still have to see if the raiders believed it."

True enough. The quality of the act would soon be judged by the actions of their audience. Jason watched the ships come at them while keeping an eye on his display. The raider's turrets remained primed, but they otherwise gave no clue as to their plans. They just kept moving. So straight and steady, Jason feared they might get run over.

Then Yarain's console beeped at her. "They're hailing us."

This should be good. "See what you can do to maintain the gambit but put em on. Audio only."

A channel opened, and a deep, heavy voice came over a line touched by static. "My, my, how the tables have turned. A second ago, I was worried. Now I'm just amused. To think the mighty Gold Group is floating in space like so many rocks to be cracked open."

Gotta admire his bravado, I guess. Jason had to swallow to stay in character. "Spare me the grandstanding. Let's talk this out before you do something you'll regret."

"And give you time to make repairs? I think not. No, we're going to bring you aboard, nice and slow, and make you our guests. Behave yourselves, and you will be granted your lives. If one person steps out of line... well, our airlock has multiple functions."

Seriously? "Do you really think we'd just float here without getting word out? We've already called for reinforcements. I'm betting you've let your coils slow down too. I imagine you'll be facing a couple of *real* frigates in about, oh, a minute?"

A rumble of laughter cracked over the line. "I think not. With your sensors down, I'm sure you didn't notice the communications jammer we're carrying. Our little gifts made sure you didn't see it activate. You're all alone, Major. Now be a good boy and sit tight. We'll be saying hello in person soon enough."

With the channel closed, Jason didn't waste time. "Can you confirm that?"

"I can," Yarain said. "I'm ashamed to admit I thought it was left over from the shells, but long-range comms are down."

"They planned well. Every angle covered."

"Except for a restless pilot and his fox," Sundale added.

Jason chuckled. "Quite right. I think we've learned all we can from our gambit. Time to say hello our way. Yarain, record orders for burst transmission. I know they'll see it, but they'll think it's us making other plans. By the time they think it through, we'll be pouncing."

After a couple of taps by Yarain, an indicator on Jason's screen showed the recording ready. "All fighters, hold for my order to execute. On my order, power up and follow me in. Start your shield generators first. Even fighters, take on the starboard ship; odd fighters, take port. Seventh squadron, shadow the transports, provide cover if required. Gold 31, activate sensor suite, watch for any more surprises. Hold responses."

Sundale fed Jason target data soon after the orders went out. *Must have snuck a sensor burst.* Though it risked breaking cover early, Jason was glad to have enemy hardpoints already plotted. Besides, he got the data mere seconds before Yarain spoke from her station.

"First called."

"Final Star," Sundale said.

Jason rolled his fingers on the controls.

"We hold the line." He then tapped his console. "Gold Group; execute!"

At first, only the shield generator got power. Seconds later, the fighter glowed to life as the group confirmed their orders by doing the same. Blue combat lights remained in place as Jason charged in on the raider frigates. His group was quick on his six, splitting to their targets like crocodiles waking from a nap. All outer lighting was gone, including a veil over the windows to further contain interior lighting.

Jason led his half of the group in formation against the port side frigate. The raider's turrets tried to intercept, but Gold Group had already gotten their shields up. They then returned in kind. Four gatling cannons per fighter sent streams of orange plasmoids flowing onto the enemy shields like a rain of fire. Scorn turrets joined the fray, compounding the pressure. Each shot created a green flare as they tried to burn away the frigate's shields faster than her generators could replace them.

The frigate's shortcomings soon became apparent. First, was the rate of fire advantage Interstar had over the rest of the galaxy. Being the only ones to solve the gatling cannon overheat problem, the Scorns were able to pour on more shots per second than the enemy. Second, was evasion. Small fighter-bombers were far more agile than a salvager frigate. Though it meant they couldn't concentrate on a target point for long, the group weaved around the defensive fire enough to greatly minimize the hits they received. What did land only flared blue, indicating reduced damage to the shield layer.

The Scorns floated around each other like a swarm of hummingbirds. Except these birds could strike at long range while twisting, flipping, and flying in all directions to avoid most of the reprisal. When a patch of shielding got thin, a change of angle gave the generator time it needed to refill the protective layer. Jason was able to keep his ship on target while also keeping their damage taken to almost nothing. He let the occasional shudder unnerve him just enough to keep him from getting overconfident as General Carson had taught him.

That same training kicked in when he saw eight hatches open in the sides of the frigate. He didn't wait to find out what was coming out of them.

"Sun, paint those holes. Gold Group, focus fire on the holes. Stand by to evade and counter."

Jason really hoped they were just hidden turrets. Instead, he got more torpedoes. Chaff was spread while their streams of fire tried to intercept the ordinance. But their own dodging made it hard to maintain fire on such small points. While the chaff caught a couple of rounds, it didn't catch them all. Jason once again had to turn his fighter belly first, so the thickest shield and armor layer took the brunt of the impact.

This time, it was a traditional round. A large explosion chipped at his shields, as did a volley of charge-pumped plasmoid rounds like a shotgun shell, hence the slang. Shaped shrapnel tried to punch through, but the shield layer held just enough to catch every one. The force made his fighter a little hard to control, which made it harder still to avoid the barrage of turret fire that came his way. Fortunately, his group was well trained. From the moment of impact, they rallied around him to absorb much of the fire while his own shields were rebuilt.

But his was not the only fighter hit. The group had to dance around each other to make sure no one took armor damage after a torpedo hit. Alarms warned the shields were having a hard time keeping up. Jason heard growls from behind him. He shared the sentiment. Enough was enough. Time to end it.

"Split up and fall back," Jason said. "Prepare to turn and pound.

Concentrate fire. Sync your missiles but hold until you see the color change."

The group scattered and got some distance, forcing the frigate's turrets to split their focus as well. It also meant the few remaining torpedoes found their hit rate plummet until the frigate ran out entirely. They tried to focus on Gold 1. It only meant members of the group could more easily cover their leader, though the status screen did warn of a heating generator. It didn't matter. He could finish the fight long before auto-shutdown.

"Sundale, target point, now."

"Already set," Sundale said. "Missiles locked. Syncro-fire engaged and ready."

"Group aligned," Yarain said. "Awaiting order."

"Engage, engage, all fighters engage."

Like a swarm of bees, the group turned from their evasion to charge in on the frigate. Cannons fired. Turrets fired. All toward one point on the starboard flank of the ship as it turned the bulk of its turrets toward them. The laser focus meant they were more exposed, but it also meant a much smaller area was getting obliterated. Scorn shields flared, but none halted their assault. The group simply rotated who was in the lead so that no one took the brunt of the damage for long.

The concentrated fire turned the side of the frigate solid white as her shields were striped. They tried to recover, but the generators couldn't replace the layer fast enough. Then the white took on a blue tint. The Syncro-fire system fired the first volley of missiles from every fighter at once. They arrived just as the last of the local shielding vanished.

The frigate's armor erupted like a thousand volcanoes under the barrage. Missiles came in coordinated volleys, blasting hull off in chunks while tearing any hope of shielding away. As the group moved in for the kill, four laser emitters per fighter sprang to life, further cutting into the frigate's exposed hull. The Scorns flew into ever thinning fire, a single force intent on erasing this frigate from existence.

The frigate made a desperate, sudden advance straight into the group at full thrust while also firing another volley of torpedoes mixed with much smaller missiles. The combined threat forced them to turn away, but not before they fired one last volley of missiles into the fire fields of the frigate's hull. Jason allowed a glance out the corner of his view. He smiled as a small explosion turned into a larger one that tore a line out of the frigate's side. The ship drifted over, and she now had a gaping, burning gash missing from her starboard side.

Must have hit an armory or magazine. Let's see what else I can blow out.

His group turned with him into a fraction of the previous turret fire as they prepared to put the ship out of her misery. The frigate shocked them all by jumping to hyper-light before they could fire another shot. No doubt they'd started spinning their drives the moment the group came to life. How they'd survived that kind of damage to engage hyper-light was a question they'd probably never get answered.

"Tough ship," Jason said with a touch of admiration. "We'll need to mention the addition of torpedo tubes to the design. Not a tactic we've seen before. Battle update."

"No damage," Sundale said. "Both magazines at fifty-four percent. Shield generator at three-hundred C."

Hot, but still plenty of room to spare.

"No fighters lost or disabled," Yarain said. "Both frigates have disengaged. No other contacts on scope. Shouldn't we go after them?"

Jason shook his head. "Not with five transports in our charge. We made our point. No sense ruining it now by leaving our ships unguarded. Speaking of which, what's their status?"

"All five in... tact. Stand by."

I know I have to know, but I really don't want to. "Problem, Captain?"

The fact that she didn't reply answered his question.

He twisted the fighter on an interception course for the transports. He didn't get far before Yarain finally responded. "Jason, you need to hear this."

A woman's hard voice broke through static clear as day. "Mayday, mayday, mayday, our ship is under siege. U.S.S. *Marco Polo* has been boarded by hostile forces. Some of our crew is assisting them. We have secured engineering and the bridge, but we don't know how long we can keep them out. We require immediate assistance. Mayday, mayday, mayday, our ship is under siege..."

Can I start this week over again? First sabotage, then Red 7 pulls their weapons on Sundale, then raiders come to exploit the sabotage, and now one of the transports is facing a mutiny backed by outside forces. The way things are going, I'm going to lose what little mind I have left. Jason let the thoughts last long enough for one quick wipe over an eyebrow, then he got to work.

Though he did look up first. "Can I get a break here, please? All second seats, gear up. Stand by to assist the *Marco Polo* with her borders. Sun, hold your seat for now. Yarain, call for reinforcements."

"I can't," Yarain said. "The *Marco Polo* has activated a communications jammer of her own. All subspace comms are down."

"Okay. What about her transit pads? Can we use them?"

"They're locked down."

"See if they can open their hanger then. We'll land Gold 1 inside, use the wing transponders to board our own troops. Have the group split among the transports, put one squad on overwatch. Have them contact the captains if they can, but no one spins their HL drives without our permission until further notice. Sundale, keep an eye on the ships. Let me know if any of them spin their drives."

While both executed their orders, Jason turned his fighter to aim at the *Marco Polo*. There was no outward sign of the fighting going on inside unless you counted a lack of movement. The members of his first squad formed up around the ship. Three of the five fighters settled near her engines just in case the mutineers managed to gain control. Jason held his position so he could make a combat landing in their hanger if he had to.

"Captain Saar will try to open the hanger but says it'll likely draw attention," Yarain said.

"We can handle that," Jason said. "They won't have any weapons that can threaten a Scorn. Stand by to board. Sun, pass your watch to Gold 8, then gear up. I want one of us in armor by the time we land. Yarain, plot for a combat landing. You know the drill."

While Sundale worked with his gear, Jason watched the hanger doors with a growing knot in his chest. Fighter crews were trained to be versatile for just such an occurrence, but it was still a big risk. He didn't have numbers, and training was a far cry from experience. Only Yarain had seen any protracted foot combat, though even that was condensed to a three-day assault on the colony of Phoenix Perch. Then again, her actions during that assault were one reason he felt no hesitation choosing his own fighter for the lead.

He and Sundale had seen some foot action in their time as well. Though it technically went against standard protocol, to say nothing of the tension it caused in his limbs, the three of them were uniquely qualified to lead this counter assault. Besides, if anyone's neck was going to be on the line, he wanted it to be his.

It was only a minute or two before the hanger doors opened. Jason waited to hear Sundale buckle in, then he rushed the fighter forward. They flew straight toward the hanger at a speed that would cause significant damage to them and the walls they would tear through, but Jason trusted Yarain's timing. Just before the fighter touched the atmospheric force field, her preset thrust program went into effect. The flight computer brought their ship to an abrupt halt dead center of the hanger. The ship almost literally dropped onto her landing pads the exact moment they reached full deployment. In less than five seconds, Gold 1 had claimed the *Marco Polo*'s hanger.

"Perfect timing as always," Jason said. "Activate the transponders. Gold Group begin boarding. Sundale, you have overwatch. Our turn to suit up."

Jason worked his armor out of its stall to his left while soft claps announced the arrival of the group's AESOs on the fighter's wings. It was nothing more than a streamlined yet blocky combat vest that sat over his combat knife. Thin plating covered the upper-most part of his arms and legs, and it carried just enough battery for a thin particle shield that wouldn't last long or resist more than one or two hits. His helmet covered his entire head save for an almost triangle cut-out over his mouth, nose, and eyes, though it had a thin display strip over the eyes for a basic heads-up display.

It was standard issue for ship crews, and nothing like true front-line armor Terrines would use on such a mission. *It'll have to do.*

He claimed his standard issue twin-barreled rifle and checked on

Yarain. She was already standing in full holdren armor with rifle in hand, waiting for her first father to lead this next hunt.

Holdren armor covered their entire torso including the hips and abdomen. Thinner protection went down their limbs to the first joint. Their helmet covered most of their head, not counting slots for the ears, with a thin layer going out over the muzzle that stopped at the mouth line. Like Jason's, the eyes had a thin display cover to allow for a HUD. Their side-arm was held in a holster, more on their ribs than their hip, by a leather strap so that it would stay there should they go on all fours in either form.

Yarain held her position, waiting for her alpha—*erm*—*her first father, someday I'll keep that straight*, to lead this next hunt.

Jason nodded approval, then wiped all levity from his face. "Do we have the hanger?"

"Yes," Sundale said.

"Very good. Lock her down, then form up. Let's get this started."

Sundale set the fighter on a security lock down. She wouldn't fly without her crew, but she'd remain primed in case they needed to use her quickly. Jason led them outside just as the hanger doors finished closing. They met up with First Lieutenant Hars Gilnt, Gold 2's AESO, a young woman whose Asian heritage and silk-smooth black hair hid a formidable soldier beneath a shell many would use to define her. Rumor said if it weren't for Sundale, she'd be flying second seat on Gold 1. In this case, rumor was right, though Jason would never admit it officially. What he would admit was the weight having her around took off his shoulders.

Lieutenant Gilnt gave him a prim and proper salute, going so far as to wait for it to be returned before speaking.

"We've secured all entry points, sir. We have reports the hostiles are focusing their efforts on the bridge. I have sixth and seventh squads setting up what defensive positions they can. The rest of the group is ready for counter assault."

Jason raised an impressed eyebrow. "You trying to outdo me, Lieutenant?"

"Wouldn't dream of it, sir."

"Oh yes you would. Scary thing is, you might just manage it. Did you send anyone inside?"

"No, sir. Figured you'd want to lead that party yourself, sir."

"Someone knows how to get promoted," Sundale said after a quiet ruff of laughter.

Gilnt couldn't stop her smile. Jason returned it before she felt she had to swallow it. The thing neither of them knew was Carter had submitted the paperwork before they left to meet the transports. It included Jason's signature and recommendation. A promotion was coming, just not from him.

"I'll think about it," Jason said. "In the meantime, separate second and third squads. Once we're inside, I want you to find and disable that communications jammer. The rest of us will deal with the assault on the bridge."

Lieutenant Gilnt saluted again before vanishing on her task. As Yarain and Sundale moved to follow, Jason made a decision he didn't realize he had been thinking on.

"Yarain, hold up."

Both stopped and perked their ears toward him. "What is it, Jason?" Yarain asked.

"Sundale and I will lead the team ourselves. I want you to stay here."

Her ears shifted back and forth as if searching. "To do what, sir?"

"One of us needs to be here in case Gold 1 needs piloting. With Sundale and I leading the teams, that leaves you."

"With respect sir, Sundale is the better pilot."

"True, but you're more than capable. Your stunt on Phoenix Perch proved you can think fast and adapt faster, and being a former first mother doesn't hurt. The way this mission is going, I'd rather have a proven leader take command in my... absence, and I apologize, Sun. I didn't—"

Sundale waved it off, though Jason saw a ruffle of his hackles that might have said otherwise. Jason felt like he had to swallow a hot coal at himself for putting things that way. He wished he had ears he could flatten to apologize further, but the situation forced him to accept Sundale's dismissal for now. *Boy, do I owe him for that one.*

Yarain, meanwhile, almost didn't stop a growl. She couldn't hide the curl of her lips. "A first mother of *holdrens*, sir. Something I haven't been for years. As for Phoenix Perch I –"

Jason held a hand up. He'd wasted time. More than he should have allowed given the situation. Now *he* had to be the first father to protect *his* pack.

He was about to repeat Yarain's assignment. Her ears and mouth corners pulling back stopped him.

"Yes sir," she said, protest lacing both words yet surrendering to her orders as well.

Jason nodded approval. "Keep the hanger safe, Captain. Leave the rest to me."

"To **US**, sir," Sundale corrected, almost ruffing the word instead of saying it.

Jason rolled his eyes but couldn't hide from the reminder. He buried it anyway while motioning Sundale to follow. The gathered teams readied their weapons as they approached while Lieutenant Gilnt gave another salute.

Jason returned it before addressing the team as a whole. *Woman needs to relax a little.* "Stay sharp. We don't know who we're dealing with so assume the worst. Check your corners, stay loose, call out if you see something. Some of the crew are in on it but some may just be trying to ride it out. Check your targets if you can but *do not* hesitate to fire if threatened. I refuse to bury any of you today. Questions?" A chorus of no sir's came back. "Prepare to move. We'll clear the exit point, then split."

The teams lined the walls one after the other. Weapons lay ready. Sundale led one line with his tails waving. Jason had seen it before. His tails said uneasy, while his forward ears changed it to ready for the hunt. Jason nodded at his friend, wished he could untie that knot in his chest, then stepped beside Sundale up to the control panel.

"May He watch over us," Jason muttered. He hit the panel to open the door.

Sundale was first out. He rushed forward at an angle into the corridor where he fell to one knee while the line filed in behind him. A member from the other side went in and did the same, pointing the opposite direction. Jason went in and leveled his rifle over the perked ears of his comrade. The two lines continued to filter in, so each direction added a member in a constant tick-tock fashion. Firing lines were made, weapons were readied, but there was no one to shoot at. *Small favors.*

Jason knelt beside Sundale and tapped his own ear. Sundale shook his head no, a motion more akin to a pendulum thanks to a lack of use. It's not that holdrens couldn't do it, they just didn't except on rare occasions for the sake of non-holdrens.

Jason turned to motion for Gilnt to move out but found he didn't have to. Just him turning around was enough for her to move.

Woman also needs her own group.

"Sun, you got directions to the bridge?"

"Yes," Sundale said. "First right."

As the team moved forward, Jason's com clicked open. "Gold Group be advised: do not trust your scanners. Reports of scramblers in action. Will attempt to confirm."

"Where the hell are they getting this kind of gear?" Lieutenant Antwan asked.

"We'll ask them when we find 'em," Jason said. "Move out! Stay alert."

The team advanced like a snake sneaking up on a kill. The smell of grit, dust, and metal permeated the air. Bland, square, industrial corridors that screamed 'work ship' were broken only by grey doors and sharp corridor intersections. As reported, their scanners couldn't crack through a scrambler field that made it impossible to be sure if a room was full or empty until you were right next to it. Thus, they had to assume each intersection had an ambush waiting for them. That meant a thirty second or less walk to the bridge took minutes to travel safely. Each corridor saw Jason's knot get tighter and tighter until it felt like it might tie up his limbs. Only his internal switch kept him focused and alert.

They finally came to the corner nearest the bridge. As the team settled in for the counter, Jason again tapped his ear at Sundale. The holdren nodded awkwardly, tilted his head, then lifted four fingers.

"Sounds like cutting tools," he added quietly.

Probably trying to slice into the bridge. Jason motioned the team into place. He risked peeking around the corner and found there were indeed only four men. All of whom were facing the bridge doors.

Jason moved members of the team to the opposite side of the corridor, then led a portion of it in picking their way forward. He wanted to get as close as he could before engaging.

The closer he got, the more he saw. Two men were trying to force their way through the door while the other two aimed their weapons in case the bridge crew tried to engage them. Jason couldn't get a good look at what kind of weapons they had, but he could see that neither was watching the corridor at all. They wore the same bright orange shirts with reflectors on the shoulders and khaki pants with more reflectors down the legs. Standard in-flight uniform for this particular cargo transport company, though the combat vests they wore certainly weren't.

Funny thing about civilians, they rarely understand tactics. Except that didn't help his nerves any. Four men was hardly a ship under siege. Even with the vests, security forces on board would have been more than enough to handle them. Something more was going on.

However, Jason couldn't find a reason to ignore the gift they'd handed him. When he was some thirty feet away, he decided to stop being greedy. He aimed his rifle, saw his team do the same, and took a deep breath to loosen the knot.

"Drop your weapons!"

The team echoed similar calls to surrender. The two with weapons turned to fire. The walls echoed with the sound of soft, sharp claps as the group riddled the fools with plasmoid bolts. The two workers reached for weapons and met the same fate.

Jason motioned for the team to advance. They checked the final intersection while others rushed forward to confirm the kills. Members of the team set up proper watch positions without anyone giving an order to do so. It warmed Jason's heart in a way only proud commanders would understand.

Sundale sent his heart falling just as fast. "Jason, we may have a problem."

Of course we do.

Jason joined him where the bodies were being examined. As far as he could tell, there didn't seem to be anything out of the ordinary about them. That is until he realized they had all been carrying long, thick rifles that ended in a gatling gun barrel. Quite a bit heavier than a standard rifle, personal mini-guns, or PMG's, were worth it for the firepower. In the right hands, it could almost act like a long-range blow torch. Even a Scorn could have its shields threatened if they took fire for too long in the same place.

"What the hell is going on here?" Jason said. "Where would a civilian get that kind of firepower?"

"And are they the only ones?" Lieutenant Antwan said.

The thought turned Jason's spine to ice. So much so he jumped out of his skin when the bridge's doors clunked open. All but those on watch trained their weapons in case of ambush. They were met with a woman whose dark brown skin and even darker black hair managed to glow in its own way. She had her hands up, but her gaze bore through anyone who might challenge her.

"I'm Captain Saars," she said. Her voice was just as hard and certain as her mayday message. "And I can tell you there are a lot more where thcy camc from."

Jason glanced at Sundale, who confirmed her identity with a scan of the badge on her uniform. Jason then told her she could relax.

"I apologize—"

"No need, Major Harlem," she said. "I can't even trust my own crew so I wouldn't expect you to trust me at face value either. However, I can vouch for everybody on this bridge. If they're in on this too, they're such fine actors they almost deserve the win."

I like her already. "Any idea how many we're looking at or where they are now?"

"No idea to both, Major. But I can tell you at least a dozen of them are raiders. Ain't no mistaking those uniforms."

"Raiders? How did they get on board?"

"My 'loyal' crew unlocked the transit pads. I'm not alone either. At least three of the other ships were boarded as well. Thanks to your alert, those assaults were snuffed out before they got a firm hold. But lucky me, I get the only batch carrying those things. I don't know where they got them, but if I find out they came from my ship, hell will only be part of the bill."

That cold chill from before nearly froze Jason solid. Over a dozen men? Armored and armed with PMG's? Who ever planned this thing really knew how to cover their bases. It also meant things were not as simple as they seemed. Neither Yarain nor Gilnt had any reason to expect such heavy firepower. And if the raiders had any other surprises, even Yarain could find herself with too many losses to adapt in time.

"Sundale, contact Yarain. Antwan, contact Gilnt. Warn them the hostiles are raiders and likely have heavy weapons," Jason said. "Captain, how well armed are you? Any casualties?"

"Got four security guards with Rinom-twelve rifles and vests," Captain Saars said. "Nothing like what you carry, but they're usually enough. No one who made it here got hurt. The rest didn't make it at all or they're helping the raiders."

"What about the jammers? Do you know where they are?"

"Jammers? This is a civilian ship, Major. Only jammers we got are the computer lock-outs I sometimes need to get my crew off the net and on their jobs."

"Curiouser and curiouser," Jason muttered.

"Jason, I can't raise Yarain," Sundale said.

Jason could literally feel parts of his body spinning faster as if powering up. "What? Can you connect with Gold 1?"

"Yes, but Yarain isn't responding. I'm trying—"

Several explosions echoed down the corridor, followed by bursts of more sharp claps. The team whipped around to erase whatever was coming toward them. Sound alone was there.

That almost made it worse.

"They're attacking the hanger," Jason said. "Fifth squad, grab a PMG and stay here to cover the bridge. Rest of you grab the others and follow me. They may need help."

Jason left his rifle with Captain Saars in favor of a PMG of his own. A deeper, high-speed popping sound joined the claps soon after the team started moving. *Well, she knows they have them now.* Jason tried to get his own PMG comfortable in his arms as the team moved fast and careful back the way they came. Corners were cleared just to be sure, but they were intent on running over anyone stupid enough to get between them and their comrades. Jason had Sundale try Yarain a few more times, but no reply ever came.

Doorways rushed by while Jason's feet kept pace with his heart. Neither liked the amount of weapons fire they heard. Either their side had gotten reinforcements, or they were pinned down by an excessive amount of fire. He'd soon learn which as the flashes from the battle began coming into view. Jason adjusted his grip on his weapon as he kept an eye ahead for an enemy to unleash it on.

He feared he was too late when the fire-fight suddenly ground to a halt. With no idea what had happened, Jason was forced to pick the next junction as a place to stop and gather what intel he could. The team collected at the corners and behind the support columns for cover while he got his breath under control.

"Sun, try Yarain again."

Sundale tapped the side of his helmet and sounded no less worried than Jason felt when he spoke. "Sundale to Yarain, what's your status, over? Repeat, what's your status, over?"

They waited a second that felt like a year before they got a highly distorted reply. "Situation secure. Enemy force has surrendered and is being disarmed now. We have casualties, but none are serious. Hanger remains under control."

Jason's heart must have heard Yarain's report because his ears sure didn't. They were too busy joining the rest of his body in relief to hear her alive and well. He wasn't alone since much of the team, Sundale in particular, breathed their own sighs at the same time.

He didn't let down his guard until they arrived at the hanger. Yarain met them at the hanger door without so much as a smudge on her fur or armor. The walls weren't so lucky. They bore the scars of several small explosions and an excessive amount of plasmoid fire. Most of the damage was cosmetic, though some of the lights were splintered, and the walls were heavily pitted. Several bodies were scattered in the hall and just inside the hanger doors. Some wore the transport uniforms, but most wore a blue uniform so dark it was nearly black. On the shoulders; down the arms; and from the boots running up the legs to the outside of the calves, the blue lightened some and looked like some kind of thin padding. No other markings were found beyond simple grey bars on the shoulders that seemed to denote rank.

Jason motioned for Lieutenant Antwan to take the team inside the hanger before addressing Yarain directly. "Told you you'd do well."

Yarain gave a gentle growl he couldn't quite decipher. "I got lucky."

"Oh? Do tell. What happened? Why didn't you respond?"

"I was busy. As for the enemy, I heard them coming down the corridors. When I realized what they were after, I acted accordingly."

"What does that mean?"

"I used their objective against them. Nothing more."

"Nothing more?!" a soldier said. "Ma'am with respect, that was bloody brilliant!" When it became clear Yarain wasn't going to tell the story, the soldier did. "She laid a brilliant trap for them, sir. When they stormed the hanger, we were waiting across the hall. With some troops hidden in the cloaked fighter, we had them pinned down before they knew what hit them. Almost felt sorry for 'em, until they started putting up a proper fight."

Jason thumped the PMG on his shoulder and winced when it reminded him how heavy the weapon was. Didn't stop him from beaming pride at Yarain, though.

"Nothing more, huh?"

Yarain's ears went back, and her muzzle dropped. She might have blushed if holdrens could. Yet when her eyes again rose, they were narrow and defensive.

"All I **_DID_**, was act in the best interest of my team. I see no reason to be praised for that."

"I can think of a few, but that can wait. We have more important issues to deal with."

"Such as?"

Jason gave her another smile before giving in to her dodge. "Transport crews assisting a raider boarding party, all of them armed with

PMG's, military grade jammers on a civilian cargo run, just to name a few. Though speaking of which, have we heard from Gilnt yet?"

"You'll hear from her now, sir," Lieutenant Gilnt said. She was coming down the corridor with second squad behind her. "But you're not gonna like it."

"Lieutenant, I think they only thing I'm going to like about this mission is the snack I had on the way. Hit me."

"In searching for the jammers, we found this ship isn't loaded with what her manifest claims it is. Thus far, we've found empty crates that stored the PMG's, two APC's, more crates stuffed with heavy weapons, and one massive crate that had all the parts needed to build a Phantom interceptor. We're checking the rest of the hold now, but early indications are the load is entirely military."

Jason could feel his brain melting with each item she ticked off. Yarain's ears grew more and more perked to show a similar mindset.

Jason looked inside the hanger as the last of the hostiles still alive were grouped along a far wall. He searched for options amidst a worsening situation. Mutinous transports he could handle, if not understand. Their being assisted by raiders presented a troubling new tactic, but nothing a few protocol changes couldn't handle. Transports loaded with tons of military hardware instead of colony construction materials? That spoke of something much, much worse. He needed answers, but kept getting questions instead. Questions no one was able or willing to answer.

Time to change that. He thumped his PMG into his hand. There was only one way to get those answers once and for all.

"Sundale, head inside, take charge of the prisoners." Sundale ticked his ears forward then slipped inside the hanger. "Did you actually find the jammers through everything else?"

"Yes, sir!" the lieutenant said. "Subspace comms are back on, and we can trust our sensors again. Our troops are sweeping the ship now with help from transport security teams. We should have full control shortly."

"Make sure they account for every crewman on board as well as enemy combatants. Transit records should give you a clear number, and keep that cargo hold on lock down. Go lead the teams, Lieutenant. Yarain..."

He trailed off when he heard Sundale bark. It took a second, more careful call to realize it was his name being swallowed by the bark. "Jason. You better come in here."

Now what? Major Harlem clicked the safety off on his PMG just in case things got ugly again. "What is it, Sun? They giving you—"

Sundale thrust a man forward for him to get a better look at. He wore a khaki engineer's jumpsuit but that couldn't hide the military in his body. Nor the face of Red 7's pilot, who Jason had seen carted off to the brig a few hours ago.

"Meet the leaders of this little insurrection," Sundale said, not quite growling.

Jason couldn't think enough to growl.

"I got this, Sun. Go borrow Yarain's seat. Get us a ship with Terrines to help us out."

Sundale hesitated until Jason stared him down enough to force his ears to fall. Sundale left, but not without a quick growl for the prisoner.

"So," Jason said, "first you pull your weapon on my AESO, then you lead an assault on my group. I hope you have one hell of an explanation, cosman."

The man thrust his chin up, no respect to be found. "Molsen, Gary J., Captain. Serial number Alpha Sierra 1-1-3-9-7-4-4-8."

Jason looked frozen. In truth he almost fell over. "You've gotta be kidding me. Do you have any idea what you're facing?"

"Molsen, Gary J., Captain. Serial number Alpha Sierra 1-1-3-9-7-4-4-8."

That's it. That's the straw. Jason shook his head in disbelief. An Interstar fighter crew... he couldn't even finish the thought. Faced with an immovable soldier, not to mention a splitting headache, Jason tossed his PMG to one of his men.

"They try *anything*, hit em, shoot em, space em, in that order."

The solider nodded understanding. He added an evil grin which more than a few appeared to take seriously.

Good. Maybe they'll behave.

Jason went for his wrist-com. "Major Harlem to Gold 2. Situation secure here, but check with the other transports to see if they fared as well. Have Gold 8 and 9 land in the hanger to take over. I want to be in the stars when back-up arrives so I can land and deliver my report personally."

"Roger that," Gold 2's POSN said.

Captain Gomez came on shortly after. "We're not hearing much, Jason. What happened over there?"

"You wouldn't believe me if you saw it yourself."

"That bad?"

"Worse. Keep the transports secure. Hopefully we can end this mission without any more surprises."

"From your mouth to God's ears, sir. Gold 2 out."

Amen to that. "Yarain, take First Squad to the bridge. Make sure it stays secure, and get me General Carson. I don't care how."

Yarain had to jog to catch up as Jason stormed toward Gold 1. "He may still be with the Command Council, sir. I don't know if I can get to him."

"Come now, Captain. You know how to get around that."

"With or without a court marshal?"

Jason stopped to slow his mind a bit. "I'll take any heat. I'm tired of beating my head against a wall. Civilian transports loaded for war and Interstar soldiers willing to draw their weapon on Sundale are all fighting along side raiders. The medals on the Command Council need to be made aware, and General Carson is our best chance to be sure they hear the full, unedited, unbiased version."

Yarain's ears perked, though her tails gave a single wave. "Understood, sir. Just don't push too hard, and don't shoulder this alone."

"I'll... I'll try. Now get going."

Yarain left with barks for First Squad to join her.

Jason approached the hatch of his fighter just as Sundale was heading out of it. The holdren's helmet bounced off his back while he scratched at an ear with one hand. The other hand set down his rifle long enough to rub his back a moment.

"Armor still bothering you, Sun?" Jason said.

Sundale huffed while turning one ear forward to say yes. "Backup is on its way. ETA, ten or less."

"That quick? You tell them we're engaged or something?"

"Found them on maneuvers close by."

"Nicely done. Take command of the group here till they arrive. Gold 8 and 9 should be landing to provide assistance while I go out to meet the ships."

Sundale feigned surprise. "You sure you don't want Yarain?"

Jason's shoulders dropped. *Okay, I deserve that.* The fact that he did is why he didn't slap Sundale down for it. "You're not going to let that go for a while, are you?"

"***NOPE***."

Sundale tried to walk away, but Jason grabbed his arm to stop him. "Hey. I'm sorry. I had to assign the best people for the right jobs."

Sundale's hackles lifted, but only enough to match his frustration. "That I can take. Having my ability to lead doubted in public is another matter."

Jason nodded while trying not to get angry at himself. "You're right. My words... my words were stupid and inappropriate. I'm sorry. I'll do better next time, I promise."

Sundale stood still for a moment. Jason braced for a continued argument. Instead, he got a weak attempt to nip at his chin. A smile from Jason, a quick ruff of laughter from Sundale, and the matter ended there. The pilot could see lingering heat in his officer's ears and tails, but he knew what the nip meant. It didn't negate the anger so much as it signaled Sundale's willingness to let it go for the time being.

Small favors, Jason thought. *Very small favors.*

Chapter 4

Jigsaw Time

Jason took the pilot seat and flew Gold 1 out alone. Gold 4 and 5 went in right after to ensure they had the hanger well covered. The quietness of the cockpit left him somewhat nervous. Yet it also let him face his own thoughts without anyone to worry about while he skimmed updated reports.

He definitely needed some time off. Even a day would do wonders for him right now. A day spent at home for a change would be even better. He could see his wife, Yarain could see her mate, and Sundale his father. Who knows? Maybe they'd have time for a hunt or two. *I know Harmus wouldn't mind.* At the very least, Jason might figure out why this mission was hitting him so hard. This wasn't his first Murphy Flight, but that comment about "having an accomplished leader" in Yarain was as much a sign of strain as anything else. True or not, it was unfair to Sundale, and something that hadn't happened to him... ever, come to think of it.

At least he could relax in the present. As promised, back-up arrived within a few minutes of him hitting space. He whistled when he saw what Sundale had gotten them. First came ten cruisers, eight corvettes, and twelve frigates around the perimeter. These Jason really couldn't see save for their sensor contacts, though they did note the usual mix of frigate variants and cruiser weight classes. Then came six battleships that looked more like dark blue sharks sporting thick, swallow-like wings instead of their usual fins and tail. A somewhat simple design when compared to the four destroyers mixed into the formation. These beasts' skins were more an ocean blue with their main hull starting as a thick, blocky oval that quickly tapered to a point at the bow. A large ring like a bicycle wheel, complete with thick spokes, was attached at the rear.

Then came the Interstar Combat Vessel *Alamo*. A last hold out from the early days of the Jantan Wars, the *Waterloo* class carrier had begun to show its age as new designs of other ships rolled out of the shipyards. Many were calling for it to be replaced, though any who cited "outdated looks" were quickly silenced. That said, Jason had to agree with their point a little.

The thing didn't even have wings for goodness' sake, which meant much of her heat sinks were built into the main hull. It was quite literally a large, dark-grey box that slowly tapered to a point at the bow. Large nacelles, four on each side at the back, served as the hangers. She'd been updated with the newest technology over the years, but despite holding her own in war after war, she looked like a relic when compared to the modern deigns. A relic that sooner or later would begin to show her age in the field as well.

Outdated or not, Jason was glad to see her. He'd asked for back-up and gotten a carrier group. He got luckier still when he was on approach for a landing without having to ask. He entered a hanger nacelle, passed between two rows of mostly empty landing pads, and touched down on his assigned space. Some of the other pads emptied further as Scorns already on station were launching to help secure the transports. Not to mention a few troop shuttles no doubt full of Terrines itching to do something besides shoot targets.

Jason silently wished them well as he put his combat armor back in the cabinet. *Note to self: have someone get my rifle back from Captain Sarrs.* He headed for the hanger door still feeling the armor's weight, or rather the weight of trying to deal with everything that kept happening.

Being a carrier instead of a Precision Strike Command or Terrine base, it was a Caelnav flight officer standing there, waiting for him with clip-com in hand. Jason was getting tried of saluting but returned it anyway when the caelor gave one.

Thankfully, this galman, while respectful as he should be, was not as tight as Lieutenant Gilnt. "Welcome aboard the *Alamo,* Sir."

"Thank you, Galman," Jason said. "You have something for me?"

"Yes, sir. Captain Yarain reports you'll have a line with Admiral Carson momentarily. In the meantime, FCO Redding would like to talk with you in briefing room three, sir."

And the day was going so well. "Did he say why?"

"No sir, and if I may be honest, I didn't feel I should ask."

"Nor should you. Whatever it is, it's my problem. Best to get it over with, I guess. Thank you, Galman."

The man gave another salute then went to continue his duties while Jason made his way to the briefing room. Unlike conference rooms, these were built for tactical planning or relaxing during downtime, though there was enough action at the moment to leave this one empty. Monitors dotted the long room to ensure those in the back could see pertinent information. Rows of chairs allowed a full group of Scorn crews plus a few more to fit without trouble. Several chairs had been retracted in favor of tables to suggest the room had been in use as a lounge not long ago. There was a large screen with a console on each side at the front of the room with walls that held far less of the blue hue the corridors were embedded with, though the room did hold a couple of drink dispensers.

Fleet Commanding Officer Admiral Redding stood in front of the blank screen as if he were about to start a briefing. The admiral's narrow eyes, which were even with Jason's, and slick hair spoke of an Asian heritage. One that seemed to conflict with his fair skin and large body and cheekbones. His rank tabs held two silver stars, noting him as an admiral in Calenav rather than a general in the PSC or Terrines whose stars would be gold.

Jason snapped to attention with matching salute, and a swallowed smile at the irony of becoming a rubber person himself. The thin state of Admiral Redding's lips left him even more unsure about how this talk was going to go. The admiral returned his salute with a smoothness that hinted at less agitation than he saw.

"As you were, Major Harlem. I'm Rear Admiral Mason Redding,

FCO of the *Alamo* carrier group." He gave Jason's hand a friendly, if stiff, handshake, then folded his arms. "So, an audience with the Command Council. You must have found something important on those transports."

Jason recoiled in surprise. "Command Council? I told Yarain to get me General Carson."

Admiral Redding laughed like the cat who was about to eat the canary. "So she did. In the middle of a highly classified meeting. Apparently, what she said to get to him piqued President Priolozi's interest. He insisted they take the report in the council chamber, once the matter at hand was finished, and they'd convinced the base commander it was a false alarm."

Jason felt his stomach sink to his feet. *There goes my career.* He could only imagine the things the suits were saying. As for the others... *Oh boy. The Marshals. False alarm? What did she say to them? That's it, I'm dead. What was I thinking?*

"So, Major? What did you find that's so important?"

Guess Yarain didn't give any details. No point in hiding them. "More disturbing than important, sir. At least one ship that should have been carrying general supplies for a colony was instead loaded up for a war."

Admiral Redding just shrugged. "So, you found a weapons shipment. Hardly cause for alarm, even with the mutiny."

"You don't understand, sir. If the entire load matches what we found already, we didn't find weapons. We found an armory. PMG's, APC's, enough parts to build a Phantom, and that's just what we know of. Raiders were given access to the transit pads so they could assist with the mutiny. And most disturbing of all, the enemy attack on our foothold was led by the crew of Red 7."

Admiral Redding's arms dropped. He looked at Major Harlem like he'd grown another head. "What? Are you saying an Interstar fighter crew fired on you?"

Jason only nodded. "Yes, sir. And that doesn't count the time they—"

"Ensign Tao to Major Harlem."

Jason shook his head to reset his mind before tapping his wrist comm. "Major Harlem here."

"Sir, the Command Council is ready to hear your report when you are. If I may say so, sir, they did not sound patient."

Do politicians ever sound patient? "Thank you, Ensign. Please patch it through to briefing room three. Major Harlem out." He stepped up to the screen and tried to look less uptight than he felt. "If you'll excuse me, sir."

Admiral Redding waved his comment off while slinking into the front row. "Not to worry, Major. Something tells me any questions I have are about to be answered. If you don't mind an audience, that is."

"I don't, sir. They might."

"I saw nothing that said this was classified. If they want me out, let them tell me."

On your head be it, sir. Jason kept his comment to himself to avoid the trouble.

He gathered his thoughts until the screen flickered on to show the inside of a large conference room. The Command Council was seated along a horse-shoe shaped table in a room with carpeted floors and walls. On the left, three highly tailored suits, two of them dark grey, represented the civilian side of the council. On the right sat four sets of blue over-jackets with silver trim, buttons, and pinstripes; blue tie; and white undershirt that served as the Interstar dress uniform. Any decorations, and they all had several, lay under the Interstar insignia and name plates, though the rank tabs were still on shoulder epulets. Three were the marshals, commonly referred to as the "medals", who led the military side of things, plus Brigadier General Rickey Carson on the end.

Jason stood straighter as the man in the center of the table, President Coray Priolozi, rose. He was a tan-skinned man with more hair on his eyebrows than his head. Yet that was the only part of him that looked at all old, which, after all, he wasn't. He alone wore a deep blue suit with matching tie and dark gold handkerchief in his pocket.

"Well, Major," he said, "you sure know how to make ripples. I'm curious to hear your explanation for them."

Jason took a deep breath, ignoring the angry look he saw on one of the suits. His mind did note it was one of two suits he had a name for:

Councilman Goodheart. His blood-red tie with black lines was somehow very distinct. Beyond that, he looked very much like someone of economic privilege. Clean, black suit; slick, black hair; and it looked like a slight bulge just above the waist. For now, he was silent, though Jason didn't expect that to last. *Here we go. Let's hope President Priolozi is as open minded as he sounds.*

Jason proceeded to explain everything that had happened over the last few days. He started with the junction boxes, then took great care to describe what Sundale encountered on Red 7, as well as how the raiders behaved. He had just gotten to the engagement, *if one could call it that*, at the bridge doors when a small-boned marshal with a heavy French accent rose with her hands on the table.

"Hold on, Major. Are you claiming that members of the transport crew were part of the assault?"

He looked at her as best he could. "More than part of it, ma'am. They allowed the raiders to use the transport's own transit pads. What little info we have so far suggests all five ships were boarded in this way. Three successfully defended their ships and are secure, but the last report I saw said things were getting dire on the U.S.S. *Oxen Vice*. Things on the *Marco Polo* are in some ways worse, however. Their counterattack on the hanger, and we believe the entire operation on board, was led by the crew of Red 7."

Yarain walked in carrying a clip-com as one of the men in suits, this one so thin and lanky that Jason had to wonder if he ate enough, raised an eyebrow in a very un-Human manor. "The same ones that drew their weapons on Captain Sundale?"

"Yes, sir. The very same."

"Where did they get their hardware? Civilians don't have access to anything military grade."

"That's one of the reasons I wanted to reach General Carson, sir. When we searched the transport's cargo hold for the jammers, we found her load did not match her manifest."

Goodheart crossed his arms and leaned back in his chair. "How so?"

Yarain stepped forward raising her clip-com. "I have part of that answer here, sir. The full manifest of the convoy is not yet complete, but I have a preliminary manifest for the *Marco Polo*. Jason, teams and fighters from the *Alamo* have taken over the securing process. The Gold Group is standing by for further orders."

"I'll handle that," Admiral Redding said. "You take care of things here, Major. Captain, let's take this outside."

Yarain handed Jason her clip-com, then followed Admiral Redding out of the room. Jason glanced at the report while trying his best to ignore the silent drumming of several fingers.

He needed only a couple of items to feel he had the answers he needed. "They had a lot more than I feared. Inspections show the first transport had at least four disassembled Phantom fighters, five heavy tanks, two dozen APCs of various classes, several tons of explosives and other ordinance—there's a lot more on here, but I think I've made my point."

"Indeed, you have," President Priolozi said. "Do you know yet if the other ships had the same?"

"Exactly the same? No, sir. Teams have only just confirmed a second transport appears loaded with the same type of cargo. We're focusing our efforts on securing the *Oxen Vice* at the moment."

President Priolozi gave a single, heavy shake of his head. "It appears you've uncovered quite a mystery, Major."

Goodheart huffed while leaning on the table and addressing the president directly. "That still doesn't excuse his actions. He was ordered to escort those transports. Instead, he ends up assaulting them. Is this the kind of message we want to send our civilians?"

"The *Marco Polo* sent out a mayday, Councilman!" General Carson said. "The ship was under attack and comms were jammed. What would you have him do?"

"Sending a fighter out of jamming range might be a good start. I wouldn't have him attack civilians."

Rickey began to reply, but the president held up a hand and called for silence. He looked down the row at the marshals. "Miss Garmon, what kind of fighters do the raiders use?"

Marshal Sharon Garmon, a fair-skinned woman whose lithe build and short, sandy-colored hair somehow did not fit her personality, leaned forward and returned his gaze. She spoke in a gentle British accent that similarly didn't match the rough face. Like all marshals, she had five stars outlined by oak leaves on her rank tabs.

"They don't use fighters, sir. At least not that we've seen. They prefer to use fast corvettes or well shielded cruisers with respectable point-defense turrets instead."

"So, if they'd gotten hold of our fighters, could they have learned to design their own? Perhaps well enough to match ours? And could they have used the ground materials against us?"

"Knowing raiders, they'd compromise several safety protocols to do it." The president's stern gaze told her this was not an answer. "Yes, sir. With enough of our ships, they could come up with designs that could rival our own. The ground assets could have made future raids far more effective."

"So, Major Harlem's actions prevented a hostile group from gaining the ability to threaten the lives of our citizens and soldiers. Not to mention the lives aboard the *Marco Polo* that he saved."

"By breaking regs to make a report," Goodheart spat.

"If that's true, we may need to revisit those regulations. Major Harlem and his group have uncovered what could be a very serious threat to our civilians and our soldiers. I for one am glad to hear about it so quickly instead of waiting to see it attached to my itinerary tomorrow morning. As for the Gold Group, they acted well under far from ideal circumstances. Such things should not, and *shall not*, be penalized."

Goodheart seethed but otherwise remained silent. Jason breathed relief while thanking the president for his support. It seemed sense had found him at last. *Guess next time, I'll have to listen to Marcy when I vote.* Jason's wife had said Priolozi would make a good president. Thinking back to his days as a senator, Jason had to admit he was one of the few that understood soldiers. Though when he ran for the presidency, Jason wasn't sure he could be firm enough with the council to get things done. *So much for that.* His "shall not," directed at the council itself, sealed all lips better than the strongest glue. Those that disagreed could only glare or squirm – or both in Goodheart's case.

President Priolozi asked for further questions or comments, though in a tone that warned the speaker to choose his words very carefully.

When no one dared risk the challenge, President Priolozi continued, "Major Harlem, continue your inspection as you and Admiral Redding see fit. Forward your full reports to General Carson. He will relay further orders soon after. Be safe out there. Earth out."

Sense at last indeed. Jason felt as if all the weight had lifted off his shoulders. He had so much still to do, yet he almost felt like he was on vacation.

He walked out of the room to find Admiral Redding leaning against the wall. For a second, Jason wondered if that weight was about to come back as the admiral stepped forward.

"How'd it go?" Redding asked.

"I think I avoided a court marshal," Jason said. "We'll see if Councilman Goodheart can manage some other kind of trouble before I rest easy. Seems the type to act out of spite when his point of view doesn't prevail. In the meantime, we've been ordered to continue our inspection as we see fit, then relay our reports to General Carson."

"Sounds easy enough. So easy in fact I can say for sure that your report will be somewhat smaller."

This is either going to be really good or really bad. "Sir?"

"I've ordered the Gold Group to stand down. You've done enough for one day. My teams can take it from here."

"I thank you sir, but this mission..."

The admiral held up a hand to stop him. "You're not trained for this like my teams are. Go to your quarters, relax, and let my men take it from here. They know what they're doing."

Jason wanted to take offence at his tone, but his body refused to let him pass on the chance at rest. He nodded with a sigh born of fatigue, not anger. "Thank you, sir. Do I have quarters set up?"

Admiral Redding looked up. "PAICCA? Have quarters been assigned to Gold 1 yet?"

"Yes sir. Deck 7, section 43, room 21-L," the non-computer voice replied. "Captain Sundale expressed his thanks for the time off, sir."

Admiral Redding chuckled. "I'm sure he'll enjoy it once his fighter checks are done. AESOs are finicky that way."

"Not this time, sir. He and Captain Yarain went straight to their quarters without delay."

"What? An AESO not insisting on fighter checks after a mission? I'm shocked."

"I'm not," Jason said rubbing his face again. "Been a long mission for all of us, sir. I myself am looking forward to something softer than my pilot seat."

Redding hummed agreement. "Then go to it, Major. We'll handle these indignant transports."

They traded salutes before Jason left for the nearest lift. By the time it reached the right deck, his body had accepted the idea of being off duty. The past few hours caught up with him all at once. His mind clouded more and more by the step. All he wanted was to find anything big enough to flop into and faint.

He entered his quarters, still digging for enough energy to take his uniform off. He froze and adrenaline returned to his system when he saw Sundale laying unconscious on the floor in his four-legged primal form. Yarain stood on four legs as well, nuzzling him and whining. Clearly, Sundale hadn't passed out the same way Jason had planned to.

Jason was on his knees beside his comrade before his mind had sent the message. He hit his wrist-com even faster. "Medical emergency. Medics to deck 7, section 43, room 21-L." He put a hand on Sundale's chest to check for breathing, then moved to his thigh to check his pulse. Nether helped his nerves any. "He's alive, but his pulse is racing, and his breathing is a bit uneven. What happened?"

Yarain whined before she spoke and continued to whine with each break. "I don't know. We were talking, then he said something about his back complaining. Next thing I knew, he was whining in pain, and then he collapsed."

Jason saw the panic in her. He knew she could do better. He forced his internal switch to flip so he could get her there, and so he didn't fall apart himself. It sounded so much easier than it was.

"Captain, get a hold of yourself. Now think. Did anything trigger it? Something hit him? Something he ate? An energy field? Anything?"

Her whines eased, but not her concern. "No. I mean, I didn't see… he whined and… and glowed. From nose to tail his body glowed."

Jason could swear his heart stopped for a second. "Glowed? You don't think he's turning into pure energy again, do you?"

Yarain's ears went back, though her breathing evened out. "This glow was stronger, external along the fur instead of from the inside. If he were changing again, there wouldn't be any pain."

"You sure about that? The accident did change you and Harmus from pure energy into solid forms. Maybe catching Sundale mid-process did something that's only now catching up with him."

"I doubt… I don't… I don't know. I just know what I saw wasn't normal… and I don't know what it means."

Yarain again nuzzled Sundale as her whining returned. The best Jason could do was watch the motionless body of his best friend for changes and put a gentle hand on his mother. Yarain stopped her nuzzling, though her whines continued to grind on his heart. He tried to find something, anything he could do. The comforting hand was all he had for her, and silent prayer was all he had for himself.

Both were halted when the doors opened to announce the arrival of the medics, one with a thin stretcher in his hands. Jason rose to his feet while indicating Sundale as the one in need of care. He nudged Yarain a few steps back to allow both men the room they needed to run their checks.

"What happened?" one asked.

"We're not sure," Jason said. "By all accounts he was fine, then he fainted."

"No warning signs or anything?"

"His fur glowed before he fainted," Yarain said.

"Which for a holdren means squat," the medic said.

"Can you help him?" Jason asked.

"Give me time to find an answer for that."

Jason kept Yarain back while the medics worked on her cub. They bounced vitals between them, creating a mixed blessing for the pilot since he knew enough to understand much of it, but it also let him share in their confusion. *Breathing labored but strong. Heart rate up, yet blood pressure isn't much. Airways clear, no bleeding or injuries found. Only consistent sign of a problem is a highly abnormal energy matrix, which for a holdren could mean anything.*

Jason wanted to be of help. His lack of training held him back.

As the medics used their scanners to find some sense among the readings, Jason realized that wasn't the only thing being held in check. He knew about Sundale changing to pure energy soon after they met. He knew it might help the medics. So why wasn't he sharing? More disturbing still, why had he spoken at all when asked? Yarain was the only one who saw anything. So, when the questions came, why him?

One of the medics finally thumped his scanner into his pack. "Where's a vet when you need one? Let's get him to sickbay. See what the doctors can make out of him. PAICCA, alert sickbay to prepare for medical transport."

"Confirmed," the computer replied. "Pad will be ready. Nearest transit point is out the door to your left."

"Thank you, PAICCA."

The other medic wasn't so sure. "You're going to flash him there? The way his energy matrix is? It's too dangerous."

"Whatever it's doing, it's stable. We won't get better. If this is serious, we need time. We're flashing him. Now."

"Not without **US** you don't!" Yarain said.

The medic looked ready to object, but he and Yarain stopped when Jason stepped forward. "She's right. The doctors are going to need to talk with us anyway. Might as well combine the trip, save time for everyone. That, and if he comes to and his instincts are stronger than his mind, she can help keep him calm."

The first medic muttered something, then motioned for them to assist. "PAICCA, we'll have two extra in the transit."

"Understood," PAICCA said. "Pad is clear. Sick-bay on stand-by."

Each medic took one end of Sundale while Jason gathered up his legs. On a three count, they lifted him onto the stretcher. They strapped him down before the second medic took one end while Jason took the other. The head medic led the way out while Yarain followed behind.

The group left Jason's quarters and turned down the hall. They stopped on a large red dot in the middle of the corridor, which marked one of the transit transponders built into the floor every hundred feet. Handy for evacuations or other emergency situations such as this. The lazy also used them at times to get to their quarters quicker.

The head medic tapped his wrist-com, and the group was enveloped by the sparkle then flash of the transporter. They arrived on a transit pad at the end of sickbay. Despite being trimmed in blue with a bar of displays and consoles lining the back wall above the beds, the walls and ceiling were white enough to make the place feel sterile. Bright lighting throughout only helped the image.

A nurse wearing scrubs the same blue as Jason's uniform, though with a silver collar and sleeve trim and no sash, arrived right after the flash faded. She, Jason, and the medics took Sundale to one of the beds while Yarain looked on, still whining her stress.

Once Sundale was moved onto the bed, sensors under the padding began to feed information onto the health monitors. Chief Medical Officer Jannet Blount approached with a clip-com at almost the same time. She was a tall woman, firm in her step, yet her face was soft and smooth with dark-blue eyes and dark-red hair that was right at the length limit. When she spoke, her tone remained gentle, keeping Jason from wondering about her bedside manner

"All right, what's wrong with the fox?"

"Not sure, ma'am," the medic said. "His vitals don't make sense. His energy matrix is a bit active, but we couldn't find anything else."

"Well, let's see if my equipment can do any better. Major, Captain, if we could have some room, please? This is sickbay. We heal, we don't perform."

Jason had to swallow a few unkind words but agreed it was still the best choice. He could do nothing for Sundale now. He stepped down the row, pushing Yarain the same way despite her many whines of protest.

"Let them work," he said. "Your presence will do him no good."

Yarain forced her ears forward in agreement. She kept her whines under control, but the rest of her couldn't be silenced. At times she would raise a paw, only to put it back down while looking at Jason with moving ears and another complaint. She didn't get any calmer when the sensor suite, which looked more like a flat slab over the bed, slid out of the wall and projected a line that went back and forth across Sundale's body.

Jason didn't bother with his hand this time. It would only let her feel his own emotions, assuming she couldn't sense them anyway. Sentient or not she was still an animal, which meant she could sense a person's "energy." Jason knew that, so he tried to use it. Though his insides were tearing him apart, he kept himself in control as if he knew an attack were coming and he was waiting for it. It was the only thing that could force either of them to forget they cared about that fox on the bed. It helped Jason. How much it did for Yarain, he couldn't tell.

Doctor Blount put her hand on Sundale's chest while the nurse injected something. A soft nod gave both worrywarts down the way reason for hope. Doctor Blount gave more orders before heading toward them with the clip-com under her arm. She pointed to her office without a word, then walked on by. Jason and Yarain followed, the holdren thankfully silent, though Jason knew better than to think she'd relaxed.

Yarain and Jason hugged the inside wall of Blount's office, which seemed strangely spartan given her position. Most of the time such an office was filled with pictures, mementos, and other things to "keep the joy" as many put it. Not Doctor Blount. A counter on the side held more than anything else, and aside from a small computer terminal, it was dominated by medical equipment. Her desk had exactly two pictures, one bonsai plant, a statue of a bear standing over a cub, and a short pile of clip-coms Jason somehow knew were job related. The walls held nothing beyond a single picture of Earth with the moon just peeking from behind. When the doctor chose to lean against the counter instead of taking a seat at her desk, Jason had to wonder how much time she spent in there doing anything other than work. He kept his thoughts internal as she gave a heavy sigh that threatened to stop his heart again.

"I'll be blunt," Doctor Blount said. "I haven't got a clue. Like the medics, I can't make sense of his vitals. They all say something is happening, but only his elevated heart rate suggests anything at all 'wrong'. Still others would seem to suggest normalcy."

"Fainting is not normal, Doctor," Yarain said, not quite raising her hackles.

Doctor Blount either didn't notice or didn't care. "I agree. Which leads me to think there is *something* going on. The only thing I have to work with is his energy matrix."

"What do you mean?" Jason asked. "What about his matrix?"

"The closest I can come is to say it's… elevated. You'd think that would be a good thing, but for some reason, it seems to be a shock instead. A shock that's messing with the entire twelve percent of his body that's made of energy, and a lot of it seems to be rushing to his back. But that doesn't make sense nor can I find a cause."

"Elevated how?" Yarain said.

"It appears to be running at a different frequency and at a stronger level than normal. My nurse got sparked by residual static electricity at least a dozen times. Run your hand through his fur, you'll set off a bigger show than the Fourth of July."

"Sounds like holdren diarrhea," Jason said. "That doesn't explain the rest of it."

Doctor Blount tossed her clip-com onto the counter with a deep breath. "Like I said, I haven't got a clue. If it is 'holdren diarrhea' then it's possible he's having a severe allergic reaction or more likely, he got broad-sided by an infection. I understand you three have been under a lot of stress lately."

"You have no idea."

"I listen to Terrines, Major. I know more than you think. In any case, it's possible the two combined to overwhelm his system. Just as a human can faint from stress alone, Captain Sundale may have had a similar reaction."

Jason had a hard time swallowing that one. He'd seen Sundale sick before. Bad enough to start losing fur even. He never had vitals that conflicted. He definitely never fainted for no reason or from pure stress. No. Something much more virulent was going on. Yet, try as he might, the only thing he could make himself say was nothing of the sort.

"So, what do we do?"

The doctor reclaimed her clip-com without a shred of emotion. "The short term? Antibiotics, take some blood tests, and the terrible 'W's; Wait, Watch, and Wonder. I'll know more about what's going on once I get the test results back. In the meantime, I'll add another 'W' by saying I *want* him to rest. I don't want him anywhere near a Scorn for a minimum of 48 hours. Longer if he's still weak or dizzy. Some time in the sun might do him some good too if he gets the chance."

Jason nodded, wondering what the weather was like back home and how she'd feel about a hunt. "I'll do what I can. Though between us, Doc; is he in any danger?"

"When can we see him?" Yarain asked.

The doctor looked first at Yarain with a stern look eliminating all question from the subject. "You can see him when he's awake and I'm sure he's stable. As for danger, my gut says no, but I trust hard facts first and I have none. As I said, for the short term, he's to remain off duty. I want him to get rest and plenty of it. Hopefully things will settle down and I can let him return to duty. If not, he may have to take a medical leave until this clears up. In which case..."

The nurse came in carrying a clip-com of her own. "Ma'am, forgive me, but you wanted to know if Captain Sundale woke up."

The doctor stood and traded clip-coms while thanking the nurse. "How does he seem?"

"A little tired ma'am, but otherwise alert and clear minded. As you can see, his energy matrix has quieted down a bit."

"Can we see him?" Yarain asked.

The doctor gave her a frustrated look, then moved to the nurse. "Can he handle it?"

The nurse nodded. "I think so. He's only tired."

"All right. If you're careful, Captain, you can see him."

Yarain wasted no time rushing out the door to her cub. The doctor grumbled while glaring at Jason, to which he only shrugged. "It may not get in the way on the battlefield, but soldier or not, he's still her cub," he said.

"Don't you mean kit sir?" the nurse asked.

Jason shook his head while walking after Yarain with the nurse and doctor. "That's a Human term. One of many we use far more than they do. No, holdrens call their young cubs, not kits. Don't ask me why. It's best to remember that they aren't really foxes. They're just canines that look, and often sound, like foxes. Only reason they use other 'fox' terms is because they have none of their own, save for their young, of course. Even then, they mind 'fox' a lot less than they do 'dog.'"

"Unless you mean a male, of course. Though they can apparently go by other names as well."

"You know a lot."

"Foxes are a hobby of mine sir."

Jason hummed interest. "Well, I wouldn't ever call a holdren a dog. Even vixen is at best tolerated. Dog... it's too easily confused with *domestic* dog. Best to avoid it."

The nurse took her turn to hum agreement. Both chuckled as they found Yarain lying next to Sundale on the edge of the bed. She was licking his head like she was trying to clean his fur. Poor Sundale tried to lean away, but with his mother sharing the bed, he didn't have anywhere to go.

His pleas, and subsequent growls, didn't get him anywhere either. "Yarain... Yarain, please. Please, ***ENOUGH*** already!"

The nurse again looked confused as Sundale tried nipping at Yarain to get her to stop. "I thought she was his mother," the nurse said.

"She is," Jason said.

"Why does he use her name instead of 'mom'?"

Jason waived a finger like a schoolteacher. "Human mind. When addressing or referencing an individual, Holdrens *always* use the individual's name. I know, it's different, but after a while you get the hang of it."

"I'm sure," Doctor Blount said. "Just make sure he gets some rest, or I'll be calling him some different things too."

Jason chuckled again while promising he would.

With Yarain no longer licking her cub to death, Jason decided it best to leave them alone to deal with the day's events in their own way. *After all, it might be the last chance they have before whatever this is turns south.*

That thought stopped him cold at the door. He stole a look back and wondered—What if it became something serious, even fatal? He'd been through a lot with that holdren. He had a hard time imagining life without him.

To say nothing of his parents. Yarain could go any direction. Harmus would likely blame Interstar again, and Jason would be unable to say for sure if he were right or wrong. Jason might even blame himself depending on what came of this illness or whatever it was. Assuming something else didn't kill them first.

Jason walked back to his quarters still trying to make sense of the last few days. One word remained in the front of his mind: conspiracy. A whopping big one, which only made it worse. Now, with their plans no doubt ruined, the conspirators could be twice as dangerous. Especially if it turned into a full-blown insurrection. Add the spice of Interstar soldiers being involved, and war with the jantans felt like a birthday party.

Seemed like the whole of the galaxy was coming undone. Try as he might, Jason couldn't avoid the sense he'd gotten caught square in the middle of something three times over. The costly raid through Coylin territory a few months ago almost ended him. How long before almost became his epitaph?

Jason went straight for the window seat in his quarters, which barely made up for the small size and single couch and table facing the window. He still got a separate bedroom and a tiny desk of his own. Better than most got on a starship, and he needed the stars today. They held the answers he so desperately needed.

First was the question he tried not to think about. Which was worse: losing Sundale as a comrade, or losing him completely? That one became moot the more he thought about it. He might get the doctor to downplay the illness, but he couldn't let himself do that. He cared too much for Sundale and his parents. Besides, doing so might bring about the very loss he wanted to avoid. No, in this case, he had to let things play out. Then he'd deal with whichever outcome he got.

Which left him with the unending questions for the future. War? Conspiracy? Insurrection? Piracy? Bad luck? Which would come for him first? He looked out into the emptiness of space in search of answers. He got a partial view as ships and fighters from the fleet competed for his attention as if representing his own mental state.

He knew he'd run out of options alone. So, Jason slid off the seat onto his knees in prayer. He never did say much. Just a single plea of, "I'm worn. Guide me."

A flash snapped his eyes back out the window. A Scorn was firing on one of the *Oxen Vice*'s pulse turrets. No doubt the enemy boarding party had gotten control of it.

Yet for Jason, it felt like a message. Right or wrong, his instincts were giving a clear warning. What he just saw, he was going to see a lot more of in the coming days. Half his spine chilled. The other half stiffened. Yeah, he knew what was coming, but he'd faced it before. Marcalla, he knew he could beat since he'd done it just a few months ago. As for this conspiracy... well, he'd just have to wait and see what they were really capable of. Not like he could do much else for the time being.

He continued to pray until Sundale's voice brought him out of it a few hours later. "Putting in a good word?"

Jason stood to greet Sundale as he entered with his mother. Jason shook his head with a laugh when he noticed that much of Sundale's head was damp. *Poor fox. At least he's clean now.*

"More like asking for one," Jason said. "How are you holding up?"

"I've been better."

"You've been worse, too. What did the doctor have to say?"

"Nothing new so far. She did insist on the monitor."

Jason turned his head as if to ask. He stopped short when he noticed Sundale's uniform sporting a device of some kind attached at his shoulders. Parts of it were attached to the back of his head with other parts going under his uniform where they attached to his chest. The strapping that went under his chin and around the base of his muzzle could not have been comfortable, especially if his instincts saw them as controlling him in any way.

Jason nodded full and complete understanding. "At least you're alive. The way the day's gone, I'll take that."

"As will I," Sundale said. "Doesn't make it any less annoying."

"No one said it should. Want something to eat?"

"Only if it's raw," Yarain said.

Jason extended a hand to Sundale, who turned his ears forward to agree with his mother. Jason turned for the cooking area—that wasn't there on a starship. He went for the door instead, tossing his head that way.

"Come on. Let's see what we can talk the galley into."

Chapter 5

A Breath at Last

As promised, Jason's report proved much shorter than Admiral Redding's, but it was Jason who heard the orders first. General Carson insisted on it.

With the *Alamo* unable to get any answers and the area already deemed not as secure as previously thought, command decided to send the entire convoy to the Sol system. With any luck, the techs at the Vernon shipyards in the asteroid belt would fare better. The transports themselves would be far too well covered for anyone to try anything stupid. The *Alamo* had some minor maintenance work and fighter juggling to do anyway, so she would head for Earth once the transports were dropped off. As for the Gold Group itself, command had them assigned to the *Alamo* until further notice with rumblings of it becoming longer term than just "until we sort this out."

Admiral Redding wasted no time using that authority. Within minutes, he'd put the whole group on stand down. Major Harlem was a bit miffed until Admiral Redding explained it further.

"I have more than enough ships to provide cover," he'd said. "Your group slept through one escort. They don't need to do it again, and Sundale isn't your only wounded soldier. Let my men handle this, Major. You get the rest you so desperately need."

That silenced all protest from Jason's mind. It would take a little over two days to get there because of the slower transports. The Gold Group would basically be off duty for that entire time. Jason would have the chance to sit back and let someone else worry for a change. He might even get a good night's sleep. He took the offer without any further protest.

Surprisingly, so did Sundale. No insistence on keeping Gold 1 keyed up this time. First thing he did when he heard was shed his uniform like a snake shedding skin, as did Yarain. Their wrist-coms remained on for communication purposes, though the sudden appearance of medics reminded Sundale he couldn't go without his health monitor either. Still, it helped. Knowing they would soon be home helped even more.

The placement of their quarters proved to be icing on the cake. They were on the edge of where the ship tapered forward, which gave them a forward view to a small degree. After the transports were handed off to the shipyards, Jason was able to use that view to see Earth as they approached. It was a pale blue dot at first, then it grew into the blue and green orb that always seemed to glow. Maybe it was just the sense of home. As if his instincts could feel the comfort of familiar territory.

He was almost glowing himself after a message came from Admiral Redding. The entire carrier group had been put on stand down, which let him grant the Gold Group full-on shore leave. Sundale was still under observation anyway. His blood work didn't show anything out of the ordinary, but the doctor didn't care for conflicting vitals. However, even she couldn't deny the benefit of being observed somewhere comfortable. So long as he took it easy, she agreed to let him leave the ship without a monitor.

Jason suspected where they were going helped. Or rather, the company they'd be keeping. Major Jason Harlem was a fine fighter pilot, but his wife Marcy was an even better surgeon. She'd have no qualms keeping a close eye on, and inflicting needed medicine upon, the fox as needed. After all, she wrote half the stuff modern medicine knew about holdrens. Thus, Jason was not surprised when Doctor Blount's resistance to Sundale joining him vanished the moment he brought it up.

All Jason cared about was that he'd be home. He'd get to really relax with the holdrens that followed him through the ship's corridors. He could catch up with Marcy, help in her garden, get stuck by thorns, find layers of dust on everything, feel the heat from above and below. He'd be home.

Jason led his crew into the transporter room with the holdrens' uniforms in a backpack and his mind already on the surface. He would have floated there himself if he didn't almost run over a fellow Cosman standing just inside the doors. Jason wondered why the man wasn't moving until a scan of the room told him a lot more than his group had been given shore leave. He could hardly see the glossy floor panels along the walls that protected the real transporter mechanics. Even the large cargo pads at the end were packed with men and materials. Operators in the raised control strip that ran down the center of the room were calling out directions like air traffic controllers, though there wasn't too much conversation they had to overpower. The transporters created a soft strobe effect as people and things arrived and left one after the other.

It was organized chaos similar to a transit hub on Christmas Eve, and status quo for a ship whose crew weren't waiting for her to dock to begin their leave.

Thankfully, everything remained organized, so Jason didn't have to worry too much about someone running over a foot or paw. Once they got their turn, they were put into the queue, waited for directions, then wove their way through the bustle to their pad.

A soft sparkle covered them, then a flash traded the transporter room for a dirt driveway in front of a simple, one story, sandstone house Jason Harlem called home. It wasn't anything spectacular, and he liked it that way. Large windows at the front marked the living room to the right and the common room to the left. He could see the many chairs and couches in the common room, as well as the bookshelves Marcy always kept well organized. A door with just enough porch to keep the rain off split the middle.

He noticed with a smile that Marcy's gardens in front of each window were as aggressive as always while still somewhat orderly despite mixing flowers and food. Yet even the vines stopped short of blocking the views. The smile turned to a headshake as he remembered Carter saying the place looked like an old bed-and-breakfast or church. For all Jason knew, he was right. Grandma never did say what the place was, just that she insisted he take it when he married Marcy. Knowing full well his grandma hadn't many days left to her, he hadn't even tried to refuse.

The other reason for the shake of the head was the heat, at least by most standards. While a pair of guardian palm trees could hide the transit transponder buried in the ground between them, their shade couldn't hide early October from Jason's senses. "Warm" would be the most used term, not that he would. He'd been born and raised in Southern California. Low 90's weren't warm. They were downright heavenly.

Though for the sake of his furred companions, Jason wasted little time heading inside. He held the door long enough for Yarain and Sundale to shake who-knows-what from their fur outside, then follow him in. The interior walls became more eggshell colored and had a dirt-like texture that looked rougher than it felt. Hardwood floors paved the way down the center of the house.

Jason hung his knife harness and P-mag belt on the wall to his right, next to a painting of the building back when it was first built. The only indication as to when that happened was the addition of a private jet plane from the early twenty-first century climbing in the distance. Otherwise, it looked as though the building hadn't changed, not counting the technology added here and there. Though the pitifully short plants in the image would have brought great insult to the bouquet of flowers and food that grew in their place.

Before he could wonder where the planter of that garden was, Marcy came around the corner from the common room wearing her usual "green sleeveless-shirt and dark-green pant combo. Clothes she'd never admit were colored to hide grass stains but not the mud of her passion. Anyone who knew her knew better than to ask and could attest to the garden god that was Marcy Harlem, despite the strain of being a surgeon. Jason always suspected it was her stress valve, just as ancient TV shows were his. It never showed on her features, though. She remained a slim, light-skinned, round-faced woman who kept her golden hair long and loose about her shoulders. It almost blended in with the wall she now leaned against, arms crossed and giving the fakest airs of being miffed.

Her even tone further failed the facade. "And where have you been?

Six months without a word, and now here you are flashing into my driveway with little notice and less explanation. That's no way to treat your wife."

Jason hung up Yarain and Sundale's uniforms and wrist-coms next to his weapons, then gave Marcy an absentminded shrug. "What can I say? Interstar keeps you very busy. I just didn't have the time."

"You couldn't find a few minutes among six months to say hello?"

"A few minutes on the border isn't easy to find. It's not like I had a choice."

Soft ticking announced the arrival of Yarain's mate from the large common room across from Marcy. Unlike the others, Harmus carried his orange on the tips of his ears as well as the leading edge of his hip and shoulder joints. Some orange was also in a stripe along the top of his muzzle from his nose to just behind his ears. He too had red bands just below his red tail tips, though his white underside went all the way up to cover the rest of his face without a single speck of grey to be found.

Jason could feel himself tense when Harmus entered. Unlike humans, Jason couldn't read holdren moods very well. The difference between joking and genuinely upset could be millimeters in the ears. And Harmus' ears rarely moved except to turn back or to do the equivalent of a holdren nod or shake of the head.

"You could have at least sent us a letter," Harmus said in an even tone that didn't help decipher his mood. His voice was just a little hard as if he were always gruff, even though experience said quite the opposite.

Jason tried very hard not to turn defensive. "You know how it is. They get paranoid about your position being discovered so any non-mission contact is strictly limited, if allowed at all."

"I don't like not hearing from my pack, Jason."

He's upset. Jason's insides tensed for an argument while Yarain walked toward her mate with flowing tails that showed she at least was in a light mood.

Jason took a deep breath that failed to relax him. "I understand that; believe me, I do. I would have sent a message had they let me. I'm sorry. Can you forgive me, both of you?"

Yarain and Harmus shared an affectionate rub and a soft whine. As they often did when greeting one another, their noses paused on a scent gland in their cheeks before starting the rub. Jason knew this was how holdrens said hello, though he never fully understood how. Mostly because he couldn't imagine how a scent could show a holdren's intent and state of mind like their cheek glands apparently did up close. The pause was short lived however, which suggested neither one found anything amiss. The rubbing that followed was no more alien than a hug.

Marcy huffed with a shake of her head. "I think that's a yes from them. As for me, I think I can manage. That is, if you still like my cooking."

"I think I'm feeling ill again." Sundale said, drawing a laugh from the humans and a quiet pant of the same from the holdrens.

Sundale put his nose on the other side of Harmus' head so he too could trade checks on the cheeks. Though Harmus examined Sundale's longer than he had Yarain's, he still didn't wait long before giving Sundale his own round of rubs and whimpers of affection.

It let Jason relax all at once. Gruff or not, Harmus never failed to show his love for his cub. It always stirred some conflicted feelings in Jason as well as a wish for a child of his own. A wish he again shot down as impractical. Hard to be a good father when you're gone for weeks and months at a time.

Jason shook the thought from his mind and turned his focus to his wife. "Well, we're here on leave, so we might as well enjoy it. First step is for me to change out of this uniform."

"Hope you remember how," Sundale said. A quick ruff of laughter followed before returning to his father. "Let's hunt."

"Oh no you don't," Jason said. "You, my dear fox, are going to rest. Ah-ah-ah, doctor's orders. We don't know what kind of affect your... seizure, for lack of better term, had on your body. You need to be sure you're fully healed before you stress it again. At least for another hour or two."

"Jason, I feel..." Jason stared him down. Sundale's ears went back with a quiet growl as his only protest. "Can I at least sleep outside?"

Jason nodded, then held the door for him and his parents as they filed out behind him.

Marcy watched them go while all lightness drained from her expression. "Seizure? What exactly happened, Jason? Your message didn't say much beyond your ETA and something about Sundale contracting some illness that made him faint."

"Didn't Doctor Blount send you anything?"

"Honestly, I haven't dug into it yet. Been busy at the hospital."

Jason sighed and led the way to their bedroom in the back. "We're not even sure it's an illness. He felt intense pain in his back, apparently glowed for a moment, then fainted."

"Glowed? Isn't that what he did when he was changing into pure energy?"

"Yes, but Yarain says it was a different glow, and there shouldn't have been any pain regardless."

"So... what? What's wrong with him?"

"No one knows, and that makes everything else all the worse."

"That requires an explanation. Care to share?"

Jason opened the bedroom door, grateful to feel real carpet even with shoes. The light fixture on the wall created a soft, yet abundant, glow which made the maroon wallpaper welcome him like an old friend. The king-size bed did nothing to dampen the spacious feeling of the room. Were it not for the conversation, the room would have put him so at ease the sudden lack of stress might have made him pass out. Instead, he had to settle for the soft bench at the foot of the bed so he could start working his boots off.

"I would if I could," he said, "but that's not making sense either. Transports aren't carrying what they should, raiders are using tactics we've never seen, entire transport crews are helping them, and Red 7 is drawing their P-mags on Sundale."

Marcy sat beside him and folded her hands in her lap. "Bet that went well."

"Depends on who you ask." Jason continued to undress while his wife held her pose in calm patience. He'd just removed his shirt when he recognized it for what it was. "What? What is it?" She didn't move. "All right, I admit it; I'm stressed."

Only her lips moved. "And? What else?"

A few thousand other things. Jason waited until he stood in just his underwear and undershirt before forming a reply. "I'm tired. It's been a long week."

"And?"

I hate it when she does this. He fought against her as long as he could, refusing to dig into the deep void within. She just sat and watched, knowing full well he couldn't survive forever. He kept it at bay until he'd folded his uniform into a drawer and pushed it closed.

Then the truth hit like a dozen torpedoes.

"I'm scared, Marcy. Or I'm exhausted, I'm not even sure which. I only know I can't help worrying what's going to happen to me or Sundale when Marcalla begins their next offensive. Forty years of off-and-on war, and we only reclaimed the last of lost territory a few months ago. Except we went full-on Hiroshima on three Marcallan colonies in the process. An act I don't see having the same effect this time, so there's waiting for that response. On top of that, we have this conspiracy that we could wind up fighting at the same time, and now something is going on with Sundale that no one can identify. For once, I think I've hit my limit. My internal switch has burned out."

Marcy nodded while rising. She put her hands on his shoulders as much to comfort as to demand his attention. "You can't change what anyone does if you don't control yourself. There's a reason they don't let me operate on friends or family. If Interstar wasn't so desperate to make sure we had enough volunteers, they wouldn't be so lax with the same rule for their soldiers. Internal switch or not, your emotions get involved. You forget what you know. Sometimes you stop thinking altogether. You ignore the fact that there are times it's best we stay out of it."

"It's not that easy, Marcy. We've been together for a long time. I can't just sit by and ignore it."

"I didn't say you had to ignore it, Jason. I *do* think you need to stop trying to fix something you may not be able to fix. You will be no good to Sundale or anyone else if you hold yourself responsible for his care. Let the doctors take care of Sundale. Let time provide options for the rest, and for goodness' sake, let yourself see that you're not alone in this."

Jason tried to form a rebuttal. What came out barely counted. "Impatience walks with disaster. That what you're saying?"

"Your words more than mine," she agreed.

Jason stared into the mirror over the dresser feeling more than defeated. Marcy had that effect on him sometimes. Mostly when she was right about something. Drove him nuts.

"I'll try," he said at last. "In the meantime, I have a lot of praying to do."

He headed for the bed, only to have Marcy again force him to look at her. "*We* have a lot of praying to do. You're forgetting me again, Jason. You can't keep fighting these battles alone. Especially if Sundale doesn't come back from one."

Jason shook his arm free with a glare. "If that happens, I'll handle it as best I can. It's all I can do at this point. Isn't that what you're telling me?"

"Not quite, but I'm not going to argue when I know better. For now, I'll just hope, and pray, that you can let us in on this."

Jason mentally brushed it off. Somewhere inside, he wanted to hear more, but when he weighed that battle against the stress and exhaustion he felt, he decided to quit while he was ahead.

There's always tomorrow, he told himself, knowing full well tomorrow would never come.

Chapter 6

A Growing Hunt

Lieutenant Junior Grade Simon Solez had to walk fast to keep up. His father, Admiral Solez, was tearing down the starbase corridor like he was angry. Simon knew better. If the Fleet Admiral were angry, he would have had to jog to avoid being left in the dust. No, the man was simply in a hurry. In some ways that might have been worse.

He'd left so fast; Simon barely had enough time to tie his boots. He had to tug on his dark-brown uniform so the soft-grey lines that went up the sides of the legs, arms, and torso were nice and straight. The lines converged to essentially outline the clavicle on the front and back before jetting up the collar as if marking primary veins. At least the Polaris insignia on the shoulder joints, as well as the long pine branch with a smaller second one attached that marked his rank on the epaulets, were already perfectly clean. One might call that progress.

Not the man he followed. Oh no. There were too many years separating them.

Admiral Timothy Solez wasn't the youngest of men, and he looked older still. Half his hair was grey with experience; the other half was half gone. His face hadn't sunk yet, but wrinkles were beginning to form nonetheless, more on the elbows than his cheeks. Not that any fool would think him incapable. There was plenty of hardness left to suggest this aging man had enough fire to burn through problems.

And apparently floors. Simon half expected to find smoke lifting from each step given his pace. The five red stars on his shoulders were like drops of blood left from a previous battle. They also reminded Simon of kill markers, which was one of the things that had begun to mess with his mind at night, some of them contradictory.

He knew what was at stake. True, some of the things to be done were less than ideal, but they had to be done. It was the only way to end the wars once and for all. He knew that. He'd accepted it a long time ago. So why were these things starting to bother him now?

"Lieutenant! You coming, or are you taking a nap?"

The admiral's voice was as hard as the man. It hit Simon like a whip, snapping him off a rabbit trail he didn't realize had slowed him down.

"No, sir," Simon said, half jogging to catch up. "I mean, I'm coming, sir. Sorry, Admiral."

Thankfully, the man waited for him. He even let Simon stop right in front of him. The relief lasted as long as it took him to realize the admiral was staring him down. Simon could see himself in those old eyes as if they were a pair of mirrors. His lines were crisp and clear, his features chiseled by hard work instead of age, dark-black hair in perfect military short cut, but there was no age there. Good lord, he even had a pimple! Simon Solez was only just beginning his career, not to mention his adulthood.

He expected to be chewed out. Instead, the forty-year-old in front of him nodded approval. "Keep your head on, Son. If half the reports I've heard are true, our first phase didn't just fail, it was D-O-A!"

Simon swallowed a sigh as Admiral Solez continued his march. "I don't understand why they didn't abort, sir. They had ample time."

"Damn ships were on EMCOM alpha, total transmission blackout. Another blunder I'll have to find the source of later. They tried to send one of our assets to stop them. Not only did they not get there in time, they themselves got captured and then blundered their way into putting half of Interstar on high alert."

"How did that happen?"

"Idiocy? Stupidity? These days, the list is as long as my arm and twice as thick."

They rounded the corner and headed straight into the communications room. Admiral Solez didn't bother saluting to the officers at the door. The rest either maintained focus or made sure they became focused at the sight of him. Admiral Solez ignored them all as he went into one of the smaller rooms in the back, a private comms room not much bigger than a lift that held one screen with one console below it. The admiral stopped and tapped at the controls, for which Simon's legs were eternally grateful.

"If I may ask, sir," Simon said with a touch of caution, "what are we doing here?"

His father only stared at the screen as it flashed 'stand by' at him. "We're getting a report from Private Glarm. He'll have the most up to date information on the situation on Earth. With any luck, what he knows might help us salvage Operation Juno."

"Isn't that risking interception, sir?"

"Some. But even if they do, they'll think it a ruse. After all, everyone 'knows' not a single Polaris soldier or civilian survived. They'll be so busy looking for the 'real' threat, they won't realize it isn't a ruse."

While his father checked the console to be sure the connection had been set and secured, Simon felt his stomach turn in that odd way again. "Permission to ask freely, sir?"

Admiral Solez cracked enough to pout confusion. "Ask freely? That's an odd wording. Go ahead."

"Are we sure about this, sir? I mean, Operation Juno is meant to put an end to the wars, but it seems like the only thing it'll do is start one."

"The last one, Lieutenant. Our enemies will weaken each other, then we'll be ready to finish them off so neither one can threaten or abandon us ever again."

"I understand the plan sir, even if I don't know all of it. But... well, sir, with all due respect, it seems like we're planning to help one enemy kill someone who might actually be able to convince his side to end it. We know United Systems would jump at the chance. I guess I'm wondering if we're sure this is the only way."

When his father drew a full breath, Simon had his answer long before any words were spoken. "That'll do, Lieutenant. I know it may not make sense to you now, I know I had my doubts when the grand marshal first read me into the *full* plan, but Operation Juno *is* the only way to be absolutely certain both threats are eliminated." He let the breath out slowly, then put a hand on his son's shoulder. "Sooner or later, one or both of them would turn on each other or us. Besides, after what Interstar did, we can't trust them to protect everyone. We can only trust ourselves. And in that, I am absolutely certain. We just need a few adjustments, and we can get things back on track."

Simon wasn't so sure. If phase one had been such a disaster, how could they possibly salvage the operation? Worse yet, what would the Admiral do in the process? That scared Simon more than anything. Even more than the fangs they might very well be facing in the near future.

Sundale's paws sank into the dirt as he settled beneath the arrow weed. His shoulders rocked as he adjusted himself for the pounce. His tails laid straight out behind, ready to keep him on balance and on target. He didn't like his distance. He crept closer in the hopes of —

The jackrabbit's ears shot up. It looked his way. He knew he'd blown it. Before his prey could register what it saw, Sundale released all the tension in his body. His legs moved faster than he could feel as his paws left puffs of dust behind with each step. The rabbit fled with all speed but couldn't lose its pursuer.

Sundale's fur bristled with wind and emotion as he followed every twist and turn his prey tried. His legs burned from the sprint yet never lost speed or balance. Another sharp turn from the rabbit, and Sundale used a hard push to change from a sprint to a leap. His legs catapulted him forward in a perfect arc. The rabbit didn't see him coming until his paws pinned it in a cloud of dust. A bite to the neck ended its cries.

Sundale panted out his exhaustion as he laid over his kill. Not exactly what one usually does after a nap, but then humans never did understand what a simple hunt meant to a holdren. Even Jason would frown on how much he was exerting himself out here.

No matter. He'd taken his nap as promised. And he had to admit, it did leave him feeling stronger than before. That was also the problem. His body demanded use. His instincts demanded food. To sit and do nothing in the face of both... well, they wouldn't understand.

Sundale's legs were just feeling ready to go again when Harmus and

Yarain caught up with him. Both were carrying their tails level and lax. Clear signs of approval.

Harmus spoke first, using their language instead of English.

"Nicely done, Sundale. I thought he'd lose you with that turn."

Sundale rose and let Yarain examine his kill. "That lunge took everything I had."

"You look like you have some hunt left in you."

Yarain tore off a leg for herself, then settled under the shade of a large tamarisk. "He doesn't need it. This will satisfy me until dinner. The rest is yours, Sundale."

Sundale reached to claim it but stopped with his ears up at his father. "You want any, Harmus?"

Harmus' ears twitched back while he laid beside Yarain. "Take it."

Sundale moved his meal into the shade beside his mother. He dug in, feeling the weight of Harmus' gaze. He tried to ignore it, but his ears remained up and alert in search of understanding. Harmus was watching him with the intensity of a hunter, yet his lax position spoke only of quiet attention. *What is he looking at?*

Harmus spoke his mind before the stare became too much. "I'm glad to see you well, Sundale. Marcy told me about your 'seizure.' I was worried it would scar you."

Sundale looked up from his half-eaten rabbit and flicked an ear. The Holdren version of waving it off. "I'm too stubborn to scar."

Both parents ruffed humor.

"As I would expect from my offspring," Harmus said. "It still worries me."

Yarain nuzzled him with a lick. "You said yourself he seems fine. For all we know, it's nothing."

"His scent wasn't entirely normal. The doctors insisted you rest for a reason."

Sundale swallowed a huff with the last piece of rabbit. "You're talking about humans, Harmus. You know how they are."

Harmus' gaze turned hard. Then, without a word, he snapped his nose up and tested the air. Yarain and Sundale did the same but found nothing out of the ordinary. Harmus however rose to his paws with a nervous wave running through his tails.

Sundale stood as well while his tails tensed in a similar way. "What's wrong?"

"A young human," Harmus said. "Wearing a sour-smelling ointment."

Sundale rechecked the air. He found only one scent that matched. He sneezed at just the thought of how much cologne the man must have used. "I smell him too. What of him?"

Harmus continued to test the air in search of direction. "He's been lurking recently. I think he's stalking me."

Now Sundale's tails started their nervous wave, as did Yarain's.

"Do you know who it is?" she said.

"Or where?" Sundale added.

"No. I've never seen him, and one does not go looking for that which hunts them."

"When alone, I would agree," Yarain said, "but this is a human that's stalking you, and you're not alone anymore. The strength of the scent suggests he's out there now. Let's split up. Sundale, you go alone, try to find him. Try not to go directly toward him if you can. Harmus and I will do the same together, but we'll try harder to appear as if we're hunting. All of you, stay hidden, stay silent unless threatened. Go."

Each holdren slipped into the wilderness like shadows. Though they knew help remained within easy reach, they otherwise vanished from each other so as to not give the others away. This left Sundale alone with the thrill of the hunt returning to him.

His paws moved so lightly even he didn't hear them. His ears and nose searched for his prey. His mouth never watered for his mind never forgot the moment. This was no rabbit destined to become his next meal. This was something far smarter and far more dangerous. He had to match it if he were to stay safe.

Sundale kept his body low, his tails level, and his ears forward during his search. He flowed around bushes and over berms like water over a river stone in search of the scent's owner. His paws sank into the ground without so much as a whiff or rustle, swallowing distance whole with each step. He'd put a fair distance between himself and Jason's home when the scent started getting fresh.

Sundale kept the scent to his side and moved at an angle that would find him getting closer without going directly for his quarry. He tested the air, and at times pawed at the ground in the hopes that it might make him appear as if he too were still hunting. He almost wished he still had his wrist-com, though when he remembered his tails, he didn't worry about it. That and he'd only need one scream to call two angry holdrens to his defense. Either would be more than enough for one human, armed or not.

Still, he remained cautious. The scent grew stronger, as did his heart-beat. He kept his instincts in check with every step. Then, at last, he found his prey. At first, the target was just a figure wearing a thin T-shirt, green vest, and khaki pants. A backpack at his side made him look like one of those bird watchers Sundale had seen several times before. He was almost dismissed as a nosey human trying to 'study' Harmus until Sundale saw a standard-issue P-mag on his belt. Then he became a very real threat.

When he got closer with no sign of detection, Sundale risked going straight toward him. He hugged the ground so he could move smooth and slow, ready to dash off after false prey or in retreat. He wanted to get a better look so he could evaluate his real prey in full, so he stayed in cover as much as possible, turning to stone any time the man looked in his direction. The man never appeared to use a scanner. The only tool he ever used was a pair of binoculars, which allowed Sundale to get close and undetected.

He soon got close enough to examine his prey.

To call the man young might have been an understatement. His face was so smooth, so clean, so fresh, Sundale had to wonder if he'd had his first pimple yet. He wasn't a large man; with thin body lines that spoke more of speed than strength. If it weren't for the military cut hair, Sundale might have let him pass as a curious, or foolish, teenager. Either that or some crazy human looking to hunt a holdren. He wouldn't be the first to try, or the first to die, in the attempt.

The man tapped on a wrist-com, and Sundale tensed to fire in case he was detected. A very young voice silenced that fear as he returned to his binoculars.

"Not having as much luck today, eh Harmus? Or did Sundale make the kill without you? No matter. I'm sure you'll get all the food you need now that Major Harlem is home. And with the three of you down here, Operation Juno should run without any more disasters."

How does he know about us?

The man's wrist-com beeped, and Sundale again tensed for danger. The man checked it, looked up as if he'd forgotten something important, then started marching deeper into the desert.

Sundale followed, careful to be silent without losing sight of his mark. The young man marched straight toward a small car hidden behind some bushes. Based on pictures Sundale had seen, the main body lines of such vehicles hadn't changed all that much in the last 200 years outside of being more streamlined. For one thing, cooling technologies removed any need for a grill, at least on a two-door sedan like the one the man headed for. Wheels had been long abandoned in favor of an undercarriage hover system that was far more efficient and required far less road maintenance.

The young man got in the driver's seat and closed the door, but like so many humans, he had lowered a window a tiny bit to prevent the inside from getting as hot. To a native like Jason, it wouldn't even be a problem, which only added to the confusion.

It also let Sundale listen in despite the hum of the air-cooling system kicking on. "Computer, identify. Glarm, Private Maddox. Asset 47988. Begin recording. Recon report. Harmus remains unaware of my surveillance thus far. Reports of Gold Group placed on leave appear to be confirmed. I have seen Captain Sundale hunting, but I believe he required rest first. Further, I was able to confirm—"

Sundale's ears became a detriment as the deeper, louder hum of the main engine drowned out anything else. To humans, civilian vehicles were quiet enough to talk over even if they stood next to a running one. To a holdren, however, they could be as loud as a music concert to perked ears, as his were. Add in the windows being rolled up, and Sundale had no hope of hearing anything more.

He hugged his cover as the car lifted a few inches off the ground and sped into the distance. Once his ears stopped ringing, Sundale gave a quick series of barks to summon the pack. Yarain matched the call to give him a direction and to announce she was heading toward him.

They exchanged glancing checks of cheek glands when they met. Mostly so the parents could confirm their cub remained in good health. Once done, they got some distance from the location just in case the man came back. They laid together in the shade of another tamarisk to let their bodies recover from the hunt and the more recent run. There, Sundale reported everything he had heard and seen.

Yarain commented the second he finished. "I wonder what 'Operation Juno' is."

"I'm more curious why he cares about me," Harmus said.

"Likely because you're 'with us,'" Sundale offered. "By watching you, he may feel they can learn something about us."

"I agree," Yarain said. "We need to tell Jason. We have to plan this together."

"You're not going after these people," Harmus said. Yarain began walking back to Jason's house. The others followed, but Harmus wasn't giving up. "Yarain! You can't hunt them."

Yarain kept her pace but did look back. "We can't ignore this."

"I agree something needs to be done, but not by you or Sundale. We can't take chances with his health."

Sundale said, "In some ways, we can't afford not to."

Both parents stopped at his comment. Yarain's ears were up and alert while Harmus' were trying hard not to go forward in anger.

"Explain that," Harmus said.

Sundale's ears fell back a second as he regretted saying anything. "Something dangerous is going on. Jason is going to need me by his side when whatever it is hits. I can't deny him that because of one little reaction."

"Sundale, you fainted and glowed! This is not a *little* reaction."

A growl formed deep in Sundale's throat. "What would you have me do? Lay in bed for days like the humans want? I'm sorry, Harmus. I refuse to let anything make me the fearful, helpless holdren again."

Harmus began a growl but was cut off by a louder one from Yarain. Sundale and Harmus immediately ducked in submission, though Harmus was more apology than true surrender. She stared at them both until she was certain she had their attention.

"You're both right," she said. "We can't ignore Sundale's seizure nor can we ignore this Private Glarm. The pack must hunt together. I trust the doctors to keep him safe."

"What about the hunt itself?" Harmus asked carefully, but with no less anger.

"Trust *me*," Sundale said. "I'm no less afraid than you are."

Yarain ruffed dismissal with an ear flick which Sundale didn't fully understand. She didn't agree with his statement, he just wasn't sure why. Meanwhile, Harmus forced his ears forward to help keep his hackles down.

"Are you? Your uniform is again forcing you to run straight at the antlers of your prey. It won't miss every time."

Sundale couldn't quite stop a growl. "I know that. I can't explain why it's worth it. I *can* ask that you trust us to be as careful as possible."

"Sundale, if you weren't as careful as you are, I would never have let you join in the first place."

Sundale's ears shifted back, in part because of the irony of the statement. If he wasn't as careful as he was, he wouldn't have let himself join either. The rest was a touch of rebellion unbecoming of a holdren. Father or first father, Harmus wouldn't have been able to stop him.

Though in a way, that's how they got stuck away from home. He'd refused to just up and leave when they found him. By the time he'd come close to a decision, the chance to choose had been taken from him. An accident changed Harmus and Yarain, then in a state of pure energy, back into the mostly flesh state all holdrens are born as. Harmus blamed Interstar, but Sundale put more blame on himself for putting his parents, and himself, in a position to be there when it happened. Without the cues they could sense as pure energy, neither Harmus nor Yarain were able to find their way home. Since then, no one had been able to find their homeworld.

And Sundale wanted to find it. He'd only been a young cub tasting his first meat when he was taken. He didn't remember much. Just the love of the pack, the thrill of play fighting and hunting, and a few dim senses of what home felt like. He couldn't even remember if the cubs he played with were his siblings or cubs from another couple.

In truth, he could recall more about his time with Karol. She'd thought him just another fox. Though by the time Sundale could tell her what he really was, he'd come to find the term 'fox' worked as well as any. Especially once he came to understand the Human need for pronouns. She may not have ever really understood him as a holdren, but she never left any doubt about how much she cared. If only it had been enough.

Sadly, even Earth, as wild as some parts still were, wasn't home. As he walked with his parents back to Jason's home, Sundale couldn't shake the twinge in the back of his mind that it was still *Jason's* home. Humans belonged there. Holdrens came from somewhere else. Some distant world as yet untouched by technology. Or it was as far as Sundale could remember. After thirteen years - *Human* years - a lot could have changed.

Little had changed in years on Earth, though. When the holdrens got back to Jason's house, they found him much as they often did when off duty on Earth. He wore a simple T-shirt and jeans and, as usual, he was on his knees helping Marcy pull weeds out of her prized flower bed. The small pile behind them spoke of a busy year for the arrow weeds. *Bad time for another bombshell.* Yet all that did was stiffen the holdrens' tails as they approached. Now or later, it had to be done.

When Jason saw them, he stood with a smile that soon vanished, though not for the reason Sundale expected. "It obviously didn't get away, so what happened?"

While Sundale tried to determine what had Jason upset, Marcy left no doubt where her feelings lay. "Before we go into that, could you three do me a favor and clean up? I don't like seeing blood on my favorite foxes."

Sundale's ears flashed back as he noticed the blood on their muzzles. He'd forgotten how much it bothered humans.

Meanwhile, Jason's face loosened with a sideways glance at Marcy.

"You perform complex surgery on a daily basis, but you can't stand a little blood from a hunt?"

Marcy glared at her husband. "Not on my friends I can't. I told you why just a few hours ago."

What did we miss? Sundale could feel the tension as if it were squeezing him from inside. Whatever was going on, it had them at odds for some reason. *As if the timing weren't bad enough.*

Before either human could provide further fuel to the fire, Yarain stepped forward, switching back to English for Jason and Marcy. "It's all right, Jason. Our issue can wait while we clean ourselves."

"Can it?" Harmus asked.

Yarain cast him a straight-eared glare of her own. "Yes, it can. We'll meet you inside."

Jason left like he'd been dismissed with Marcy following, a bit stiff.

"I wonder what they fought over," Harmus said as they started working each other's fur clean.

"You never know with humans," Sundale replied. *"I've seen them fight over the most trivial of issues."*

"I hope this issue doesn't leave either of them harmed. I like them too much to see them injured."

On that, Sundale had to agree. Humans could too easily turn a simple argument into a "serious problem." The thought of Jason or Marcy allowing that to happen made what they were bringing them weigh all the more.

The weight grew further as they used a paw-pad trigger to open the door. They went into the living room looking for Jason and Marcy. Mugs on the coffee table reeked of the name-sake drink with other, much sweeter scents mixed in. *He never does take it black if he can help it. Probably why he drinks so much tea.*

The room was otherwise open save for one sofa against the front window and another couch along the wall. A couple of short cabinets with minor adornments dotted the other walls and held pictures, mementos, and other things humans liked to collect. The wall opposite the couch held a monitor for viewing whatever entertainment was desired.

The room connected to the dining room without any border beyond a change from carpet to tile where the dining table and chairs resided. Large cabinets on the wall held most of the dishes used as well as a few they only brought out for certain occasions. Beyond the table lay a large kitchen separated from the dining room by a counter. Three people could cook in there and still have room to spare.

It was still Marcy's domain, which one entered with great caution when she was cooking. The kitchen was walled with tile but the dining room walls were all wood planks that looked like they were freshly cut. Even at a distance, the holdrens could catch an air of fresh wood, which helped make the house feel just a little closer to home.

Sundale wished he could go there instead of bringing more stress into Jason's home. Sadly, he had to make his report, no matter how much he might like to ignore it.

Jason and Marcy were found on the sofa of the living room, hands together as they shared a passionate kiss. They turned decidedly red when they saw they weren't alone anymore, to which the holdrens ruffed amusement.

"I guess you're done," Jason said.

"That lasted less than I expected," Harmus said.

"That's the other thing about humans," Sundale said. *"They can 'make up' just as fast as they get angry."*

Jason and Marcy leaned forward still looking embarrassed, mostly unaware of the Holdren conversation.

"So, you had something to tell us?" Jason said.

All ears twitched. Sundale felt the duty fell to him to make the report, so he began. He "forgot" to mention the amount of hunting they'd done. Last thing they needed was to argue about Sundale's health again, and Jason knowing would change absolutely nothing. While not quite a lie, it did push the boundaries of how Holdrens operated. One does not hide information from a first parent. It keeps them from acting properly and speaks of ego that could be a threat to the pack. But knowing the details about their hunt would not change Jason's reaction, thus it was acceptable—barely.

The red faces before him turned serious the moment Sundale mentioned the scent belonging to who he was certain was a soldier. He recounted the report he'd heard, adding the sidearm as further proof this wasn't another crazed scientist trying to study a holdren without permission or a hunter looking to die. He also admitted he couldn't get close enough to catch the license plate.

Jason's head fell into his hands when Sundale ended his report. He didn't need his nose to know how Jason felt.

"Is there some rule that says we can't relax for more than twenty-four hours?" Jason said.

"It's getting hard on me too, Jason," Sundale confessed.

"I'll bet it is. I take it you didn't get anything else from this guy."

"*NO*," Yarain said. She then added, "We couldn't break cover. I'm sorry, sir."

"No, no, that's what you should have done. We've been blessed with a series of fortunate events thus far. Let's not press our good fortune more than we have to."

Marcy ran her hand along Jason's back. "The question is what we do now? It's not like we know who to go after."

"Which is why we can't act until they do. Contacting command might tip off this Private Glarm or his friends. Not that we have much to tell them anyway. I might be able to send something to General Carson, but the best we can do is wait and see if we can figure out who this guy is and what Operation Juno might be." He looked right at Harmus, and the corners of his mouth lifted. "It's just like hunting a heard of elk. You can't blindly charge into the herd. You'll wind up finding the wrong end of someone's antlers. You have to stalk them, find a target, then wait for the right moment to attack."

Harmus' ears turned forward. Subtle changes in his whiskers changed the 'yes' into the Holdren version of an approving nod, but most humans wouldn't have noticed. "Not a bad analogy for a Human."

"I'm a soldier," Jason said. "We're not that different."

Harmus' ears flattened for a second, only to rise with his hackles. Jason raised a hand to surrender the subject, to which Harmus turned and walked into the common room with his mate close behind.

Marcy sighed while rising to her feet. "Well, if we're going to do nothing, then we might as well eat. I know you three just ate, but I still intend to cook dinner."

"Cheese-noodle casserole?" Sundale asked, almost pleading.

"What do you care? You can't eat much. Your system can't handle it."

"There's always leftover cheese."

Marcy shook her head while a laugh slipped through her lips. Sundale ruffed and swished his tails, obviously faking excitement. Marcy continued to control her laugh despite her head continuing to move. She then tried to ignore him on her way to the kitchen.

Sundale kept his stance until he saw Jason's chin resting on his folded fingers. His eyes were focused on nothing.

"What is it, Jason?" Sundale asked.

Only his reply said he'd heard anything. "The clouds are thin and the air still, yet I am as blind as if it were the darkest night."

I hate it when he does that. "What does that mean?"

Jason shook his head as if to snap himself out of a trance. "Sorry. I'm just thinking. There's a lot going on out there, none of it making sense. That's without your little seizure. Combine the two, and I'm looking at more risk than I like and a headache growing worse by the day."

"Sounds normal to me," Sundale said without emotion. "We've faced this kind of thing before."

"We haven't always come out intact," Jason noted. He tapped his left shoulder where a Jantan 'Auro,' or four-star Admiral, by the name of Jals had almost killed him in a sword duel. Only his rib and a bluff from Sundale had saved him. It wasn't their only close call over the years, but it remained the closest Jason had come to meeting his god thus far.

Sundale knew that. He also knew how little he cared about it. He was a Holdren. They didn't run from a threat they could handle just because of a few scars. If anything, those scars reminded them what they were protecting. To Sundale, this was no different. Nor was the reason for his lack of fear.

"A scar is nothing more than pain left behind," Sundale said.

"You wouldn't say that if you had one of your own."

"Perhaps. What matters is the now, and right now, I know that no matter what, you and Yarain will be there for me just as I will be there for you. The rest will be dealt with when it finds us."

Jason leaned back. Though his arms did fold, they were loose like they were settling in rather than turning defensive. "I guess you're right. I still can't stop worrying, though. There's a lot we don't know about this Private Glarm and your condition. Promise me you'll be careful?"

Sundale came around the coffee table to lay beside his friend on the couch. He rubbed his head against Jason and let out his 'purr,' as Jason called it. "Always, Jason."

Jason pulled him in close like he would a beloved dog, and Sundale only continued to rub. Any other human would have been bitten for trying. Jason was the exception. True, they never did meet at the same level as real packmates, but that didn't stop Sundale from dropping his defenses. From allowing Jason to stroke him like a dog, or hug him like a dog, without the slightest comment. Heck, there were times Sundale thought he might even play fetch with Jason if it meant they could feel bonded. Though if he ever did, it would be just the two of them. He had to retain *some* dignity.

A beeping from down the hall broke the moment. With Jason's wrist-com inactive, the message had been sent to his personal computer. Jason sighed, gave Sundale another hug, then dragged himself up to see what trivial detail needed his attention this time. They always had a way of finding him while on leave.

Sundale waited long enough to be sure he wasn't included. He lifted his nose toward the kitchen but found only hot water, steam, and expended cooking fuel. At best, he'd get a shred of some vegetable out of Marcy. He decided he'd rather have the cheese, so he went back outside to be in the wild.

He found a comfortable place under the setting sun where he couldn't see any sign of civilization. It took some effort given the Human need for lights, but he'd looked for such a place before. His usual spot under a tamarisk provided as much shade from humans as it did from the sun. Once he was alone on his belly, he let the outdoors swallow him whole.

As the clouds ceased to glow over the mountains, his eyes fell shut, and the desert came alive in ways no human could comprehend. In the trees he heard the screeches of owls and the soft chirps of bats on their own hunt. In the distance, he could hear the chirp of crickets, the yips of a young coyote, the growl of an angry bobcat, and a diamondback's rattling warning. The wind in the palm trees rustled the branches in a steady rhythm and rattled the leaves of a nearby cottonwood, no doubt claiming a few stray leaves. Yet the same breeze only lightly touched his fur and whiskers. As the wind grew more constant, it carried with it the acrid-sweet scent of a desert rainstorm brewing in the mountains. Mixed in were traces of wet clay and dust that still held the warmth of the afternoon as well as the pale scent of old arrow weed.

Sundale basked in the moment, letting all that lay there flow over and through him as if he weren't there. He felt himself lift as if he were floating off the dirt he lay in. Thought fell away in favor of the animal. The 'fox.' The untamed creature that had been born in such a land. He felt the air brush him much like Jason had a moment ago. He felt the wild, soft sand beneath his paws. He felt the urge to hunt, to explore, to claim, to be. If Jason's heaven did exist, Sundale imagined it would feel a lot like this.

"Taking in the wild?"

Sundale was so deep in the moment, that he hadn't noticed Harmus settle in beside him. Well, not quite true. His instincts had said something was there, but they'd also known it to be a friend and thus not important. A Human might have been insulted to have it described that way. A Holdren would know it to be the truth and, like Harmus, not care.

His father's words, while far from startling, were enough to break Sundale's trance. Though his use of the wild language let him hold onto more of the animal than he wanted to surrender right now.

"Yes," Sundale said.

"I do the same. It helps me when I... when I worry about you."

Sundale's ears flicked back. *Here we go again.* "You don't have to. I know what I'm getting into."

"I know you do. That's what scares me the most. Interstar has never learned to treat us like the wild beings we are. I worry they expect you to act like them."

"Jason doesn't. He lets me have my wild moments wherever possible."

Harmus huffed and scratched at his ear. "Holograms, force fields, but no scent or sense to it. Sim rooms aren't the same, Sundale."

Sundale gave a short growl with a flicked ear. Of course it wasn't the same. It never is. "It's close enough."

"And this new hunt? You don't know who that private answers to or what they have planned. You can't underestimate them."

"I won't. Harmus, trust me. When the time comes, I'll have a pack behind me." Sundale leaned over and rubbed his head against his father's. "And I promise I'll be careful."

"See that you do, Sundale."

Chapter 7

Cheese Noodle Casserole

Jason couldn't see them, but he knew they were out there. He'd watched Harmus slip into the wild through the living room window. With Sundale nowhere to be found, he knew where they'd gone. As always, he wished he could join them. But that was their element. His had found a way to catch up with him.

While he used the opportunity to send a vague report to General Carson, the message was a copy of the doctor's final report to headquarters. She again stated that she found no sign of infection, illness, or anything that could explain Sundale's "seizure." Her best guess was an allergic reaction to something, or perhaps stress combined with an adverse reaction to the magnetic storm and the EMP torpedoes. Both could have messed with his matrix enough to trigger a sneeze of sorts. She repeated her insistence on rest, observation, and added an order for another test of his matrix in a few days, which is the main reason Jason got the full report.

Command accepted her confidence that Sundale could remain on duty for the time being. Jason wasn't so quick. His own swirling concerns drove him to stare out into the wild desert wondering where they were. He could imagine them together. Hunting, playing, sleeping, or perhaps sharing affection as they often did. It created a bitter-sweet moment strong enough to threaten the onset of tears. If only he could share it with them.

"Wishing for something, Jason?"

Jason closed the curtain and snapped around to face the tall, dark-skinned, fairly-well-built man that was his old friend, Major Carter Gomez. Carter had his arms crossed, which allowed some of his muscles to show through the vest and sleeveless shirt he wore. His pants and shoes were well worn, though far from wearing out anytime soon. Jason could never tell if he belonged on a hiking trail, in a boxing ring, or on his own mountain no one dared climb. Too bad he was clean shaven or the choice would be easy.

"No, not at all," Jason said innocently. "Just checking after Sundale. After all, he did – "

Carter held up his hands. "Easy, Toro. I know how you feel about the whole 'family' issue."

Jason recracked the curtain. He knew Yarain was out there too, though he somehow felt she wasn't with the others. "Not sure you do. I can't see them, but I know what I'd see if I could." Jason huffed resignation, then closed the curtain again. "You'd think by now I'd know better. Every time I try to watch, I wish. And when I wish, I wonder, then I ask, then I think, then... you know the rest."

Carter nodded while pulling his CO away from the window by the shoulder. "Hey, it's not so hopeless. You already found a wife that will tolerate you and remains as fiercely loyal to you as you are to her. Now if you can manage that despite your career? Then this little chica of a home will be filled with laughter, sighs, and dirty diapers in nothing flat."

"Yeah? Then what? I get pictures. I get videos of his first step, first tooth, school awards. Hell, I probably won't even be there for his wedding."

Carter shook his head trying to control a laugh. "We both know nothing would stand in your way, Toro. Not even God. Now we both know where this conversation is going, so let's skip it, eh? Let the foxes have their moment and trust me when I say I am certain you will someday find a way to make it work." He grinned, then added a boisterous laugh bordering on evil. "Then, Toro, I will be there to save you from the evil diaper monster."

Carter backed up so he could extend his arms and rock from one leg to another. He groaned, moaned, and growled before chanting, "Change me, change me" in a slurred tone. Jason sighed, then pantomimed drawing a sword and calmly slicing Carter in half three ways. Carter groaned again before dropping his head and arms.

Jason resheathed his 'sword' with equal lack of emotion. He flopped onto the couch and folded his arms with great suspicion. "So, diaper monster, what are you doing here?"

Carter tossed out his hands looking positively injured. "What? Can't a guy visit his best friend while on leave?"

"Not out of the blue, no. Not your style."

Carter folded one hand under his arm while waving the other in a circle. "Well, you know. I found out about Sundale, so I decided to drop by and see if he was doing all right."

Jason barely moved. "Uh-huh. You called Marcy and learned she was making her casserole, didn't you?"

Carter shrugged again. "No speak English."

At last, Jason laughed. He tugged at Carter's shirt, to which the burly man pretended to be thrown onto the couch like a doll. He faked being stunned while Jason sat with folded arms, basking in victory.

"It's a good thing you're not like this when you're on duty," Jason said. "I'd send you in for a psych-eval."

"They'd only confirm just how loco I am," Carter said.

"Not to mention a strong addiction to a certain wife's cooking. Still, hard to say no when Marcy already said yes."

"Who said she did?" Carter said. Jason pointed at Marcy as she grabbed a chair from the living room. Somehow chair number six always found its way out of the dining room unless it was needed. "Guilty as charged, sir."

"Plea accepted." Jason slapped his friend's knee with another laugh. It was nice to have Carter around. Call it a cliché of a tale, but like Sundale, they shared a bond forged in fire. Though in their case, it was more like a lava flow.

When they met, Carter was a young officer under the control of Jantan technology and brain-washing techniques that were apparently hard to achieve and even harder to maintain. Meanwhile, Jason was a ripe-cantaloupe shade of green and proof of how fallible the techniques were. Both wound up prisoners of the jantans until Jason broke them and Marcy out in the then prototype Scorn heavy fighter. To say the following days were rough would be to say the early space wars between Earth alliances had been minor disagreements. The only highlight was when they found Sundale, though that relationship didn't exactly start well either.

Despite all that, it wasn't long before the two of them found common ground. They were both soldiers, both dedicated, and in Carter's case, royally pissed off. Yet it was Jason's bull-headed determination that had gotten them home. That's how he'd earned Carter's nickname of "Toro." Why he only used it when off duty was a question Jason never got around to asking. He had his theories but preferred to keep it a mystery. In this case, not knowing was more fun than true understanding.

Jason gave his friend another pat on the leg after his thoughts returned to the present. "Well, I'm glad you're here. I'm sure Harmus will be too once he finds out."

"In or out of my uniform?" Cater asked, a touch of seriousness in his tone.

Jason let his stern commanding-officer face touch his features. "Overall, he doesn't care, and you need to lighten up on that subject."

"Jason, he hates us. You can't tell me that doesn't bother you."

"Not enough to get in the way, no. He has plenty of reason to resent our uniform. Don't forget: someone else in the same clothes stole his cub from him. And that's only the first thing our insignia did to him. Add three years of being held captive by raiders, and I can't say I blame him." Jason blew out more stress as if he might deflate it like a balloon. It didn't work. "He doesn't hate *us*. He hates what the life demands of his pack. He's a worried father and husband who's already lost a lot because of people in uniforms. I can't fault him for that. Nor should you. Give the fox a break, all right?"

Carter threw up his hands to surrender the topic, at least for the time being.

A creak and clank sent both men sitting up toward the kitchen. A wave of melted cheese and hot sauce hit their noses, which drew a pair of delighted hums.

"Stand down, boys," Marcy said. "Your 'first hot meal in forever' needs to get a little hotter first."

"No, it doesn't," Carter said.

"I have a spatula, and I'm not afraid to use it."

"I've faced worse."

Jason thrust a hand onto his friend's chest. "Trust me, old friend, you haven't."

Carter replied by folding his arms and pouting like a scolded five-year-old. Jason scoffed at him before standing with a stretch onto his toes.

"Should I call in the foxes?"

"Might as well," Marcy said. "They can help you set the table. Dinner should be ready when they are."

Carter did a stretch of his own while Jason stuck his head out the door and tried not to feel like a father, or a farmer calling his dog. *I'll just keep that one to myself.*

"Dinner will be ready soon! If you want that cheese, best head this way."

He left the door unlatched as a courtesy. There was a control pad outside they could use, but they always appreciated not having to. He returned to the dining room to do his part for dinner.

Carter was already setting placemats on the table, so Jason went for the plates. He stopped at the first cabinet, though.

"You need anything for serving?" he called into the kitchen.

"Got all I need, Jason, thank you," Marcy said. Jason closed the cabinets, only to have Marcy's voice freeze him a second later. "Although, would you grab a big bowl? I forgot to account for Carter."

"And what does that mean?" Carter asked.

"Exactly what you think it means. One of these days, I'm going to give you a whole sack of potatoes and call it even."

"I'm a soldier. I need the energy."

"You're a professional mooch that needs a spanking."

"It's your own fault. It smells like combat in there. It sends my body into 'prepare for war' mode."

"You try anything, and you'll *see* combat."

Jason laughed while carefully lifting a large white serving bowl trimmed in gold from a short stack. Flower and tree patterns in the same color decorated the sides, as it did much of their dinnerware. It always seemed like over kill to Jason but it actually hadn't been that expensive. Nor was it the best they had by far.

He took it into the kitchen and set it beside the stove where Marcy was working with several things: a pot of potatoes bubbling nicely under a glass cover, a savory soup that would become gravy soon enough, and of course, the glaze for her meatloaf. She never served her casserole without her meatloaf. Even now, he could find hints of what smelled like cooked bread coming from the oven. How she achieved that was a family secret she refused to share. The glaze smelled of hot ketchup, which only made his mouth water, knowing what it was going to taste like.

Carter's right, it does smell like combat in here. The thought drew another chuckle. Soldiers often ate well unless in the field, but any time a battle was expected, the mess hall always found a way to set out the best of their cooking. Many a soldier knew they'd be seeing combat based on the smell; thus, the phrase was born. Forty years of war was enough for it reach the civilian populace, where it was now a common way to comment on how good a meal smelled. And today, Marcy's cooking smelled like a suicide mission.

"You really need to patent that, my dear," Jason said, offering an affectionate kiss on his wife's neck. "You could retire."

Marcy put a hand on his in reply. "Then you'd be the only one saving lives. No, Jason, I'm happy enough seeing my guests drool."

"Speaking of which. What have you got for our furred companions?" Jason was not relenting on his affection.

"The usual. They aren't as picky as we are, remember."

"And Sundale?"

"Don't worry. He'll get his cheese." Jason moved to her ear, which drew a short giggle. "Now come on, Major. Get out." He kept going. "Jason! Jason, get out of here before you make me burn something."

"As if you'd allow it."

She grumbled at him while he stopped at the fridge long enough to get out the butter. *Might as well save a trip.* A knife for serving, and back to the table he went. He returned to the cabinet once the butter was in its place and pulled out six plates adorned much like the serving bowl, though with far less artwork. He slid them into his arm like a running back, using his other hand to grab three tall glasses. Carter went into the kitchen for the silverware as Jason laid out the pieces he had. He went back for three wide mouthed glasses. Really, they were supposed to be wine glasses but experience had found them to work quite well for his holdren comrades.

Those holdrens entered right on cue and took their seats in finesse form after being assured the humans had things under control. Yarain, as usual, took one head of the table, with Sundale and Harmus taking a side for themselves. Right where their glasses had been placed. Having nothing to do, Sundale stared into the kitchen with a lick or two of his lips, to which Jason chuckled.

"You know what you look like," he teased.

Sundale only made a point of growling at him, which drew another laugh. *Protest all you want, you still do.*

He and Carter were just finishing with the settings when Marcy's voice came with authority from the kitchen. "All right boys and foxes, you may help take dinner to the table. No snitching! I see a single lid come off; you will pay."

Everyone volunteered to help.

A line formed to take parts of the meal to the table for serving. Each member took a covered bowl, pot, or metal sheet, and arranged them on the table. Jason was first, taking the bowl he'd gotten for her. Even now, he could see steam leaking out from under the lid, and he breathed in the smell of buttered potatoes as it wafted to him.

It only got better from there as the meal was assembled. The sweet scent of steamed carrots, corn, and melted butter joined with the potatoes. Then came her famous meatloaf with its signature smell of fresh baked bread, though moist, cooked meat was there as well. Just like the promise of a juicy steak from the grill, though this one had hot ketchup already applied on top. Real bread, in this case a few simple though hand baked rolls, only helped the smell as it came from under a handkerchief cover. Pungent, spicy-smelling – though not spicy-tasting – gravy sat in a bowl, mostly for the potatoes.

Then it came. The one dish Marcy carried herself. A large casserole dish filled to the brim with noodles, pieces of meat, and a layer of cheese garnished by a thin layer of green powder. Bits of corn and carrots were in there as well to round it out, though Jason knew the cheese wasn't just on top. Below, it would become more like a sauce with just a tiny bit of marinara mixed in for a touch of extra kick. It always smelled closer to pizza than anything else, yet not a one of them could agree on what it smelled like. Truth be told, it had its own aroma that seemed to change depending on the individual.

The entire meal was mostly holdren friendly, though they couldn't eat much without paying for it. Still, to give them something they could eat without consequence, a large, uncovered bowl was added to the meal. This one was full of meat with one-hundred percent holdren safe vegetables mixed in, all of it uncooked though still warm to make it more appetizing. Jason could only smell the vegetables and wondered, like always, if that was a good thing. A small bowl of shredded cheese was added for the holdrens to add as desired. A pitcher of water and a second of milk, and the meal was complete.

Jason took the other head of the table while Marcy and Carter took the remaining side. Married couples sat closest to each other, which meant Sundale was on Jason's other side. A welcome side effect he'd always enjoyed but would never admit to if asked. *Well, maybe if they really pressed, I might.*

Marcy and Carter folded their hands before looking to Jason.

"Jason," Marcy said, "given how rarely you get to, I think it best you give the blessing."

Jason nodded his agreement, then bowed his head with Carter and Marcy. "Dear Heavenly Father, I thank you for giving us this time to come together, and I thank you for watching over us all these years. I ask, Lord, that you may continue to watch over us and that you may bless this food to the nourishment of our bodies. And Lord, I hope that you will remain in our lives from now until forever. Amen."

Carter and Marcy echoed the amen while the holdrens sat in respectful silence. They didn't share the belief in God, but they also never minded being respectful of those that did. From the start, it had taken no effort for them to remain in silence as they had now. Even to not eat until the blessing was complete was done without protest. It wasn't their way, but they didn't mind adapting out of respect.

Though once the meal was on, both races were very much the same.

As such, Marcy took charge. She reached for the cooked veggies and began to serve herself. "Okay, you all know the drill. I'll start things off, and no overloading on a single item."

She looked at Carter and Sundale as she said the last, causing both to lower their heads, and ears in Sundale's case, in submission.

All hail the queen of the dining room, Jason thought with a smile. Marcy never did stand for much when it came to plants or dinner. In an odd way, Jason liked it. For once, he was the one taking orders. The pressure belonged to someone else. True, dinner was nothing like combat, but Jason didn't mind forgetting that, if only for a while.

Marcy began the passing. Each dish went around the table, and the attendees served themselves before passing it on to the next. The potatoes went next, followed by the veggie-meat mixture for the holdrens. Plates were filled as desired, Carter and Sundale as always staring at the casserole until it finally made the rounds. Harmus and Yarain stuck to their holdren mix, the assorted vegetables, and maybe a bite each of the casserole and potatoes. As for Sundale, he took what might be called a tiny helping of the casserole. On its own, not really a problem. It was when he added a healthy sprinkle of cheese to his holdren mix that Marcy started glaring at him.

"You know what that does to your bowels, Sundale," she said.

"A little irregularity is worth the taste," he said.

"Carter has a little irregularity. *You* spend the next two hours growling from your hips."

"Hey, don't bring me into this," Carter protested. "I'm behaving myself."

"Oh really? And how many potatoes do you have there? Three? Four? And I suppose you'll be drowning them in salt and butter."

"And gravy!"

Marcy and Jason both shook their heads at them. *Peas in a very strange pod those two, at least when it comes to Marcy's cooking.* Not that anything around him could ever be called normal.

How could it? He was having dinner with alien foxes, that weren't *really* foxes, who after failing to manage any other way, still lapped their drinks instead of sipping them from their glasses. Being canines, they didn't exactly chew either. Be it the vegetables, the casserole, or their holdren mix, they more chomped at their food than the grinding motion humans called chewing. Nothing ever spilled, though. They'd learned to achieve that much. Even so, it was hard to see anything but the animal as they ate. At least they'd learned the mysteries of silverware. While the bites were perhaps bigger than most would try, they had no problem using fork and spoon instead of eating right off the plate. Though that too had been an adventure.

Jason huffed at the memories as the conversation around him turned trivial. *My gosh how time has flown. Seems only yesterday Sundale and I were beginning to recognize our bond. Guess that makes it today we got the three of us assigned to the same fighter. Wonder where that leaves tomorrow?*

Stop thinking so much, Major, he scolded himself. *You'll get yourself into trouble.*

Too late, he replied. What may be coming tomorrow had already entered his mind. The sleeper escort, the transports, Red 7, now a mysterious private. He couldn't help fearing the next bombshell. Add Sundale's whatever it was, and he felt more terrified of the near future than he could ever remember being.

He forced himself back into the conversation before those fears consumed him. He then wished he hadn't, for it allowed him to see the tightness in Harmus' ears and tails. He had something on his mind, and Jason knew full well where it had its basis.

Thankfully, Carter provided hope that the issue, at least during these last moments of the meal, may go unaddressed.

"You've outdone yourself this time, Marcy," he said, dabbing his mouth a moment. "I can see why you don't use the food printers."

Marcy shrugged off the praise. "They're convenient, but they never can get my recipes right. While it can do a passable meatloaf, the last time I printed my casserole, I nearly threw up. It does ingredients per-fectly but a full meal? I don't trust it."

Jason swallowed his last bite before adding his own opinion to the mix. "Depends on the dish. I've had some meals that are as good as the real thing. Though I will admit, the more complex the meal, the harder it is to get a close approximation. Then there's the times something goes wrong, and you get macaroni and cheese that tastes like chicken."

"Even so, Jason," Sundale said, "you must admit, the real thing is often better."

"Only when it's cooked by Marcy."

The humans gave a chuckle, and the holdrens a few short ruffs.

Harmus reached for his glass with too much intent for Jason's nerves to trust. "So how long will you three, I mean four, be enjoying Marcy's cooking?"

And behold, the elephant. So much for avoiding the issue.

"Just what are you asking, Harmus?" Jason asked, meeting him head on for once.

"When are you going **BACK** on duty?" Harmus said, half ruffing a word.

"I don't know. That depends on your friend out there. We may be gone tomorrow for all I know."

"With or without Sundale?"

Sundale raised a hand between them before either could respond. "**WITH**, Harmus."

Marcy cleared her throat while tapping her fork on her plate. "Perhaps now is not the time for such things. You are all here to *relax*, not to con-tinue old arguments."

A beeping from down the hall drew a heavy sigh from Marcy, and Jason breathed out his own frustration. *Of all the times for an "urgent matter."*

He rose, trying to form an apology. "If it weren't for the hour..."

"Just, go Jason," Marcy said with a wave. "Get it taken care of."

Thanks a lot, Harmus. Jason went to his office trying to keep his anger from going any further. *Some relaxation.*

His office was at the end of the hall. It was a room with little more than a work desk and computer. There were a few token pictures as well; Marcy of course, his parents, Rickey back when he was just a pilot in command of the Red Group, Carter the day after they got back with Sundale standing beside them, and one large picture on the wall of the Red Group, taken shortly after Jason had been assigned to it straight out of the academy. Most had died in battle the day he was captured by the jantans. Many of the rest had died later, save for a few that were now retired or generals and admirals.

"PAICCA, this better be a real urgent," Jason said as he took his seat.

"I think it is, Major," the computer said. "It's General Carson on a secured channel, but the carrier wave is civilian, not military."

Great. It's so top secret he doesn't want command to know he called me.

"Match the encryption and receive the transmission."

"Stand by."

In the moment it took PAICCA to do so, Jason glanced at his father's officer blades and side-arm on the wall behind his desk. Like Jason, he was well practiced in sword and dagger fighting and was thus given matching ceremonial weapons. *What I wouldn't give for five minutes with you right now.*

Rickey Carson's image then flickered onto his terminal. By the weight of his eyes, Jason guessed his day wasn't going much better.

"Good evening, sir," Jason said, failing to sound cheerful. "What can I do for you?"

"Nothing right now, Major. I'm just letting you know about some big happenings going on."

"Define big." Jason turned around to see Yarain standing in the doorway with Sundale just behind her. "Marcy suggested we join you. She said it might be a good idea for us all to listen in, though I'm not sure that's her original thought."

No, I'm sure it's not. Jason motioned for them to come closer while facing Rickey again. "You were saying sir? Unless you want them—"

"No, they're fine. I was saying..." Rickey paused to shake his head. "You won't believe this."

"I'll believe anything at this point, sir," Sundale said.

"All right. I will tell you something you never heard, understand?"

They all agreed to not hear a word. "Remember that high-end escort mission I mentioned? Apparently, the jantans are coming to Earth in four days to begin negotiations for a peace treaty."

"That's a bit sudden," Yarain said with erect ears.

"Actually, I'm told it's been in the works for weeks. They kept it secret to prevent complications. Now that they're ready, command wants to be sure peace gets every chance, which means Interstar assets flying escort."

Jason felt his eyes turn dark as he tried to control his rising anger, mostly because he felt sure command was again ignoring clear signs of danger. "An escort for the jantans. The same guys who brainwashed Carter? The same guys we've been at war with off and on for the past forty years? Those jantans?"

Rickey just kept nodding. "It gets better. I'm told the commander of the ship transporting their representatives is none other than Auro Jals himself."

Yarain and Sundale both raised their hackles and began growling at the mention of Jals' name. A sentiment Jason shared though could not so easily express.

"You can't be serious," Yarain said. "Surly the jantans know about his history."

"History with the three of you, maybe, maybe not," Rickey said. "History for them, better than we do I'd wager. Jals is as much a Marcallan war hero as you three are United Systems war heroes. Believe me, I'm not enthusiastic about it myself, but to them, he's the perfect man for the job."

"Which begs the question, sir," Jason said. "Who are you going to send on this mission? I can't imagine Red Group would get the job after what happened with Red 7."

Rickey tried to rub the tension out of the back of his neck. "I understand they have someone in mind, but I haven't talked with them yet. My first priority has been to put everyone under my command on stand-by alert in case this thing blows up by any definition. Only those with the highest security clearance, and a few trusted souls like Yarain and Sundale, are being told the details."

From within, an intense sense of urgency took hold. Before Jason knew why, he had drawn himself up to the best professionalism he could manage. "Sir, I highly recommend that you assign the Gold Group to this mission."

Rickey shook his head. "Not possible, Major. This mission needs the lead crew to be there."

"We can be there, sir. This mission is important enough to skip some shore leave."

"Shore leave isn't the issue. It's Sundale's health I'm worried about. A temporary replacement won't do for a mission like this. If the Gold Group takes the mission, he has to be there. That's not possible with him still recovering."

Jason looked at Sundale and Yarain, silently asking permission to speak for them. Both nodded, or rather dropped and raised their muzzles, in reply. His stomach turned, but he knew this one was concern not a warning he was ignoring. Despite his words, he'd still be taking a risk with his friend's health. It felt right. It just didn't feel safe.

"With respect," Jason said, "the doctors are overprotective. He's fit for duty, sir, the doctor from the *Alamo* said so herself. We can handle this. We *need* to handle this. If peace is to be achieved, both we and Jals will have to learn how not to kill each other. This will be a perfect time to begin that road – for him, us, and both governments. Not to mention the little matter I messaged you about this afternoon."

Rickey sighed as he slumped in his chair. "All right. I'll trust your judgment. I can't give you any more details over the comms, though; command doesn't want to risk it. Report to Earhart Station Monday morning at oh-eight-hundred hours. You'll be fully briefed then. General Carson out."

The screen flickered off, and Jason walked out of his office with holdrens in tow. Words began to form but were stopped by Harmus standing just outside his office, ears straight, eyes boiling, and hands slightly curled as if ready to strike. He had no doubt listened to the discussion from outside. *Gotta stop underestimating those ears.*

Jason rubbed his eyes with another frustrated sigh. "Harmus, I'll be blunt. Now is not the time for this."

His hackles rose while his lips curled in an echoing snarl. "You are taking a **BIG** chance with my cub's **LIFE**! This is **JUST** the kind of situation that could complicate Sundale's condition. Now explain to me why this mission is worth that risk."

Jason formed a reply but was stopped again by Yarain's hand on his shoulder.

"Think how you'd feel in his position."

If only I could. Jason swallowed the resentment with what would have been a growl of his own. "All right. This Private Glarm in the desert spoke of an Operation Juno, and he noted us being on leave. Hours later, we learn the jantans are coming for peace negotiations. That's way too much of a coincidence. They clearly care that we'd be out of the way. The best way to counter their plans is to be there when whatever they have planned goes down. Believe me, Harmus, if there was another way, I'd take it, but I don't see another choice. Do you?"

Harmus' snarl slowly faded into a frustrated growl while his hackles relaxed. "No."

When he offered nothing further, Jason took it as his cue to say... something. He took Harmus' hand in his in the hopes of making a connection, especially when his words sounded so very wrong. "I can't promise we'll come back alive, but I can promise our best effort and that we will be excessively careful. Another thing I can promise is this: I will do my best to protect the lives of your pack, even at the cost of my own."

"Then you would break your promise," Harmus said without missing a beat. When Jason looked up confused, he added, "You too are a member of my pack." He placed his other hand on Jason's shoulder and looked him straight in the eye. "Good hunting, Jason."

Jason could only manage a soft thank you in reply.

Part 2: Let Slip the Dogs

Chapter 8

We're Doing What?!

Because of the looming escort mission, no one would call Jason's last days of shore leave entirely relaxing. Then again, nothing else happened, so he couldn't complain, nor would he have. Marcy managed to get a few uneventful meals out of them, with Carter crashing every one. Sundale, Yarain, and Harmus were able to spend a good piece of the time being as wild as they could on an alien world. Jason even managed to go to church for the first time in months. All in all, they were able to enjoy the time until Monday came and demanded an end to it.

A quick breakfast was served, fond farewells were exchanged, then in no time at all, Jason and his crew were walking into the briefing room with the rest of Gold Group chattering about what they thought this was all about.

General Rickey Carson was already waiting for them there in a uniform so clean it appeared brand new. As the crews took their seats, Jason took his position to one side of the screen while his crew took their place farther off to that side. Rickey stood to the other side of the screen by the controls. Once the group was seated, he activated the main monitor with cool control and precision. His voice held not a single waiver or touch of lightness as he began the briefing.

Hasn't changed a bit.

"Good morning, everyone. I'm sure by now most, if not all, of you have heard rumors of an impending mission regarding Marcalla. This time, the scuttlebutt is right. In fact, your group is going to be running that mission."

Carter raised his hand but didn't wait to be recognized. "If I may ask, sir, what kind of mission would that be?"

"Wait a little bit, and I'll tell you, Major."

Carter dropped his hand with his shoulders following a little.

"As you also know, Interstar has been put on standby alert. No details have yet been released because the reason for that alert is the same mission you are about to undertake. You see, ladies and gentlemen, the Gold Group is going to be escorting a Marcallan negotiation team to Earth for the preliminary stages of what is hoped to be a final, *lasting*, peace treaty."

The room echoed with mutterings as well as a few sarcastic chuckles. Jason couldn't blame them. There had been six cease fires over the course the of Jantan Wars. Only one lasted longer than five months, and rumor suggested it only did because Marcalla had its own internal problems to deal with at the time.

Rickey no doubt felt the same, since he let the rumble make its rounds for a moment before clearing his throat to silence it. "I share your initial reaction. I didn't believe it myself at first. But this one feels different, and command is adamant that we give the peace process every chance to succeed. So, I suggest you swallow any snide remarks you have in mind. I won't tolerate a single one during any point of this mission."

Rickey tapped on a console, and the screen changed to a map of the border area between the Republic of Marcalla and the Untied Systems Republic. "At outpost 371, you will meet a Marcallan heavy cruiser, codename 'Hillside,' which will be commanded by Auro Jals. Yes, *that* Auro Jals, stuff it! Your group, codename 'Rainbow,' will assume escort formation around the cruiser and ensure she safely arrives at Earth, Waypoint 'Riverside'"

Gotta love these code names. Jason stayed quiet, though. Now was not the time to lose his composure. His group needed him to be an example, especially now. *Bet Sergeant Tillman will love this.*

"Jals is commanding a heavy cruiser, sir?" Carter asked. "That's not exactly a small ship or a small man."

"That's kind of the idea, Major," Rickey said.

"I don't understand, sir."

Rickey pulled up a diagram of the ship in question, which did no justice to how she looked in person. She was a long beast with a thick, half-circle shaped bow and backward curved spikes running the length of the hull along the sides. The spikes ended where three sets of wings resembling Earth battle-axes sat at the stern of the ship, and the hull was painted a dark violet color with a very slight purple sheen to it. Jason had seen a lot of that ship in his time. Enough that he had to take a deep breath to silence some bad memories. Not to mention a phantom ache from the scar near his left arm pit.

"The Histmar class heavy cruiser," Rickey said, "is, as many of you know from experience, both fast and resilient. There is a lot of space between the border and Earth. Space filled with people who would love to blow any Marcallan ship out of the stars. After lengthy discussions with their leaders, it was decided that the Marcallan delegation would use this vessel, under the command of their best man, to ensure they make it to the negotiating table."

"Seems like a light escort for a ship that could do a lot of damage," another officer said.

"The escort's job is to *protect* the ship, not engage it. The more weight we send, the more attention it will draw. But should that attention come anyway, she'll have the bulk to handle it without relying only on you."

"And if it decides to attack *us*?"

"I doubt they'll risk it, Captain. She'd be swarmed by half the fleet in nothing flat. More to the point, I feel quite certain the jants are sincere about wanting this treaty."

Sundale flicked a curious ear. "May I ask why, sir?"

"Because I've just learned that the Marcallan negotiation team will be led by one of their military commanders, Hilahshan Forin, *and* their prefect."

Jaws dropped, holdren ears went erect, and eyes bulged. No one said a word or dared laugh. Talk about big happenings. So little was known about Marcalla's supreme leader, some wondered if they were even a jantan. Some went so far as to question the existence of *any* prefect, citing the scarce examples of Jantan soldiers in any way mentioning a single leader. Even when they did, it was always the English "prefect."

Not a one ever used a Jantan term for the role. They spent far more time talking about Hilahshan Forin, one of Marcalla's five-star admirals. Never mind humanity meeting its first alien; this was bigger than the invention of the hyper light coil.

Rickey, ever calm, just nodded his amusement. "I see I'm not the only one who was shocked to hear about that. It's true, people. They'll be on that ship. So, it's imperative that you get it to Earth safely. The I.C.V. *Spartan* will join you as a mobile sensor platform, and we'll have task forces ready to join you should you need them, but they won't know why they're on alert unless you call for them. We don't want any surprises here. Gold 1 will remain in command of the mission, however, so any orders you get will come from Major Harlem or be relayed through Captain Yarain or the *Spartan*. All others are to be ignored for the duration of this mission. Don't listen, don't respond, nothing. It's the best way to ensure the right information gets to you at the right time."

"No ship for us to land on, sir?" a younger officer asked. "What about sleep and food?"

"This isn't your first rodeo, Lieutenant. You've eaten on the wing before, and your AESOs can fly from their chairs long enough for sleep rotations while you're away from colonies. Speaking of which..." Rickey changed the screen to show their general course through United Systems Territory. "As you can see, we've decided to have you get past the Sagittarius arm, then spend the rest of the trip between arms as much as possible. We're hoping to limit, if not eliminate, problem encounters with civilians."

This time, Jason interjected on behalf of the group. "And if we do have a problem encounter, sir? I've already dodged one court marshal for firing on civilians. I don't want me or my men to face a second one."

"Your mission is to escort the jantans to Earth, Major. If anyone, military, civilian, or otherwise, jeopardizes that mission, you are to pacify that threat by whatever means you deem necessary."

The weight he put on the last part left no question how much freedom they had on this one. Jason nodded silent understanding, feeling the full weight of the mission for the first time. *In other words, if I feel I have to blow away a civilian yacht to protect the prefect, I have full clear-*

ance to do so. Not exactly the kind of thing one signs up to do. Jason again kept his thoughts to himself. Rickey trusted him to make the call. That mattered.

He knew he'd make the right call. Being able to live with himself after... Well, he'd cross that bridge if he came to it.

Rickey, meanwhile, deactivated the screen, then stood at its middle with a clip-com pressed against his belly. "Inter-group communications and call signs will be unchanged but are to be highly encrypted at all times, used only when necessary, and contain as little information as possible. If you must mention the cruiser, use her codename only. Further, the cruiser will communicate with Gold 1 and *only* Gold 1 unless different orders are received *from* Gold 1. Sorry to put so much of this mission on your team's shoulders, Major."

Jason gave him a wry smirk and huff while waving it off. *I'm getting used to it.*

"Twenty minutes before the mission, you will all receive clip-coms with the details I have outlined as well as anything else that has changed or was not mentioned. The differences and missing information will be highlighted, I assure you. However, I expect you all to be familiar with the updated mission profile before you launch. That's it for the briefing people, not that I think you need it. You're the best we have. I have no doubt you will conduct yourselves like the expert team you are. And let's face it, your orders here aren't that difficult. Meet the cruiser, make sure she gets to Earth in one piece. How you do it is up to Major Harlem. Any questions?"

Did we really need to be reminded whose neck is on the line here? Jason's mind flashed from Rickey's hidden reinforcement of his command to the soldier in the desert. From there, a thought on their plans sent a shudder down his spine. *Could they be that foolish?* At first, he thought not, until he remembered the kind of equipment those transports were loaded with.

The shudder grew while Rickey answered, in great detail, a question regarding the cruiser's normal compliment of fighters, including the reasons for their absence on this mission. Possible? With the kind of mindset he'd seen so far, an attack on the Marcallan delegation seemed almost certain. It could even be what all that gear was meant for. To say nothing of the captured Scorns had they not caught the faulty junction boxes. Any or all of them could have been used in a successful assault on the Marcallan cruiser. Even thwarted, they may yet still try something.

Part of him considered allowing it. For a fraction of a second, he even thought about helping. Then sanity took hold.

Peace. Real, actual, peace. Marcalla had "made peace" before, but not like this. Not with their prefect. Not without a massive, crushing loss. And not once had they been willing to go to Earth for it, never mind agreeing to leave their fighters behind or be escorted by Interstar forces. Either they were trying a whole new angle, or they may have finally had their fill of war.

The thought felt odd in Jason's mind considering how angry he had been at being pulled from the line only a few days ago. Yet somehow, call it a sign from God or plain wishful thinking, he couldn't help feeling like this time was different. That maybe, just maybe, he could go a year or more without burying a member of his group.

Part of him still didn't trust it, and who could blame him? Jals and Forin on the same heavy cruiser? *There's a pair of red flags if ever there was one.* Even so, if there was even a sub-atomic particle of a chance this was real and would last, he had to make sure it did. So, history with Jals or not, that cruiser would make it without so much as a chip in the paint. Anything less would be unacceptable.

I just pray it's real, or that I can see through the trick before it's too late— No, really God. Help me out here. I could use it.

When Rickey finished explaining why the cruiser would have only non-combat vessels aboard, he called for more questions. Jason raised his hand, hoping to ensure these mystery men didn't have a single chance to accomplish their mission.

"Just one, sir," he said. "Will my crew still be escorting their party to the negotiating table? It is how it's written in the regulations, sir."

Rickey gave him a scanning, sideways look. "Want a look at your old enemy, Major?" Jason didn't move, didn't even blink. "Yes, you will. You're our flagship unit on this one, which is why so much of this mission is on your shoulders. Despite some misgivings, I want it done right, start to finish, by the book, no nonsense. Any other questions?" Silence. "Very well. You leave in one hour. Take the time to go over your ships with a fine-toothed comb. I want them in peak condition for this one. Dismissed."

The group filed out of the briefing room, all talking about the mission. Carter made a point of walking beside Jason, which left him waiting for whatever he had on his mind. Carter walked beside him all the way to the hanger, sneaking a glance at both him and Sundale along the way. Not knowing why, Jason didn't want to risk opening another can of worms, even though it might become a bigger can later.

When they got to the hanger doors though, the can came out. "Can you three do this, Jason?"

One question, yet his tone, more reprimand than question, asked all the others.

It was Jals who led the attack on the Apollo Research Station. Jals that oversaw the brainwashing of Carter. Jals that nearly killed Jason in a sword duel. And Jals that was directly responsible for the deaths of half of Jason's original group. Sparrings with him over the years had grown a fair amount of hate. Jals would do anything, absolutely anything, to achieve victory. All three of them had lost good friends and seen some despicable acts, all under the order of Auro Jals.

There was some question as to how much Hilahshan Forin had been involved, but Jason had only heard his name in passing. Forin had never been directly involved that he knew of, save for some minor oversight of the brainwashing program that had corrupted Carter and failed to corrupt Jason. It was during this time Jason got his only look at the man outside of enemy leader profiles.

Jason paused for a moment, his crew silent and patient behind him. He felt them, and the answer came. *Just imagine,* he told himself, *never having to worry again. Never having to fear for their lives again.* He could so imagine it. Sundale could take all the time he needed to recover. Harmus could spend weeks with his pack. For goodness' sake, maybe Interstar could mount a proper expedition to find their home world.

Do this? If it meant all that and more, he'd give Jals a song with a full-on French kiss and flowers! *Wouldn't that be a sight?*

"Yes," Jason said, no doubt in his mind. "We can do this."

Carter nodded his approval. "All I needed to hear, sir."

"You know, I could ask the same of you."

In a rare moment, Carter's eyes got heavy. He closed them with a deep breath and a brief drop of his head. "I'll be all right. I put my doubts behind me long ago, and I know how to fight past it now. They can't own me again."

Jason put his hand on his friend's shoulder. "And that is all *I* needed to hear."

"Then we're settled. Let's go make peace."

From your mouth to God's ears.

The group went inside and parted ways as if nothing had happened. Jason led the way to his fighter, which they found already being looked over by technicians. Every one of them snapped to perfect attention with a salute the moment they arrived. Jason tried to mute his head-shake as much as possible. *Another group of rubber people.*

Jason returned their salute with a half-hearted one of his own. "As you were, people. Except for someone willing to give me an update on your progress."

A young, blonde-haired woman approached while the others returned to their work. "Little has been done so far, sir. We're just about finished with armor analysis and were about to begin looking at the control thrusters and main sub-light engines."

"Very good. I was planning to run computer and control checks of my own in the cockpit. Would that interfere with your work?"

"No sir. Just mind the hazard tags."

"I promise. Carry on."

The technician saluted again before rejoining her team. Jason led his own crew inside, motioning for them to check their stations while he went over his. The consoles hummed to life as they began the diagnostics, though several controls were physically blocked by small red tags to make sure the crew didn't do anything they shouldn't. Sundale was the first to dive underneath his station to check the physical components. Jason settled for basic system checks to start, though he knew his own dive was forth coming. Not that he expected problems, but with a mission of such importance, and given what happened the last time they looked, he wasn't taking any chances.

Yarain meanwhile chose a broader beginning to her checks. "Everything looks good. Not reading any residual problems with the sensors or comms."

"Make sure there isn't," Jason said, surprised by his reserved tone. "We need this bird in perfect shape for the mission."

"Yes, sir."

An uneasy silence enveloped the cockpit, broken only by the consoles themselves responding to input commands and the strangely echoing conversation of the techs outside. At times, it seemed as if Jason was listening through the ears of the ship. Or maybe it was his nerves making it appear that way. Whatever the case, each passing moment left his chest feeling more and more solid. As if it knew something important, or disastrous, was coming.

He tried not to think on it. His checks and rechecks of even the slightest glitch made it difficult.

Sundale stood over his console with a shake, drawing Jason's attention, and his thoughts, away from his current set of diagnostics.

"Everything checks out here," Sundale said. "All magazines are fully loaded and secure." He settled into his seat, and Jason knew he wasn't done. "Do you think it's real this time?"

That diversion didn't last long. Jason's hand went to his left shoulder. "I hope it is. It's encouraging that they're sending their prefect this time. Though it could be a fake, or it could be them even more dedicated to the ruse than ever before. I suppose we'll see."

"Assuming it doesn't blow up because of bad posturing or old wounds."

"If it does, it won't be because of me. I've buried too many friends already. I won't let my hatred for Jals or anything else force me to bury anymore."

"I hear that," Yarain said. "The idea of going more than a few months without a funeral would be a dream come true."

"Indeed it would, Yarain. Indeed it would."

"Just one problem, though," Sundale said. "Once peace is achieved, we'll have to learn how to enjoy a full and complete shore leave. I don't know about you, but I'm not sure I can take that."

Jason stared at him until he gave a playful ruff with a swish of his tails. Then Jason found a broad smile with an amused huff of his own.

"Sun," he said, "sometimes I don't know what to do with you."

"There's nothing you can do. I'm here for life."

"You're a crazy fox is what you are."

"Now until forever."

Jason laughed at him while Yarain ruffed amusement. They each returned to their individual work, and while he couldn't be sure how they felt, Sundale's antics had loosened the knot in his chest considerably.

A respite that proved to be short lived as the promised arrival of the clip-coms caught him off guard some time later. As was her position, Yarain got the chance to look it over first. That, and Jason needed a moment to extract his hands from the innards of his own console.

Jason was just sealing things up when he noticed her go stiff. Her ears were straight up, and her tails were frozen. With not a single hair raised, he knew this to be shock instead of preparation for attack.

Given the strength of her shock he didn't want to ask, but knew he had to. "What is it?"

She handed him the clip-com with shifting ears. "You're going to love this."

Jason read over a section at the top noted as containing specific orders for Gold 1. He had to read it three times before he could accept it. Even then, his mind couldn't fully believe it.

"This is a joke, right?" Jason said. "Some prank Rickey's playing on us to lighten the mood?"

"I don't think so, Jason," Yarain said.

Sundale looked up from his work with his ears perked in search of clarification. With no words to explain it, Jason handed him the clip-com with a shake of his head. When Sundale finished reading it, he stared at Jason with his ears slowly going more erect than Yarain's. Even with the lack of usual facial expression, Jason could see the "you gotta be kidding me" in his eyes.

"Sun," Jason said, "I'm right there with you."

Chapter 9

A Strange Curtain

Jason's chest got tighter by the second. Worse yet, it couldn't decide why. Part of it wanted to be excited, another part wanted to be terrified, and a third part sat in the middle trying to bring them together. It felt like three equal halves locked in a tug of a war inside his chest, with his throat standing by for round two.

His group settled into position on their side of the border, with his insides wishing they had tails to wave. At least then the energy could be expressed. When the Marcallan cruiser appeared on his sensors, he had to breath deep to keep breathing at all.

"Take it easy, Jason," Yarain said. "Try to calm yourself."

It took a pair of deeper breaths to get enough air to respond. "I'm all right. Really."

"You don't smell all right."

"It's just nerves and conflicting instincts. Don't worry, I'm ready for this."

Yarain remained silent, but Jason had no doubt she had an ear turned his way. All the better, for in a strange way, it forced him to get a hold of himself. He took deeper, longer breaths that were held for a second to loosen his chest. Success there brought success in clearing his mind for the upcoming exchange. By the time the cruiser arrived in person, only his fidgeting fingers betrayed his nerves. Not counting whatever the foxes could smell on him of course.

Though they too calmed when Jason saw the cruiser in a way he never had. For years, she'd been the silent assassin. A dark figure lit only by weapons flashes and fires burning from within. Not this time. Today she floated before him, lit by lights shining from windows all along the hull, with the sides in particular being well lit. Running lights he never knew about, or perhaps never cared about, also announced her presence by illuminating insignias and registration numbers in alien writing. Simple flashers and glowing points on all sides let others know she was there. All the lighting made her paint glow, much like the fire nebula with a soft purple shimmer that went up and down her hull as she moved with a grace befitting a ballerina.

"My goodness," Jason said softly. "She's beautiful."

"We sure that's the same ship?" Sundale asked. "I've never seen her look like that."

"We've never been on peaceful terms with her before. What a difference. I don't think I've ever noticed but check out their directional lights. Twin blue top, red and blue port, green and blue starboard, blue always pointing 'forward.' Makes you wonder; was it always that way, or did they like what they saw on our ships and adopt it?"

"I doubt they'll ever tell us."

"Can't hurt to try," Yarain said. "They're hailing us."

Jason took the deepest breath he could while shifting to get as comfortable as possible. Once certain he could be no more ready, he motioned for Yarain to open the channel.

One of Jason's side screens flickered on to show a deceptively humanoid head and upper body. The body, when one ignored the extra pair of arms and dark grey color, wasn't that different from his own except that everything, arms included, were much thinner and smoother than a human's. When one's gaze traveled to the head, the face rounded out as expected though it tended to be longer, and the back and sides appeared to be more carapace than skin. However, none, including Jason, could see past the layer of short antennae that lay flat against the head in place of hair and filled the role of their missing ears.

Jason mentally had to shake off his crawling skin, among other emotions, as he stared at the dark purple eyes of the jantan on his screen. He couldn't help noting the disgust buried beneath the horizontal, blue colored slits of this particular jantan's pupils. The thicker looking antennae layer, as well as the longer, rounder face, and silver adorned armor with touches of green told him exactly who he was dealing with. Judging by a ripple that went through his antennae, Jason guessed that Auro Jals had not forgotten him either.

"Greetings, Major," Jals began in a deep voice that was more loud whisper than rasp. "As Commander of the Marcallan vessel, *Histmar*, I request permission to enter United Systems territory."

Let the false hospitality begin. "Auro, I am authorized to grant your request. You are hereby given permission to enter United Systems space and to make your journey to Earth. We will be flying escort to ensure no harm comes to your vessel or those aboard."

"Thank you, Major. We appreciate your assistance. My operating chief should be requesting a data link now. This is to help ensure our formation travels the same course at the same speed without disrupting each other."

Jason looked back at Yarain while ignoring the sneer behind Jals' words. "Can you handle that, Yarain?"

"Not a problem," she said, casting a straight-eared glare toward her screens. "I'll keep everyone in line."

Jason returned his focus forward. "We'll have the link in no time, Auro. Is there anything further before we get underway?"

Auro Jals' eyes narrowed, and Jason's fingers hovered over the triggers. "I assume your leaders were informed about the prefect's request."

Oh yeah, that. "Yes, but we received few details. Just that he wanted to meet with me and my crew before we jumped to hyper-light, and what we were, or rather weren't, allowed to bring with us."

"There are no details, Major. You will receive landing instructions shortly. That is all."

His voice got harder with each word, leaving Jason more uneasy than ever. It's a good thing Jals ended the conversation right there, or Jason might not have continued to retain control. Though the prospect of those last-minute orders didn't leave him feeling much better.

"Are we really doing this?" Sundale asked.

"So it would seem," Yarain said. "I've already got the landing protocols, and we're being cleared for approach by their flight operator."

"Are we sure we can trust them? This is Jals we're talking about."

"Not much choice," Jason said, pulling up the landing information. "We've been ordered to give the peace process *every* chance. To back out of this would be an insult we can't afford."

"And if things turn ugly?"

Jason thrust his thumb at the armor and weapons lockers on the wall, and nothing further was said. Although they knew they weren't allowed to carry them, the point was made.

Per their instructions, Jason flew toward one of the curved spikes on the cruiser's starboard side. He kept their speed low and watched as the spike split across the middle and open up to expose a hanger void of any ships or equipment. Only a pair of fully armored jantans awaited them in a surprisingly bright hanger that held the same industrial roughness to it that Interstar's hangers did. Though if he were honest, the Jantan hanger appeared to be better maintained aesthetic-wise. The deep violet paint on the walls appeared clean, and not because it was fresh as evidenced by a particularly large stain on the back wall.

As much as the hanger proved interesting, the jantan guards themselves held Jason's attention. No matter how many times he saw them, he never got used to them. Their grey colored, carapace-like skin continued to a thick, long lower body full of short legs like an oversized millipede that trailed behind them for a few short feet. They wore armor much as Interstar did, but theirs appeared more straight up metal than the ceramic/metal mixture Interstar used. Naturally, it's contour matched their different physiology too, such as plating down their entire body and broader plates to accommodate the extra arms. Yet they also held markings and insignias on their shoulders, arms, and chests, almost as if this bulky armor was their normal uniform. Jason couldn't say for sure since, having only seen jantans on the battlefield or in a situation where combat was just one wrong word away, they'd never exactly had any reason to wear anything else.

I suppose in this case, ignorance really is bliss. If he knew whether or not the armor was standard issue, he'd know if seeing them in it was a good sign or a bad one. Though when he noticed their belts held the standard issue energy weapon but no blades, he decided to take it as a good sign.

Jason prayed he was right as he set the fighter down while the doors, or rather the spike, closed behind them. *Guess we're committed now.*

Once everything was powered down, and a few security protocols set in place, Jason lead his crew out the back hatch with sweaty palms and six tails waving behind him. He couldn't blame them. After all, his hand kept forgetting he didn't have a P-mag or blade and he hadn't even said hello yet. The holdrens behind him were equally unarmed, aside from their natural weapons of course.

Wonder what they'll do with that, Jason thought still trying to settle himself.

He approached the guards, trying very hard to walk normally. To a human or the holdrens, he probably looked stiff. To a jantan, only they knew.

However he looked, the two jantans watched with quiet attention. Both stepped, or rather trickled, forward on their many legs to meet them with very human smiles.

"Welcome aboard the *Histmar*," one said in a surprisingly cheerful though still raspy voice. "I am Araf Malook, what your Caelnav rank system would call a full lieutenant, and I will be your escort during your time here."

Okay, this is too much. He sounds like a tour guide! The way Malook spoke left Jason half expecting him to mention some random fact or go into the 'don't touch this or do that' speech. He felt embarrassed because he could only stare, unsure what to say.

Thankfully, the soldier had more to say in his place. "Our prefect is most anxious to meet you. However, there are some security concerns he wanted to address. In addition to what was already sent to you, I'm afraid the holdrens must remain in their four-legged form at all times while on board."

Sundale's throat released the beginnings of a growl, which Jason silenced with firm hand held in front of him. He then faced the araf and allowed himself to still appear stern.

"May I ask why, Araf?"

"The prefect did not say why," Malook said. "Only that it is required."

"Nothing else?"

"Nothing else."

Jason stared at them, trying to find some sign of danger or deception. Neither gave off anything but neutral patience, which included four hands casually folded in front of them. If they were laying a trap, they were making a good show of it.

With no reason to argue the matter, Jason shrugged at Yarain and Sundale. "Seems reasonable to me, guys. What about you?"

Malook and his partner were again scrutinized and again held their stance without so much as a ruffle from their antennae. At last, Sundale gave a growl-laced sigh before he and Yarain dropped their muzzles in agreement, then assumed their primal forms as requested.

Araf Malook nodded with a soft smile before gesturing toward the door. "If you will please follow me."

Malook and his partner led them out into corridors painted the same violet as the hanger, but in a thicker, fuller coat that was just a touch lighter. Despite the color, the corridors felt far from dark. Lighting tucked into the corners of the ceiling was almost hidden, yet the effect chased all shadows from the room save for those cast by individuals. While the floor looked like metal, it felt like a thin layer of artificial turf without the fake grass. *May want to suggest this to the guys at R&D.*

He continued to examine his first undamaged jantan vessel interior. How different it was from the burned-out wreckages Interstar had seen before. The more he looked, the more he realized just how little it differed from their own. Besides color, a squarer appearance, and egg-shaped doors trimmed in silver, the only real difference was they seemed to keep their ship a few degrees warmer than Interstar did. Not uncomfortable – not to him anyway – but noticeable.

Jason couldn't say the same about what greeted him as they rounded a corner. At the end of the corridor stood four guards, all in heavy armor, though no more armed than Malook, in front of two highly adorned doors. Some of the detail was Jantan text, but most of it appeared to be pure decorative engravings of plants, some creature he didn't recognize, and the unmistakable silhouette of a jantan demanding full attention right at the break.

When they reached those doors, Araf Malook and his partner split off to join the other guards, who were all watching Gold 1 like they expected trouble. *That is their job,* Jason reminded himself, trying to steady his quickening pulse. A glance back found Yarain's and Sundale's waving tails betraying their own uneasiness.

Jason's nerves didn't get any calmer when he noticed a jantan at the far end of the guards he soon recognized as Hilahshan Forin. He wore a deep purple armor that covered his torso and lower body. It held silver accents on the shoulders and top arms, as well as several medals on the sleeves of the bottom arms and more green accents than any armor anyone had ever seen. His rank tabs had the admiral spiral of three lines, almost like a tight braid save for the very top where it was only two lines, thus making what looked like a hole in the braid. Unlike Jals, this man's face was long, thin, and even more squished than Jason's. In fact, his entire body seemed oddly thin when compared to the bulk of the guards near him.

Hilahshan Forin stared at the entourage in a way that left Jason even more unnerved. It wasn't a glare, or an 'I'm watching you' warning. It actually looked patient and respectful, yet still aware of every move made. It kept Jason from relaxing, and he couldn't figure out why.

Malook on the other hand, stayed as calm and friendly as he'd been the whole time. "Please enter. The prefect awaits you inside."

No turning back now, Major. He rolled the tension out of his shoulders, then led his crew through the doors.

The walls inside were bare and colored a dark violet trimmed in green with light pouring down them and into the room as if it were water. His boots found soft, purple carpet which appeared fresh yet smelled like sawdust. He reminded himself where he was while drawing his attention to the pitch black, crescent-shaped desk at the back of the room. Jason soon realized that it, the chair and ottomans in front of it, and the jantan coiled behind it were all that occupied the room. No other furniture or visible signs of protection were present. There weren't even any banners on the wall, which surprised him.

Don't get complacent yet, Major, he thought as he led his crew forward.

The jantan behind it looked up from reading something, then uncoiled into a standing position and brightened as if he and Jason were old friends which slowed Jason's pace a moment. *This is their prefect?* Seeing him in clothes instead of armor Jason half expected. The simple looking sleeveless, purple shirt with silver-colored top shoulders he wore, had Jason expecting more. The prefect had the same braid on his shoulders as Forin, though his was a full braid with no holes. Upon closer inspection, Jason saw a green belt at his waist and thin green pinstripes running down his clothes, which he noticed covered his entire body. Aside from these things, Jason saw no other highlights he would have expected from a man of such rank.

The prefect didn't look the part, yet the way his body stood perfectly upright, his hands folded in front of him, the calm, almost disarming smoothness of his face, silenced any thoughts about him being a fake. Granted, it would explain their lax attitudes with Yarain and Sundale, but Jason had a hard time believing anyone, human or jantan, was that good an actor.

Real prefect or not, the man watched Jason with careful attention and a warm smile the pilot never thought he'd see on a jantan. Jason stepped right up to the desk, unsure how to start the conversation. He was again saved by the other guy.

"Welcome aboard, Major. My name is Giller Colark, Prefect of the Holy Republic that is Marcalla." His voice was a bit heavy but held no rasp at all. He extended his hand while maintaining his smile.

Jason took his hand, surprised to receive a firm grip and a soft shake. "Major Jason Harlem, pilot of the Interstar fighter Gold 1."

"I've heard a lot about you, Major," Prefect Colark said, "as well as your crew. Let me see if I read my briefing right. The solid gold holdren is Captain Yarain and the one with orange is Captain Sundale. Am I right?"

This cannot *be real.*

Jason couldn't help staring for a second. Never in his wildest dreams had he imagined such... normalcy from *any* jantan. He had to shake the cobwebs from his mind before he could reply.

"Almost, Prefect," Jason said. "You have the holdrens backward. Sundale is the one that's solid gold."

The prefect brought a hand to his chin like he'd pulled it from a flame. "Oh, my apologizes. I guess I got confused."

"No apology needed, Prefect," Yarain said. "If it helps, Sundale, being a male, has bands on his tails where as I, a female, do not."

"Thank you, Captain. I'll try to keep you two straight. Please, sit. I hope I found something comfortable for you all."

Jason took his seat with a satisfied hum, while Yarain and Sundale spun around on their ottomans before laying down with their tails hanging off the back. The tips continued to wave out their nerves.

"Do you always do that before you lay down?" the prefect asked.

Sundale tilted his head with erect ears. "Most of the time."

"Does that mean they're comfortable?"

"They're fine," Yarain said. "Thank you."

"I'm happy to hear that. We know so little about both of your races, I wasn't sure what you would find agreeable. I'm sure you've faced your share of people treating you like dumb animals to exploit, and I wanted to avoid that."

"Some humans have acted poorly, but the vast majority have surprised me." She looked at Jason with a warmth in her eyes that made him blush. "Some more than others."

Prefect Colark's chuckle was just as light. "I see now why you three have given our military so much trouble. I envy you, Major. That kind of loyalty is a rare thing I pray I might someday find."

Jason couldn't fight it anymore. He rubbed his eyes, trying to again clear the webs from his brain. He looked up again to see the prefect regarding him with a curious tilt.

Note to self: remind command I am not *a good diplomat.*

"Forgive me," Jason said. "Rough night. Now then, I assume there's a more specific reason you wanted to meet with us."

"Worried I'm not as direct as most jantans, Major?" Colark replied with a raised eyebrow. Jason nodded once as the prefect coiled into the jantan sitting position. "That's the problem with the military. It's a rare case when you can be anything but direct. If you saw our civilian life, you'd see that not all of us are like that. Some even hate the military and all it stands for. I'm sure your people are no different."

Sundale's and Yarain's tails slowly began to cease their waving. It seemed they too were beginning to nurture optimism regarding this prefect and perhaps the talks themselves. Jason held his best poker face, not willing to drop his guard just yet.

"More or less," he said. "Of course, we don't try to conquer other races. We prefer to live peacefully and explore the galaxy. We arm ourselves only because we know that not all share our love of peace."

Colark's shoulders slumped with a sigh. "Your attacks are well hidden, Major. I suppose I shouldn't be surprised. Your feelings about Auro Jals, as well as your history on the field, are not unknown to us. But let's not dwell on the past. I asked you here to help me protect the future."

Sundale's tails started waving again. "What do you mean by 'protect the future'?"

Prefect Colark leaned forward while folding his hands again. "For years, I have wanted to end our wars. All they've brought is destruction and death without providing a single reason for us to fear you."

"We didn't start those wars, Prefect," Jason noted. "When a civilization is threatened with essential slavery after a few minor infractions, you can't blame them for wanting to defend themselves"

"Or for being slow to trust that race in the future," Sundale added.

Colark nodded. "Our leaders then were arrogant fools. They sold the populace on the idea that we were the supreme race in the galaxy. An idea I thought had died with the worst of our race long before I was born. Your 'minor infractions' were simply the excuse they were waiting for to begin their plans. When you began to effectively challenge that belief, some hardline leaders just couldn't let go."

Jason raised a curious eyebrow. "You seem to have let go."

"I was of the minority back then. I never saw you as a threat or inferior. Something your race proved again and again. How many times did you punch through our defenses but refuse to inflict serious damage to our civilian populace? When we finally called for a truce, you let us be without retaliation. Only safeguards to prevent future wars."

Sundale ruffed dismissal. "A lot of good those did."

"As I said, some people couldn't let go. But I stayed in the fight, hoping to get my chance to end it. Two years ago, I got it. The previous prefect committed suicide because he felt he had failed his people. When the competitions for prefect became available, I saw my chance to stop the river of blood once and for all. When I emerged the newly anointed leader of our people, I began the steps I had so longed for. I ordered our diplomatic core to begin exploring how we might end our mistrust."

Jason leaned back while loosely folding his arms. "I bet that went over well."

Colark sighed again with a shake of his head. "I didn't expect it to be easy, nor was it. Military leaders still hold a lot of power. They continued to hatch plots and go on small raids to test your resolve. Not once did they listen to my calls for peace. That is... until recently when you... when you did something you'd never done before."

Jason didn't need him to say what it was. He was there for it, though had been spared from taking part.

Interstar had pushed deep. So deep they were in easy striking distance of three Marcallan colonies. Before talk could begin about what to do, an order came down that Jason had been very public about condemning. All three colonies were flattened. Blasted off the surface of those worlds. No survivors. A comparison was made to the bombing of Hiroshima and Nagasaki during World War II. "A point had to be made," their leaders said.

Jason agreed with the choice in history. He didn't agree with this one. Having fought them for so long, he knew jantans better than most. Such an act would only make them dig in deeper. Interstar would have to burn down every colony, which would gain them nothing but genocide. They would have been better served by treating the Jantan civilians well or ignoring them all together. Despite his rant to Rickey, one he was now feeling quite ashamed of, he'd seen Jantan soldiers behave honorably. Some had even been *very* honorable. Showing the same or better to civilians would have dealt a major blow to Jantan moral, rhetoric, or both. Either way, he had no doubt such a slaughter served absolutely no one but those like Jals.

"I wish I knew who gave that order," Jason admitted. "I'd like to give them a piece of my mind."

Prefect Colark nodded gravely. "I know. I tried to use it to further my goals, but like before, I got nothing. Then three months ago, a new official in the diplomatic corps came to me and offered to, in his words, 'retry first contact.' With my permission, he contacted your leadership, and a few weeks later, I was talking with your president. A few weeks more, here we are. On our way to peace negotiations, on Earth no less, with the full support of the civilian sector and strong support from the military. Even Hilahshan Forin expressed his approval despite leading just about every campaign against your fleet."

"That's a pretty sudden change," Yarain said with shifting ears.

"Too sudden. No doubt someone thinks I'm a fool. I'm certain these negotiations have some part to play in their plans for the next war. I intend to disappoint them, but I will need your help to do it."

I think there's a spider in my head. As Jason shook another set of cobwebs from his brain, he noticed the tails of his comrades had fallen still. His would have too, come to think of it. The more Prefect Colark talked; the more Jason believed him. He saw a cold confidence in the jantan's eyes he almost remembered seeing in the mirror. His words held not a single waiver of deception. Either he was an exceptional actor, or he truly wanted to make peace.

Jason refused to accept the former, going on instinct more than thought. Yet he reminded himself to tread carefully lest his actions cause more harm than good.

He finally leaned forward with his hands clasped together. "I assume you have some sort of plan in mind?"

"Not exactly, Major." The prefect picked up a Jantan device much like the United Systems clip-com. "I recently uncovered evidence that suggests a conspiracy is developing. As of yet, I have little to go on. However, I have come to suspect that elements within your republic are working with elements in mine toward some unknown goal."

Jason slowly leaned back while going on the defensive again. "That's quite an accusation, Prefect. Not to mention a little far-fetched."

"I agree it seems unlikely. Nevertheless, agents I trust have confirmed secret transmissions being sent between Marcallan space and United Systems territory. They've also picked up other signals going from both of our territories into space neither of us has charted or claimed."

"With respect," Sundale said, "we need more to go on than secret transmissions."

"I have little else to offer, Captain. Whoever they are, they know how to stay hidden. However, my agents were able to capture a few messages. I was hoping you might recognize something in them."

The prefect slid the clip-com-like device to Jason across the desk. Jason read through the messages first, silently laughing at one of the code names. *Multi-step? Really? Then again, it doesn't say which jantan it is, so I guess it does work.* The rest of the messages were bits and pieces that meant little to him.

He soon found one message with an image that stiffened his back. It was a dark-navy bear silhouette outlining the full constellation of Ursa Major with a bright star above the bear. The insignia of the Confederation of Polaris, one of the many factions from Earth that held colonies in the early years of human deep space exploration.

When Earth started to unify under the Untied Systems Republic, Polaris declared independence. Partly because their old rival Interstar, being the most effective thus far at holding the line, was essentially given full control of the military. While it soon became nothing more than a name that wouldn't go away, for Polaris, the past remained just as rooted. Controversial policies and highly questionable choices saw Polaris stand alone only to see every man, woman, and child killed by Marcalla or themselves not long after. At least, as far as anyone knew.

When Jason's concern faded into a huff of doubt, Sundale asked, "More trouble, Jason?"

He turned the device so Sundale could see for himself. "I'm not sure."

When Sundale saw the image, his ears perked at Jason, as did Yarain's when she got her turn.

Prefect Colark looked at each of them before throwing his hands out. "May I know your thoughts?"

Jason set the device on the desk with narrow eyes. "I'd share them if I knew what they were. I assume you know about the Polaris Confederation?"

"Unfortunately. No doubt their... destruction is one of the reasons your fleet destroyed our colonies."

"Now that you mention it, I wouldn't be surprised. But this is… I have a hard time buying it. At least Orion's Arrow had some refugees that preferred life to pride. Polaris died to the last. Why would anyone fly their flag now?"

"To cause confusion, perhaps? Or people who were sympathetic to their plight seek what they believe is justice? I understand many thought Interstar should have tried harder to save them."

"Possible, but still weak. It feels like a smoke screen. In a jumble of messages hopelessly encrypted, we get a nice, clean image? Feels like they wanted us to see it. Then again, I'm not sure we can totally ignore it either, which leaves me back where I started. We don't know enough to act, so we can't. But even as that seems the best choice, we're fast approaching a point where that's not an option either. If we wait too long to know more, we may not know enough when they launch their plans."

All calm and friendly expressions drained from Prefect Colark's face. The confidence Jason saw before had been replaced by a glaze over his eyes. "I'm afraid I don't know much about Polaris outside of threat reports and propaganda. Even if it were them, would they be that big a threat?"

"Depends on what they have," Jason said. "When they fell, their technology wasn't that different than Interstar's. They've had, what? Not quite twenty years? That's a lot of time for unhindered research. They could match or even beat our ships, or yours for that matter, pound for pound by now. More if their manufacturing technology is anything like ours. And that's assuming it's not some new entity entirely using the Polaris flag as a smoke screen. They could even have allies we've never heard of just waiting for the chance to pounce."

Prefect Colark's hand went to his temple, and he wavered enough for Jason to worry he might fall out of his coil. The pilot rose in case he needed catching, but the prefect waved him down.

"I'm all right, Major. The stress of my position occasionally catches up with me. Causes a headache. Give me a moment."

Definitely off the mark. Jason retook his seat while watching a man he never expected to see. This was their prefect? A man so like humans he got cluster headaches? Seemed impossible, yet for a moment, Jason almost forgot he was a jantan. He couldn't help staring as the prefect rubbed his temple, wondering how many more like him there might be among the ranks of their most hated enemy.

Prefect Colark had long since stabilized, but it wasn't until Sundale muttered something that Jason returned to the present.

"What was that, Sun?" Jason asked, having to clear his mind of cobwebs again. *I gotta find that spider.*

"Jason, show me those messages again," Sundale said. Jason held the Jantan clip-com so Sundale could read it. He scrolled upon request until Sundale barked a word so much even Jason barely caught it. "***THERE***. The third message. Make you think of anything?"

Jason read over the message. It appeared to be orders for someone to check on the status of two "assets" and, if possible, have them abort their mission. When he re-read details he had skipped before, he saw it had been sent only a few hours before they ran into Red 7. A further skim suggested it used similar carrier waves to the ones sending messages out of unknown territory. *Way too much coincidence.*

Jason hesitated while his eyes rose to the prefect. His mind quickly decided how much he could, or should, share. "You mentioned communications going in and out of United Systems territory? Here's proof you're right. Looks like a run-in we had with raiders might have been ordered by your unknown entity. And if that's not bad enough, it involved an Interstar fighter that turned hostile *and* led a mutiny."

Jason threw the clip-com onto the desk. It felt like the back of his brain was literally sizzling like a steak on the grill. This was way worse than one mutinous fighter crew. This spoke of a vast fifth column that could have significant reach within the ranks of Interstar, if not further. Part of him somehow knew he could trust his own group, but there was still that seed of doubt. If this became public, others might turn that seed into more, which could cause its own kind of damage.

Prefect Colark blew out two breaths worth of stress in one long wind. "It would seem things are worse than I feared. Unfortunately, I'm not sure I know how to act. Plot or not, I can't pass up the chance at peace. I have to try to put an end to this blood shed before it destroys us both."

Never thought I'd find an idealist jantan. Jason had to admire the man's conviction, even if he might be a little naive. Then again, sometimes a wise man must become naive to get what he wants.

Try as he might, Jason couldn't find a good reason to cancel the peace talks. It would only tip their hand and prevent what was still their best chance for a lasting peace. More to the point, the enemy's plans were being salvaged now. If they postponed things, whoever it was would have time to prepare a new plan. One that might go off without a hitch this time.

That said, little could be done without hard intel, which left Jason with quite possibly the worst idea he'd ever thought of. Worst of all: he felt sure it was the best choice they had.

"The hard part is preventing this conspiracy from succeeding," Jason said. "Unfortunately, we have so little to go on I fear we have no choice but to let them make their next move."

Prefect Colark's eyes narrowed as his antennae rose. "I don't think I like what you're suggesting, Major."

"Prefect, *I* don't like what I'm suggesting. I'm getting tired of feeling like I have to wait for a knife in the back to act, but if there's one thing I've learned from my foxy comrades, it's that the best way to fight a predator you can't see is to let him think he has you fooled. Both sides want these negotiations to happen, that much is certain. Let's play our part for the time being. Let them think we're in the dark. That way, when they act, we'll be the ones who have surprise on *our* side."

Colark's antennae settled down, though his eyes remained narrow. "That's not a reassuring suggestion, Major."

"We're open to a better idea, Prefect," Yarain said.

The prefect gave a heavy sigh, then nodded while rubbing his temple again. "Very well. We'll wait and see what they do. In the meantime, I'll see what my personal guard can find. Don't worry. They're the best of the best and unwaveringly loyal. They won't spoil the surprise."

Jason nodded his acceptance. The moment he was on his feet, his body felt like a pillar of certainty as if he'd just claimed land. "Then unless you have something further, I suggest we return to the escort so we can jump to hyper-light. The sooner we get to Earth the better."

Prefect Colark uncoiled with his calm demeanor slowly returning. "Any information I obtain will be immediately shared with you, Major. I hope I can expect the same."

"Superiors permitting. I don't have the freedom your position affords you."

"Fair enough. Take the attelza. It contains everything I know as well as ways to contact me without anyone knowing. But only your crew may view it, Major. Do not share it with anyone unless you have no choice."

"Attelza, sir?" Jason asked. Colark pointed to the clip-com like device on the table. "Ah. We call them clipboard computers, or clip-coms for short. We've never heard the Jantan name for them."

"Then we have both learned something new about the other. Perhaps these peace negotiations have a chance after all."

Jason tucked the attelza under his arm as Yarain and Sundale hopped down from their seats. "Perhaps they do. Take care of yourself, Prefect."

"Live strong, Major," the prefect said. "I pray that Galla will keep us safe until your predator comes for the kill."

"Just keep your ears perked. We'll do the rest," Yarain said, drawing a curious tilt from the prefect. "A common phrase among Holdrens. It means to stay alert and cautious."

Colark nodded with a smile. "A chance indeed. Thank you, Captain."

Jason bowed his own thanks, then led his crew back to their fighter under Lieutenant Malook's escort. They rejoined the formation and jumped to hyper light with Jason's mind swimming in enough thoughts and feelings to fill a lifetime.

Forty years we've been at war. Forty years we've hated each other. Forty years we've been unable to stop the bloodshed. It all gets undone by ten minutes of conversation. Never in his wildest hallucinations could he have hoped to have a Marcallan prefect willing, able, and determined to achieve a lasting peace. More than that, he seemed the type to actually pull it off. Yet with all that hope, obstacles remained strong.

This secret conspiracy kept him more on edge than the potential problems they faced on the mission. The idea of jantans and humans working together had him uneasy. The knowledge that the humans were working under the Polaris flag, fake though it may be, sent a shiver down his spine.

It helped that the more he thought about it, the more fake it felt. However, that brought up a new concern over who they really were. Who could be out there that would want to ally with the jantans? Did he really want to know? Jason doubted that he did even as he knew he needed to find out as soon as possible. One thing remained certain: if he hadn't seen everything yet, he probably would by the time it all reached its end.

Chapter 10

Atypical Diplomacy

The convoy saw very little excitement over the next two and a half days. The closest they came to an incident were some less than friendly messages from a small transport ship. It kept pace with the convoy for a while, even threatened to open fire unless they did something about the "filthy jants." A stern reminder of who was leading the escort brought a quick end to their courage. From there, it was smooth sailing.

Even so, seeing Earth in the window brought a great sense of relief for all involved. At last, it wasn't just the Gold Group watching over the cruiser. Earth's standard patrol of ships, as well as its own defense platforms, offered reassurance that they were not the only ones on alert.

Yet as Jason had Yarain get their landing instructions, he couldn't shake his nerves. He scanned the view through his window while keeping a close eye on his sensors, making sure no one beside his group came anywhere near the *Histmar*.

"You all right, Jason?" Sundale asked.

"Fine," he lied. "Just a little nervous."

"Your scent says you're staring down a pride of lions."

Again, I forget what they can do. "I'm not sure. It's like I can sense something in the air, as if another battle is coming my way. I don't know, I could be imagining it."

"Perhaps not," Yarain said. "Command has changed the landing site. Instead of the shipyard in Germany, we'll be touching down at the support base in the Kolyma mountains."

"The Russian icicle?" Sundale said. "That doesn't make sense. They only have one pad big enough for the *Histmar*, and it won't have room for us."

Which means we'll have to land in hangers that are a fair distance from the main pad. Jason's stomach sank to replace his bladder. For a time, the prefect would be on an exposed landing pad, dealing with protocols he doesn't know, unguarded by any who do. With two conspiracies out there, Jason didn't trust those circumstances for a second. Something had to change, and without anyone knowing about it.

"We've got our landing profile," Yarain announced. "Any orders, Jason?"

I think my lungs just joined my stomach, Jason thought as he contemplated his next move. After a quick scan confirmed the absence of transport inhibitors, he chose one.

"We'll follow the plan as instructed," Jason said, "save for a slight amendment. Sun, take center chair." Sundale unbuckled out of his seat and took the pilot seat as Jason released it. "Follow the flight plan, don't give any indication anything's amiss."

"Understood, sir," Sundale said.

Jason turned to work on Sundale's console as they began their vibrating trip trough the upper atmosphere. "Yarain, you're with me. We're going to flash down and greet the prefect personally just as protocol demands." He handed Yarain her armor as she rose out of her seat. "And you are going to be my honor guard."

Yarain tapped her armor with flattening ears. "Bit of a stretch, don't you think?"

"They met us in full armor; I see no reason we can't do the same. Besides, someone needs to wear something that can take a shot, and that can't be me."

"Diplomatic risk *and* a living shield. I'm **NOT** liking this side of you, Jason."

"Nor am I. Unfortunately," Jason indicated the fast-approaching Kolyma mountains through the forward window, "I don't have enough time to come up with a more acceptable plan. If you have a better idea, I'm all ears."

Yarain stared at her armor with a growl before strapping it on with a sigh.

"Thank you," Jason said. "I won't forget this."

He stood over Sundale's shoulder as much to keep an eye on things as to get closer to him. A glowing speck on the horizon had since grown into a small complex of concrete buildings settled into a gorge as if a large ship had crashed there. The glaring exception was the spattering of landing pads, not even enough for a task force, built at the leading edge of that complex with the largest of them sitting farthest out. Pulsing lights along the floor and walls of the gorge were already guiding the *Histmar* in for a landing on that pad with more lights on the complex itself reminding the fighters where they were going. All the other pads were occupied by transports or other small craft, leaving no room for Gold Group to go against those instructions.

Too much coincidence, Jason thought while staring at the view. Someone had to have had a hand in all this. More than ever, he feared what might be waiting for the prefect on that pad. If only he had more time to prepare.

With their group about to break for the hangers as ordered, Jason breathed out all his stress while putting the last pieces of his plan into place. "Sundale, when you land, don your own armor before joining us. I want you both serving as honor guards once we've met up."

"Weapons?" Sundale asked.

Jason raised his voice to be sure Yarain heard him. "Knives only for both of you. Your tails are enough for our purposes. I'll be leaving my weapons behind, so I'm counting on the two of you to keep me alive. That said, keep your shields off unless you're certain of immediate danger. Understood?"

"Understood," Yarain said with another growl.

Sundale only flicked an ear, either at the order or her. "Will do, Jason. Anything else?"

A wry smile formed on Jason's lips. "If our hidden predator tries anything, go for its jugular."

Sundale a gave soft growl Jason didn't want to translate given his raising hackles. Its meaning held too much risk for an already sensitive stomach.

After making sure Yarain was in full armor but had only her combat knife on the back of her hip, Jason tapped his holster to remind himself it was empty, then activated the transporter just as the group pulled off for the hangers. A flash later found Jason and Yarain standing in one of the smaller transit rooms on the base. Jason wasted no time marching out toward the main landing pad with Yarain tight on his heels. Once outside, they were greeted by a cool breeze that added enough chill for Jason to switch on the heating system in his uniform.

They went to the edge of the landing pad and watched as the *Histmar* made her approach. The Marcallan ship he now considered majestic glided in like an osprey waiting to catch a fish. A great rumbling hum grew louder as she approached, vibrating his ribs and sending birds scattering from near by pads and tress.

Yarain flattened her ears as the *Histmar* came on its final approach, and Jason didn't blame her. His ears were already complaining, and they weren't as good as hers. Yet she stood firm with him as her fur bristled in the backwash from the *Histmar's* braking thrusters.

The great ship slowly hovered over the pad, then touched down on landing legs the size of oak trees. An eerie silence fell over the pad when the rumble of her engines quickly faded away.

Jason almost jumped when PAICCA's voice chimed in with its automated announcements. "Engine output: zero. Shields: inactive. Countermeasures: inactive. Starship: at standby. Pad clear to accept support staff. Caution: access points unfamiliar. Be alert for open air locks and boarding ramps."

Jason rocked on his heels as he waited for the Marcallan prefect to choose his exit. No doubt, they were scanning for possible threats, but that didn't make the waiting feel any shorter.

Just when he began to wonder if he should try to contact them, a ramp lowered from the underside of the bow. Four heavily armored jantans walked down with Jals and Forin leading the way and the prefect walking among them in the same clothes as before. He at least appeared to be enjoying the moment. He checked the surrounding area with the absorbing eyes of an explorer. His guards, on the other hand, scanned the same area like any particle of dust could jump up and destroy the ship. Jason half expected one of them to shoot a passing bird when it squawked at them. Only Jals appeared stoic, which in many ways had Jason more worried than anything else. Last time his face held that little emotion, Jals nearly killed him.

Jason tried to put the past out of his mind as he stepped out onto the pad with Yarain behind him. All eyes instantly locked onto them with just one set brightening at their presence. The two Admirals actually got a bit darker in their gaze. Jason ignored them in favor of the man in the middle of them.

Jason clasped his hands behind his back and took a deep breath to settle his nerves. *Here we go.* "Welcome to Earth, Prefect."

Prefect Colark pushed his guards aside so they stood beside him instead of in front. "Thank you, Major. I admit, it's not what I expected. I thought I'd see more infrastructure."

"Don't let a small outpost fool you, Prefect. We have several large cities to our credit. Some of them are quite extensive."

"Then why are we here?"

I'd like to know that myself. "I am not privy to that information, sir. My job is to make sure your party makes it to the negotiations and has as pleasant a time as possible."

Prefect Colark bowed, then looked past him while his guards went for their weapons. Jason turned around, fearing the worst, only to relax when he saw nothing more than Sundale running down the path from the complex. *He made good time.* Though he ran on all fours and in full armor, a keen eye could tell he was still in his finesse form. A pair of Interstar technicians were walking out behind him to care for the *Histmar.* Both seemed to stop cold for a second when they saw Jason and Yarain among the group.

"It's all right," Jason said. "He's just catching up."

The guards didn't relax until Sundale slowed to a trot as he got close. He stood upright and removed a clip-com that was tucked into the back of his armor, which he handed to Jason with a soft pant.

"The negotiating team is waiting for us," Sundale said. "They're in conference room five just down the hall."

Jason thanked him while looking over the information on the clip-com. It turned out to be little more than a list of the negotiating team members, a couple of trivial details, plus a note about weapons not being allowed inside the conference room. *So much for my honor guard.*

He tucked the clip-com under his arm. "Everything's ready, Prefect. I'm afraid your guards will have to leave their weapons at the door, however, as will our own people."

"Of course, Major," the prefect said. "Tell me, did they give a reason why they chose this site for our negotiations?"

Sundale answered before Jason could search for it on the clip-com. "Security, sir. They felt it best our first meeting be conducted away from large populations."

Sure they did. Jason didn't buy it for a second, but the prefect seemed to as he nodded understanding.

"Seems reasonable. Perhaps these talks will bring an end to such precautions."

"We can only hope," Jason said.

"Hope is important, Major, but it's not our only option. If we want it, we must make it happen."

Colark looked at Jals, who responded by bowing his head in respect. Or was it surrender? Jason couldn't tell for sure, though based on the ruffle that went through Jals' antennae, he guessed whatever it was had something to do with a disagreement between them. If so, this prefect definitely had a chance to succeed, for it appeared as if he had won that argument.

Prefect Colark returned Jals' nod, then drew himself up. "Now then, Major. Please lead the way to the conference room. That wind is getting cold."

Jason indicated the path Sundale had taken before leading the way. Yarain and Sundale walked just behind him with Jals and Forin between them at the head of the prefect's party.

The technicians stood at the sides of the door and saluted as they passed, though one of them twitched his head as if he was trying not to look. Jason glanced back to see why and found Sundale and Yarain staring at him with forward ears and waving tails.

"Problem, Captain?" Jason asked.

"Just a familiar face," Sundale said slowly. He forced his ears to relax while returning the young man's salute. Jason on the other hand had no trouble picking up the bread crumbs. *Seems our mystery private got a new assignment. Terrific.*

Jason entered the base with an eye scanning every wall and support beam, almost forgetting to turn off his uniform's heating system. He only saw grey colored square hallways with silver highlights and blue stripes down the sides. Terminals were built into the walls every few feet to allow soldiers, or visitors, access to a computer should they need it. All in all, a standard ground-base layout. No sign of anyone or anything else, which made him even more on edge than before.

Knowing about a conspiracy was bad enough. Knowing a member of that conspiracy was present left the door wide open for all kinds of possibilities. Worse yet, he couldn't say anything about it. What would he say? "This kid was parked in the desert near my home?" The best he could hope for was increased security, and that would get him nowhere. So, he continued to lead the Marcallan party toward the negotiations with a silent prayer that he could somehow stop whatever these people had planned.

They were met at the doors of the conference room by two Interstar guards fully armed and armored. Admiral Carson was also there, wearing the same formal blue over-jacket with silver trim, buttons, and pinstripes as the last time Jason saw him. He had quite the collection of decorations under his Interstar insignia and name plate, though his rank tab held only a single silver star. His presence was a minor blessing given the years of experience he had both in the field and with Jason. At least Jason knew of one man he could trust without question. That still left him four or more that were in doubt, however. Not to mention the threat of unseen foes waiting to make their move.

Focus on what you see, Major. He tried to put his fears aside, or at least control them, while standing to attention with salute for Rickey.

"Sir," Jason said once his salute was returned, "allow me to introduce

Prefect Giller Colark of — let me see if I remember this right — the Holy Republic that is Marcalla. Prefect, this is Brigadier General Rickey Carson, commander of the Forty-Third Strike Wing."

The prefect stepped forward with his guards right beside him. The prefect shook Rickey's hand with a familiar, warm smile.

"A pleasure to meet you, General. Your soldiers appear to be worthy of you."

Jason could swear he saw Rickey blush, not that he'd ever admit it. "They have their moments. On behalf of the Untied Systems Republic and Interstar, I bid you welcome to our little corner of the galaxy."

"Thank you, General. I hope this will not be my only visit here."

"So do I, Prefect. If you will, please follow me in. Any guards you want to have join you may, provided they leave their weapons with our men here. I will be the only one joining you inside."

Prefect Colark bowed his acceptance, then pointed at two of his men and his admirals. They proceeded to disarm and hand their weapons over to the guards. It was only then that Jason noticed Rickey didn't have his officer sword. *They're really not taking any chances. I don't blame them.*

As Rickey punched a code into the door controls, the prefect glanced at the Human guards, then at Jason and his crew. He faced Rickey with folded hands.

"Excuse me, General," the prefect said. "I would like Gold 1 to accompany us inside."

Rickey cocked his head as the door control beeped acceptance of his code. He stared at the prefect a moment, then shrugged. "I don't see why not. Major, follow us in. Yarain, Sundale, join the guard unless you receive other orders."

"Excuse me, General. I said I wanted *Gold 1* to join us. Only together can they be known as such. They *all* join us."

Ears rose, as did jantan antennae. Jals and Forin in particular had their eyes grow in size, though Jals was the first to voice the issue. "Prefect, with respect, that can't be done. You can't confiscate their weapons."

The prefect glared at him with vibrating antennae sounding much like a rattle snake. "Are you questioning me, Admiral?"

So that's what Jals looks like when he's scared. Jason had to swallow a smile as Jals retreated, dropping his head and hands. "I meant nothing of the sort, sir. I am merely pointing out that the humans are not permitting weapons of any kind inside the conference room. The holdrens have tails and fangs which cannot be surrendered."

Hilahshan Forin chimed in with the heavy voice of experience. "We ourselves suggested a ban on weapons, Prefect. To go back on that now makes little sense."

Rickey stepped forward. "I must agree, Prefect. We're taking every precaution here, which includes treating everyone like a possible threat. As much as I trust the captains, we can't take the chance. It's for your safety as well as ours."

The prefect halted his antennae, but his voice remained hard. "I understand your concerns, General. However, they are unfounded. Both have already proven they can be trusted. If a lasting peace is to be achieved between us, such acts must be rewarded."

Rickey stuttered for a moment before his hand went to the bridge of his nose. "You're putting me in a difficult position, Prefect. How can I allow them to enter when my superiors, not to mention you yourself, made it clear no weapons are to be allowed for either side under any circumstances?"

The prefect turned to face Rickey directly while drawing himself up again. "They join us, or I return to my ship. Make your choice, General."

Rickey again failed to form a sentence. Meanwhile Jals recovered from his surrender with a soft vibration seeping into his own antennae. "You can't allow it! You can't trust them. All it takes is a flick of a tail and—"

The prefect's antennae vibrated a moment as he glared his officer into silence. "Next time you dishonor me in front of another race, I will not be so kind, Admiral. You say they can't be trusted? Then explain why they met with me alone, as they are, aboard the *Histmar*, without so much as a menacing growl."

Jals stared at his prefect with wide eyes and straight antennae. He tried to speak, but he didn't even manage a sound much less a word. Shock had frozen his body solid, which left Jason squinting in confusion. *Jals knew we landed on the Histmar. Did he not know about the meeting? Or the why? Or that the prefect had met with us alone?* Jason's head swam with many more questions that threatened to drown him. Rickey wasn't far behind. His eyes also threatened to pop out of his head as he looked at Jason unable to voice his own question. The pilot answered with a nod confirming that yes, they did meet with him in private.

Rickey had to physically shake off his shock while Jals found his defiance replaced by submission to his leader's glare. *Shame looks don't kill. Jals would be a smoldering puddle if they did.* Instead, he and Hilahshan Forin were bowing before the prefect, their lower bodies on the floor with their legs flat in what Jason took as the jantan version of kneeling.

The prefect held his glare until Jason saw, of all things, a shudder run through Jals' body. Then the prefect returned his focus to Rickey, reassuming a neutral, if more stoic, demeanor.

"Now then," he said. "What is your choice, General Carson. Are we entering, or am I returning to the *Histmar*?"

Rickey glanced at the still cowering Auro Jals before letting out a sigh the size of a cruiser. "We're entering, Prefect. However, I must draw the line at their blades."

"To that, I will agree, General. So long as the captains are willing to give their word they will not harm myself or anyone else while inside."

Seemed like an odd request to Jason, but neither he nor anyone else was brave enough to say so. Yarain and Sundale, meanwhile, gave the requested promise on the spot. They handed over their blades, then the chosen party followed Rickey inside the conference room.

Jason soon realized how a little decoration could change a room entirely. The normal circular conference room had been transformed into an elegant hall with blue and purple drapes hung beside each other all around the walls. The blue drapes bore the United Systems logo – an image of the Milky Way with three tiny arrows streaking halfway across. The galaxy lay inside a yellow lattice ring reminiscent of an atom's electron orbits on a black background contained by a silver ring.

The purple drapes held the Marcallan insignia of an eye much like a jantan's in silver. A deep violet line, also outlined in silver, flowed above and below the eye, with a break coming only where the green pupil sat. On opposite walls lay large monitors with the respective insignias on each side, but only the United Systems side of the table had chairs of any kind. The last highlight came in the middle of the ceiling, where a silver curtain trimmed in blue and purple circled around a single light in the middle. *One thing both sides share is a love of silver. While hardly an instant path to peace, friendships have been started on less.*

A long table sat against the far wall with drinks and refreshments, much of it the usual sandwiches and pastries every official function seemed to require. *I hope the prefect likes turkey and bagels.*

Standing just inside the door were three Human officers Jason didn't recognize, as well as Marshal Garmon who he remembered from his conference with the Command Council. She, like the officers beside her, was in dress uniform, though her decorations could almost form a full shield over her heart, and they were all without their swords. Jason met her with salute as did his crew, which she returned with a nod as Prefect Colark entered behind him. Jason stepped aside as the doors closed so the prefect could approach.

"Marshal Garmon," Jason said. "Allow me to introduce Prefect Giller Colark. Prefect, this is Marshal Sharon Garmon."

They shook hands, though the prefect added a bow of respect. "An honor, Marshal. I assume you know of Auro Jals and Hilahshan Forin. These are my aides and bodyguards, Bevsit and Flugul."

No ranks or first names for them? I'll have to ask him if there's a reason for that—assuming I get the chance.

Each bowed as called which Marshal Garmon returned. "A pleasure," she said, "You've met General Carson already, as well as Major Harlem and his crew. Behind me you have Staff Sergeants Gary Miles, Lou Shin, and Joe Vasquez, my aides." Bows were again traded, then Marshal Garmon indicated the table with a heavy glare settling on Yarain and Sundale. "Please, let's take our seats so we may begin. You are dismissed, Captains."

As the jantans went to their side of the table, Rickey leaned in to whisper to Marshal Garmon. "Actually, ma'am, the prefect insisted they and

Major Harlem remain for the proceedings. It was either that or let him return to his ship. I had no choice but to agree."

Marshal Garmon nodded, then bowed at the fighter crew. "I apologize, Captains. I was out of line."

"A testament to your leadership, Marshal," the prefect called from his position. When Jason looked his way, the prefect carefully brushed his antennae. "They're as good as a holdren's ears, if not better. It's always good for a leader to admit their mistakes. I see why your president sent you in his place."

Yet he thinks eavesdropping is okay? Then again, given the sensitivity of these talks, I guess I can't blame him that much. Jason again kept his thoughts silent for the same reason. A minor knock on one's morals was not enough to undo all the good signs he'd seen thus far.

Marshal Garmon took her seat as did her aides and General Carson. The jantans coiled afterward while Yarain, Sundale, and Jason stood behind their delegation in a relaxed state of attention.

"A necessity he greatly apologizes for, Prefect," Garmon said. "Critical issues required his direct attention. I can assure you he puts the highest importance on these proceedings and hopes you will –"

The prefect waved her down before she started to diplomatically grovel. "Please, Marshal. I meant nothing by the comment. I understand there are things only the supreme leader can handle. Were it not for the exceptional staff I now employ, I too would have been forced to abstain from these negotiations."

Another coincidence. Their leader was able to make it but ours wasn't. At this rate, I need to start expecting them no matter how improbable. If only I had some idea what they were all leading to.

Marshal Garmon continued with a breath of relief she didn't try to hide. "I appreciate that, Prefect. I'm glad we could continue these talks despite the last-minute change."

"For the time being," the prefect said. "I will need to meet with him face to face before anything is finalized."

"One small step in a long journey. That's all this is. I think we can agree on that, can we not?"

"Indeed we can, Marshal."

Jason soon found himself drifting as the talks progressed past the initial moments. Politics were never his strong suit, and he had to stand there while a pair of experts talked about issues he couldn't always follow. He had to give Rickey credit. He and the jantan admirals seemed to be keeping up with them pretty well. *Guess all that time behind a desk hasn't been as useless as I thought.*

Though by an hour into the talks, Jason felt pretty useless. The conversation centered around political issues and potential ways to earn trust with thoughts on the viability of trade starting out between the two nations. He tried his best to hold his pose, though he noticed Yarain and Sundale were starting to let their tails gently rock back and forth. No doubt they were trying to release the same tension he felt. They stayed focused and alert, for the most part, because they knew a plot was likely in motion.

The talks hit the ninety-minute mark, and soon after, Rickey's ability to keep up ended. The prefect explained why an idea wouldn't work, and Rickey's head shook as he rubbed his eyes. He quickly apologized, but the prefect looked around the room and pouted.

"Perhaps we should break for a time," the prefect said. "I sense many are starting to lose focus. Myself among them."

The prefect uncoiled as did his party. Interstar's side rose to their feet, with Rickey stretching out his back. Marshal Garmon gave him a soft glare to which he shrugged with an apology.

Garmon shook her head at him before addressing the prefect. "It would appear you are correct. We'll break for a few minutes. Share some refreshments."

The prefect bowed, then motioned for his men to take their turn first. Rickey and Yarain both took their turns while Garmon turned to face Jason.

"What did you do, Major?" she said.

Jason couldn't tell if he should be worried or defensive. "Ma'am?"

"The prefect is the one who insisted no weapons be allowed at the talks. How did you and your crew manage to earn his trust so quickly?"

I think he took a happy pill. "I really don't know, ma'am. He had the same amount of trust when we met him aboard the *Histmar*. He never gave any reason for it."

Marshal Garmon turned to watch the prefect take his turn at the refreshments while his men walked away with cups of water and sandwiches. "He does seem to be a man that makes his own way."

"He's certainly not afraid to exert his position," Jason said. "His men respect him or fear him. It's a hard line to separate."

"Do you think we can deal with him?"

Jason looked over at the man in question. He seemed to be getting some kind of explanation from Sundale on how they brewed coffee, including a look inside the coffee maker. He guessed an explanation of why they still brewed it fresh despite food synthesizers was in progress. *I just hope Sundale is patient with having to go into so much detail.*

"Definitely," Jason said. "He'll take a hard line at times, but he's committed to ending the wars. In fact, I'd bet he'd go so far as to…"

He trailed off when he saw Sergeant Miles approaching the prefect with folded arms and a stiff upper body. The prefect turned to face him as Sundale's tails started waving.

"Does the food meet with your approval, Prefect?" the man said in a mocking tone.

"***SERGEANT***!" Sundale barked. "Stand down."

The prefect held a hand up. "It's all right, Captain. I expected this. Yes, Sergeant, it does. I thank you for your attention to detail."

"Detail," Miles echoed. "Yes, I pay close attention to detail. Such as the detail of your crazy eyes and unnatural body!"

A growl formed in Sundale's throat that quickly filled the room. "Leave, Sergeant! I must apologize for this, Prefect. This man will be disciplined, I assure you."

Now when did he make Major? Jason almost didn't want to intervene so he could watch Sundale work. However, he stayed behind Marshal Garmon as she marched toward the table with fury in her fists.

Sergeant Shin stumbled into her way, knocking both the marshal and Major Harlem down and setting off all kind of alarms in Jason's head.

"No, sir, I won't," Miles said. "Because I have news for you, Prefect. You may approve of the food, but *I* do not approve, of *you*!"

He had raised his arm up, a finger pointing upward for no clear reason. He started to bring it down to point at the prefect, but he never got close. Sundale sprinted around the prefect and into the sergeant's chest so fast, the man was on the floor before Jason realized Sundale had moved. At the same time, Sundale and Yarain's armor shimmered as their shields came online.

Sundale's voice shattered the peace and flipped Jason's internal switch. ***"COVER** the prefect!"*

The prefect's guards dropped their refreshments and stood around and over their leader as he coiled like a snake preparing to strike. Sundale had Miles pinned with a snarl on his lips, while Garmon and Jason found themselves having to do the same to a suddenly violent Sergeant Shin. Things got worse when weapons fire erupted from the door, missing Jason's head by inches. He never did see where the Jantan admirals went.

Cover fire from Yarain's tails gave Jason the moment he needed to land a knockout blow to Shin's temple. Then he and Marshal Garmon ducked behind the table as another volley went where they had been. He peeked over to see Vasquez had opened the door so the Interstar guards from outside could rush in with plasmoid rifles they didn't have earlier. Behind them, the Jantan guards were dealing with a pair of humans hanging on them like cowboys trying to tackle a pair of bulls.

Both Human guards continued to fire while one of them began to work his way around, step by slow step, to get a better angle. Yarain tried to return fire, only to be pinned down each time she raised so much as a tail above the table. The jantans held tight to their prefect as their armored mound took hits, though the rifles were mostly focused on those who could still fight back.

Rickey and Jason crawled over to where Sundale was ripping the Adam's apple out of Sergeant Miles' throat with his jaws. When the man reached for the wound, Sundale used his now free hand to land a punch that snapped his neck like a twig. He then joined the others behind the table as cover. He managed to add short bursts of fire that halted the second shooter's movement for the time being, but neither he nor his mother could get a clean enough shot to pierce the armor or shields of the attackers.

"Got any ideas?" Jason asked the room.

Sundale glanced around, then handed him a half-full bag of coffee grounds. "When I bark, count five, toss that at the guards."

"That won't be much of a distraction, Captain," Garmon said.

Jason huffed a humorless laugh. "They don't need much."

Sundale and Yarain got down on all fours before taking up positions at the outside ends of their limited cover. Marshal Garmon managed to reach a second bag of grounds, while Rickey grabbed a couple of mugs. Both nodded at Sundale to indicate their readiness. Sundale then barked, bringing a brief pause in the weapons fire as both rifles centered on his location.

"*NOW*, Jason!" Yarain barked.

No one hesitated. Two bags and two mugs went flying with surprising accuracy. One of Ricky's mugs smacked one man dead center of the forehead, while Garmon's bag was deflected by the other. Both men grunted at the contact.

The holdrens made their move at the moment of impact. Yarain sprinted around the edge of the room and leapt into the closer guard's chest with a snarl before he could get a shot off. Their shields fizzled, they hit the floor with a thud, Yarain got a firm hold on the man's neck. The man's cries turned to gargles at the holdren crushed his neck with every ounce of pressure her jaws could manage.

The second guard turned to fire at Yarain, then turned back to save himself from Sundale as he too bolted around the room. The guard fired, but the angle caused the shots to skip off Sundale's shield into the walls. Sundale never slowed as he plowed into his prey like a furry linebacker with his own snarl. He too wasted no time crushing his prey's neck.

Sergeant Vasquez rushed to try and pry Sundale off only to be plastered against the wall with a resounding thud by Marshal Garmon. Sergeant Shin had begun to rouse, but Rickey was already there with a plate he'd appropriated to make sure she stayed down. That left Jason to watch with mixed feelings as the guards pushed and pulled at

Yarain and Sundale while gasping for air. The holdrens just bit harder through their growls, severing arteries and sending blood gushing from the wounds with each twist and turn of their muzzles. When cracking from beneath ended their struggles, Jason stared at his holdren comrades as they released their holds. Their muzzles, fangs, and chests were dripping with blood, sending his stomach into a twist.

Why are you surprised? he asked himself. *You know what they are, you've seen it before.* Somehow that didn't help. He'd seen them be very precious and gentle, too. At times, he almost thought of them as intelligent pet dogs. *How easy it is to forget just what they're capable of.*

Yarain and Sundale held their growls while watching over their kills. Then their heads snapped up, their ears perked toward the open door. Jason followed their gaze to find the battle outside had ended with the Jantan guards getting stabbed in the back. The humans were nowhere to be found, but when Yarain and Sundale tore down the corridor, he knew where they'd gone. He also knew what the holdrens had in mind.

Jason ran to the door trying to catch them. "We need them alive!"

A great thundering followed by loud snarls told him the poor saps didn't get far. With the corridors clear, Jason turned back into the room, unwilling to guess if the traitors were alive or dead. The sight that greeted him wasn't much better.

The table and much of the far wall were horribly charred by weapons fire, which matched the scent of burnt fabric that had just found his nose. On the far side he could see the jantans tightly gathered around their prefect with Rickey making his way over to them. Their armored shells had taken multiple hits, but based on the movement of the mound, all had somehow come out alive. Hilahshan Forin laid on the floor behind the mound but was moving far too much to be badly injured. Marshal Garmon still had Vasquez squished against the wall, while the blood of his comrades began to soak into the carpet. Much as their vacant eyes would no doubt be soaked into Jason's memory for some time.

He tried to put it all out of his mind while he helped Marshal Garmon wrestle Vasquez to the floor beside Sergeant Shin. The man continued to resist, even when Garmon made a point of planting his face in the carpet.

"You move, you join your friends!" Garmon said, nearly growling herself. Sergeant Vasquez looked at the remains of his comrades and decided surrender was preferable to the same fate. "Good. Major, grab their sidearms and hand me one."

Jason nodded and retrieved the weapons from both guards, thankful they had avoided getting too much blood on them. He tossed one to Garmon who stood and trained it on her captives, while Jason raised his own, ready for any more surprises.

Satisfied the situation was at least currently secure, Jason eased his way over to check on the prefect. General Carson was kneeling beside the tangle of jantan bodies as they began to relax their cover over the prefect.

"Everyone all right?" Jason asked.

"No apparent fatalities if that's what you mean," Rickey said. "Looks like their armor prevented any serious injury. As for the peace talks, I'd say those were just put on life support."

"Don't tell me the prefect blames us for this."

Jals stiffened as he rose first from the pile. "Security was your responsibility, Major! If you had done your job—"

"Quiet, Admiral!" the prefect said as he rose from under his guards, some of whom had limbs tucked against their bodies. "It is my opinion that matters here, not yours. Interstar had no part in this. In fact, in case you missed it, their officers saved our lives!"

Thanks for that. Jason never thought he'd hear a jantan give him or any human a vote of confidence.

Jals bowed but did not retreat into himself this time. However, it was Forin, now clearly untouched, that spoke next. "Respectfully, Prefect, that doesn't excuse their lack of security. They allowed assassins to earn a place at their table. We can't let this go without a response!"

"Nor shall we," Jason said, thrusting his weapon into its holster. "I promise you, Admiral, we're going to find those responsible, and we are going to bring them in to answer for their crimes."

"And we have a great place to start looking," Sundale's voice said.

Jason turned to see him leading the same young technician he saw on the landing pad into the room. He breathed relief when he saw the young man and Yarain's captive behind him bore nothing more than scrapes on their faces. They no doubt went nose first when Yarain and Sundale tackled them. The rest of their faces were white with fear as both holdrens had a hand on their necks with claws pressing into the skin. The still wet blood on their muzzles and chests made them all the more intimidating. The shimmer of the shields was gone, but that only meant they'd been turned off or had exhausted their power supply after taking hits.

Jason approached the young man Sundale had, giving him an evil grin that drew a sharp breath from the man. "So. I finally get to meet the mystery man. Tell me, *Private*, how do you like the Coachella Valley?" More color drained as the man's eyes grew wide. "That's right, Private. The captain here saw you out in the desert near my home. We know you are a part of a conspiracy, and part of something called 'Operation Juno'? Now how about giving us a little more info, like where we might find your friends?"

The man shook his head, which the other man echoed when Jason looked to him with the same question.

Yarain licked her chops with a growl bordering on a purr. "We'll get it out of them."

"Not right now, Captain," Marshal Garmon said, dragging one of her captives to their feet. "We have a few things to deal with here first."

"More than you know," Sundale said. The levity of his voice made Jason feel like his heart literally stopped.

Something Marshal Garmon seemed to pick up on as well. "What's wrong, Captain?"

"This room... and I, have been exposed to dangerous radiation, ma'am. We should clear the room. I've already alerted a hazard team."

The private in Sundale's hand swallowed so hard it's a wonder it didn't include his tongue. Jason, meanwhile, wished he had a defibrillator so he could get his heart going again. Only then did he realize that Sundale had been carrying his right arm out and away from himself more than usual. It didn't take much guess work to theorize why.

"How do you know that?" Jason asked.

"Sergeant Miles had a nano-beam."

Of course he did! Jason rubbed his hands across his face as a wave of stress hit him. As if the whole fiasco wasn't bad enough. Now they had a martyr in the mix. What else could— *Let's not ask that.*

"Clear the room!" Garmon said. "Carson, Harlem, take charge of Shin."

Rickey and Jason approached the now awake, if a bit woozy, Sergeant Shin. Sundale collected the plasmoid rifles while a glare and growl from Yarain kept their two captives from trying anything on their way out. Marshal Garmon took personal charge over Vasquez. Shin was dragged to her feet, and though she stumbled, she let herself be led outside with the rest of the delegations. The jantans maintained a close circle around their prefect on his exit.

Once the room was empty of anyone alive, Sundale hit the control panel while the jantans reclaimed their weapons. The doors closed, and after Sundale input a few extra commands, a lock clanked into place. A force field flicked on over the door soon after to bolster the shield.

"PAICCA, is that enough?" Sundale asked.

"Confirmed. Room clear. Radiation contained."

He sighed relief, but his ears fell as if he were still concerned. Jason almost literally dropped Sergeant Shin against the wall.

Sundale tossed Admiral Carson a rifle while the many captives were made to sit together. "I have half a mind to shoot em where they sit," Rickey said.

Jason stepped forward to agree, but Marshal Garmon cut him off. "Stow that, General. We need answers. For starters, where did they get a nano-beam?"

Jason couldn't help asking a question he knew wouldn't get a good answer. "Assuming it was one. Sun, I have to ask: how can you be sure?"

"The glow is unmistakable," Sundale replied.

"It's not possible," Rickey said. "That project was terminated years ago."

"I know what I saw and felt."

"Could have been something else. We'll wait to see—"

"I *KNOW* what I saw and felt, sir!"

"You've been wrong before, Captain. It's just as likely you saw—"

"Stop!"

Everyone snapped toward Prefect Colark as his antennae started vibrating again. Only Yarain went back to the prisoners just as fast. The rest stared at the prefect, more startled than anything else. The prefect stood with his hands out, breathing hard with every exhale. His glare could have bored through armor.

The prefect held his pose as his breathing slowed. At last, he let out one huge sigh that seemed to calm him. "We have more important things to address. Marshal, I suggest these combatants be taken somewhere they have no chance of causing more harm. I don't care what your radiation protocols say. They cannot be allowed to remain."

Marshal Garmon nodded agreement and pointed to Rickey and Yarain as the ones tasked with doing so. With a snarl from Yarain to keep them honest, all four captives were led away.

Jason motioned for Sundale to join them, but the holdren ticked his ears back. "I can't."

"Why not, Captain?" Prefect Colark said.

"I was in close proximity to the nano-beam. I'm certain I've been exposed."

"Which reminds me, just what is this nano-beam?" the prefect asked. "You spoke as if you think it's the source of the radiation."

Jason took over before Sundale got bogged down by a dozen questions in search of the full answer. "A nano-beam is just what it sounds like, Prefect. It's a laser weapon designed to be extremely small yet still able to cut through thin armor. The project was abandoned because no one could solve the radiation problem."

"Radiation problem?" Jals asked.

Jason had to take a deep breath of his own to keep his composure. *I'd forgotten he existed for a while there. Felt good.* "The crystal required to make the device work emits high levels of radiation when charged. Anyone using it would receive a lethal dose of radiation."

"How is that possible?" Prefect Colark asked. "Laser weapons don't put off radiation."

"I'm sorry, sir. Poor choice of words on my part. They call it a laser weapon, but it isn't actually a laser. It's a focused beam of intense particles. The only way we've found to do it requires a special type of crystal to force the beam into a tiny stream. But as I said, it gave off too much radiation, and it never performed as expected anyway. Basic armor was enough to stop it."

Perfect Colark nodded grimly before facing Sundale. "Captain, you said something about a glow."

"I saw a faint glow under his sleeve, sir," Sundale said.

"And that's how you knew?"

"*THAT*, and as a predator, I know a hunt when I see one."

On that, Jason had to agree. He too had seen the intent in the man's actions. Once Shin "got in the way", his instincts recognized the combined threat and went straight to condition one internally. Had he been in Sundale's place, he wondered if he would have recognized the specific danger in time, though he was not at all surprised that Sundale had. While the peace talks were almost certainly dead, the words "for now" were attached to that sentiment, all thanks to holdren instincts.

Before he could think of the next step, Jason's attention was drawn to the arrival of two medics and a four-man radiation team. The latter came in wearing thick suits that made them look like samurai warriors from some bad Chinese movie minus the skirt, though the face shields were clear enough to see their faces. They wore thick backpacks for radiation cleaning as well. All of them paused a moment when they saw the jantans. One of the medics couldn't help staring at Sundale, or rather the blood still on him.

"I take it things didn't go well," the medic said.

"Just wait till you see the room," Jason said, a laugh escaping through the adrenaline crash. "Tend to the Jantan guards first. They've taken several hits."

"Not until we do our thing first," one of the radiation team said. "All of you need to be scanned for radiation poisoning."

"I'm the only one that needs to worry about that," Sundale said. "My right arm came into close contact with an assassin carrying a nano-beam."

"No one else touched him? Or you?"

"Only one who lived and never with my right arm."

Jason wasn't surprised when they didn't ask for more details. The blood on his muzzle and chest probably answered their questions.

They motioned for Sundale to step forward while Jason felt his heart for the first time. Close contact? Sundale had ripped his throat out! To say nothing of the tussle that had come before it. He knew what the man would have gone through, but what about his favorite fox? Just how much exposure did *he* receive? What about Sundale's energy matrix? It was a natural born radiation shield, though no one knew why. Would it protect him from this? Would his armor's shield protect him? Jason watched with an aching heart as two suited men ran a scanner up and down Sundale's body in search of radiation.

He forced himself to check the area as the other members of the radiation team began scanning the rest of the living. He noticed for the first time the carnage outside the room. The Jantan guards had not gone quietly. Two more human bodies were on the ground, sliced open like steers ready for cleaning. One had lost an arm. Their blood mixed with the brown blood from the jantans to form a puddle that turned Jason's stomach. Both jantans had Interstar knives in their backs. More than standard training, those blades had found their way through armor with the pinpoint accuracy of special forces. *Not a good sign.*

Prefect Colark had since leaned over one of the dead guards. He spoke softly in what Jason assumed was the jantan native language. Aside from a couple of hard syllables, he couldn't even determine where one word ended and another began. The rest of it sounded like the mixed Latin still used by fantasy stories for casting spells.

Jason felt his stomach sink, then latched onto the only thing he had. In truth, he hoped to somehow save the peace talks.

"Guess I was wrong," he said. "We shouldn't have waited for them to act before we did. I'm sorry."

"Don't be, Major," Prefect Colark said, anger deep in his words. "You prevented them from succeeding. These soldiers gave their lives doing the same. We did the only thing we could."

"It shouldn't have been necessary."

"It is who they are. Those who wear this armor dedicate their lives to one thing: the preservation of mine. *I* am still standing. Nothing else matters to them. They fulfilled their duty and shall be honored for it. Now it's up to us to finish the job." He looked toward Sundale, who was without his armor or uniform, still being scanned by the radiation team with Marshal Garmon standing nearby. "Perhaps you should check on your... do you say fox or man?"

This guy is unreal. "Fox, sir. Even in their two-legged form, it's more accurate despite the fact they aren't really foxes."

"I see. Well, whatever you call him, I think you should get an update. That doesn't look encouraging."

Indeed it doesn't.

Jason left, slightly embarrassed he did so without a word or reaction. Okay, he was worried, and he didn't have a battle to focus on. He still could have at least bowed thanks or even saluted before marching off. The damage was done, though. Hopefully the prefect would forgive him for it.

Jason buried those thoughts as he approached the group. *I'm getting too good at that.*

The medics were having a hard time talking the Jantan guards into removing their armor for treatment while one medic ignored Marshal Garmon's assurance she did not need to be scanned for injury. Other members of the radiation team were at the door, scanners in search of leaks. A crate of equipment had since arrived, including one for stowing contaminated materials, as well as additional suited soldiers. Jason went past them all, until he was stopped by Marshal Garmon.

"Sorry, Major, they won't let us get closer," she said.

That was all the answer Major Harlem needed. "Then he was exposed."

"Yes. They're not sure how much yet. Between his armor and his energy matrix, it may not have gotten to him. They crated his armor and uniform and called for holdren-compatible radiation gear. He won't like it, but they'll be able to take him to the infirmary without leaving a trail of radiation down the..."

She trailed off as one of the scanners started beeping. Even a laymen knew that to be a bad sign. It got worse when the radiation team member tapped at his scanner as if trying to stop the beeping. "What the—"

He too was cut off, this time by Sundale yipping with a cringe. The cringe turned into a whine as he fell onto his hands. Radiation or not, Jason started moving toward his friend but stopped when Sundale started glowing. Every eye turned his way as Sundale's whining became mixed with growls. The glow began to run along his body toward his back. All through it, Sundale continued to cringe like he was fighting it, without success by the looks of it.

Jason was breathing almost as hard. "Can you do something?"

"I don't know what's happening, sir!" the medic said. "By all accounts, his energy matrix is going crazy."

"Can't you at least help the pain?"

"Sir, right now, I'm afraid to touch him."

Jason had to admit, so was he. More so for Sundale's sake than his own. His heart wanted to help. His time around Marcy told him that was exactly the wrong thing to do. Anything he did could and likely would make it worse. That left him with the hard choice of watching his best friend endure intense pain with no way to stop it.

Sundale seemed to continue fighting as if he could somehow prevent whatever was happening to him. Then as fast as it had started, his ordeal ended. The glow faded, and Sundale rolled onto his back, panting heavily with his eyes closed tight. A medic pushed her way in, as did Jason, the second Sundale hit the floor. Marshal Garmon waved the radiation team down despite loud protests about contamination. The medic outright ignored them as she started her own scans. Jason knelt beside Sundale's head, preparing a glared challenge to be moved. When the radiation team surrendered to Marshal Garmon, Jason focused on Sundale.

"Easy, buddy, easy," he said. His hand rested on the holdren's forehead to keep him still. "Let it fade. You all right?"

Sundale waited until his panting had shallowed before opening his eyes to glare at Jason. "Ow."

Jason burst out laughing. *Only Sundale could give a complex answer in a single syllable.* "Point taken. Given the circumstances I suppose 'all right' is a relative term. You still in one piece at least?"

"Ask me in an hour," he said between pants. "I'll know if it actually hurt by then."

"If it actually hurt?" the medic said. "What do you mean by that?"

"It didn't really—" He tried to sit up but cringed with a soft whine at the attempt.

Jason gently pushed him back down before he tried again. "Let your body recover first, then we'll explore movement. Now, you were saying?"

Sundale thumped his head on the floor with a growl-filled sighed. "Beyond the initial onset of the attack, I'm not sure how much was pain and how much was my body fighting me. It felt a lot like when I was turning into pure energy, yet totally different at the same time."

A different voice asked, "Could it be the radiation?"

Jason turned back, surprised not only to hear Prefect Colark offering the thought but hearing real concern in his voice. Had they really made that much impact on him in so little time?

Meanwhile, the medic tapped on her scanners. She motioned for one of the radiation team to take a look. After a long moment, the man nodded with a hum of agreement. "It appears possible. Before the... attack, we were reading definite signs of radiation exposure. Now I'm reading almost none. It's as if whatever happened counteracted the exposure."

"Impossible," Marshal Garmon said. "You can't just reverse radiation exposure even with modern medicine."

"*We* can't. Maybe holdrens can."

The medic asked, "Could the contamination on his armor have thrown off our readings? Made it look as if he'd been exposed when he wasn't?"

Jason felt an endless circle of debate on the horizon. One he didn't feel Sundale had time for. Cured or not, he had to get to the infirmary for answers and treatment. Not to mention a thorough decontamination just in case. All of a sudden, he couldn't decide who he felt more pity for: Sundale, or the nurses who would have to deal with him during the process.

As the prefect asked about other possible explanations for Sundale's attack, Jason did decide he had to end the debate while he still could.

"Whatever happened," Jason said in a firm tone, "he still needs to get to the infirmary as soon as possible. They'll be able to learn more than we can, and he still needs to be scrubbed down to be sure he's clean. Sergeant, can we carry him out of here yet?"

The medic gave the radiation team a sideways look. The man checked his scanner again, then nodded. "Yes sir, I think we can. Whatever happened seems to have cleaned his fur enough for my tastes, and he's stable. Even so, I want him isolated until he gets there. Corporal, get a bio-barrier on a stretcher."

"I can walk," Sundale said, trying to sit up again.

Jason put his hand on Sundale's chest, but the prefect spoke first. "Be sensible, Captain. A moment ago, you looked like you might explode. Don't risk further injury by overexerting yourself."

"He's right, Sun," Jason chimed in. "Let your body rest. There's no shame in being carried."

Sundale growled at him with a glare to match. "Jason, really. I think I can manage."

"And if it happens again on the way? Ask yourself this: you want to be carried on a stretcher or by your paws? In any case, it's a moot point. You're going to be carried. That's an order, Captain. Now lie down and wait for the stretcher."

Sundale growled again but gave in by easing himself back onto the floor. When the stretcher arrived with a thick device attached on the end, the radiation team member regarded those gathered with great suspicion.

"You're not going to let us lift him, are you?"

"Nope," Jason and the medic said. Prefect Colark added his own, "No, I'm not."

Jason continued, "We're as contaminated as we're going to be. Might as well let someone he trusts handle him. He also doesn't respond well to gloves."

"And I owe him my life," Prefect Colark added.

The suited man grumbled, then surrendered Sundale to the others. "You're lucky the scanner is in your favor."

Jason took Sundale's head while the medic took his legs. Prefect Colark took charge of his middle. The three of them gently lifted Sundale onto the stretcher, with Prefect Colark sparing an arm to keep Sundale's tails from folding under him. As the medic strapped him down, Sundale gently grabbed the prefect's hand.

"Thank you," he said. "Humans tend to forget those."

The prefect bowed. "My pleasure, Captain."

Absolutely unreal. Utter trust, true concern, now almost insisting he help with Sundale. More and more, Jason got the sense that with this prefect on board, peace was not impossible after all.

The device on the stretcher flicked on to create a low-level containment shield over Sundale. A sighed growl from Sundale suggested he saw it quite differently.

"Hey," Jason said, "it doesn't hold you. You could break right through if you wanted. Now lie there, relax, and let them do their work."

"Yes, sir," Sundale growled.

Two of the suits took Sundale down the corridor in the direction of the infirmary. Another stepped up to Jason with a scanner in his hand.

"This, I am going to insist on, sir," he said. "I need to know how much exposure *you* just got."

Jason bowed his agreement. "Fair enough."

One by one, he, the medic, and Prefect Colark, submitted to a detailed scan. Each passed with only minor exposure. They were given injections as a precaution but were otherwise cleared to leave.

As corpsmen arrived for the bodies, Marshal Garmon turned to the prefect. "Are there any arrangements you would like for your guards?"

The prefect slowly shook his head. "Just bring them and their equipment to the *Histmar*. I will see they are properly honored for their service." Marshal Garmon offered him one of their side-arms, but he pushed it away. "That is not mine to take. It belongs to their children, so they may remember the sacrifice their fathers gave in the name of peace. Keep them with the bodies."

Marshal Garmon nodded and placed the weapon beside its owner. She paused a moment before gently removing each knife, not even trying to keep her uniform clean. "These don't belong here anymore," she said.

The prefect nodded with a smile, as did his remaining guards. Hilah-shan Forin didn't react at all while Jals just rolled his eyes. *Well, there's a shocker.* Jason wondered for a moment if Jals may even be this "Multi-step." Then again, he couldn't honestly say that wasn't colored by their brutal history. The scar Jals had left behind went deeper than the physical. While it was indeed a scar rather than a festering wound, until he learned to see past it, he couldn't be objective about Jals.

Meanwhile, the prefect gave another sigh while a hand went to his temple. "I think it best I return to the *Histmar*, Marshal. This has been a trying day for all of us. More so for your fox."

Jason answered before his brain noted the decision. "I wouldn't worry about him, sir. He's tougher than he looks. He'll be back on duty shortly."

"True or not, I think it best we all let ourselves recover from this before moving forward. I've come this far and waited this long for peace. I can wait another day for the dust to settle."

Jason sighed frustration but nodded understanding. He didn't want Polaris, or whoever they really were, to win even the smallest of victories. *So much for that.* The prefect done for the day, Sundale exposed to radiation, nerves frayed beyond tolerance, not to mention the state of the conference room. He should be thankful more didn't happen.

Jason chuckled at the thought. *Let's not jinx that.*

Marshal Garmon stepped forward. "I'm sorry things went the way they did. I hope we can try again in the future."

"We *will* try again, Marshal," Prefect Colark said. "That's a promise. We just won't be doing it today."

Jason stepped to her side at attention. "In that case, sir, if you'll follow me, I'll see that you make it to your ship."

Prefect Colark shook his head with a hand up. "Not necessary, Major. My guards can handle it."

"I'm afraid this time, *I'm* going to be the one insisting, sir. We've already had one attempt on your life. I will not allow a second to succeed while I'm on duty. Please, sir. Humor me."

The prefect raised his antennae for a second, then bowed his permission. Jason nodded his thanks before turning to salute Marshal Garmon. "With your permission, ma'am, I'll escort the prefect and his party to their ship, then return here to assist as needed."

"Negative, Major," she said. "The rad team has this under control. Assist the prefect however he needs, then tend to your officer. I want a full report on his condition by eighteen-hundred."

"Understood, ma'am."

She gave a salute of her own then went to the equipment cart to oversee the operation, with protests from the suits of course. Jason motioned for the prefect's party to follow. He led them back the way they had come, checking every corridor more closely than before. His hand remained tense, ready to draw the P-mag it had missed before. No reason to do so was found, though. In fact, by the time they reached the *Histmar*, Jason's instincts said he could relax. Not that he listened to them just yet.

He stood at the gangplank with his hands folded in front of him. As the prefect and his party boarded their ship, he stopped and bowed. "I thank you for your assistance, Major. I have nothing further I need for the moment. You may return to check on Captain Sundale."

Jason bowed his thanks. "Be well, Prefect."

Jason left for the base but stopped when the prefect called after him. "Major. When you determine his condition, I want to be informed."

Jason nodded. "When the doctors send their report to Marshal Garmon, I'll be sure you receive a copy as well."

"Thank you, Major. Live strong."

Jason again bowed, then continued on his way. He kept a steady pace for the infirmary while trying to deal with a startling thought process.

A week ago, he would have regarded any jantan he met with mistrust and a plasmoid rifle. A little over two days ago, he expected a trap aboard a Marcallan vessel. Instead, he found a Marcallan prefect willing and able to end the wars once and for all. A couple of days later, Jason helped save his life. Now as he walked through the base, Jason realized that the two of them were forming a sort of friendship.

So many years fighting them, at times hating them, to be heading for a time where he was on a first-name basis with their supreme leader... he couldn't quite come to terms with it. It would be like a wolf and a caribou suddenly becoming friends. Yet he couldn't deny that feelings of affection had brewed over the last couple of days. Based on his words and tone, Jason had a feeling the prefect felt the same way.

And they say God doesn't like irony. Jason had made his name fighting the jantans. Now he could end up making it again by being the first to befriend one. *Let's hope I'm not the last, or there's no chance at peace.*

Jason's mind buzzed with the possibilities as he entered the infirmary. The place was dead quiet save for a conversation between nurses down the row. He saw Sundale lying on one of the beds, Yarain standing beside him and again nuzzling him. *She's still a mother.*

He found the doctor standing in his office with a clip-com against his chest. The short, bald-headed man had skin as black as black men naturally get, and had no wrinkles on his face or scalp. The type of man that looked the same at 70 as he did at 30. He was staring at a display on the wall, biting his lip in deep thought.

When Jason approached, the doctor held up a finger, then waved the pilot out of his office. There, Jason was forced to wait while the doctor finished whatever he was doing. Jason soon found himself rocking on his heels with nothing but Yarain's conversation with Sundale to keep him occupied. It would have been enough, had he been able to hear any of it.

At last, the doctor came out, still carrying his clip-com and biting his lip. Jason opened his mouth to speak, but the doctor spoke over him. "I don't know."

There's that spider again. Jason shook his head for a mental reboot. "What?"

"I don't know if the radiation triggered his reaction... or not. I don't know if his reaction cleared his exposure... or not. I don't know if he's going to die... or not."

I think the spider just had kids. "Do you know how he is right now?"

"Stable, clean, and alive."

And now they're eating my brain. "Look, Doc, if I caught you at a bad time, just say so. I'll come back later."

The doctor sighed while a hand went to his forehead. "I'm sorry, Major. I'm under a lot of pressure to make sense of something no one knows anything about. How can I say what his condition is when I don't fully understand half of his physiology?"

"You work with the half you do know. As for the rest, try contacting my wife, Marcy Harlem. See if she can help you. She knows more about holdrens than anyone."

The doctor nodded with another sigh. "Thank you, Major. I'll give it a try."

"I hope it helps. In the meantime, mind if I see him?"

The doctor looked down the way at Sundale, then gave Jason a sideways glance. "Hope you've got insurance."

The doctor returned to his office while Jason went in search of what he meant. He shook it off while approaching his old friend. Yarain saw him first, though her ears rose before her head did. Sundale didn't react.

Jason decided to address her first for Sundale's sake. "You got here fast. Weren't you escorting prisoners?"

"I got back right after you left," she said. "Marshal Garmon told me what happened. With her permission, I came straight here."

Jason shook his head with an amused huff. "A mother you will always be."

Sundale stirred between them for the first time. Jason leaned on the bed beside him, thankful to see him moving without whines.

"Hey, Sun," he said. "How you feeling?" Sundale glared at him with forward ears and a soft growl. Jason didn't understand why, until he remembered it was him that had suggested Sundale still needed a scrubbing. *So that's what the doctor meant. I should have realized given the state of his fur.* "Sun, it had to be done. When it comes to radiation, we can't take any chances. The only way to stem the tide is with a scrub down."

His growl faded, but the glare didn't. "They're lucky I didn't bite anyone."

"Though by what I'm told," Yarain said, "his growls gave them all a good heart test."

Jason might have laughed if he weren't dealing with an angry holdren and friend. "What am I supposed to say, Sun? Sorry doesn't cover it, so I'm left with nothing but my guilt."

Sundale sighed, then grabbed his hand. "It's all right. Just don't expect me to feel very chipper for a while."

Oh yeah. That makes me feel better. "I suppose I'll take it considering what you just went through. Can you tell us anything more about what happened? What it felt like?"

Sundale sat up without so much as a cringe, which ended many of Jason's concerns. "It felt like my back was trying to open up like a hanger. But it really didn't hurt. I mean it did but... it's like when a joint pops."

"What about your energy matrix?" Yarain pressed.

"If anything, my energy matrix is the only thing that *did* feel right. I could feel it rushing to my back much like it does when we get an infection. Except it felt like the whole of my matrix was being sent to the one area. I'm sorry, that's all I can tell you."

Jason's heart sank as he decided he couldn't risk Sundale's health any further. Long friendship or not, he had to ground him.

Or did he? As Jason tried to form the words to tell him, he got a sick feeling in his gut. Every time he tried to push past it; the feeling got worse. He didn't understand why, only that on some level he knew he had to listen to it.

Was it God, his instincts, or his subconscious refusing to let Sundale go? He'd need a shrink, a priest, and about a week to figure it out, none of which did he have. The only other factor was that every time he'd ignored such a feeling, he soon learned why he shouldn't have.

In the end he bowed to it, though not all at once.

"At least you're alive," Jason said. "In the end, that's all that matters. Although that does bring me to an important question that concerns us all."

Sundale's ears went erect before he could ask any form of the question. "Not a chance, Jason. This reaction is no different than any other trial we've faced before. None of them could stand between us, and neither shall this one. I won't ***LET*** it!"

Now how do you ground that? Even without the sick feeling, Jason didn't think he could have. Never mind having enough heart to do it. To ground someone after they gave a vow like that would be torture.

A sheepish smile formed as Jason finally surrendered to his gut. He could only pray it was right. "You're going to make me blush yet. All right then. Doctors permitting, you'll remain on duty, but I want you to rest this time. No stressing, no hunting, and forgive me because I must also include, no shifting. Until we're sure your energy matrix is stable, I don't want you using it unless you have to. I'm sorry. You'll just have to endure this... trial, as well."

Another sigh, but Sundale's pulled back ears said he was submitting. "Understood, sir."

"Thanks. As for me, I'm going to do the only thing I can, and that's pray. I hope you don't mind since I'll be spending a lot of time on you."

Sundale waved it off. "Your beliefs are your own, Jason. We decided that a long time ago."

Jason nodded his thanks while rubbing Sundale's shoulder. "Take care of yourself, old buddy. I'll be back tomorrow with... I don't know, something."

"Cheese noodle casserole?"

"Don't push it."

Chapter 11

Counter Strike

Simon sat outside his father's office with a growing knot in his stomach. He'd come to deliver a report only to hear his father having the mother of all arguments with the grand marshal. Though he wasn't able to understand any specific word or identify one voice from the other, he had a pretty good guess about the topic.

Operation Juno was falling apart. Instead of being on leave as Private Glarm had reported, the Gold Group had been there to mess things up again. Worse still, some of the operation's assets had been captured. Not two days later, thirty-two more had gone silent. Their fifth column, carefully formed over several years, had been reduced by almost half with more likely to follow. Admiral Solez had informed the grand marshal he was going to pull the plug on Operation Juno while they were ahead.

The grand marshal demanded a conversation less than an hour later. It didn't take a genius to guess why. Simon worried that his father might stand his ground this time and be reprimanded, which could create a cascade of effects, none of them good for either of them, or Polaris for that matter.

A part of him wondered if it was just as well that Operation Juno had collapsed. He had his doubts about the plan, and maybe this would give the Marcallan prefect a chance to make it unnecessary. He shot that thought down as fast as it came. Marcalla and United Systems were in the best place they'd ever been. Now was the time to take them both down, and this was the way to do it. Unfortunately, every attempt thus far had made things worse. Even if it was the best time, he couldn't see how they could pull it off anymore.

When his father finally emerged, Simon snapped to attention with his clip-com under his arm. Admiral Solez chuckled with a half-hearted salute. "At ease, Lieutenant. I assume that's the latest reports?"

"Yes, sir!" Simon said. He handed the clip-com to his father. "It's about as bad as we thought. We've explored every option we could think of. There's no way to neutralize the Gold Group without a direct attack."

"Might almost be worth it. What about Gold 1?"

"We don't know how, but Captain Sundale remains on duty. They are very much in play. May I assume the grand marshal wishes us to continue?"

Admiral Solez came close to breathing fire. "Worse. Four fleets are on their way here. The order to drop the curtain won't be far behind."

"What? We're not ready. Surely, he can't be that... I'm sorry, sir. I was about to say—"

"Nothing I'm not thinking myself, Lieutenant. It's been one disaster after another. But the grand marshal is adamant that we press on anyway so, God help us, that's what we're going to do."

Simon's stomach felt like it was literally rolling. The initial assault was meant to take advantage of a confused and weakened Interstar already dealing with a renewed Marcallan offensive. They were none of the above now. When the attack began, Interstar would be in a position to counter with full strength and focus.

When he thought of the lives to be lost, his mind touched on the thought he'd shot down before. "Couldn't we somehow delay or cancel it anyway?"

His father shook his head with sinking shoulders. "He'd just replace me with someone who wouldn't. No, Lieutenant, whatever the outcome, Operation Juno will proceed as planned."

This time, Simon's stomach sank. Orders, however misguided, had been given. There was nothing to do now but their best with what they had to work with. Polaris had been preparing for years, and Interstar still had no idea where they were or how well equipped. Surprise could still see much of the plan succeed, and it wasn't like the Gold Group could do any more damage than they already had.

Just keep telling yourself that, Lieutenant. You might actually believe it.

"I still don't know how the guy didn't faint."

Sundale turned an ear to listen as Jason continued to talk about the interrogation he missed. It was a welcome distraction as the fleet traveled to their target.

Apparently, Rickey had used a pile of meat and a fake human hand to convince Private Glarm that Yarain was going to eat him if he didn't talk. He bought it hook, line, and sinker. So much so, some said the man was still shaking the next morning.

I might have preferred his position to mine. While his mother was getting answers, Sundale was having his patience tested.

Marcy had arrived to help diagnose his condition. Despite the cleaning, he'd soaked in enough radiation to make it hard to keep food down that night. However, there wasn't any lasting damage from it or his latest "seizure." Even without treatment, he'd have been fine within a day or two. With treatment, he was discharged by sunrise.

Though discharged did not mean free. Marcy and the doctor agreed that the exposure was what had triggered his second seizure. With a scanner catching the beginning of it all, Marcy was able to deduce it was based in his energy matrix. Thus, she came up with a rather unorthodox, though effective, treatment.

Sundale almost wished he'd been grounded. The monitor she'd insisted on wasn't that bad. This time, it only meant an extra sensor on the shoulders of his uniform. The treatment however, meant a collar that was not only somewhat bulky but delivered a gentle shock to his system every few minutes. The shocks were forcing his energy matrix to realign more than usual, which did seem to be settling things down. His back hadn't bothered him in the slightest since.

The problem is, he was receiving a shock to his system every few minutes via a collar that felt like it was rubbing his fur off. Marcy insisted there was no other way since it needed to deliver the charge to several major arteries at once to be effective. That way it would run through as much of his blood as possible and thus affect the parts of his energy matrix that ran through it as well. If that wasn't bad enough, she didn't want him shifting forms for another ten days unless his duties required it.

In other words, he had to stay in a form that didn't feel as natural, wearing an equally uncomfortable collar that kept shocking him, while making sure he wore some kind of monitor whether he wore his uniform or not for *at least* ten days. The phrase 'stir crazy' came to mind. However inaccurate, it came as close as any term Sundale could think of for how he felt. Missing his mother in action just made it worse.

At least she'd been effective. Private Glarm had given up quite a bit. First came details on how he got the weapon past the scanners; second came the name "Admiral Solez" as being a man in charge. After the first crack, everything else came pouring out. What it was, who was involved – though he stopped short of naming the group he was working for – and his contacts within Interstar which had led to multiple enemy agents being arrested. More importantly, he told them where it had all come from.

That last bit of intel was what they were dealing with now. Marshal Garmon had chosen them for this mission. Best of all, unlike so many times before, they were far from alone.

The Gold Group was hitching a ride on board the I.C.V. *Berlin*, a battleship borrowed from the *Alamo* carrier group. The task force was also joined by a pair of heavy cruisers, which Sundale knew carried assault weapons and a sizable ground force. Beyond that, those ground troops were led by a contingent from the Field Logistics Assault Recon Echelon, otherwise known as FLAREs or the slang 'zeros.' The Gold Group themselves had been outfitted with two heavy assault cannons, one on each dorsal side between the engine nacelles and the central spine. After so many surprises, Marshal Garmon was done playing nice.

Sundale had to agree with her there. Ever since the sleeper escort that was anything but, he was tired of being bitten by hidden predators. Now at last, it was their turn to do the biting.

The task force was traveling under cloak to prevent the enemy from reacting. They would be able to capture an enemy outpost assuming their misinformation campaign worked. Though far more difficult than flattening the place, if successful, they might finally get some real answers for a change.

I just hope that happens before this collar rubs my neck off. As he'd done time and time again since first putting it on, he moved the new collar around in a vain attempt to get it to settle.

"Best to just leave it, Sun," Jason said in response to a soft growl. "Fighting with it won't do you any good."

Removing it sure would. "I've tried that, Jason. The discomfort just gets worse."

"It's like a burn. It stings at first, but if you let it sting long enough, it stops."

"There are ointments for burns."

"We could always numb your neck. Then you wouldn't feel it."

Sundale growled, but it came out like a ruff because he was trying not to chuckle at the same time. Jason's joke had helped, if only for a moment.

He got a better distraction as the task force dropped out of hyper-light at the edge of the solar system. While it meant waiting for the attack to begin, it also meant they would arrive undetected. With any luck, they could get the drop on the enemy before they could mount a proper defense.

The Gold Group launched less than a minute after dropping out of hyper-light. Sundale watched his screens for any changes as they made their way toward the target planet. He had nothing to react to beyond his own status board that kept a close watch on their emissions. If it got too high, their cloak wouldn't keep them hidden. Despite the occasional sensor burst and running passive sensors, he wouldn't need to do any power juggling to maintain stealth just yet. Though he already had a few ideas prepared in case that changed.

"No bogies detected," Yarain said. "Comm traffic clear. I think we got the drop on them, Jason."

"We'll see," Jason said. "We get orders yet?"

"Yes. All ships will stay in high orbit until otherwise ordered. Our group will go in first, confirm target, then we and the *Berlin* will provide cover for ground insertion."

"Sounds easy enough. Of course, we know how long that lasts. Well, best get to it. Sun, get what you can on the planet without breaking cover. Yarain, plot us a nice stealthy approach vector and watch your screen for any new arrivals. Last thing I want is another surprise."

Yarain confirmed her orders while Sundale used low energy scan bursts to gain intel. He couldn't get much, but anything more would give them away. About all he'd gotten was the topography and more empty space suggesting they were alone. *Doesn't mean we are,* he reminded himself.

He set one sensor to remain active for any visual distortion. If a cloaked ship was out there, that would be their best way of finding them. *Of course, if we had a corvette with subspace scanners, we'd have a better chance.* Why they didn't send a larger or better equipped force was a question that now didn't matter. They didn't, so the task force would have to make do.

As they approached the planet, Sundale got his first look at it through his turret screen. It was little more than a brown swirl of a rock. If it weren't for white clouds and a random spattering of green and blue, one would think it incapable of supporting life.

Yet life it held, and not all of it natural. On a continent in the south lay their target, right where Private Glarm said it would be. It was a small base built into a mountain. A faint energy signature most scouts wouldn't have seen gave it away. If it weren't for details on the exact location and frequency, Sundale had to admit that even he and Yarain might have looked it over.

"Target located," Sundale said. "Energy signature minimal. Either their base is shielded, or they still don't know we're here."

"Or our intel is way off," Jason said. "Private Glarm didn't know as much as we thought he did."

"Nor did the others they picked up," Yarain said, a silent growl hidden beneath her words. "Orders are to hold. Captain Cane wants to see if anything changes before we advance. I don't like it, Jason. We're charging blind into an enemy facility we know too little about."

"It's just a small outpost," Jason said. "The *Berlin* could probably handle it alone if she had to. As for any other surprises, that's what the assault mods are for. We may be going in blind, but not without teeth."

"Teeth soon broken once our soldiers are on the ground. It's not right. We're risking half a division when a little more intelligence work could cut the risk."

"We can't lose the trail, Yarain. Once they learn their operation failed, they may pack up and leave. For all we know, they already have. We've got to act, now."

"It's their lives we're putting on the line, not ours. We should do more to protect them."

Jason leaned around his chair with raised eyebrows. "You're talking like a unit commander back there. Maybe you should try it someday. I bet you'd do well at the head of a group."

Sundale didn't have to look. He heard Yarain's ears fall in her tone. "I could never be the first mother of humans."

"Oh no? You led a pack, didn't you? You took charge on Phoenix Perch, didn't you? You defended the hanger of that transport, didn't you?"

"*PHOENIX* Perch was instinct. I was acting under your orders on the transport. I led a *PACK* of *holdrens*. I wouldn't know how to handle leading a pack of humans."

Jason huffed amusement that Sundale didn't understand. "You think I did? You remember when we got this assignment. Rickey said 'Gold 1' and my heart stopped. He later told me what I'm gonna tell you: none of us really know what to do with the command chair until we're given our own to sit in. You'll do better than you think, I guarantee it."

"If you say so, Jason," Yarain said. Her voice held more fear than Sundale remembered ever hearing from her.

Jason threw his hands up in surrender as he returned his focus forward. Sundale meanwhile watched the status reports with his mind ablaze.

As strange as the notion sounded, he agreed with Jason. Yarain would make a fine unit commander. She possessed a steady mind, a warm heart, and a will strong enough to overcome rank. Family relations aside, serving under her would be wonderful.

Only problem is, he never would. If she ever became a unit commander, she'd do it away from them... from him. They'd built a pack around their Scorn fighter. The thought of losing a member of the pack, even if it was better for her, left a hole inside him that Sundale didn't care for.

The dread of such a situation grew until Yarain reported orders to enter atmosphere. He might have been grateful for the distraction if it weren't the beginning of a dangerous mission. However, the time had come, and his duty required he push all else aside for the sake of the mission. Things didn't go aside without protest, but they did relent.

"Let the games begin," Jason said gravely. "Any sign of defenses?"

"None that I can see," Sundale said.

"Yarain?"

"System remains clear," Yarain said. "No bogies."

"All right. Here goes nothing. Gold Group inserting."

Jason angled the fighter in a straight down dive toward the planet's northern hemisphere with the rest of the group close behind. Locator beams too weak to be detected spanned the distance between fighters to maintain the formation. Though low speeds tried to minimize it, the atmosphere still flared around their navigation shields as the planet's surface came into view.

"If they're alert, they saw that," Jason said.

"Still no change in the energy signature," Sundale said.

"Let me know if that changes."

"Aye, sir."

Sundale watched his screens closely as they leveled off over the planet surface. The landscape looked like some kind of painted canyon, the land containing swirls and lines of blood red and tiger orange among rusty rock. As the group proceeded south, the rock rose and fell in rolling hills, deep valleys, and several mountains; a couple of which were tall enough to force an altitude adjustment lest they clip the peaks. Every valley contained large rivers with shrubbery and trees growing all around them like oases tucked into a corner. Then came lakes, no bigger than some of the smaller lakes on Earth yet containing the same shimmering blue one might expect from a large body of water. They, too, were surrounded by foliage, as if someone had created the lakes for the sole purpose of watering their garden.

"Not too bad a place after all," Sundale said, mostly to keep the mood light.

"No," Jason agreed. "Don't know that I'd want to live here, though. Too much nothing between the somethings. Then again, the oases might not be too bad. Still, I'll stick to my own desert."

"Doubt there'd be much game either," Yarain added.

Jason hummed agreement, and the conversation ended.

The mountain that contained their target appeared on the horizon soon after. On the surface it looked like all the others: tall, jagged, almost a naturally built castle with spires dotting the taller points. Yet as they got closer, caves could be seen that were too uniform to be natural. In addition, many points held a subtle glow, likely from external or landing lights on the base. When the group got to within a few hundred feet, Sundale could see evidence of recent traffic around the caves, as if the prey inside had just left or entered.

Jason began an order for another scan but stopped when he saw Sundale was already on it. It didn't take long for the sensors to confirm their intel.

"Crystal deposit confirmed," Sundale said.

"How big?" Jason asked.

"Can't get a full reading without breaking cloak, but it's very big."

"Sounds like we found the place. Any details on the inside?"

"Nothing useful."

"Skip the twenty questions."

Sundale growled annoyance, but his ears fell in submission. It was the more relaxed way they worked around their different mindsets. It didn't annoy Sundale any less, but it rolled off of him far better than it had during the sleeper escort—an indication of just how tired they'd all been back then.

Though considering his collar, Sundale was surprised by how little it annoyed him this time, and how many details he was able to give without trying. "I can tell you there are people in there. How many and how well armed is eluding me. I also can't identify anything more than where the base itself begins and likely access points."

"A blind hunt into a scorpion's den," Yarain said, holding her growl. "I have a hard time believing they don't know we're here."

Jason breathed out his stress, but his voice betrayed little of it. "Oh, they know, but they may not know who or what we are. They may be passing us off as a scout they don't want to tip off."

"Or they could be ready to spring a trap."

"Not much choice. Signal the *Berlin* we're ready to poke the bear."

"They're already en-route. The *Appalachian* and the *Stanovi* are prepared to drop for troop insertion. We're to hold for their order to engage."

"Roger that."

Sundale waited with waving tails as the ships moved into position. Yarain remained on the comms to coordinate the movements of the group and maximize their effect. Sundale gave Jason a set of target points to choose from, then watched his sensors for any change. His hands were tight on the turret controls, however, as he expected to need those first. *No way they don't know we're here now.*

The longer they waited, the more Sundale felt the thrill of the hunt. His every fiber stood tense, ready to pounce at a moment's notice. His ears stayed forward, watching for sounds he knew he couldn't hear but his instincts looked for anyway. His heart thundered, his tails went stiff, and his eyes locked onto his target. He was a watchful hunter, stalking his prey, waiting for the chance to strike.

Then at last, the order came.

The group decloaked first, three of them coming down from high altitude to mask their true fleet size. After a second to let the combat shields reach full, Jason fired two vilon missiles into one of the caves. The blast jetted out of the hole, though it did little to the primary rock. Seconds later, the *Berlin* decloaked high above the engagement zone. An order to surrender was sent but apparently ignored.

However, at the same time, a thick combat shield covered the base while dozens of points on the mountain retracted. A few large plasmoid cannons and a massive number of Point Defense Fire turrets took their place with additional small missile tubes pocketing the mountain side.

"Oh shit!" Jason said as he pulled the fighter in a hard ascent with the rest of the group the moment holes started opening up. "So much for a small outpost. Sundale—"

"Prioritizing targets," Sundale said. "Preference?"

The fighter shuddered from the initial hits.

"Do I really have to answer that?"

"Roger."

Sundale left his turret on point defense mode for a moment so he could focus on marking every Point Defense Fire turret they were facing. It was an extensive grid, but it was spread across the entire group as well as the additional fifteen Scorns arriving from the other ships. Getting some distance and altitude allowed the combined force the room they needed to evade much of the enemy fire. However, unlike the raider frigates, these turrets were top of the line, meaning the group took a lot more fire this time.

While the group turned to engage, Yarain announced new orders. "***DISARM*** the base! Try to minimize damage, but ending the threat is our primary goal. *Stanovi* and *Appalachian* moving in for assault."

"They better hurry," Jason said.

The group fired their heavy cannons both barrels at a time while the *Berlin* pummeled the base with her own guns. The base's shields flared so much, it almost disappeared beneath them. The *Berlin* herself was also taking hits, but most of the fire was chasing the Scorns. The exchange of fire between the two sides quickly turned into a light and firework show with neither side quite able to punch through the shields of the other. A saving grace that kept the enemy missile tubes silent for the time being since none of them were big enough for torpedoes.

Jason twisted and rolled their fighter around the spread of fire as best he could. Sundale and Yarain tried to focus on the same turret cluster, but it was hard to do when facing a thick screen of fire that continued to rattle the ship. The group was already weaving around each other to cover thinning shields while the *Berlin*... did not care. She sat up there and absorbed the fire from six single-barreled plasmoid cannons like it was nothing. Had the other four not been busy trying to score a lucky hit on a Scorn, she might have had to do more than roll. Even a few PDF turrets would have made a difference. Instead, she got to sit and bombard without a care in the world.

After a few minutes, an alarm on Sundale's station told him they weren't so lucky. "Shield generator at 600C! At this pace, we're less than five minutes from critical temp."

"Gold 3, 9, and 24 are already there," Yarain added.

"Have them fall back," Jason said. "Remind the *Berlin* we can't hold like this for long."

"I just did."

"And?"

"They said we won't have to."

Both cruisers decloaked to reveal a pair of ships with a long, thick fuselage that had pods on either side; wings extending out from those pods; and a short and thick conning tower toward the aft. They were painted dark blue and grey, and unlike most ships, were somewhat customizable as evidenced by the massive cannons attached to their hull just above the pods.

The base shifted the bulk of its fire toward the cruisers, but the turrets became splintered in their focus. Each time they came off a fighter, said target held their position and let 'em have it. With how much they were changing targets, it appeared the fleet had rattled the base crew's nerves as well as their leadership.

Right after the cruisers appeared, large heat sinks at the rear of the cannons began to glow. A weakness perhaps, but when a ship is packing that much firepower, they become a prime target anyway. Once Sundale warned of the charge-up, Jason had all fighters clear the firing line but continue their assault. Sundale held his line on his chosen turret cluster and watched as the cruisers absorbed additional punishment from the base.

It came too late. The cruisers began firing thick bolts of blue energy. Each shot created a thunderclap Sundale could hear through the hull. The bolts exploded on the base's shields, further obscuring it in smoke, dust, and shield flare. Torpedoes from the capital ships made it almost impossible to see the base at all.

The shields continued to flare at the onslaught, but they ran out moments later. The combined weapons fire began chipping the mountain away chunk by chunk, creating a cloud of dust big enough to swallow a carrier.

Swarms of missiles streaked forward to erase defenses several turrets at a time. Rocks of various sizes started raining down around the mountain, at times bouncing off Gold 1's shields. Sundale's scanners registered damage to the base itself soon after. Much of it cosmetic, the rest significant. He fed choice targets to the fleet while watching the base disappear bite by bite on his screen.

When all fire from the base ceased, Jason called for a halt to their own just ahead of the *Berlin* doing the same. Smoke began lifting into the air as the dust settled. The task force hovered and waited, holdren tails waving and fingers adjusting on the controls in anticipation of the next move. Sundale fully expected another round of resistance. It was just a question of when and how much.

A repeating pair of beeps from Yarain's station shattered the silence. Sundale's ears turned back to listen while his eyes watched for any change.

"We're being hailed by a Captain Suto," she said at last. "He says the base commander and his number one are dead. As the default commander, he is offering the unconditional surrender of his facility."

"Sounds like someone has a brain," Jason said. "Can't wait to hear how Captain Cain handles this one."

"Roger that. Patching us in."

She knows him too well.

Yarain tapped into the channel so they could hear the conversation, but not participate. Jason would want to know just to know and to react to anything they might hear.

The first thing they heard was alarms in the background of the conversation.

"Captain Cain," a Korean accent said. "With the Gold Group no less. I should have known you'd both be here for this."

That sounds personal. Or is it stress? Sundale's attention floated a little as he felt his tails getting restless again.

Captain Cain's burly voice responded after a soft laugh. "Yes, well, here we are. And we're not happy either. I wanted a simple mission, and I get a fire fight. I don't like surprises, Captain."

Sundale swore he could hear the man seethe over the comm link.

"You did fire first, Captain. How else would we respond?"

"A fair point, I suppose. But then, you could have accepted our request to surrender. *And* you did play a crucial role in the attempt on the Jantan prefect's life. Now how would you expect me to respond to that?"

"Whatever our motives, the point is we are no longer a threat to you. All I care about now is the safety of the men and women still alive in this facility. I'm ready to let you in, Captain. I just want to know my soldiers will be protected and cared for."

Drop the act, little bird. We know your wing is uninjured.

If Captain Cain had reached the same conclusion, his voice gave no indication of it. "We don't make war on the unarmed, Captain. Show me troops without weapons, and no harm will come to them."

A sigh of relief came from the comm link. "Thank you, Captain. We'll proceed with the evacuation momentarily."

The channel closed, and Sundale couldn't hold his tongue any longer. "It's a trap."

"Of course it is," Jason said. "They've probably got a full division gearing up for round two. Don't worry. Cain and I haven't lived this long just to act stupid now."

"And yet," Yarain said, "that's what we're going to do, isn't it? It's the only way to achieve the mission. Call the bluff, force them into a battle they may not expect."

"Yeah, it is. For once I'm with you, Yarain. I hate the idea of sending our troops into battle with so little to go on and no way to really help them."

Yarain responded with a steadiness that silenced Sundale's tails. "I don't like it, but they have their orders, so all we can do is trust them. They'll carry out their mission. If we show them that confidence, they'll be fine."

Jason's head appeared on Yarain's side of his chair. "I'm telling you; you'll be a great group leader someday."

"I still don't agree. However, future hunts don't matter right now. The longer we wait, the sharper their antlers get."

"I will never get used to that perspective," Jason said while facing forward again. "Do we have orders yet, or do we need to pass on your wisdom?"

"Coming in now. Stand by... Cruisers are moving to deploy their troops. Gold Group is to provide what cover we can. Miller, Rivet, and Zeus Squads are on over watch, Berlin standing by to hit any turrets that wake up."

"Copy that. How's our generator, Sun?"

"575C," Sundale said.

"And me without my marshmallows. Keep an eye on it. Trim down the power a little unless they start shooting again. Should help it cool off faster."

Not much. Then again, when a generator got that hot, not much could be enough to keep you alive when the plasmoids started flying again. You just had to be careful since less power meant a slower rebuild of the shield layer.

The fighters moved in over what was left of the mountain side while the cruisers touched down several yards back. The mountain itself looked the part of a range target with charred rock and craters in what remained. As dust cleared further, Sundale could see the beginnings of the facility within. Several portions were now exposed, showing extensive damage through newly formed holes. Smoke lifted from the higher portions of the base, though it had begun to thin out as the soldiers within battled the blaze. The area between the base and the cruisers was littered with so much rock, it looked like a quarry. A rather odd one since weapon fragments were mixed in as well.

Sundale scanned this span and the base within in search of trouble. Unfortunately, what had been masking their signature before remained functioning, further increasing the chances of a trap. He watched the troops assemble, then march toward the base, feeling glad to be in the air and then guilty because he was. For a creature accustomed to sharing risk, the idea of another taking it for him left his heart sore.

Sadly, he could do nothing to help but his duty. Sundale continued his scans, hoping by some chance his fears were wrong. Instead, they were confirmed as the troops were met with small arms fire right at the door. The ground troops took cover behind the few tanks they'd brought as well as well armored walkers and power armors piloted by the FLAREs. At Jason's order, Golds 4 and 9 hovered over the entrance and laid waste to the enemy soldiers in the doorway.

With air support maintaining pressure, the troops charged the facility. Infantry and power armor hit the entrance the exact moment the fighters ceased fire. They filed into the base where Sundale's scans could no longer track them. A sobering fact he relayed to Jason.

"It's all on them now," Jason said. "We can do nothing more for them."

"Except pray," Sundale offered.

"You converting on me back there?"

Sundale ruffed amusement. "No. But I know how much comfort it brings you."

Jason hummed, and nothing more was said.

Sundale kept a close eye on the scanners in case he might catch some sign of the troops progress or potential dangers to them. He found nothing but dead rock and a soon-to-be dead fire atop the facility.

Minutes passed like days. No word came either way regarding their progress. For a time, Sundale wondered if they'd met with disaster. Then all of a sudden, his scanners were able to penetrate the base. He now had a full layout, location of people inside, damage taken, everything. This included a base full of Interstar soldiers, and not a single shot being fired.

"I think they did it," Sundale said. "Their sensor jammer has been deactivated. I'm showing a heavily damaged base under full Interstar control."

"Confirmed," Yarain said. "Master Sergeant Calfree is on the comms. She's reporting full containment of all enemy soldiers and fires. The base is ours."

A deep sigh of relief came from Jason. "Excellent. Any idea how we did?"

"She's reporting very minimal casualties. No specifics yet."

Another sigh came from Jason, and Sundale heard the smallest of smiles creep into his voice. "Guess we'll take it. At least we'll be leaving soon. Then we can stop waiting for—"

"Uh, maybe not."

"—the other shoe. Why?"

"Between damage and security protocols, they're estimating three days before they can get any data."

"We may not have three days," Sundale said.

Jason added, "I'm assuming we can't just yank out the core and take it with us."

"*NOPE*," Yarain barked. "And... you're going to love this; command wants us to assess the damage."

"Do I want to know why?"

"No. The enemy soldiers are wearing Polaris uniforms, right down to the insignia. Command wants to convert the base into a forward outpost for future operations they expect to follow."

So not one other shoe but two.

Jason almost growled himself. "Great. So, either Polaris isn't as dead as we thought, or somebody is trying *really* hard to sell the lie. Well, if we're going to hang around, might as well do our best to prepare for an attack I hope never comes."

"And if it does?" Sundale asked, regretting it the moment he did.

"Then we'll do what we do best."

Serves me right. Ask a silly question, get a silly answer.

Transmission detected.
Static file, scale fifteen encryption... stand by...
Encryption broken.
Monitors active.
Attempting trace...
From: Commander Interstellar Defense

To: All units
Classification: TOP SECRET BLACK 1 Eyes Only
Message:
Drop the curtain.
End Message
Transmission successful...
Multiple reply pings found...
Message being repeated...
ALERT! Numbers exponential...
ALERT! Forwarding to executive of combat operations...
ALERT! Initiating level two alert...
ALERT! Pings match parameters 88972...
Forwarding to office of the prefect...

Kor'Agel, or "Prefect" when speaking English, Colark stared at the report for the entire night. Wasn't much there. Just a simple, one line order to someone.

A lot of someones.

An army.

He knew what it meant. He prayed to the great Galla it wasn't so, but he knew it was. What made him sick was that he could do nothing. He had one of his guards forward what they had to Marshal Garmon, but he knew it would be vague at best and likely to not reach her quickly.

Which meant it would also be too late.

Kor'Agel Colark uncoiled from behind his desk and headed for the back of the room. Here, in the estate for the Marcallan 'Champion of the Ancients,' or Kor'Agel, he had the one thing he'd wished he'd thought to bring with him on the *Histmar*: a small shrine that bore a silver eye much like his own pressed into a slate of solid black agate. To each side of this were small quivers of incense. Just below lay a shelf with candles, two on each far end, and a wooden box with holes along its top in the middle. The rest of the shrine was made of simple wood outlined in purple marble.

Kor'Agel Colark brought a match to the top of the shrine. He chuckled at the report he'd gotten years ago about humans using almost exactly the same formula for it. In truth, after consulting the holy attendants, he'd found the human's round candles far more appealing than the spiral design most Jantan shrines required. The attendants assured him it wasn't the style of candle that mattered, only that the flame was created by one who's heart lay open.

He struck the match, bringing a soft light to the darkness coming through the windows. He first lit the candles, alternating to each side just as Galla had made her people. He dropped the still burning match in a metal bowl at the bottom of the shrine so that the remaining flame may be sent to Galla. He then took a stick of incense from one of the quivers, used a candle to light it, and put it inside the box.

As the smoke lifted through the holes, Kor'Agel Colark raised his hands up as if he might clap a bug between them. He breathed deep of the musky incense, taking in the spirit of his godess so that she may see the open state of his heart.

"Galla, priestess and creator, I ask of you: help my people. Keep us safe. Keep Major Harlem and his crew safe. Your creation cannot survive another war. Not if it comes to our shores. Please, my heart aches for your help, your guidance, your wisdom. Fill my heart with your presence so that I may preserve that which you have created. Fill the hearts of Gold 1 and all they hold dear. Let them feel your courage so that they, and I, may save your creation. Seeking, I come. Humbly, I await."

Await he would, for the full hour it would take the incense to burn to its end. He didn't have to, but the longer he waited, the louder his request would be. When the last of the smoke lifted, the Kor'Agel blew out the candles but did not leave. Auro Jals would find him there the next morning, still praying silently.

Still praying that what he knew was coming would not be the end of his people.

Chapter 12

The Polaris Insurrection

Jason tried to rub the sleep out of his eyes like he had the last couple of nights. Once again, he'd spent a lot of time staring at the ceiling. It wasn't the room or the fact that it had recently belonged to an enemy soldier. The room itself was undamaged and the beds were comfortable, he just couldn't sleep.

Spending the entire time in full uniform probably didn't help, but he'd done that before. This was something different, though he couldn't figure out what. He only knew sleep didn't come easily. It did come eventually, and he was getting enough, but this time especially, his body refused to relax.

As morning dawned where the base resided, he dragged himself out into the tiny common room where his crew fared much better. For them, it had been the same every night. A couple of turns, an occasional itch, then as soon as the head hit the paws, out like a light. Well, at least for Yarain anyway. Sundale still had to contend with sleeping in his finesse form. Though even that only caused a minor delay. *I could only be so lucky.*

Accepting that he'd gotten all the sleep he was going to, Jason let his mind take him... somewhere. He wandered the hallways, most of which still had plasmoid burns and/or blood on them. He traded salutes with other soldiers he passed, still not aware of where he was going.

That is, until he walked through the doors of the command deck. Or what was left of it. The place had been improved, but many workstations were still buried under debris or missing altogether. At least the bodies were gone, though not all the blood. Techs were working on the functional consoles, no doubt still repairing or reprograming the computer interfaces.

Jason tried to avoid thinking about those that died here while stepping up to Master Sergeant Calfree in the middle of the room. She was the only one in the room whose top two rank lines had merged into a much thicker chevron.

"Report, Master Sergeant," he said. "How are things going?"

She gave a prim and proper salute without becoming another rubber person, which somehow came as no surprise. Maybe it was her smooth, narrow face and eyes and the calm confidence that just screamed "lady" underneath her armor. Even after Calfree relaxed, she carried herself so highly, she took on a somewhat regal aura.

Her voice, however, was pure hard soldier. "The work is going well, finally. We're still working on the encrypted files, but the computer is ours now. We should have the shield generator and some of the weapons back online by the end of the day. I'm told reinforcements and a reconstruction team should arrive by then as well."

"No offence," Jason said, "but I've heard that before. They said three days or more. Then they said four for sure. Today makes day eight. We can't keep tempting fate like this. Sooner or later, Polaris, or whoever they really are, *will* come in force. We need to be ready for them."

Sergeant Calfree looked around the room as if it might hold an answer. "Permission to speak candidly, sir?"

Jason nodded. "Keep it respectful."

"I don't know what you want me to do. I can't hold a weapon to their heads and make them work faster. With all due respect, I know the risks, but if we are to get this place up and running, we must allow our technicians the time they need to do it right. Otherwise, we may as well pack our things and leave."

Some small part of Jason took exception to her tone. The rest dropped his head when he realized how he sounded. Likely a product of all the rough nights he'd been having.

"I'm sorry," he said. "You're right, we can't rush it. But at the same time, we can't wait forever. That attack *is* coming. It's just a question of when."

Master Sergeant Calfree nodded while relaxing again. "I understand, sir. I've been pushing them as hard as I can. I *do* think their latest estimate is accurate."

No sooner said then fulfilled. An officer walked over, saluted them both, and handed Sergeant Calfree a clip-com. "Sir? Ma'am? We've got it. Once the *Alamo*'s machine shop finishes with the field coil, we'll have full shielding again. ETA: ten minutes. They're loading the armored panels now so we can finish patching some holes. We should have an actual base within the hour."

About time. "Any progress on the data?"

"Not much," Calfree said over the clip-com. "They only just cracked the codes. Thus far, it's pretty trivial stuff. A crew manifest, we have that. Armory status, we blew that up. Vehicle bay inventory, blew that up too. Hanger inventory, piles of scuttled scrap. And of all things, their menu for that night's dinner."

Jason couldn't resist. "Really? What were they having?"

"Pizzas, apparently. Regular sauce on all, lightly spiced. Standard cheese, pepperoni, mushrooms, and... oh my God. And a chef's personal special – liverwurst, pickles, and anchovies on a crispy thin crust glazed with ketchup."

A few "eews" rolled around the room while Jason pretended to turn grave.

"They are truly evil beings. They must be stopped, no matter how many ships it takes." Chuckles replaced the disgust, including one from Jason soon after. "Although that does remind me. What's the status of our fleet? I understand we lost a ship?"

Calfree tapped at the clip-com before nodding. "The *Appalachian* left to have her guns taken off as well as drop off our prisoners. I understand she took her FLAREs, Vespers, and a lot of Terrines with her. Before you ask, I don't know why, but I wouldn't worry, sir. With the arrival of the *Alamo*, we basically have a full group in orbit. Shouldn't be a problem."

Indeed not. A flotilla of almost forty ships was a welcome security blanket. Any attack would be hard pressed to get past them. Any that did would take significant damage and then find themselves facing two full groups of Scorns who were all one transit away from their ships at all times. Real Polaris or not, they were ready for them.

"Nice," Jason said. "I'm sure Admiral Redding is happy to have the *Berlin* back."

"Very, sir. He said something about missing his big child. Though he's still nervous about having your group here instead of on the *Alamo* while repairs are finished."

"Ironic, since he endorsed my suggestion on the spot. Thankfully, it looks like he's worried for nothing. Repairs will reach a point where it doesn't matter soon enough. Carry on, Master Sergeant."

Sergeant Calfree saluted and walked off to oversee the operation. Jason knew his group would be in combat relatively soon, so he stepped up to the gaping hole in the forward section of the command deck in search of some peace. He looked out over the landscape to absorb the view as best he could.

Wasn't much of a view, really. An endless horizon of rusty rock broken by the remains of half a mountain scattered below like a layer of confetti. The only highlight was a purple haze that seemed to be lifting off the edge of the world in the distance. This planet's version of a sandstorm. Still, despite what he'd said when they arrived, he'd always had a soft spot for the desert. Maybe it wasn't so much the desert itself, but how it reminded him of home. For a moment, he was able to float across the cosmos to his own house.

In his daydream, Marcy sat next to him, smelling of whatever flowers she'd been working with that morning. Carter was crashing dinner as he often did. *That man needs a wife of his own.* The holdrens lounged in the desert, assuming they weren't hunting. It was warm outside, just as it was on the edge of the base he stood in for real, but that only served to relax him that much more.

As the vision colored what he actually saw, the real view once again added that little bit extra to trigger something he hadn't realized he needed. His body began to settle, as did his nerves. Though it often lasted only a few seconds, it was a few seconds he was at peace. Even the haze helped, mostly thanks to it twinkling as if snowflakes were—

Wait a second. Jason stepped up to the edge of the hole to get a better look at the haze. He'd looked over that exact view every morning. Never had he seen such a sparkle.

Not once.

He held out his hand. "Glasses!"

A pair of binoculars appeared in his hand, which he immediately put to his eyes.

"What is it, sir?" Master Sergeant Calfree asked.

Jason didn't answer. He was too busy trying to convince his instincts they were wrong. That the entire carrier group in orbit hadn't messed up that badly.

He examined the haze in the distance. He went as far as the binoculars would go. A moment to stare, and his fears were confirmed. That twinkle turned out to be exactly what his instincts said they were.

Glints off hulls and windshields.

One ship floated out of the haze to remove all doubt. An obvious combat fighter but of no design he'd ever seen unless you counted the heaps of scrap metal in the hanger. The fuselage reminded him of the basic shape of a shoe, except it was rounded off on all edges. It did have wings, but they were on top and at the back of the fighter about where the ankle would be on this shoe. These wings held all the fighter's weapons, except for a turret under the wing on each side of the fuselage. Tiny engine nacelles were tucked against the wings. A fraction of a split second allowed him to analyze his soon-to-be-target enough to come up with the word 'fragile.' That said, there seemed to be a lot of them out there. Two groups minimum, probably more, flying in way too tight a formation to be anything but hostiles.

His blood chilled when he saw the insignia above the cockpit. Not Marcallan or even alien. Instead, the Polaris bear beamed proudly from above the enemy cockpit.

"Shit! PAICCA, set condition one! Hostiles inbound! Alert the fleet. We need cover ASAP. All hands evacuate outer walls now! Get your butts out of here. MOVE!"

No one offered a word of question. Workstations vanished and wires were removed as the techs began packing up as fast as they could. With the walls of the base still open, no one could safely remain.

Jason turned for the nearest transit pad. He'd made this run a couple of times to develop some muscle memory since they'd arrived. It would take twenty seconds or less to reach a pad, transport to a transponder near the hanger, run the rest of the way, and reach his chair on Gold 1.

At least it would have, until PAICCA came over the PA just behind the bleating tone of the base evacuation alarms. "ALERT! ALERT! Begin evacuation. Base transporters non-responsive. Lifts and transits to hanger bay also unresponsive. All forces proceed to hangers for extraction. Cruisers *Musala* and *Hood* moving in for cover fire. Evacuate immediately. Be advised, enemy fighters detected on approach. ETA: less than two minutes. Additional forces detected in orbit. Condition one in effect."

"Dammit!" Jason snapped, too full of adrenaline to feel guilty about his cursing. "You heard him, move for the hangar. Keep calm, but keep it moving! Move, move, move!"

Jason turned to help only to find the last tech tossing a case under his arm and joining the dash out the door. He followed close behind, ensuring all were out before leaving himself.

The rumble of engines penetrated the walls as the two cruisers came in to provide cover fire. When the stairways or corridors allowed a look outside, Jason could see them and a couple of corvettes. The latter were little more than six sided boxes bristling with scaled up PDF turrets, a twin barreled heavy cannon battery top and bottom, and a pointed bow. All four ships were moving in to cover the base they'd fought so hard to capture. At one point, he saw a cloud of Scorns fly toward the mist.

Keep em busy, boys. I'll be along in a moment.

Jason kept pace with the evacuating troops, impressed with how the flow kept moving without degenerating into a panic by any definition. There was speed to be sure but control through it all. *Small favors.*

Another small favor was finding Yarain and Sundale waiting for him at the bottom of one of the stair ways. From there, it was a straight shot to the hanger, and they were directing traffic to keep things organized. Somewhere, he made a note to scold them for it since they should have been at the fighter getting her ready. For the moment however, he couldn't deny he was glad to see them.

The three of them waited for the rush to thin, agreeing without a word between them that they'd go back for anyone left behind. An agreement made void by Carter's arrival with a platoon of Terrines behind him.

"That's all of them, Jason," he said. "We swept through the quarters to make sure no one slept through the alarm. The base is clear except for us. You don't have to stay any longer."

He knows me too well. Satisfied, Jason and his crew matched speed with the rest. They stood together like the pack they were as they continued with the evacuation. The corridor had multiple gashes in the walls, allowing him passing glances at the dogfight happening out there. He couldn't tell who was winning, but the claps from the cruiser's cannons suggested they weren't being detained enough.

"How did they get past the fleet?" Sundale said.

"Don't know, don't care," Jason said. "Right now, we need to get out there and cover the evacuation. We can yell at people later."

"I thought we had the computers," Yarain said. "What happened?"

"More questions we'll have to wait to get – *hit the deck!*"

Jason dove for cover as an enemy fighter that had snuck through appeared to their side. It fired a short volley of plasmoids and missiles into the side of the base. Must have been a hurried shot, because most of the fire landed on the sides of the walls and under them. Even so, a few rounds got through. Sparks showered over everyone except for two who were hit directly and blown apart. Jason turned his head away from the blood spray as the missile impacts knocked down anyone who hadn't heard his order. Sundale rolled to a corner to avoid parts of the roof falling on him. Another missile hit, and Jason felt the floor buckle. He waited for it to fall, but it never did.

At least not under *him*.

He looked up in time to see the floor below Sundale collapse. Jason heard it hit as well as a sharp yip from Sundale. Jason crawled over to look down the hole, then his internal switch flipped hard to keep him from losing it.

He saw Sundale lying on the stone slab one floor down. He wasn't moving, but Jason saw chest movement that meant life.

Yarain and Carter appeared next to Jason a second later.

"He's not—" Yarain started to say.

"No, he's alive," Jason said. "I think there's a stair well just ahead. We can get to him there. Yarain, you stay here, grab a medic if one passes. Carter, with me."

Jason and Carter turned to run for that stairwell as the last of the troops passed them. They didn't get to take a step before a glint caught Jason's eye. Another enemy fighter. It twisted on its course to point his way. He and Carter froze, waiting for confirmation of their fears.

Eyes were meeting despite none being seen. All knew what came next.

Jason and Carter both reached a hand toward Yarain long before they saw a flash from the wings. Softer, but unmistakable. *Missiles!* Both hands moved on their own as if possessed by another. Had to be. Part of Jason's heart was still in that hole.

They yanked hard on Yarain's collar the moment they made contact. Yarain yipped surprise as her body flew with them in their leap for relative safety. She landed on Jason, and they shared a bounce on the floor that knocked the wind out of him for a second.

The floor shuddered from two impacts. Several more shook the entire base. Jason rolled over to shield Yarain. His eyes forced his head to look back at the hole Sundale fell into. Just in time to see a stream of fire erupt from it.

A second fireball engulfed the corridor. It seemed to be heading their way, until half the mountain fell where they had been. Though it blocked the fire, Jason's eyes were forced shut against dirt and dust.

Then... silence.

Jason let the dust settle before he looked back again. His heart prayed for a miracle. What he got was a wall of mountain.

No corridor.

No hole.

No chance.

The words hung on his heart for hours even as the clock only marked a second. Somehow, his mind pushed it aside. He had no choice. Staying there... his training wouldn't allow it.

"Come on, we gotta go," Jason said, his voice a thousand light years away.

Yarain gave a soft whine. She stole a look back as she dragged herself to her paws, yet her ears were up the entire time. "Aye, sir."

They sprinted the rest of the way to the hanger. They had to dodge another volley of plasmoids that brought down more of the corridor, but they remained untouched. At last, they made it inside their fighters. Jason skipped the preflight entirely. He turned it on, deployed the shields, then blasted out before anyone got another chance at him.

He never did remember the rest of the battle. He barely remembered finding enough safety to get a replacement for Sundale transported aboard. There were pieces that remained. Alien ships also bearing the old insignia. Fighters proving to be more of a challenge than first thought. Reports of a widespread invasion across multiple fronts.

Condolences from Carter.

Jason didn't retain any of it. All he felt that day was the vacant seat behind him. Even when it was filled by another, it still felt empty. It wasn't a holdren there. It wasn't his friend there. There was only a hole that pierced deep into his heart. One he feared would never again be filled.

Part 3: Allegiance

Chapter 13

"The Enemy"

What happened?

It was the only question Sundale could ask at first. His back hurt... he thought. His head certainly did. The latter created a cloud that made the fog that much harder to sift through.

Time brought awareness in parts.

Nothing smelled familiar. Not the metals, nor the floor, nor the scents he found on the air. His uniform was gone, though he still wore a thick collar. Yet that too felt different. Instead of frequent jolts to his matrix, this felt more like a constant tingle that seemed to run through him. He was laying on his chest for some reason, but it was definitely the floor. Too dirty to be anything else.

Being in finesse form, he tried to push himself up, only to realize his hands were locked in metal cuffs behind his back. When his eyes finally came open, he was able to confirm the presence of a muzzle. It didn't keep him from opening his mouth, but he'd have a hard time biting anyone through the cage around his jaws.

Anger at his restraints cleared the fog. What little was there came back in a rush.

He was running for his fighter. They dodged weapons fire. He rolled to avoid getting crushed only to see the floor he'd been on fall away from him. A sharp pain, then nothing. Next thing he knew, his head hurt, his back hurt, and he could barely concentrate. He was still in the base — then he wasn't.

A transporter flash took him. Must have fallen to the one on the floor below. *But they were inactive, weren't they?* He was in a new place after that. Wrong smells, wrong uniforms, wrong everything. He still couldn't think, nor could he really move. Too many things hurt too much. Loud shouting didn't help. Then something else came. A prick in his neck? He couldn't quite find it through the fog. Then... here. Wherever "here" was.

With his hands bound, Sundale rolled into a sitting position to get his bearings. He found himself staring at the door of a holding cell. Bars and a force field blocked the entrance, but he didn't see or hear anyone else. Inside the cell, he found only a toilet, much like the "bucket" on a Scorn, and a cot in the corner. No other clue as to where he was or who had him.

Deciding to chance it, Sundale tried his best to aim his middle tail to slice through his bindings. He kept the energy low to prevent damage until he had the aim right.

Except a beam never formed.

Try as his might, Sundale couldn't get his tails to fire. He couldn't even get them to glow. Panic came up his throat, only to catch at the back of his throat and be swallowed down with a breath. *Focus on the moment. You're a Holdren. You're better than this.*

Once the animal side of him settled down, he tried again to alter any part of his energy matrix. He found that what used to be subconscious maintenance had become an action needing deeper concentration the more he tried to do. Basic adjustments to keep his body safe required little effort, yet the most he was able to achieve was a slight glow in his tails, and that took near meditation to get there.

In trying, Sundale realized why. The collar was different than Marcy's treatment. This one was delivering a weaker, constant current into his body. While he didn't know what kind of long-term damage it might do, in the short term, it was keeping his energy matrix from moving enough to do anything.

Hands bound, and now disarmed, Sundale had to settle for a bit of awkwardness. He rolled back onto his chest so he could get the angle he needed to try and scratch his collar off with his legs. His first swipe found only metal. Solid metal at that. When he tried prying it off, he found it too tight to push off, and too thick to pry off without breaking his own neck.

"You can stop that," a young voice said.

Sundale looked at the entrance to find two men. One was an obvious guard with a rifle and an uneasy stare. The other carried only a side-arm and appeared to be no more than a year out the academy. Much like the soldiers in the captured base, both men wore a uniform of nearly solid dark brown save for soft grey lines that went up the sides of the legs, arms, and torso. The lines converged to essentially outline the clavicle on both sides, as far as Sundale could tell.

The young man folded his hands in front of him as if he were a greeter. "It's welded on. You won't be getting it off without a cutting laser."

Sundale growled at him before working himself up onto his paws. It took a little effort with his hands bound, but he managed to stand and face his captor. The guard gripped his weapon tighter as the holdren stepped up to the entrance. Sundale ignored him in favor of the younger one. The man rolled his shoulders, but otherwise showed no reaction.

For a brief moment, they locked eyes. Sundale allowed the animal in him to glare challenge at the human. The young man still didn't waiver. Really, there wasn't much of anything to be found in his gaze.

Then the young man hummed what sounded like approval, and Sundale decided to break the silence.

"That's it?"

The young man turned oddly grave. "For now. The rest is up to my fath... to Admiral Solez. He'll be conducting your... interrogation."

Silence hung between them like a hangman's noose, more so because of the shiver Sundale had to swallow. *Interrogation*. The weight of the word promised there would be no gentle ruses in his future. Try as he might, Sundale couldn't keep his ears from twitching back ever so slightly. It didn't help that his insides were dropping as the reality of his situation hit like a warship.

He was helpless and afraid. The two things he'd joined Interstar to avoid becoming. Now here he was, ear deep in both.

He had no contact, no idea where he was, and no way of resisting. The cuffs on his hands were too thick to break through. The muzzle didn't have much give either. Without his tails, all he had were the claws on his paws, which could too easily be held down. His only hope was to endure until Jason and Yarain could mount a rescue. A thought soured by honesty from within.

Given the suddenness of the attack, the chances of a quick rescue were pretty much zero. The chances of rescue at all... His heart had one answer. His mind had another.

Sundale ignored both since the topic was making him queasy. He could only offer a soft growl, as much for himself as for his captors.

Then an older voice came from around the corner.

"Well, I see you got a response out of him."

An older man stood beside his son. Sundale saw the bond through the military discipline even without any physical contact. His uniform was almost exactly the same as the others except it appeared so clean as to be brand new. He also wore five red stars on his shoulders versus what appeared to be a long pine branch with a shorter, second one attached for the young man.

Sundale let his growl grow, taking an early stand of defiance hollow though it may be. He glared his challenge at this Admiral Solez for he had little else he could do.

Admiral Solez folded his arms as if about to scold a child. "You do know you're not scaring anyone with that?"

"Are you sure?" Sundale said.

He glared at the guard, waited until he had the man's attention, and then nipped at him. The man flinched while starting to aim his weapon. Admiral Solez gave a glare of his own at the guard with a sigh of frustration. Sundale dropped his growl, satisfied to have gotten a win, however minor. *I doubt I'll be getting many chances.*

"I see I can skip any kind of appeal to your better nature," Admiral Solez said. "Too bad. You really are a pretty thing." He turned to the young man with deep thought in his eyes. "What about you, Simon? What do you think of our guest?"

Again, they locked eyes. This time with Simon going deeper, searching. For a moment, Sundale thought he saw what he could only describe as a shadow. It was as if a thin cloud flashed across the back of the man's eyes. It held Sundale's attention, and he didn't know why. Stranger still, for the smallest fraction of a second, he forgot where he was. In the time after, he couldn't decide if that was good or bad.

Then Simon said, as if making a discovery, "He's a scared stray."

Sundale ruffed in surprise with a tilt of his head. Half of him was mad at himself for letting his fear be seen. The other half was curious how the young man had seen it, and what he meant by the comment. Scared, of course, was accurate, but stray? That one didn't make any sense.

Admiral Solez recoiled in surprise as well. "What? What do you mean 'scared stray'?"

"I don't know, Dad—er, sir. He... he looks like a stray dog you find on the side of the road. I... I'm sorry. I can't put it better than that. It's what I see in his eyes. He's a scared, stray dog."

Sundale tried not to take the comparison personally as he tried to understand the comment. It was touching something inside that he couldn't find. An emotion that couldn't, or wouldn't, show itself. Whatever it was, it brought out a reply he couldn't stop.

"I'm a Holdren," he said. "There is nothing more to me than the fur you see."

Admiral Solez smiled for reasons Sundale couldn't discern. "Lieutenant Gordon would disagree. You tore his throat out a couple of weeks ago."

Must have been one of the guards. "As I would any threat to my pack. I'm only your enemy because you've made me your enemy."

Admiral Solez shook his head with a laugh, and Sundale realized he'd said too much. "You see what he tries? 'I'm not your enemy.' Technically true, I guess. Interstar never actively attacked us. At least not after the Jantan Wars started. They just didn't step in either."

Again, Sundale couldn't stop it. Curiosity won out, spurred further by the solider seeing a chance at intel, regardless of the slim chance he'd ever get to report it. "What are you talking about?"

"Don't you know? 'Pay up or face Marcalla alone.' Not the exact words, but that's pretty much what they told us all those years ago.

Interstar left us to be wiped out. Then, when the war went their way, they claimed many of the very worlds they refused to defend."

"I doubt it was that simple."

"Don't fool yourself, Captain. We both know the truth."

"***THE*** truth, or *your* truth?"

"It's the same thing. Interstar, the United Systems Republic, they only care for their own. If you don't toe the line, they'll abandon you. It's all about *their* goals, *their* desires. Anyone else is left to die."

Sundale wanted to debate that. He wanted to hold up Jason helping him as proof to the contrary, but he knew better. Further conversation would do nothing. It might even lead to a further disadvantage. While walking away could be seen as a surrender, staying was just as bad.

So, Sundale ruffed away the conversation and headed for the cot in the corner. Granted, that too was a surrender, but he didn't care anymore. Comfort was going to be hard to come by pretty soon. Might as well take what he could while he could.

He laid down on his side since it was the only position he could come close to calling comfortable. He couldn't quite relax, though. His glare remained on the men that still stood at his cell door. He refused to surrender to them any more than he had.

Admiral Solez huffed as well, probably enjoying *his* victory. "Well, I have a war to lead. You stay here, Simon. He's responded to you already. Maybe you can find something we can use against him."

Now Simon's voice held nothing but doubt. "Do you really have to... do you have to? Surly there's another way."

"There isn't, Son. As second seat on Gold 1, he knows things. Locations, codes, plans, schematics, things we could use to strike our enemies where it hurts. Armed with such information, we could end this war before it starts. He won't give it up, which leaves us only one way to get it. It's a grizzly job, but it must be done. That's why you have to bury your heart. You can't let him, or what you see in him, deter you from your mission."

Simon nodded and recited by reflex, "'Compassion is a weakness'. I'll remember Dad—er, sir."

His father patted him on the back, and then left.

Sundale stared at the young man for a while longer to further evaluate him. The word 'cub' kept coming to mind, but that shadow had gone from his eyes. For now at least, Simon was committed to his cause.

That left Sundale to close his eyes in search of sleep. He could do nothing now, and if he was going to hold out, he'd need to be at his best. That, and when the rescue came, he'd need to be as mobile as possible.

The hope was still as hollow as his chest. Admiral Solez did not look like a man who would let his prisoners be rescued. More likely, when the attack came, Sundale would stare down the barrel of a P-mag, and then he wouldn't be staring at anything anymore.

Jason won't let that happen. I just have to make it until he gets here.

It was as hollow as an empty belly, but for the moment, it was all he had.

Jason held the picture close to his chest as if he might find some warmth within its frame. *Is this really all I have left?* It still didn't feel real. He looked at the fox staring back at him, no emotion on his muzzle but Jason could see it in his eyes. It had been a happy day. A rare time when they'd been able to leave the wars behind, and just — be. He could see the lush forest in the background. The same one they'd all hunted in that day. "Fang and claw only," had been the rule, or in Jason's case, two daggers. Jason had even gotten the kill. How strange that on a day they were trying to forget death, he had taken such joy in causing it.

It wasn't the kill he'd enjoyed. It was the time spent with his closest friends, the feast they'd had from the kill which he almost over cooked for himself. He'd blushed so hard as the three holdrens laid there watching him go frantic as he attempted to save a slab of meat from the fire. Marcy was enjoying it too, without any offer to help him of course. It was a good day.

There weren't going to be any more of them.

It refused to sink in. Maybe because, with the onset of another war, a formal service couldn't be held. The best they'd been able to manage was a gathering of the group, a toast to Sundale and the others that hadn't made it out, followed by a scramble to their stations as another attack canceled their plans for the night.

Try as he might, Jason couldn't get his mind to accept it. His heart still prayed for the report they'd found him alive and well. Maybe left behind on that planet, forced to dig his way out of a 'den' that had saved him. Yet he knew it wasn't going to.

Sundale, his closest friend, was gone forever.

Jason set the picture on the table as he fought the urge to cry for reasons he didn't understand—or didn't want to face. Maybe it was for Yarain. He looked over to where she laid on the windowsill with her head on her paws. There was no life in her ears, no spring in her tails. Just eyes gazing out into the stars as if their owner were among them. As much as Jason was hurting, he could only imagine the pain she held underneath.

He dragged himself over to sit beside her with a heart of stone. An ear turned his way, but nothing else acknowledged his presence.

Jason looked out into the stars and found words rising from within. "Ya know, it's funny. A view like this almost ended my career. I was a deep-green lieutenant, who had no chance of becoming anyone worth anything. After a rough mission I looked out at those stars and thought, 'It's not worth it. There's nothing to fight for out there.' Then I found Sundale. A half-dead fox with gator bites in his hip, and a lot of blood, on the ground of some remote planet. I saved his life, and he saved mine. Gave me something to fight for."

Yarain again turned an ear his way but gave no other indication she'd heard a word. When she remained silent, Jason knew he couldn't dance around the issue anymore.

"Yarain, we can't mourn forever. Sooner or later, we have to find a way to... live on. Continue to build a future."

"The future of the pack is our cubs," Yarain said. Her vacant gaze turned his heart inside out several times over. "How can I build anything when my cub is dead?"

Ask me something easy. "Yarain, I don't know what to tell you. I'm hurting as much as you are. You know what he meant to me."

"I was his **MOTHER**! And first mother. It was my job to protect him — and I failed."

All Jason could do was offer a hand between her shoulders. "We both did."

They sat together for what felt like hours. Somewhere deep within, Jason wondered how he was going tell Harmus. By now, he'd gotten the dreaded two-soldier visit. Probably did a number on Marcy's emotions too. But Jason owed him a more personal touch. He deserved to hear from Jason how his cub died and how much the failure hurt.

But what could he say? How could he possibly apologize? Jason had promised him he'd protect his pack, and now his cub was dead. Jason had to wonder if Harmus would ever speak to him again — assuming he let him live.

Old memories of Sundale soon pushed their way to the forefront. They started with the early days when Jason was still getting used to him, then moved through the years to the more recent moments of insanity they'd enjoyed together. Somehow, tears never formed, though he could feel them there, just waiting for the right circumstances. *What the hell am I gonna tell him?*

His attention was drawn by alarms and a shift to blue lights, followed by PAICCA. "General quarters, general quarters. All hands to battle stations. Set condition one! Outpost one-four-seven is under fire. Prepare to engage!"

Jason swung his feet off to follow the orders but stopped when Yarain didn't move. His switch must have flipped, because he found a level of control he hadn't had a moment ago.

Control he used as best he could.

"Come on, Captain. It's time we did our job. It's time we made sure Sundale didn't die for nothing."

For a brief second, he feared he'd lost her. Then she seemed to flip the same switch he had and hopped down to follow him. Her only delay was to shift into her finesse form.

"In Sundale's stead," she said, quoting what had become their private battle cry.

One that Jason feared would never stop hurting.

Chapter 14

Scared Stray

Simon had to focus just to keep his lunch in his stomach. His father continued to stab a shocker stick into Captain Sundale's side over and over until Sundale's whines were ringing in Simon's ears. Whenever the shocks stopped, Sundale panted heavily with pulled back ears.

The few times Sundale spoke, he recited the same thing. "Sundale, Captain. Serial number, Beta Alpha 6-1-6-1-0-0-3-8."

Simon's father once again sighed his frustration. "Come now, Captain. All we want are the secret transmission codes for the Marcallan Prefect. Tell us that, and this will end."

Captain Sundale glared at him and tugged at his bound hands as he laid on his back. Unable to do anything more, he held his ground the only way he could.

"Sundale, Captain. Serial number, Beta Alpha 6-1-6-1-0-0-3-8."

Another sigh from Admiral Solez. "Stubbornness will get you nowhere."

Admiral Solez stood over him. Another stab, center of the chest, and more gut-wrenching whines from the holdren. Sundale pulled again, but the cuffs held. The shocker was withdrawn, the whines stopped, and Sundale again panted.

He's the enemy. This has to be done, Simon told himself as he had several times over the last two days. He often chanted it in is head as if it were a spell that would change his perception. It never worked. As the whines echoed again, he forced himself to watch and saw nothing more than an animal in pain.

What am I doing here? What possible gain can I get from enduring such a sight? Am I going to be here for everything? Simon prayed to anyone or anything that would listen that he be spared more of this torture.

His father set the shocker stick against the wall while motioning one of the guards to leave. Any hope of an end died when the guard came back with a small case, three lengths of rope, and additional men.

Admiral Solez faked disgust while staring at Captain Sundale. "I'd hoped to spare you this, Captain, but you've forced my hand. Since simple pain won't convince you to talk, we'll try more aggressive means. Hold him down!"

Sundale struggled as best he could, but two soldiers held him on his back while two more contained his legs. Simon's father took the rope and began to wrap it around the captain's paws. Sundale struggled harder, snarling so fiercely many faces lost color. The guards lost their grip on Sundale's legs for a moment, but by then, his paws were tightly bound together. Another moment later, and Admiral Solez had tied one rope just above the ankle joint, what many thought of as the backward-bent knee, and another just above Sundale's actual knees.

When the soldiers withdrew, Sundale pulled and tugged against his bonds, but accomplished nothing except to scrape his paws on the floor. Meanwhile, the case held a set of claw-clippers and a shaver. When Admiral Solez held up the clippers, Sundale's snarl grew so loud Simon put a hand on his chest to stop his ribs from vibrating.

"Come now, Captain," Simon's father said. "We're only trying to make you look pretty."

The holdren's glare sought to erase Admiral Solez from existence.

The admiral ignored it, again calling for him to be restrained. Captain Sundale fought as best he could as the man proceeded to clip his claws, one by one, at times drawing yips of pain. Once done with his paws, the men rolled Sundale onto his chest so they could do his hands next. By now, Sundale had surrendered to his fate. He only gave token squirms while his eyes found Simon's.

The young man's stomach sank when he saw it. Sundale's eyes were pleading for help, though the rest of him refused to admit it. They begged for rescue like a lost puppy looking for food. His ears were so flat they could barely be seen. A soft whine escaped his throat, and Simon couldn't bear to watch anymore.

"I'm sorry, Father, I really need to go. I'll be right back."

Simon dashed out of the room while hugging his crotch as if he needed to pee. It was the only way he could think of to escape the room without his father questioning him. *Thank God we're not in combat, or I don't know what I could have used to get away.* He made his way down the corridors to the nearest bathroom, surprised to find he had some real urine to offer the stalls.

It didn't last half as long as he'd hoped. Nor did the most thorough hand-washing he could manage—done twice. Simon waited until the air-dryer started to burn his hands before slowly walking back. He tired to find something, anything he could do or say to exempt himself from being there. Yet as he stood just outside the cell block, he knew his father would never allow it. For whatever reason, he wanted him there.

When Simon passed through the doors with a cringe, he found the cell block strangely quiet. Sundale's growls had stopped, as had his whines. Simon didn't want to think why, but he knew he had to find out one way or another.

He tried to get control of himself while walking past the empty cells to Sundale's. There, he was met by his greatest test yet.

"Ah, Simon," his father said, almost giddy. "You're just in time. Isn't he beautiful?"

Admiral Solez held Captain Sundale up by the scruff of his neck so that his paws swayed just above the floor. A floor now littered with sandy gold, white, and red fur. Small clumps clung on everyone's uniforms, especially Admiral Solez's.

The worst of it was Sundale himself. His once pointed claws were mere stubs at the end of his paws. His thick fur had been reduced to a thin shell covering brighter, gold colored skin underneath. Even his whiskers had been shaved off, as well as the fur on his ears. His bushy tails had been reduced to three dangling sticks holding just enough fur to make them look like they were infested with mange. Dozens of red pores, where his energy matrix could be allowed to interact with the crystal-like fur fibers, dotted the tails where red fur had once been.

Barely visible through the remaining fuzz, they looked more like puncture wounds. Whether this was better than rat tails was a question Simon didn't want to ask.

On top of all that, Sundale's eyes bore into Simon, with silent pleas hidden beneath shame. Simon swallowed down his lunch before it got back to his mouth, though his stomach was two decks down by now.

Why am I here?! Why do I have to watch this? What purpose does it serve for me to see another being in so much pain?

Simon tried his best to keep his thoughts internal while his father looked at the captain like he was a prize. "A fine job if I do say so myself. And best of all, Captain, I have another surprise for you. Sergeant!"

Two men dragged a small cage into the cell and opened it up. As Admiral Solez and his men forced Sundale into it, Simon realized the inside was shaped to match his body. Sundale again resisted but could manage only a token struggle and a soft growl. In no time at all, he was locked into the cage and unable to move so much as a tail.

"I think we'll leave you to consider what continued resistance might mean," the admiral said. "If you still won't cooperate, then much more will be in store for you."

"Sundale, Captain. Serial number, Beta Alpha 6-1-6-1-0-0-3-8."

It was weaker than before, but no less dedicated.

Admiral Solez stood over him with Captain Sundale growling and testing just how much he could move. Admiral Solez stomped his foot on the cage, nodded, then rolled the cage over so that Sundale was on his back. There, the man smiled at him. Sundale replied with another fierce snarl. They held their stares for a moment, then with the speed of an expert, Simon's father drew his side-arm and shot the captain in the chest. Sundale went limp with a yip, followed by an eerie silence.

Simon's insides turned to stone. He was staring at his father like he'd gone mad, as were all the other guards in the room.

Simon couldn't contain his horror, though other soldiers reacted as well.

"Sir!" one guard said. "With respect, don't we need him to—"

The admiral raised a hand to stop him. "Relax, Sergeant. It's just a stunner despite what it looks like. You'll all be getting one by the end of the day. He'll wake up in a few hours."Simon held his chest again. His mind raced to save his own skin. "With respect, Dad—er, sir, I wish you would have told us. Command would not have liked you shooting our only high-value captive."

"If I had, Sundale would have known as well. The key is to get inside his head, Simon. We must break him in order to get what we want. Making him face death time and again will help us."

"Understood, Sir. I'm sorry I doubted you."

Simon's father holstered his weapon on his way to Simon, then rubbed Simon's shoulder. "Were I in your place, I might have felt the same. You stay here, Lieutenant. Let me know when he's conscious. The rest of you, come. We have an offensive to mount."

The cell was closed, and the block was cleared save for Simon, his father's shocker left on the console outside, and a chair to sit on. One Simon gladly took the second he had the room to himself. He waited a minute longer before hugging his chest as if he might keep himself from throwing up by physically plugging the hole. He breathed so deeply his sides hurt. By the time his stomach agreed to hold onto lunch, he felt like he'd run three marathons at once. As his insides settled, he took a long look at "the enemy" in the hopes of making his own private judgments.

Simon never quite found one. He stared at Sundale, eyes closed, body still in the cage. He tried to find an enemy there. He tried to find a selfish, evil being. He saw nothing more than a naked, helpless fox, locked in a cage. Hours of staring found the same. Even as Sundale stirred, tested his cage, then relaxed with growl-filled breaths, Simon saw nothing more.

Compelled to learn the truth while he could, Simon grabbed the shocker and opened the door of the cell. Captain Sundale's eyes locked onto him, for he could move nothing else, and his breathing became more erratic. As Simon stood beside him, he realized Sundale wasn't looking at him, but at the instrument of pain in his hand. Simon tried to ignore it, reminding himself just who he was dealing with.

"What's wrong with you?" Simon demanded. "Can't you see what you're doing to yourself by resisting? Why are you fighting so hard?"

Sundale's eyes never left the shocker. His breathing slowed though it remained labored. "I'm protecting my pack."

"Pack? You can't mean Interstar. They don't care for us, they proved that when they left us to die. They don't deserve your loyalty."

"And you do?"

"We're fighting for our survival. We're not like United Systems. We intend to take humanity to its rightful place in the galaxy. We're a force of order, Captain."

Sundale tugged at his bonds, drawing Simon's attention to them, which he then realized was the point. Sundale then spoke with a ruffed word. "Does **THIS** look like something a force of order would do?"

Simon tried to remain undaunted, even as his stomach did another turn. "We must do whatever it takes to protect our way of life. You and the bureaucrats of the Untied Systems Republic left us to die. You only care for yourselves. You could have helped us survive! You did nothing. We can't let that stand. We're strong enough now. We'll do what you didn't. We'll see that humanity, *all* of humanity, reaches its full potential. We'll see the Jantan Wars end once and for all. We'll create a lasting peace, for everyone."

Sundale stared at him, not moving for once, though his eyes once again bore into him. "Except me, apparently."

For a moment, Simon swore his heart and lungs were joining his stomach in its summersaults. Then he shook all thoughts from his mind. "Compassion is a weakness. This is the only way. It's the price we pay to protect our nation. You'll see. Our nation will be one built upon peace and order. We'll punish you for what you did to us by doing what you should have done! We'll make everyone see the truth."

"*The* truth, or *your* truth?"

"It's the same thing."

"You don't fully believe that."

"Enough!"

Too confused and now too angry to think, Simon stabbed Sundale through the cage. Whines again echoed down the cell block while Sundale fought to get away. Simon withdrew the shocker stick, suddenly overwhelmed by shame he didn't understand. Sundale's breathing grew heavy while soft whines continued to escape his control.

Simon's breathing matched the holdren's. He looked at the shocker in his hand with confused horror. Unable to understand what just happened, he dropped the shocker and sprinted out of the room. He nearly ran over the guard entering to investigate the noise.

He kept running. He didn't care who he ran past or knocked down. He wanted to get away from whatever just happened in there. Away from the man he'd almost become.

Simon ran all the way to his sparsely furnished quarters where he plastered himself in front of the bathroom sink. His hands shook so much, he could barely turn the water on much less splash any on his face. He ended up putting most of it on his neck and chest, though some did get where he aimed. With his uniform now soaked, he stared at the young man in the mirror.

"Who are you, Lieutenant? What kind of person are you? What are you becoming?"

He didn't get an answer. How could he when he didn't even want to think about it? For the first time, *he'd* been responsible for Sundale's pain.

So what? He's the enemy; he deserved it. It has to be done.

"You don't fully believe that."

The holdren's words echoed in his head more than his whines. They haunted him like some ghost floating in the wind. Simon could almost feel Sundale standing there, questioning him.

Simon nearly jumped out of his skin when he felt a hand on his shoulder. He whipped around, ready to knock that blasted fox on his tails. Instead, he swallowed hard when he saw it was his father who had entered the room.

"You all right, Simon? You look like you've seen a ghost."

No, just touched by one. "I'm sorry, Father. You startled me."

"Obviously. The question is why? What's wrong with you?"

Simon forced his breathing to relax while leading his father back into the living area of his quarters. They sat in chairs facing each other while Simon tried to find words to give him.

"Dad… are we sure Interstar is evil?"

Admiral Solez looked horrified for a second, then his shoulders dropped. "You spoke with him, didn't you?"

"For a moment. Then he tried to lie to me."

"And you shocked him for it. Bravo, Son. You acted well."

Simon shook his head and walked to the window full of stars. "Not that well. I ran. The worst thing is, I don't know why."

Simon's father stood behind him with his hands on Simon's shoulders. "You let him in, Son. For that brief moment, you let him get inside your head. In that, I am disappointed. You can't forget what he is."

"How can I do that when all I see is a beautiful creature I can't believe would do me harm?"

"There are frogs on Earth that are lethally poisonous, yet very colorful. There are fish on Seltis that are gorgeous, but are as deadly as piranha. Beauty can hide danger, Simon. Especially when that beauty has intelligence. Our only defense is vigilance. We must remember: compassion is a weakness. It gets in the way of what we have to do. It's not easy, but it is required to keep our nation safe."

Simon put his hand on his father's. For the first time in hours, his stomach no longer churned. "I know, Dad, I know. I just wish it wasn't so hard."

Admiral Solez turned Simon around and looked him in the eye. "These are the moments that test us, Son. Allow us to become the men we're meant to be. I have great faith in you, Boy. I know you won't disappoint me when the time comes to act. But enough of that now. You have been through a lot. Perhaps it's best you get some rest. Take some time to clear your mind of Sundale's lies."

Simon nodded his agreement, more than willing to accept a bed. "Maybe it will. Thank you, Father. Goodnight and… I'm sorry."

"It's all right. You're young. You'll learn. Goodnight, Simon. Sleep well."

Simon retired to his bedroom which held even less furniture than the living area. His insides had settled, but his mind was making up the difference.

His father called Sundale the enemy. Simon only saw a scared fox.

His whines were still echoing in his ears. The fear, the silent pleas for help, they haunted him even as he changed into his sleep wear. The fur on the floor, the scattered claw clippings, those thin, fur-less tails, Simon had to wonder how he'd ever stomach a meal again.

He tossed and turned that night as the conflict raged within. *Inter-star is the enemy. Captain Sundale is the enemy. They only care about themselves. They abandoned us. They left us to die. They're not protectors. They're not worthy of loyalty. We are. We stand for order. We stand for peace. We stand for the truth.*

"The *truth, or* your *truth?*"

Chapter 15

Whatever it Takes

Simon couldn't decide if Sundale was getting more used to the pain or if he was just getting more used to seeing it.

Almost a full week later, Sundale had spent the entire time bound and often caged. He'd been mercilessly shocked, at times beaten, and through it all, Simon had been left no choice but to watch in silence. His father wanted him there. "We need to help you overcome yourself," he'd said.

In other words, Simon was supposed to watch his father work so he could learn to take their mantra to heart. Admiral Solez wanted Simon to see the lengths he himself would someday have to go to for his nation.

What Simon saw was the slow fading of Sundale's will.

Already gone were his snarls, as well as his rank and serial number. Now there was only labored breathing and his cries echoing off the walls, which themselves were less frequent. He wasn't even cringing away from the shocker anymore, like somehow the pain had become natural to him. The fur remained, mixing with urine and feces since Sundale was almost never free enough to use the toilet. The worst of it was cleared away every day for the admiral's sake, not Sundale's, though the fur remained on Admiral Solez's orders. At times, he even had them clean it off and bring it back "so the captain could see what he'd lost."

As for the holdren himself, he'd been unable to clean himself because the muzzle always remained. He'd tried once when Simon was alone with him for a moment. Getting the angle with bound hands was an obvious effort. Getting anything done on top of it proved impossible. He'd fallen into the muck with a whine that day, and Simon had very nearly lost his lunch again. As if the stench of singed fur and skin weren't bad enough. The burns on Sundale's sides and chest didn't help either. Simon would have given anything to provide comfort, a bucket of water, something to ease the pain of this innocent creature. Except his uniform demanded that he stand guard and swallow lunch and emotion alike so he could follow the orders of his superior officer.

The nightly ritual only made it worse. Admiral Solez never changed it, yet it never seemed to lose its effect. Whether in his cage or not, Sundale was offered water through a tube fed out of the wall and a few thin strips of raw meat were slipped through his muzzle. Each time, he initially resisted, then gave in when his body acknowledged the need.

Then, Admiral Solez would hold him down with his foot or stare at him through the bars of his cage. He'd draw a stunner that looked like a regular single barreled side-arm. At times, he'd put a round from a real weapon into the wall or close enough to graze Sundale, but only earlier in the day. He'd always find a way to switch it out for a stunner. Sometimes using misdirection that would make the best of magicians proud.

Sundale couldn't help his reaction. Every time the weapon was drawn, his ears went flat while his body shuddered. Simon wondered why he never realized it would never be real. Then again, given the way his father acted, there would always be doubt, which was enough for the body to fear.

Admiral Solez kept the routine exact. After a glare, he'd aim the weapon at Sundale. "You've had your last meal," he would say. "Care to add any last words?"

Sundale never offered any. Be it out of pride, sheer terror, or resignation, he just watched the weapon with an ever-increasing breathing rate. Admiral Solez would wait a few seconds, sometimes longer, then add another shot to Sundale's chest. The holdren always gave a soft yip that sent another arrow into Simon's heart. Only then, while Sundale was unconscious, would the bare minimum be done to prevent infection. No other treatment was ever done, and nothing remotely good ever happened to him when he was awake.

We're in the right. Compassion is a weakness. We're doing what we must.

The words held no effect, for others came on their heels, sometimes even coming first. *Why are we doing this to him? What did he do to deserve this?* Try as Simon might to see Sundale as an enemy they had to break to win the war, he continued to see nothing more than a scared fox, held in constant agony, for no good reason.

He began to wonder if Sundale knew it. Or maybe Simon was just the weak link he hoped to exploit. Either way, Sundale's eyes often fell on him during the worst of the torture. They asked, pleaded, got on hands and knees and begged him to help their owner. Each time, Simon looked away, unable to bear the shame of denying their request.

He had a hard time escaping that shame on the night of day six, or rather seven since he chose to count the day Sundale arrived. Sundale had spent the entire day locked in his cage but still tortured. When the hour grew late, Simon expected the ritual again. This time, however, Admiral Solez left Simon on watch while taking the guards away for some undisclosed reason.

Simon waited until he felt confident they were gone, then knelt beside Sundale with the water tube in hand. "Drink," Simon said. "Drink what you can while you can."

Sundale didn't resist this time. He swallowed what Simon gave him until he tried to turn his head away. Simon removed the tube and was rewarded by the first stare that didn't bore through him. This time, there seemed to be a lightness to Sundale's eyes despite deep, labored breaths that shook him from time to time.

"Thank you," Sundale said.

The words hurt more than seeing his current state. His hide remained covered by no more than a thin layer of fuzz heavily soiled by waste. As for his tails, their scrawny look made Simon sick. The burns on Sundale's side and chest turned Simon's stomach further, more from the memory of what had created them. Then he had to deal with where Sundale's ribs were starting to show. The meat he'd been getting was enough to keep him alive but little more. When Simon put it all together, the words of thanks felt as hollow as his heart.

"I'd rather you didn't," Simon said.

Sundale's breathing eased as his ears rose within the cage. "Why not?"

I don't deserve it. "Because I'm not doing it for you. I'm just trying to keep my father from killing you."

Sundale turned his head as much as he could while his eyes went the rest of the way toward Simon. "I thought compassion was a weakness."

Simon latched onto the reasons his father gave and formed his own lie. "It is. But command wants the information you hold. My father won't get that if he kills you. I'm just making sure he's able to complete his assignment."

Sundale didn't even blink, though he did ruff. "You're getting good at lying to yourself."

Simon raised the shocker from the wall, to which Sundale dropped his ears with a shudder. "Be careful, Captain. I won't tolerate any of your tricks this time."

Sundale rested his head inside the cage as his eyes drifted closed with a growl-filled sigh. Simon set the shocker back against the wall before returning to his chair outside. There he stared at Sundale, watching him shift around as best he could, no doubt searching for a comfortable position. Either that or he was testing his bonds again.

It didn't matter why. What mattered is it further enforced the image of just a fox Simon saw in him. An image held as an exhibit for the debate raging inside his head. One side spouted the same rhetoric his father did: "Compassion is a weakness. He's nothing more than an enemy. We have to do this." The other remained strong in their single position: "He's just a fox. He'd never hurt us. We're in the wrong here." The two sides could never break the stalemate. As the minutes passed by, all they could accomplish was draining Simon of his energy.

When the guards returned and passed on his father's order that he be dismissed for the night, Simon gladly made his exit from the cell block. More than ever when he saw them choosing the strips of meat that would serve as Sundale's dinner.

Turns out, Sundale ate better than Simon did. No matter how much he stared at the food dispenser, Simon couldn't stomach more than a glass of warm milk. Even that couldn't break through the knot in his chest.

Again, Sundale's words hounded him through the night and tainted his dreams. Time and again Sundale questioned him. Even the times where Admiral Solez killed him, his ghost rose from his corpse to challenge Simon's beliefs. "You don't fully believe that," he would say, forcing firm denial and even raging reprisals. A nightmare in which Simon made the killing blow woke him long before his alarm did.

Simon held his head in his hands much of that morning, until his father came in to be sure he hadn't missed his alarm. Funny thing was, in a way he had. The repeating tones were still going when his father appeared in the doorway of his bedroom.

"Simon?" his father said. "You all right?"

Simon could barely give his father any attention. His alarm got even less. "Rough night."

His father turned the alarm off before folding his hands in front of him as if on inspection. "Brush it off, Son. The sooner you're up and about, the sooner we can start the captain's big day."

I can hardly wait.

After dragging himself into his uniform, Simon forced his stomach to accept a shallow bowl of cereal for breakfast. Between fear for Sundale and fear of how he'd handle it, he never tasted a bite. He put what energy he had into an act of professionalism for his father as they returned to the cell block for day eight of Sundale's time.

Simon expected to find Sundale still woozy from being shot the night before. Instead, Simon was surprised to find him very much awake, staring at them with the clearest gaze Simon had seen since he arrived. His breathing had also calmed as if he no longer felt any pain at all.

Did a full ration of water do that much? Simon searched his mind for an answer while his father opened the cell door and led them in. Sundale's ears fell again, and his breath grew deeper as they approached with more guards. He, like Simon, was expecting another round of torture and questioning.

They both got the surprise of their lives.

"Get him out of there," Simon's father said. He almost sounded like he didn't want to give the order. "Be careful not to hurt him."

Be what now? Sundale's raised ears held a similar question. If anything,

Admiral Solez had insisted the guards be rough with him before. Now he wanted them to be careful?

Simon didn't trust it. Nor did Sundale, he wagered. When the cage was opened, Sundale growled protest while testing his bonds for weakness. Instead, he found weakness within his own body. So much time spent with limited food and water combined with almost no movement had taken its toll. As he was placed on the floor of the cell, he cringed and whined anytime he moved. Just the tilting of his shoulders closed his eyes with the pain of muscles held still for too long. His legs in particular showed signs of stiffness, and their skin seemed to be a slightly darker shade than everywhere else. Attempts to move his legs resulted in more small lurches than the lithe movement Simon had seen before. Nevertheless, Sundale continued to work his body loose, and Simon continued to hide his pity.

As Sundale tried to remind his body how to move, he pushed the fur and filth around into a slurry that made Simon wish he'd had gelatin for breakfast. At least then it wouldn't be so rough if it came up. It only got worse as he considered the fact that he'd played a part, however small, in Sundale's fate.

It didn't get any easier when he had to bury those feeling lest his father subject him to the same or worse. No matter how Simon felt, he could only watch Sundale fight with a fading body that was already running out of strength.

"Untie his legs and help him up," Simon's father said. "Be careful about it. Don't let go until he can stand on his own."

Wait, what? The guards gave him the same confused look Simon did, to which Admiral Solez repeated his order. The guards, not wanting to risk his wrath, removed the rope from Sundale's legs as instructed. Simon's cereal did a few more summersaults as he saw the ropes had left deep, dark purple marks in Sundale's skin, including what was certainly rope burn in some places.

Sundale moved his legs apart but didn't try to move his paws until he was very gently lifted off the floor and forced to stand on them. He cringed and whined again as his legs bore his weight for the first time in over a week. The guards held him steady, at times lifting him off his paws again before he could crumple to the floor. Sundale cringed and growled through the forced rehab until at last he was able to stand on his own, albeit uneasily.

"Better, Captain?" Admiral Solez spat.

Sundale gave him a dark glare fueled further by his pain. "Sundale, Captain. Serial number—"

Simon's father almost growled himself. "There's no need for that, Captain. I have been ordered to discontinue my interrogation. You are to be treated as a prisoner now, nothing more."

Even Sundale couldn't stop a moment of confusion. His ears turned up while his gaze lost some of its fire. Simon tried to get his mind to reboot enough to think.

"And this changes things how exactly?" Sundale said.

"Allow me to show you. Guards? Get the poles and bring him along, gently."

These poles turned out to be dog catcher sticks which Sundale growled at the moment he saw them. The growl became a snarl as they approached, but he could do nothing to stop them from tightening the loops around his neck. Once secure, they tried to get Sundale walking.

Sundale's snarl grew while he pulled against the poles as hard as he could. Except his body had nothing left to give. When dragged forward, he tried to plant his paws, only to have his legs collapse and send him to his knees. Twists and turns Simon had seen shake a full-grown man off his back now did little more than test the guard's grip. Sundale was dragged to his feet, and the cycle continued. They'd pull, he'd resist, he'd hit the floor, he'd drag himself up to try again, each time with his ears falling lower than the last.

After almost landing on his side for the second time, Sundale stared at each of the guards in turn. They replied with another tug to get him moving. His eyes fell on Simon next, who was forced to give a face void of emotion lest his father see just how much this bothered him. He didn't allow their eyes to meet. There would be no hiding his reaction then.

At last, Sundale dropped his head and ears. His eyes closed tight as a soft whine escaped. They reopened to glare at Admiral Solez as he heaved himself up without any assistance. Only a shuddering of the legs betrayed the pain they still felt. Simon's heart broke in two as Sundale walked with the guards without complaint, only growling when they pulled on him.

Admiral Solez and Simon took the lead as they left the cell block, then turned for the nearest lift. Simon stole a few glances at Sundale as they walked. He found a far different fox than he had before.

Although his balance and stiffness improved with each step, his tails had once held a slight but proud and elegant curve as if they flowed out of his hips. Now they hung low behind him, only just staying above the floor. His head remained up, but he couldn't keep his ears from pulling back no matter how many times he tried.

A proud creature has surrendered. Whatever more Simon's father was going to do, he had managed to break Sundale's will to fight. To see nothing but fear remaining tested Simon's control. More so because as much as he wanted to, he had no way to ease that fear.

When Admiral Solez ordered the lift to deck twelve, Simon feared they were heading for the medical bay for some purpose he didn't want to imagine. Instead, he led them the opposite way to the gym of all places. The guards paused and looked at each other when Admiral Solez turned for that door though a stiff order quickly got them moving. Only their captive was unresponsive.

Those inside snapped to attention at the Admiral's presence. He ignored them as he drove the captive convoy into the showers. Simon looked back in time to see a few cover their mouths with their hands and not in surprise either. Given the stench and Sundale's physical state, it's a wonder that's all they did. *Bet they won't be eating much this morning.*

Inside the showers, a pair of officers in jump-suits were waiting by a stall.

"Clean him up," Admiral Solez said. "Be gentle and respectful, but get him clean. Make sure to dry him off as well."

What the hell is going on?! As Sundale for once didn't resist direction, Simon stood staring at his father, unsure if the man had lost his mind.

After days of being as brutal as possible, going out of his way to induce pain, suddenly he was telling people to be gentle? To be *respectful*?

The admiral only stood and waited while the cleaners drew the curtain out of habit or some other reason Simon's mind didn't have energy to think of. Steam and the sounds of rushing water filled the air, punctuated by a few growls and three sharp whines. Simon couldn't help counting because each one was followed by a blink from Simon that took the place of the equally sharp cringe his body wanted. With no word of explanation given, Simon and the guards could only stand and wait as well. Simon just about sprained his neck as it fought over whether or not to look anywhere but the stall.

Finally, air blowers announced the drying phase. A few minutes later, the curtain was drawn back to reveal a fresh-looking Sundale. Or he would have been, except now there was nothing hiding the effects of his torture.

First was the straight layer of fuzz thinner than a horse's summer coat. *Holdrens just aren't meant to be naked.* His tails looked so thin; they appeared ready to fall off. The fact that they hadn't risen so much as an inch didn't help any.

Then there were the burns. Scalding marks all over his sides and chest. Clear of filth and loose fur, they were easy to see now. How they still held even the thin fuzz was a curiosity Simon managed to focus on in order to keep his breakfast down. About the only thing that wasn't worse was the smell. The stench of month-old toilet had been washed away with the rest of the muck. All that remained was the slight musk even holdrens had as well as wet fur. *A miracle in and of itself come to think of it.*

"Better?" Admiral Solez said.

Sundale only glared at him with a ruff in reply.

The convoy moved back into the corridor with Simon still searching for answers. His father took them a few doors down to the very last place he ever expected Sundale to go. The moment they entered the mess hall, even Sundale couldn't keep his ears from perking. In much the same way, Simon scanned the room in search of whatever surprise his father had prepared.

Try as he might, he could only find the sweet smells of buttery pancakes, rich eggs, and the spicy ingredients for breakfast burritos, all of which reminded him just how little he'd eaten lately. He almost felt envious of the array of soldiers sitting at the rows of long tables, all eating their meals or engaged in small talk. One table appeared to have an arm-wrestling tournament going with a plate of croissants, twin over easy eggs, and a very rare helping of perfectly-cooked hash browns sitting to the side as if it were the prize. *I wonder if Martinez will ever master those.* Despite the battle for the perfect meal, the non-existent line at the kitchen and the cleaning of serving trays within announced the morning meal was coming to a close. More than a few soldiers were already taking their plates to the end of the kitchen or heading for the door to leave.

These were the first to notice Sundale's presence. They stood still and stared when they realized just who had entered. These in turn drew the attention of others in search of what they were looking at. A landslide of silence followed as Sundale was forced to take a seat at the end of an empty table facing away from the room. Sundale's growls of protest grew into a constant complaint as he felt the stares of the room fall on him. His ears actually went up and forward while the corners of his lips flashed the fangs beneath when a few of the braver soldiers inched closer for a better look.

"As you were!" Admiral Solez called into the room.

The mess hall returned to action quickly, though not at the volume it held before. The few remaining eaters continued to steal glances at Sundale, costing one man his spot in the battle for the perfect meal.

Simon stood on the opposite side of the table and waited for his father to spring a trap, or slap Sundale, or do... something. He couldn't believe this was all it seemed. Nor did Sundale by the looks of it. His growl may have faded away, but those ears of his went up and alert right after Admiral Solez's order. Broken spirit or not, he couldn't help being on the lookout for the next step in his torture.

Simon's father again surprised him by standing at the head of the table with his hand out. He sounded no less frustrated, however. "Take your seat, Lieutenant. The captain might as well have some company for breakfast."

Simon's eyes dashed from side to side, now more worried about *his* fate than Sundale's. "You won't be joining us, sir?"

His father nearly spat his words as he spoke. "No, I will not. I have some things to arrange, including the captain's meal. Guards? When the captain is served, I want you to remove the poles, as well as his muzzle and cuffs. Then you are free to eat your own meals at your leisure. I'm sure my son can handle the captain on his own." Simon's father leaned on the table while staring at Sundale. "As for you, Captain... if you cooperate, you will be allowed to eat in peace. If you don't, this nice young man will not hesitate to shoot you."

Sundale huffed while looking away as if uninterested. Only his flattened ears betrayed any feelings he held within.

Simon's ears would have been all fear if they could move like that. His father was leaving him in charge of a soon-to-be unbound and unmuzzled holdren? All the collar would do is make him use his fangs instead of his tails. Given a choice, Simon decided he'd rather have the tails.

"Have a seat, Lieutenant," his father said. "I'll bring you something too if you'd like."

Simon swallowed hard while taking his seat as instructed. "Just some pancakes, eggs, and toast will do."

Admiral Solez hummed, then marched for the kitchen. Sundale watched him go with his ears rising until he disappeared behind the kitchen doors. Sundale then looked at each guard in turn before resting his gaze on Simon.

"So, what now?" Sundale asked.

"I... I don't know," Simon said.

"*DON'T* toy with me!"

"I'm not! You know as much as I do."

"I doubt that."

Sundale's ears perked back toward the kitchen as Admiral Solez brought two trays out to them. He set one before Simon with a stack of sweet-smelling pancakes, steaming scrambled eggs, and crisp toast swimming in the scent of butter. The other went before Sundale and held only plates of raw beef and uncooked chicken legs. His also held a bowl of water as opposed to the glass of milk for Simon.

Admiral Solez pointed at the guards, who began loosening the loops and lifting them off Sundale's neck. Sundale watched them and Admiral Solez very carefully as his muzzle was removed next, much to the reluctance of the guards. Sundale opened his jaw wide to stretch it out, then watched again as his hands were also freed, though his collar was never touched.

Sundale kept his hands behind him until the guards had dropped the bonds against the wall and left for the kitchen to get their breakfast. Satisfied they were staying away, Sundale began the long, slow process of reminding his arms how to move. He cringed with frequent wines as he seemed to push them forward as much as he could, reset and pause for a moment, then push again with growing success. An act that normally took seconds took several minutes, until he was able to set his arms on the table, and then gently lean on them. He rubbed his chaffed wrists while casting a flat-eared gaze at Admiral Solez.

The admiral folded his hands in front of him. "Feels better, doesn't it?"

"You don't expect me to trust this do you?" Sundale said, hiding a silent growl within his words.

"What you trust is irrelevant, Captain. What matters is I have been ordered to grant you more freedoms during your time here. You will be fed better rations and permitted free movement during certain times of the day. You will also be allowed to reclaim your fur and will no longer be subjected to interrogation. You are now just a prisoner."

"Superiors got tired of failure, did they?"

Simon's father sighed fury before storming back into the kitchen. Sundale watched him go, then turned to face Simon with a huff Simon was beginning to recognize as amusement. "I think I struck a nerve."

For once, Simon felt no guilt in punching him across his muzzle. "Watch your tongue, Holdren! I won't allow anyone to disrespect my father."

Sundale shook his head before rubbing the point of impact. As he did, his ears perked forward. "That makes three," he said, approval heavy within the words.

Three? Three what? Simon stared at him trying to understand what he meant. Three times he'd reacted? He couldn't see how that would warrant approval considering what each reaction had cost Sundale. It had to be something else—right?

A rumble from Simon's stomach reminded him about the food on his plate. He pushed the search for answers to passive while spreading half melted butter around his pancakes. Sundale, meanwhile, sniffed at his own meal still staring at Simon.

"What's the game here?" Sundale said.

Simon swallowed a bite before waving his fork at him. "I told you; you know as much as I do. He hasn't said a word to me about it. I've never seen him this upset, though. I think he's sincere about his orders."

Sundale huffed again. "That man doesn't know the meaning of the word."

"Watch it, Captain! I've already hit you once. Look, I don't know why he's doing this. But what does it matter? You're free to move, and you have a full meal before you. If I were you, I'd enjoy it while you can. Even if there is some ulterior motive, you might as well build up your strength while you have the chance. You may not get another."

Sundale stared at his tray with frequent glances back at Simon as he cut through his pancakes. Eventually, Sundale chose a chicken leg, sniffed at it for almost a minute, then proceeded to crack his way into it.

He didn't hold back from there. Sundale crunched through legs and chewed on hunks of beef straight from the plate very much like a hungry animal. He only paused when he took a moment to lap at the water in his bowl. Yet he never achieved the wild frenzy Simon expected. What he ate, he ate quickly, but the food remained on his plates and in his mouth every time. Only the cracking bones bothered Simon, and even that didn't prevent him from enjoying his own breakfast.

Sundale never lost sight of him, though. Nor anyone else for that matter. Any time an officer came close, his ears went back, and he cowered like he expected them to hit him. He held his fear until they were gone, then resumed his eating at a slower, more careful pace at first.

Otherwise, his eyes remained on Simon the entire time, though Simon couldn't tell if they were watching out of fear or curiosity.

It only fueled the debate within. Simon still saw only an innocent fox. No trace of an evil enemy to be found. He still couldn't understand his father's hatred. Sundale had acted about the same as anyone else might in his position, perhaps better. After all, how many humans, after suffering the kind of humiliation Sundale had endured, would still have an ounce of pride left to show?

Simon had to admit, he didn't think he would as he finished the last of his eggs. He took the toast as it came while watching Sundale lick whatever was left off his own plates. Simon couldn't help a quiet laugh as he remembered an old family dog that did the same when he was young. Ironically, she too had had sandy colored fur.

"How was it?" Simon said.

Sundale licked his lips while sitting straight up, his guard very much in place. "Acceptable."

Simon wiped the residue of breakfast from his mouth, then reached for the last of his milk. "That's it? Just acceptable? I thought you lived on meat."

"*Fresh* meat, from a recent kill."

"Just being raw isn't enough, huh? Well, next time we'll see if we can get you a live rabbit."

Sundale gave several short ruffs, which Simon remembered from reading was indeed a laugh, while his ears pulled back halfway. "What is it with you? First you seem to care, then you seem like you don't, then you do again. What's coming tomorrow? You going torture me yourself?"

The idea of doing so sent Simon's stomach to his feet. "I hope not. I'm lucky I haven't lost my lunch as it is."

"Then which is it?"

I wish I knew.

Simon sighed with a drop of his head. His uniform, his insides, his mind, his heart, they all went to war with each other all at once. Lord knows where his stomach went. When he looked up at the holdren, it fell so far it had to have created its own dimension. Worse yet, Sundale just sat there, ears up, eyes attentive. No mistrust, no fear, just waiting. It only made the debate rage harder.

It got to the point that Simon had to halt the debate entirely so he could at least offer *some* kind of response.

What came out... it didn't feel hollow, but it wasn't him either.

"I'm only following my commanding officer's orders. He says we're to treat you well, so that's what I'm going to do. More than that is irrelevant."

For the first time, Sundale sat back. His ears were up, but relaxed. His tails curled around to lay beside him. He settled in his seat with a soft slump as if a large weight had fallen off his back. He even managed a single windmill stretch of his arms that, while slow and painful based on the cringe, was otherwise smooth.

"That's four," he said halfway through the stretch.

Simon got the oddest blessing he never knew he wanted. His mind went blank. Utterly devoid of thought. There was some shred of a question, but he got as far as *what does that mean?* Before the void swallowed it again. Sundale didn't offer any help. He sat there like the cat that ate the canary. *Or perhaps, in this case, the fox that ate the rabbit?*

The chuckle got his mind going in time to notice Sundale snap a straight-eared gaze to the kitchen. Simon followed to find his father marching toward them without a trace of his earlier frustration. If anything, he was carrying himself more proudly, as if he'd just won a major victory. *This can't be good.*

Simon snapped to attention when his father stood at the end of the table. Sundale only glared at him with falling ears and a shudder he couldn't seem to control.

Admiral Solez returned his son's salute before addressing Sundale. His voice was once again hard and condescending. "How was your breakfast, Captain?"

Sundale's ears fell further as his glare fell on Simon. When he spoke, he sounded so distant he almost couldn't be heard. "Just do it."

Admiral Solez nodded with a laugh, and another shudder went through Sundale's body. "As you wish."

He snapped his fingers, and soldiers sprang from two tables over.

They descended, and before Simon knew what was happening, Sundale was on his face with his hands cuffed behind him and a muzzle back in place. Growls echoed off the walls as Sundale fought against his captors like he'd just arrived. A fight that ended with a sharp yip when Simon's father punched him in the back.

His growls remained, however, as he was hauled to his paws then forced to kneel after the dog-catcher poles were tightened around his neck.

Simon hid his horror behind the confusion he truly felt. "Dad, I don't understand. What's going on?"

His father shot him a narrow-eyed glare, then held Sundale by the throat. "I hope you enjoyed your breakfast, Captain. You won't be getting another for a very long time. Take him to the medical bay. I want him properly prepared for our next session."

The entire room watched Sundale spit and snarl like never before as he was dragged away by the poles. Once the doors closed behind them, Simon's father told the room to carry on before facing his son. His eyes narrowed again, and Simon saw his life flash before him.

"I expected more from you."

Shame instantly turned to anger that left Simon terrified of the consequences. "That's all? After everything you've put me through, all you have to say is you expected more?"

"You've gotten too close to the holdren."

"And you've pushed him too far!"

"I am doing what I must to see that our enemies are crushed before us! If that means I must shatter every bone in that fox's body, so be it!"

Simon couldn't even feel his insides. *He means it. By God, he means it!* Sundale may be the enemy, but what his father had in mind... that had to go beyond "the needs to defend our nation."

The holdren had done no wrong. He didn't deserve to die. He didn't deserve any of this. Captive yes, as with any enemy solider, but this? He couldn't accept it. Abused dogs were treated better than what Sundale was going through, and now more than ever, all Simon could see in him was their family pet after she had broken a leg. Except Simon couldn't provide comfort for Sundale like he had for her.

"You can't just throw away his life," Simon said. "He wasn't there when Interstar abandoned us."

"I was!" Admiral Solez said. "So were you. Because of them, your mother went to be one of the fallen. She was forced to leave us just when you needed her most."

"You're blaming Sundale for Mom?"

"Interstar threw their lives away. They stood by and did nothing while *five* million families were broken. If I have to do the same to Sundale to prevent it from happening again, then that is what I'll do. I thought you understood that."

"Mom was going to become a vegetable a few weeks later anyway. She volunteered to make her death count for something. I didn't understand that then, but I certainly do now."

"There were treatments. There was a chance. Instead, she had no chance because they did nothing!"

"She was gone, Dad. You can't possibly blame—"

"That's enough, Lieutenant!"

Simon stood in perfect attention. Fear won out to end his outburst. His father glowered over him while all eyes watched his fate unfold before them.

"I see I've been careless," Admiral Solez said. "Let you be alone with the holdren too often. He's clouded your judgment."

Simon held his stance and threw everything he had into one last prayer. "What do you expect? One moment you're *telling* me to find something to use against him, which not only requires I earn some trust but is something you have yet to *ask for*. Then you come out with this ruse, that you didn't clue me in on by the way, which makes it appear as if we are indeed ending his interrogation. When you told me to sit with him, I took that as an indication that I should start treating him like a respected prisoner." Simon glared at his father with far more confidence than he felt. "With all due respect, if anyone has clouded my judgment, it's you, *sir.*"

The two of them locked eyes while the room stood silent as a tomb. Admiral Solez tore into his son with his eyes, searching for something. Simon did his best to show him cold confidence. Deep inside, he was dead. Probably going to be rooming with Sundale after that outburst. Any other man might have already been on his way there. Not much he could do about it now. He'd dug his grave. Best he could do was lie in it and hope his father didn't grab a shovel.

After seconds that felt like days, Admiral Solez broke the silence.

"Either you're the best liar I've ever seen, or you're telling the truth. From any other officer, I'd believe the former. From you, I don't know what to believe."

Simon didn't miss a beat to press his advantage. "Believe what you will, sir. I stand in the truth. If that puts me in the wrong, then I'll go get in bed with Sundale."

Simon's father nodded as the corners of his mouth lifted. "Perhaps you're not as lost as I thought. Very well. You'll get a reprimand for your insubordination, and I wouldn't expect to get promoted any time soon. As for the rest—I expect you to do better, Lieutenant. We need information only Sundale can give us."

"I understand, sir," Simon said. "I won't fail you again, provided you give me more to work with, so I don't assume the wrong things."

"I'm sure you won't. I'm sorry if I wasn't clear, Lieutenant. And I'm sorry I took my frustration out on you, Son. I'll try to be better."

Simon's heart beat so hard he could feel it in his whole body. Talk about close. For a second, he thought he might have doomed himself. Now by some miracle, it sounded like he might have earned his father's respect, however tiny.

Take the advantage where you can get it.

His father headed for the door, then stopped and tossed his head through it when he noticed Simon hadn't moved. Advantage or not, Simon didn't dare say no. He followed him down the corridors and half-way across the base to the medical bay. Scratches on the floor showed signs that Sundale still had some fight left in him. Something soon confirmed as his growls met them the second they entered the medical bay. However, it was the sight of a soldier being rushed into the surgical wing with a face full of blood that caught Simon's attention.

Admiral Solez saw it too. He grabbed a nurse by the arm before he could follow a doctor inside. "What happened?"

"That fox has more kick than we expected," the nurse said. "Literally. Caught the man right in the eye. Even clipped, he had enough claw to puncture the eyeball. He may lose it. Depends on how deep the claw got."

Definitely has some fight left in him.

Admiral Solez let the man continue without comment. He and Simon walked down to the other end of the medical bay where Sundale had been strapped to a bed on his back. He tugged and pulled at his restraints with more energy than they'd seen in recent days. His growls filled the room and drained color from the nurse and guards.

Fear seeped into his ears when Simon's father stepped beside him, though his growls remained furious.

"You're quite a piece of work, Captain," Admiral Solez said. "You've messed with my son's mind, and now you may cost a solider his eye. I must admit, I am impressed."

"Just think what Yarain will do when she finds you," Sundale said.

"Now, now, Captain. Is that really necessary? After everything I've done for you, do we really have to resort to threats?"

"It's not a threat if it happens."

Admiral Solez faked a sigh, then nodded at the nurse. Sundale snarled and fought with all he had, then stopped both when the nurse applied an instrument to the burns on his side. A few seconds later, the burns appeared less red than before. Sundale's ears rose and fell like he didn't know what to feel.

"There, you see?" Simon's father said in a soothing tone. "We only have your best interests at heart. Now why don't you return the favor? All we want, are the transmission codes for the Marcallan prefect."

Sundale's ears went back as far as they would go while his growl returned. Yet as he breathed, his gaze shifted to Simon with more silent pleas. "You won't stop there. I won't doom my pack by helping you."

Admiral Solez's tone lost all semblance of benevolence. "By being in Interstar, you already have. Face it, Captain. You've doomed your entire race by siding with them." Admiral Solez took a sharp breath Simon didn't understand. It was as if it had caught in his throat and he had to clear it before he could continue. Before Simon could think enough to ponder, the breath came out in a sigh. "I could stop that. I could even let you go home. All you have to do, is give me what I want!"

Sundale's ears came up, and he snarled full on at Admiral Solez as he barked more words. "As you humans say, over my ***DEAD BODY***!"

"As you wish."

Admiral Solez pointed to a guard who pulled out a much shorter version of the shocker stick. The nurse pulled back just as the soldier stabbed the shocker into Sundale's chest, drawing a new round of crazed whines from him. They rang in Simon's ears so much he could almost feel the pain himself. *Please God, or whatever being is listening, put an end to it. Stop this madness.* The whines softened when the shocker was removed, and he again tried to pull himself free. The restraints held firm, and his breathing returned to a frantic pace.

The nurse administered another treatment while Simon's father leaned close to Sundale's ear. "The transmission codes, Captain." Sundale only glared at him. Simon's father dropped his head, then stood straight. "Clear!"

The nurse retracted, and the shocker returned. More whines, another headache for Simon, but Sundale held his ground. Admiral Solez demanded while the nurse treated. He only got defiance.

"Clear!"

More agony for Sundale. He was tugging so hard; it was a wonder he didn't snap a tendon. Simon held his stance as best he could while feeling a lump in his throat the size of a small moon. He swallowed several times, but he couldn't get it to drop down. *Compassion is a weakness. Compassion is—*

"Clear!"

Another short burst of pain. Sundale's breathing was becoming erratic. He cringed in pain with a yip when the nurse again administered treatment, almost as if his body could only feel pain now.

Admiral Solez pounded into the bed beside him. "You can end this, Captain! One bit of information. One small morsel, and it will all be over."

Sundale turned his head to look straight at him. He took several deep breaths before finding one he could hold. Then he went still. He opened his mouth as if he might speak, and when Admiral Solez leaned in close, Sundale nipped at him. The tip of the muzzle bounced off the Admiral's chin.

"Gotcha!"

Simon's father rubbed his chin, and took a deep breath like he did when he found out a then six-year-old Simon had just broken the family vase. The current Simon couldn't help closing his eyes for a second. Back then, there was no threat of violence. Today, it was a foregone conclusion.

"CLEAR!"

More echoing whines. Simon forced his eyes to open in case his father was watching. Instead, he saw the man holding the shocker just below Sundale's throat. The whines were quieter but only because Sundale couldn't catch a breath. They still got Simon's ears ringing so much he feared he'd hear that sound for the rest of his life. He didn't know how much more he could take.

One of Sundale's whines turned into a squeak, and then he went silent. His mouth remained open, but no sound came forth. The convulsions were different too. They had become weaker and localized as if caused by the shocker and not a mind trying to pull away. Admiral Solez withdrew the shocker, and Sundale slumped on the bed. Everyone, even the Admiral, stared at him a moment.

"Is he... dead?" Simon asked, almost hoping he was.

The nurse, much to the admiral's disapproval, removed Sundale's muzzle and checked under his chin and in his mouth.

"No, he's alive."

"But that sound... what was that?"

The nurse continued to examine in and around Sundale's throat as he spoke. "Him fainting most likely. For a moment, I thought his trachea might have been seared shut. Looks like he just couldn't take it anymore, and his body ran away and hid."

Admiral Solez threw his hands in the air. "Wonderful. Again, he defies me. Take him back to his cell. We'll try again later."

The nurse and the two guards proceeded to unstrap Sundale from the bed while Simon's father took him aside. "Tell me, Simon. Did he say anything to you that might help us? Did he maybe mention some fear we can use against him?"

"Not that I can think of," Simon said, glad he could sell him on the truth.

"Think hard, Son. It may not be anything clear. It could be as simple as a wince at a particular moment."

Simon shook his head, now hiding Sundale's fear of the other soldiers in the mess hall. *The poor fox has suffered enough.* "I'm sorry, Dad. I can't think of anything. I'll keep trying though."

Admiral Solez sighed frustration. "All right. Let me know if you think of something."

Simon promised he would, to which his father turned and followed the guards as they dragged Sundale down the row of beds.

Simon turned away. For once, he didn't care what they thought. He just couldn't bear to look at Sundale anymore. Even in the silence, he heard him crying out in agony. Saw his eyes begging for help. Simon pounded on the wall, feeling the weight of the debate waging inside his heart.

This has to be right. This has to be—

His thoughts were interrupted by yelling from the far end of the medical bay. One of the voices belonged to his father.

Simon looked down the row to see the guards and his father on the floor with a very conscious Sundale charging toward him. It didn't matter that his hands were still bound behind him. The rest of him more than made up for it. Though his muzzle was slightly lowered, that only let his eyes tear into Simon as if they could slip into his skin and take over. His ears were so flat they'd vanished, and every fang was showing, ready to tear Simon's throat out. His snarl vibrated through the air like some perverse siren's call seeping into Simon's soul.

Simon didn't think. He didn't have time. His hand acted out of pure self-preservation. In less than half a heartbeat, he drew his stunner and fired. Sundale yipped as the impact imbalanced his upper body. With no mind in control anymore, the rest of him convulsed, twisted, and thundered onto the floor from the remaining forward momentum.

Simon's hand remained frozen, terrified at what he'd just seen, then mortified at what he'd just done.

One of the guards rushed to Sundale's body, training a real side-arm on him while the other guard was being tended to by the medical staff. The nurse from before knelt before Sundale and very hesitantly checked for a pulse.

"He's still alive," the nurse said.

"He'll soon wish he wasn't!" Admiral Solez said as he rose from the floor. "Tie his legs, wrap his muzzle closed, then lock him in his cage. Let me know the second he's awake."

Both guards acknowledged, then carried the limp Sundale out of the medical bay, though not before they replaced his current muzzle of their own accord.

Simon, meanwhile, felt his body weaken by the second. The shock of the moment was fading, allowing thought to replace instinct. Except, there hadn't been any thought. The terror of what he'd seen was so fresh he was almost reliving it. *What changed? Days of pleading, now suddenly Sundale wants to kill me? Why? What could possibly drive him to...*

Realization, worsened by memory, hit like a battleship. Sundale never intended to kill him. The display, the charge, all an act. No wonder his eyes were tearing into him. But Simon had missed the message. Sundale was telling him, begging him, "Don't move." He should have realized it. Sundale's ears weren't back to keep them safe; they were down in submission. A stance no canine would show in any kind of combat.

Simon couldn't figure out the endgame, but it didn't matter. He'd made that irrelevant. Worse, he'd guaranteed even worse treatment from Simon's father. The thought of what that might look like sent a shiver down Simon's back that caused the stunner to slip out of his hand onto the floor.

I can't do this. I can't be here for this. I don't care what he thinks of me. I'd rather be on the line than watch another day of... I can't do this!

Simon's father appeared before him. He took Simon's extended hand in both of his and rubbed the life back into it.

"Simon. Simon, snap out of it." Simon shook his head, though neither his breath nor his heart would slow their pace. He did manage to look up at his father, though. "Are you all right?"

Not by a billion light-years. He could only thank whatever being was around for the ability to speak. "Such fury. Such... such... What was that?"

"That," Admiral Solez said, "was his true self. The beast I told you lay within. That's the enemy we're facing."

"I've never seen anything like that. What... what was he planning?"

"I doubt he was. Not deeply anyway. He knows he can't escape. He must have faked fainting so we would let down our guard. He took advantage of that and tried to secure a hostage he thought would earn him a chance."

Simon's eyes widened as he heard the undertone in Admiral Solez's voice. *A hostage he* thought *would earn him a chance? Is his life more important than mine?* Simon's mind tried to reject what it heard while another nurse appeared behind Admiral Solez.

"Sir," he said, "you'll be happy to know Sergeant Suko will be fine. Sundale only left gashes on his arm. As for Lieutenant Sanders, I'm afraid it doesn't look good. We're still checking, but it looks like the claw got all the way to the nerves. Even with a prosthetic, he may not—"

Admiral Solez held up a hand to stop him. "Just let me know if he'll be able to serve or not. I don't need the rest of it."

That's it? A man may lose his eye, and all you care about is whether or not he can still serve? Simon stared at his father while his insides felt like a solid hunk of rock. His hands went to his chest as if he didn't believe he was still breathing. His mind was too far away to know. His legs started shaking as the war raged within.

We stand for humanity. We stand for justice. We stand for the truth.

"The *truth, or* your *truth?*"

Sundale's words knocked Simon to his knees. He couldn't hide anymore. He couldn't lie anymore. He looked at the bear on his arm, at the glowing North star, and felt his stomach outright vanish. Eight days ago, it was a point of pride. Today, the moment he saw it he turned away even as he felt it burn into his skin.

Admiral Solez was on a knee next to him a moment later, a soft voice the only clue he cared. "Simon? Simon, what's wrong? Lieutenant!"

Simon dropped his hands to his knees and waited for the pancakes to come up. When they finally admitted they weren't going to, he slowed his breathing enough to lie once more.

"I'm sorry, sir. I still can't get over that look on Captain Sundale's face. He might as well have been a demon."

Admiral Solez stood him up. "Come on now, Son. You're stronger than this. Pull yourself together. I can't have my son collapsing on the floor while I'm breaking the captain's will."

Simon swallowed his throat so he could keep his face from showing the horror in his heart. "You're going to continue the interrogation?"

"Of course I will. I'm going to make him pay for what he tried to do!"

When he saw the anger, the hate in Admiral Solez's eyes, Simon declared a winner for the internal debate. He couldn't do it anymore. Nor could he just stand by anymore. This had to stop. He had to act, and fast. At best, he'd have a week, but he had to try. There was no choice left.

Simon took deep breath after deep breath to settle himself. When he could feel his lungs again, he stepped to attention to appear the proper soldier Admiral Solez wanted.

"Request permission to be there, sir! I wouldn't want to miss the show."

Admiral Solez threw his arm around the man. He even offered a brief hug. "That's my boy! Come on. Let's see if he's awake yet."

They walked together to the nearest lift. The admiral went on about how he planned to break Sundale's will. Simon pretended to go along, showing more comfort than he'd ever shown, all the while making his own plans.

Chapter 16

That's Only the First Shoe

With the *Alamo* in need of resupply and minor repairs, Jason had the chance to eat a slow lunch in the mess hall while he looked over the personnel updates Yarain sent him. With the pilot of Gold 3 getting tapped for her own squad on the carrier, they were going to need to move someone else into the position. They also were getting replacements for those who hadn't come back from the last battle.

The latter is what had his sandwich and salad sitting like lead pellets in his chest. Or perhaps more correctly, it was the message.

On this day, June 24, 2263, the following soldiers are to be remanded to the Gold Group until otherwise assigned. Exact deployment to be determined by Group Command no later than twenty-hundred hours.

Jason read every name in detail. Good men and women. While some were coming straight out of the academy, they all had the exemplary marks required to earn a posting in a group of such stature. Yet each one, save for the promotion, meant he'd lost more of his group.

It helped that he had a rare chance to choose the replacement for Gold 3. While it didn't happen often, especially in wartime, his group's record earned him the very rare chance to be pickier. They had time to spare, and because the first seven ships each led a squad within the group, HQ liked to give group leaders some choice in their replacement when they were able. Jason only had a few hours and a very short list, but that was still enough for HQ to grant him that chance to fill his command staff however he wanted, provided he did so in a timely fashion.

He liked having a personal touch, even though he hated it every time he had to because it almost always came after a funeral. Doing it so soon after replacing Sundale in the field didn't help any.

At least Carter had come with him. The man had a knack for choosing the best candidates or helping Jason admit he knew who he wanted. Either way, his presence was making up for the rest. What could have been an hour-long search was over in minutes with Jason deciding on Yarain's plan. Gold 3 would be covered from within while the new vacancy would be filled by a young "flipper" – a slang term for a rookie referencing the single falcon wing on their rank tabs – who had some very high marks, but not as many in POSN duties.

As he finished his meal, Jason poured over the clip-com with her information just to be sure. At last, he handed Carter the clip-com while nodding agreement.

"Not my first choice to be sure, but war never allows for such things."

Carter tucked the clip-com under his arm with a shrug. He'd already absorbed it before Jason even got there. "You know the saying, Jason. Better a flipper than a void."

"Not by much. Still, she shows promise. Put her with Gold 12. I'll see if I can get Yarain to work with her, help her get up to speed. The rest are pretty much contained units, so they can take the fallen call signs. Lieutenant Ming, or rather *Captain* Ming, just got promoted, so she can take the open spot on Gold 3. About time she earned that star between her wings."

"Will do. How is Yarain doing by the way?"

Jason dropped off his empty tray, then led the way toward the nearest lift. "Better. She's not as depressed as she was. Still spends a lot of her off hours staring out into space, though. I think the worst is over, but she's a long way from healed."

Carter nodded his understanding with a grim sigh. "She lost her cub and she's been in combat almost every day since. I can't imagine that's easy for anyone. Has Harmus spoken to you yet?"

"Not since I told him. I'm not sure if I got lucky or not. He was out hunting when the bad news pair arrived. Marcy, once she got over them not being for her, insisted it was best *I* tell him. Ironic, really. Right after we lost Sundale, I was thinking I owed him a personal conversation. Can't say I agree with the idea that it include me telling him his only cub is dead, right after I'd promised to protect him, over a comm link no less. I'd give a lot to know if he's angry or just in pain. At least then I'd know in part how to apologize to him."

"Give him time, Jason. He's not the kind of fox to hold a grudge forever. He, like you and Yarain, must first find time to mourn."

"Which I have done as best I can. Every chance I get I bring him up, try to move forward in the grieving process for both of us. We've made some progress. Still, having only one holdren back there has been hard. As have... other things."

"Like *your* promotion?"

Jason stopped short of the lift while he reached for one of his epaulets. He ran a finger along the full silver falcon that now resided there. The ethos said it was a sign of the command presence the soldier now had as well as the combined support of those under him. In practice, he'd yet to feel that second part somehow.

"He always said he felt it coming," Jason said. "Like someone was waiting for the right moment. Now that it has... I never thought reaching Lieutenant Colonel would hurt so much."

Carter put his hand on Jason's shoulder which helped but also threatened another round of tears.

"Sundale would be proud, Jason," Carter said. "Just as we all are."

Jason managed a weak smile, though it did push back the tears. "In Sundale's stead, eh, Captain?"

"Something like that."

Jason nodded his thanks while calling for the lift. Before it could arrive, PAICCA chimed in from his wrist-com. "Lieutenant Colonel Harlem. Marshal Garmon wants to see you in her office."

"How urgently?" Jason said on reflex.

"I believe her exact words were, 'PAICCA, I need you to get Colonel Harlem in here immediately.' And before you ask, she did *not* sound angry."

Might almost be worse. Last time a higher up wanted to see him that urgently, he was sporting a new scar a few days later.

"Tell her I'm on my way." Jason turned to his wingman. "Guess I'll have to get off early, old friend. The new recruits are on board and settled, so they should all be waiting for you. You know what to tell the group, right?"

Carter folded his arms over the clip-com like he'd been slighted. "I think I can manage it. I know I'm only a captain, but I'm still useful."

"As a decoy maybe," Jason said, returning the tease.

"Careful Colonel. 'In Sundale's stead' has a lot of meanings."

"Yeah, I know. When he shot at me, he also missed."

Jason stepped into the lift ahead of Carter who was faking a wide mouthed look of disgust.

"Well," Carter said, "that's the last time I come to *your* house for dinner."

"Good, we'll save a fortune in potatoes."

Jason grinned like the cat that ate the canary to which his wingman pouted with a grumble as he entered the lift. They held their poses until the doors closed, then laughed with shared shoves while Jason ordered the lift to deck seven. There, Jason stepped off alone and made the long, long walk over to the starbase, up a few decks, and eventually into Marshal Garmon's office.

Despite her position, Marshal Garmon kept her office quite spartan. Chairs for those coming in with reports, a small couch against the wall for more casual conversations, and only a small smattering of pictures on her desk. The rest of her desk was all work related, though the neat piles of clip-coms suggested a rather detailed system for herself. Otherwise, she had brought no personal touch at all, save for a small British flag on the wall over the door to the outer office. Despite Earth being unified, the nations remained somewhat separate. It allowed national pride, and a few old feuds, to remain. Still, once off world, they had learned to work together peacefully.

That did not mean Jason could relax, however. He entered the office wondering what she had in store for him while holding on to his light mood as long as he could. One is rarely called to a marshal's office 'immediately' without the topic being important. Often it meant bad things for someone, usually the person being called.

Jason stepped up to her desk with a perfect rubber-man salute. "Lieutenant Colonel Harlem, reporting as ordered, Ma'am."

Marshal Garmon returned his salute without standing. She indicated one of the chairs in front of the desk. "Take a seat, Colonel. You're going to need it."

As if the comment itself wasn't bad enough, her voice held so much gravity it sounded like she was about tell him Earth had been destroyed. Jason took his seat, now more than ever convinced the meeting was not going to end well.

Marshal Garmon continued once he was seated. "Five days ago, we received an encoded message marked urgent. We didn't know what to make of it at first since it wasn't sent from anyone in the United Systems Republic."

"Who was it from?" Jason asked, more than a little confused.

"No one knows. We haven't been able to identify the signature on it. All we knew for sure, is it held over fifty gigabytes of information."

Jason's eyebrows raised in mixed curiosity. "That's quite a random message."

Marshal Garmon nodded. "Indeed. Obviously, it piqued our interest. With dozens of safeguards in place, we opened the file, and found scores of tactical information inside. We have since spent every effort we could spare into confirming it. Including one very specific item."

Here comes the first shoe. "And what item is that, Ma'am?"

Marshal Garmon looked away as if she were ashamed. Jason waited with folded hands, not wanting to pressure her or think about how bad this was about to get.

"Colonel," she said, coming back to him. "We have just confirmed that Captain Sundale is alive."

That's... quite a shoe.

At first, Jason's mind went into some deep dark void trying to make sure everything was working right. Then it pressed the ears for confirmation, followed by furious refusal from the heart. Even his internal switch couldn't figure out what to do.

At last, some corner of his mind stepped forward and said, "With all due respect, that can't be possible. He was hit with a missile, then buried under a mountain. There's no way he survived that."

Marshal Garmon gave another heavy sigh. "The message explains that. The transporters were taken over by Polaris forces during their counterattack. How, we don't know, but that's why you suddenly couldn't use them. They were hoping for prisoners, and they got one. More than that, we've already confirmed it. A scout fighter on the border was able to detect Sundale's energy signature within a Polaris base, which the messenger so kindly pointed us to. There's no doubt, Colonel. He's alive."

At last, Jason's heart began to accept it. Somewhere, he apologized for his lack of professionalism since he was more stuttering than talking. His mind kept replaying the fireball followed by the avalanche that had—that he *thought* had killed his best friend. Part of him tried to mention the idea that he'd left him behind, but it couldn't get through the confusion.

Sundale was dead. Had been dead. Okay, they still hadn't managed a proper funeral yet, but everyone was going about their lives as if he were dead. Because he was. Jason had seen him die. Now, apparently, he hadn't. Worse, Sundale was a P.O.W.

The thought of what Sundale must have gone through since his capture turned out to be a blessing. It cut through the emotion to allow the mind to process the moment. Marshal Garmon was known to care about her soldiers but not this much. Admiral Redding could have given this report just as easily. She wanted something more from him. Something that could still be rated as 'not good.'

Jason still had to fight through his emotions to ask the question he feared the answer to. "I... I get... I get the feeling you didn't call me here... just to tell me this."

Marshal Garmon offered a soft smile that left Jason feeling a touch optimistic. "Indeed not. The base in question is just under two days from here at fleet maximum. The message came with a detailed rescue plan that we are preparing for as we speak."

Now it was Jason's heart that took over. It snapped him into perfect attention while his switch flipped enough keep himself under control. "Ma'am! The Gold Group would like the rescue mission!"

Marshal Garmon nodded while rising to her feet. She handed him a clip-com. "That's why you're here, Colonel. I had a feeling you might need a chance to calm yourself before you addressed your group. Don't worry, Colonel. Your record more than proves your ability to serve together, and this is quite the shock. More to the point, I thought you'd want to tell them yourself. I understand your group has already assembled?"

Jason was already skimming the information, a little embarrassed at the disrespect though not worried since Marshal Garmon wasn't reacting to it. "Only some of them, Ma'am. We have some new additions and reassignments that need to be worked out. I was on my way to do that when you called. Carter—Captain Gomez should be doing that in my absence now."

"Well, then I suggest you gather the rest of the group. The task force leaves at oh-six-hundred tomorrow. They'll need to be briefed before then."

Just wait till Yarain hears this one. "Understood, Ma'am. I'll make sure..."

Jason trailed off as the thought soured much of his mood. Yarain had been hit hardest by Sundale's loss. To have her find out in a bombshell like this... no, he couldn't do that to her. She needed to be told in a private setting.

When Jason read how they planned to extract Sundale, his heart sank further. In a matter of seconds, his mind added Sundale's situation, plus how long he'd been in it, plus what had been done to him, multiplied by what he knew about the Holdren mentality. The result he came up with meant he had another reason to talk to Yarain alone, provided he could convince Marshal Garmon.

"Something else, Colonel?" she asked.

Again, Jason felt embarrassed for standing still so long. Then he buried it under professionalism. "As a matter of fact, yes, Ma'am. I see here we plan to use a Vesper team to extract Sundale?"

Marshal Garmon again nodded. "That's right, Colonel. COB Team is already gathering their gear."

"With all due respect ma'am, I'd like Yarain to lead that team."

Marshal Garmon now stared at Jason long, hard, and with shrinking eyes. Then it vanished in favor of folded hands, though the eyes hadn't returned to their normal size. "Are you sure that's wise, Colonel? This is her cub we're rescuing. I know she's proven it isn't a problem, but it may still impair her judgment."

Jason shook his head. He knew he'd put himself in a minefield, but he stood firm in it all the same. *No turning back now.* "Quite the contrary. Nothing will focus her mind more than being responsible for her cub's life. In addition, she is naturally built for stealth, she's led small teams before, and I've seen the talents of a unit leader within. I think she'd do well."

"We can't be sure of that, Colonel. A mission of this magnitude has to be flawless."

"All the more reason for Yarain to lead it. If this random message is to be believed, then Sundale has endured severe and possibly damaging torture. If his mind has been adversely affected by it, then the best thing for him to see kicking down the door is his mother. Better still, his *first* mother. No one, not even me, will hold the kind of instinctual trust she does.

"More than that, she herself spent three years held captive by raiders. She'll understand exactly where Sundale's mind will be and how to deal with it. It will guarantee a calm and cooperative disposition from Sundale. Something they may not get with an all-human team."

Marshal Garmon folded her arms while looking at her stack of clipcoms. Jason tilted his back and forth in his hands, unable to keep a lid on his nerves. He knew he was right. The moment he gave the reasons it made perfect sense. Not only would it remove a variable from the mission, but it might force Yarain to admit she's ready for command.

Not if Yarain becomes a variable herself.

The thought did make its case, but Jason rejected it almost at once. The prime example was the time they had to defend a ship from a boarding party. When Sundale took a round to the chest, Yarain didn't flinch. The only reason she'd gone to him was that she was near him, and he had fallen out of cover. Once he was safe, she'd gotten back to the fight without missing a beat despite not knowing if he were dead or alive. It wasn't the only time she'd proven a clear head in the heat of battle either. Having her there to provide an anchor for Sundale would only make the mission more likely to succeed.

The problem was—did Marshal Garmon agree?

Her pout was going in and out in almost perfect rhythm. The longer it went, the more worried Jason got. Being sure was easy. Convincing a Marshal to agree took a good argument and a whole lot of luck. Jason could only stand and wait, unwilling to risk upsetting the balance by offering more without invitation.

About the time Jason wondered about her lips getting tired, Marshal Garmon snapped her head up to look at him. "Are you confident she can be an effective and clear minded commander?"

"Yes, Ma'am!" Jason said without hesitation.

"Very well. I'll inform Captain Harrison of the change and the reason. Have Yarain report to me so I can brief her on the specifics. In the meantime, I'll make sure the Gold Group is gathered and waiting for you."

"Thank you, Ma'am. You won't regret it."

"See that I don't, Colonel. Dismissed."

Translation: If this goes wrong, it's your fault.

The thought was a bit sobering as Jason gave a salute before leaving. He still had no doubt it was the right call, but there was always that one voice asking if there really was *no* doubt. It didn't help the flurry of emotions that hit him as he started the long trek back to his quarters aboard the *Alamo*.

Despite his conversation with Carter, he now realized that in his own way, he'd started to bury Sundale. He was clicking with Captain Gilnt who had assumed Sundale's position after her promotion. The nightmares were far less frequent, and he could look at Sundale's picture without falling into tears... most of the time. There were moments, sure, like his promotion ceremony. There were supposed to be two holdrens there, not one. His quarters felt a little emptier too, but that had fallen into the background. Just yesterday, he'd walked in, and throughout the entire day, he didn't once feel a twinge.

Now all of sudden, it was all different.

Sundale wasn't just alive; he could be rescued. He *needed* to be rescued. A part of Jason finally cursed himself for not being sure of Sundale's death. He'd left him behind to be tortured, brutalized. It was his fault Sundale was in that condition.

Fireball, followed by avalanche. What were you supposed to think?!

Only made it worse, really. Now he was mad at himself for being mad at himself. A vicious cycle that was always hard to break. Then, even when he did break it, he still had a hard time getting his mind to accept the change of Sundale's status. Yesterday, he was dead, still without a proper funeral. Now, he was alive, and in need of help no less. Jason had to wonder if he'd be able to accept it, even when he finally saw his old friend again.

That left him more uneasy than ever about breaking the news to Yarain. How do you tell someone their child, who they watched get killed not that long ago, was actually alive and in enemy hands? To say nothing of what'd been done to him during that time. If Jason held himself responsible, what would Yarain think? Where would he start with her? With Harmus?

Jason instantly put a pin in that thought process as he made his final approach toward his quarters. *Telling Yarain is going to be hard enough. I'll deal with him later... somehow.* He almost deleted the section about Sundale's torture but decided to leave it since she'd find out sooner or later. *Might as well let it all come out at once.*

A tactic he finally decided on by the time he entered his quarters.

As he often did, Jason found Yarain laying on the window seat with her head on her paws and her gaze drifting through the window. At least it didn't demand her attention anymore. When the doors closed behind him, Yarain looked his way with her ears up and eyes alert.

"Jason?" she said. "I thought you were talking with the group about the new members."

Just let it all out. Just tell her... what and how?

Jason walked to the couch while holding the clip-com to his chest like it might offer protection. "Yeah. Will you come here please? I need to talk to you about something."

"*SURE*," Yarain said, more yip than speech. She hopped down and sat in front of him as he sat on the couch.

The words got stuck in his throat, several times. *Where do I start?* The lump grew into a boulder as she waited with nothing but curious attention.

When he couldn't speak, she did.

"What's wrong?"

"Nothing's wrong," Jason said. "That's the problem."

"Jason, take a deep breath, and start at the beginning. Don't try so hard."

Oh, I wish it were that easy.

Jason set the clip-com beside him while swallowing the asteroid in his throat. When he still couldn't get the words out, he took her suggested deep breath and leaned forward with his hands folded between his knees.

"They found him, Yarain," Jason said.

Yarain's head tilted in confusion while her ears flicked thought. "Found who?"

Jason somehow kept his tone calm and level. "I... they found Sundale. They... they found him."

This is going well.

Yarain's hackles started rising as did her ears. "Jason don't toy with me."

"I'm not toying with you, Yarain. I'm trying to find a way to say it. They found him. He's in enemy hands but... he's alive. Yarain, he's alive."

Jason could almost see her mind rebooting behind her eyes. *I wonder if I looked like that a minute ago.* As it did, Yarain's breathing grew heavy only to calm a moment later. Her fur fell flat, but her ears hadn't moved.

None of it kept her voice from wavering when she spoke again. "What's being done?"

"A rescue mission is being prepared as we speak," Jason said.

"And us?"

Jason allowed a wry smile to form. "We'll be there. The task force leaves at oh-six-hundred tomorrow. I plan on going straight to the group from here to brief them on the mission. Marshal Garmon already has them gathering."

For a second, Yarain went stone still. Then she sprinted toward the door, stopping as it opened to look at Jason like a dog waiting to play. "What are you waiting for?"

The strength to drop the second shoe. Jason rose to his feet with the clip-com in his hand, surprised at how calm he sounded considering the thunder in his chest. "You're not going to be there."

"*WHAT*?" Yarain stared at him a moment, only to have her ears and tails fall in total submission. "Jason, no. I *HAVE* to be involved in his rescue!"

"And you will be. In fact, you'll be playing the most important role." Yarain's ears wavered between submission, anger, and perked curiosity. Jason knelt before her with a confident smile that froze her ears forward. "You're going to lead the extraction team."

Yarain's ears perked further. "Excuse me?"

Jason raised the clip-com. "Marshal Garmon is sending a Vesper team in to extract Sundale. I convinced her to give you command of that team."

Jason braced for a different kind of battle when Yarain backed away with falling ears. "Thank you, Jason, but no."

"And why not? Sundale is likely to be a bit feral when they find him. They're going to need you there to keep him calm."

"I'm not a commando."

Jason stood up and folded his arms over the clip-com. "No. You're a Holdren. A naturally built predator, and by your own admission, the former leader of a pack. To say nothing of your little stunt on Phoenix Perch and the training you did with Terrines early on. This mission is going to require speed, stealth, precision, and someone who can not only adapt to whatever happens but can ensure Sundale's emotional wounds don't jeopardize his own rescue. By my calculations, that fits you perfectly. You know what it's like to be a Holdren held captive. I can't think of anyone better suited for this mission."

"I'm not a commando, Jason," she repeated. "I'm not ready to command either."

Jason rolled his eyes. He nearly growled himself as he dropped the clip-com to his hip. "You ever thought about what might happen if you did well? No, I'm serious. Yarain, sooner or later you're going to be tapped for command. It's inevitable. You have too much to offer to sit behind me the rest of your career. Now, despite your fears, I have *full* confidence in you. You *are* ready for this."

Yarain's ears tried to come up but failed. She seemed to be fighting with herself as much as fighting him. Jason searched for some way to help her through it. He found few he liked and fewer still he had confidence in. If only he knew why she was so hesitant. At least then he could attack the core issue.

"I don't know, Jason," she said. "I'm... I'm just not sure."

But I am. Time to let us go, dear friend. Jason sighed out his stress and latched on to the only idea that held any traction. She seemed determined to keep things as they were. If she wasn't going to accept the chance at growth, then he wasn't going to leave her any way to avoid it.

He prayed he wouldn't come to regret it.

"You better get sure," Jason said. "I need my best people on this mission, and that's you. You *are* going to lead that team. That's an order, *Major.*"

At first, Yarain's hackles rose. Then they fell as her ears perked in surprise. "You're promoting me?"

The corner of Jason's mouth lifted as he nodded at her. "They recently rewarded me for my efforts. Carter should be hitting Major by the end of the week for his. It's high time you got the same. Besides, that second star between your wings will come in handy when you take command. Now, are you going to accept the promotion, or shall we argue some more?"

Yarain's ears shifted a moment, but that didn't last long. They soon settled on a forward perk, this one more a show of confidence than dominance—*I think. Sometimes I wish I could speak Holdren.* Regardless, her tails were level and her fur flat.

"All right, Jason," she said. Her words were heavy but void of anger. "I'll do my best."

Glad that's over. Jason nodded at her with a sigh to match his relief. "In your case, that's more than enough. Come on. You need to talk with Marshal Garmon to get the specifics, and I need to make your promotion official. I'm sure you'll be sent straight to your team soon after to get acquainted. I suggest you use every second you have to get to know them. It'll help you lead them better."

"And if they don't accept me?"

"Why wouldn't they?"

"I am swooping in to steal command."

Jason shrugged, understanding her concern but not sharing it. "Be assertive. You'll have orders by then to back you up. Sometimes humans are just like holdrens. Once you show who's boss, they'll fall in line."

"And if assertiveness doesn't work?"

"That's what your tails are for."

Somewhere inside, Jason had a feeling he *would* regret that one.

Chapter 17

First Mother

Yarain stopped at the doors so she could try, and fail, to keep her ears up. Her claws were on the verge of digging into the clip-com in her hands. *There has to be someone else. Someone who can do the job better than me.*

The words held as much weight with her as they had with Marshal Garmon. After the marshal was reminded of Jason's confidence, as well as her own after she made the promotion official, Yarain knew the truth. This was her mission to lead. Her mission to carry.

Her pack to protect.

Let's hope I do better this time.

Yarain found enough courage to force her ears up, then walked inside, trying to appear the confident first mother she lost long ago. She still couldn't find her as she scanned the room and the soldiers in it.

In general, the space looked like a locker room with a separate stall and cabinet for each of the four men and two women inside. The stalls themselves held equipment for each soldier as well as a personal item or two that, as in the case of a shirt hung on the wall, were displayed more like decoration than anything practical. Otherwise, they all seemed to have the same collection of light and heavy weapons, a few armor choices, and other secondary gear. One solder in particular seemed to have half the armory stuffed in her stall, including a couple of weapons Yarain didn't recognize.

The team was busy checking their gear or, in one case, arranging sev-eral vials and medical utensils into a pack as if they might explode if not put in just right. All of that stopped when Yarain stepped into the middle of the room and gave a soft ruff to announce her arrival. The team offered a silent salute, then returned to their work without a word or reaction when it was returned. All except for one soldier on the far side that set his rifle down and headed her way.

Yarain worked hard to keep her ears forward as this tall, slender man walked toward her. He had a head of short, dark-brown, almost red, hair that went with his hazel eyes almost perfectly. It made his full, yet not chubby, face seem firmer than it was. Though that also came from a smooth gait that spoke of confidence as well as agility. She half expected to learn he was a gymnast or figure skater. Were he a Holdren, he'd make a fine first father.

Her eyes fell on one of the four tabs above his nameplate. A falcon with swept back wings that had a shield on its back with a blade sneaking from beneath the top of the shield and a grenade tucked under the bottom of it. "The Falcon," which was different than '*a* falcon' for officers, was not easy to earn. It made Yarain's simple pilot's wings and POSN tab feel cheap. Her only other tab was one she earned passing a combat infiltration course in the academy. *Probably better than me even at that, yet here I am to take his place.* The thought didn't make her task any easier as the man snapped into a picture-perfect salute before her.

"Ma'am," he said. "Captain John Harrison, leader of COB team, affectionately known as the Cobras."

Yarain returned his salute, still trying to keep her ears all the way up. "As you were, Captain."

Harrison stood with his hands behind his back, stiff as a board. "I'm honored, Ma'am. It's not every day we're graced by one of the greats. Is there something I can do for you?"

I thought Jason said they were expecting me. Yarain couldn't understand how they didn't know she was coming. The only thought that made sense was that Marshal Garmon didn't say *why* she was coming, though that too had her confused. Why wouldn't the team be alerted to a command change, however temporary?

Whatever the reason, it appeared that Yarain would be breaking the news to the commander herself. *As if this wasn't going to be hard enough.*

She swallowed a sigh at being called a "great" while handing Captain Harrison the clip-com. While he read it over, she decided to sum it up for the team as much as him. "By order of Lieutenant Colonel Harlem and Marshal Garmon, I have been placed in temporary command of COB team for the upcoming mission."

The team burst out in protest.

"What?"

"They can't do that!"

"What's wrong with them?"

"She's not qualified!"

Captain Harrison motioned them to silence while staring up at Yarain. This time, her ears were easy to control. They were straight and forward in response to the challenge she saw in his glare. She could almost see his ears turned forward just as hers were, even though human ears didn't move. Were he a Holdren, he almost certainly would have been growling. Yarain kept hers silent, half because she couldn't find the confidence to back it up, the other half because she knew it wouldn't help.

"I was hoping the marshal's message was a joke," Harrison said.

Since when do marshal's joke? "It's not."

"So I see. Apparently, I'm going to need to go up the food chain before an unqualified pit gets my team killed."

Yarain almost thanked him. His use of the less polite term for fighter crews gave her enough fire to fight past her fears for the moment. She allowed her hackles to ruffle a bit, even letting a growl seep into her words as she spoke.

"I have more experience on the ground than you think."

"More than me and my soldiers who have spent hours training our skills, learning to anticipate each other's moves? I don't care how many missions you've been on, Ma'am. You need a few more tabs to lead Vespers."

Yarain's growl grew loud enough to fill the room. An irony that was not lost on her considering how much she'd resisted this assignment. "That'll be enough, Captain. I ***AM*** leading this team. That's an order from *three* superior officers."

Captain Harrison didn't even flinch. If anything, he stood straighter.

Yarain had to keep a tight hold on her instincts. If he were a Holdren doing that, she'd have her jaws on his throat before he knew what hit him. In the present, she merely let her hackles rise in full. To his credit, Captain Harrison still didn't react nor did his scent change.

He drew a breath to speak. Yarain barked first. "***STUFF*** it! You have your orders. If you don't like them, you can stay behind."

"With all due respect, Ma'am, I'm going to do one better. I'm going straight to the marshal to save my team from a dangerous element."

He walked past Yarain for the door, and she felt the first mother blood boil within her. When she turned to face him, she didn't see a soldier. She saw a young pack member she'd be biting hard enough to draw blood. She almost pinned him anyway, though she knew it wouldn't work.

Her training had one way to deal with him, but her blood and Jason's joke gave her one she liked better. She curved her outside tails around and fired two short bursts over Harrison's shoulders. While the 'setting' wasn't enough to cause any damage to the wall, it was more than enough to make her point. Harrison dove for the floor while his team rose, some going for their own weapons.

"As you were!" Yarain said in full snarl. All froze in their stance, though none lost any color – something she noted with approval behind her anger. "Do I have your attention yet, *Captain*?"

Harrison sprang to his feet heaving equal fury. "Are you insane?!"

Yarain let her lips curl up, showing the fangs she so very wanted to put against his skin right now. She also reminded herself that humans needed more words than a Holdren would.

"No. I am in command. By order of Marshal Sharon Garmon, I have been directed to lead ***THIS*** team, on ***THIS*** mission! You can accept that and help me integrate, or you can sit in the brig while we do our best without you. Your choice." While Harrison seemed to consider that choice, she took a breath so her snarl could fade, but not her glare. Again, her training wanted to say one thing, but her blood had other ideas. "I know I'm swiping your command from under you. ***THAT'S*** why I want *you* to help me lead them well. It's the only way I can keep them alive *and* rescue my cub. So, what will it be?"

She and Harrison stood locked in battle for a moment that felt like hours. Both glared their challenge, neither stepping away from their packs. The lack of fear she found made her respect him all the more. He clearly knew what she could do, but he refused to back down. She could only imagine what he was like on the battlefield. She hoped she would get the chance to learn even as she prepared to pin him, Holdren or not. *If that's what it takes, then that's what I'll do.*

As if he could read her mind, Captain Harrison suddenly dropped his glare, which then became a nod. "Colonel Harlem was right. You do have an iron will." *Huh? What does that have to do with anything?* The confusion sent her ears up and kept her from reacting as he again walked past her to stand before his team. "As you were, Cobras. I've seen all I need to."

The team returned to their checks like nothing had happened. Yarain on the other hand traded all her anger for pure confusion. Her fur had fallen, but her ears were only getting straighter.

Captain Harrison turned to face her with a slight cringe. "Sorry about that, Ma'am. Marshal Garmon ordered me to test your ability to handle an insubordinate officer. She wanted to see if you could *take* command. And take it you did. A soldier would have to be a fool to think you incapable."

Yarain had to wait for her mind to catch up. When it did, her growl returned, but softer and not meant for Captain Harrison. *I'll have to log a letter of complaint about this.* A threat she knew she'd never act on. Deep down, she understood the need. A proper pack always had those that tested the members. They would make sure a first parent could take charge, a necker – what humans would confuse as a 'beta'— could end a fight, a blunter could prevent one in the first place, and so on. The need to ensure a first parent could *be* a first parent made sense to her. She just didn't like the way humans did it nor did she like Jason being a part of it.

Whatever her future actions, Yarain let her anger and confusion fall from her like lost fur. She met Captain Harrison with a more even, respectful stare. "Thank you, Captain. But let me be clear; I am in no mood for practical jokes or any more tricks to test my ability."

Harrison nodded, though otherwise remained stoic. "I know. I've already explained the situation to the team. They know what this means to you, and with your service record, we know you won't lose your mind because of it."

"You sound awfully sure of that, Captain."

Harrison chuckled while folding his hands in front of him. "I know I'm right, Ma'am. When you do this job long enough, you learn to tell. In you, I see a great soldier who's only just begun to bud. Case in point: I have *never* seen an infiltration tab, pilot wings, and POSN tab on the same uniform. It's nuts. And it's damn impressive."

It's a good thing holdrens can't blush. Well, they could, but for them it was a soft fall of the ears with the whiskers pulling back a touch as well. Most humans would think it fear or submission. Could have been worse. The thought of her white face suddenly going red left her ruffing amusement, further fueled by the description that had just been used for her.

"I'll try not take that personally, Captain," she said.

Harrison nodded with laugh of his own. "Come on. If you're going to lead us, it's best you get to know us."

Captain Harrison indicated an older soldier with a full six tabs above his nameplate, and plenty of bulk. It wasn't even muscle-builder bulk like some humans had, the man was simply huge. As he rose, his eyes very nearly met Yarain's, yet his shoulders were wide and his hands bigger than hers. His hair was a soft-black and cut military short, which only added to a head that looked thick enough to crack through a wall. Yarain knew his position long before Captain Harrison spoke because of the air he gave off. The man was a perfect necker and not someone she ever wanted to see angry.

"Major Yarain," Captain Harrison said, "allow me to introduce COB Two, Captain Harry Fickle. Though most of the time he goes by 'Master Yoda', or just "Yoda.'"

"Why does that name sound familiar?" Yarain asked.

Captain Fickle folded his hands against his chest while appearing very confident. "A pleasure to meet you it is, Major Yarain."

Yarain looked to Harrison for more answers, to which he just closed his eyes in a cringe. "He's an archiver, Ma'am. Much like Colonel Harlem, I understand, though, in the case of Captain Fickle here, it's much worse. Colonel Harlem, like most archivers, just has a focus on which kinds of old shows and movies he likes."

"Now I remember," Yarain said. "Jason has an interest in some old show called Star Trek, though anything with a fighter seems to appeal to him."

"There's a shocker. As for Yoda, he not only has a laser focus for what he likes, in this case something called Star *Wars,* but he's probably the only man alive who can quote all of the movies, word for word. I blame his father."

"As well you should, sir," Captain Fickle said in a normal if heavy voice. "He was the one that indoctrinated me, just like his father before him."

Yup, that sounds like Jason.

Captain Harrison continued after a shake of his head. "All that said, it's more than just his fandom. Despite the crazy person you see before you, there's a reason he's my number two. When I'm being stupid, this guy saves my neck. And on the field of battle, he has no equal, not even me. You've heard of people you don't want to meet in a dark ally? You don't want to meet this guy in *any* ally. He's that good."

I don't doubt it. By now, Yarain's nerves had begun to fade. Enough that while she didn't know anything about Star Wars, she knew that masters were often supposed to get a bow of respect. As such, she offered one to Captain Fickle as a gentle tease.

"Nice to meet you, Master Yoda," she said.

Captain Fickle returned to his earlier persona with a broad smile. "A good addition to our team, you will make."

Chapter 18

Last Stand

Sundale stared at Admiral Solez from inside his cage. He tried desperately to pull together another ounce of resistance, but neither his will nor his body had any left to offer.

His ribs were showing more than ever, a testament to how long it had been since his last full meal in the mess hall. His mind had little more to offer. His arms screamed any time he moved for even a token struggle. His legs weren't much better. Both had been bound since his desperate attempt in the infirmary. They had begun to swell more than before, the color wasn't right, and they hurt with even the tiniest of movements. This also meant he continued to suffer the indignity of his own urine and feces staining his body with no hope of ever getting clean again.

Even if his limbs didn't hurt, it wouldn't change anything. He had no reason to move. He couldn't stop them. He couldn't fight them. He could only watch the shocker in Admiral Solez's hand, drop his ears – which also hurt, and wait for another burn to be added or made worse.

The admiral's son stood behind him like he always had. He still hadn't participated, but he hadn't tried to stop it either. In fact, he'd done nothing but stand there, every day, and watch. The man stood still like everyone expected him to, but Sundale could see the turmoil in his eyes. He could sense the tension, feel it with every step transmitted through the floor as if it were sent via a comm link. It was a battle to maintain control, to which Sundale could relate as he held on with the last shards of his own.

Shards Admiral Solez continued to remove one at a time. "I grow tired of this, Captain! I want those codes. I want them now!"

Sundale stared at the young man behind the admiral. Once again, the holdren made sure to make eye contact. It was his only way to beg for help. But Simon Solez never moved. He remained still like the good soldier he'd become since the infirmary.

I should never have shown my fangs.

The wounds Sundale gave himself only made the real ones that much worse. His plan to show his true self, maybe even break the admiral's "compassion is a weakness" rhetoric, had backfired in the worst possible way. Instead of creating doubt, he'd been shot by the very man he'd hoped to influence. It wasn't even a real weapon, either. At least then he'd be dead. But he'd awoken hours later, bound, muzzled, and caged once more.

The first man he had seen was Simon. The young man had knelt in front of his cage, their eyes had met, but when Sundale pleaded for help, there was no shadow there. The holdren had heaved breath after breath trying to find it again. It had to be there. Buried deeper perhaps, but still there. It never was. Even in private, the eyes, turmoil or not, never wavered. That moment had hurt more than all the days of torture combined, for it was the day his hope died.

Sundale's one mistake had cut off his only chance of escape. Where there had been a raging battle, now there was only irrelevant resistance. There was no weak link to exploit. Even now, as Sundale tried in vain to find that shadow, he found a firm soldier awaiting orders.

Simon had made his choice. He'd chosen his father.

Sundale closed his eyes in acceptance. He wanted to recite his rank and serial number, but the words never even made it to his lungs. Instead, he could only wait for the shocker and feel his skin burn with fear. More than anything, he wanted it to end. He didn't care how anymore. He just wanted to stop feeling pain. He wanted to stop being afraid. He wanted... he wanted someone to kill him.

He got the shocker instead. Sundale could feel a new bruise coming as his whines again echoed off the walls. Ironic that the only sound he could easily make anymore was one of pain. When it stopped, he could only pant and cringe as he tugged at his bonds again. Each movement felt like he was losing skin. His stomach was long gone to some safe place he wished he could follow. When he tried to find it, he found only more fear.

What little thought he had floated to that one moment in the mess hall. The few seconds he'd allowed himself to believe, to hope. He was free then. Freer than now, which wouldn't take much. He'd had a full stomach too. Cold or not, he was fed. For that single moment, he'd let himself think it was over.

Then it ended. Admiral Solez had come out again and restarted the whole thing. Sundale longed for that moment now. He'd give anything to go back there. Even a minute with no fear, no pain, would be worth everything.

"The codes, Captain. Now!"

Sundale tried to growl. He whined instead. There was nothing else left.

Admiral Solez tossed the shocker against the wall with a clamor. Sundale let his eyes open. They found the admiral with his hands on his hips. Every guard shuddered under the weight of his glare. The anger was real, but Sundale feared what it would bring.

Except Admiral Solez didn't do anything else. He stormed out without a word or even a half-hearted motion toward anyone. Those in attendance looked at each other, some asking what they should do. Simon suggested they give it a minute, then he'd check.

Meanwhile, Sundale got his moment. Though he tried to stop himself from feeling that grain of hope, he wanted it too much. *I did it. I outlasted him. He'll kill me, keep me here, let me starve, it doesn't matter. It'll end. Finally, it will end.*

He was close to crying, even though holdrens didn't cry in that way. For the first time since the mess hall, he could feel himself again. He could feel his skin, what remained of his fur, even his bare tails. He was beginning to feel like a Holdren again.

Then it all came crashing down.

Admiral Solez soon returned, large clippers in one hand, and a dagger in the other. One look at the tightness in his face, at the fury in his eyes, and Sundale knew it was far from over. He tugged as hard as he could, whimpering through the pain. It was more of a weak withering, really. Fear constricted his chest into the size of a gain of sand. His lungs got even smaller, though they still found the breath to whimper. The struggle became a constant shudder as he wondered just what was in store for him. He tried to reclaim his will, but he'd relaxed too much. He had nothing left to fight with.

Admiral Solez knelt beside him, set his tools down, then dragged Sundale out of the cage. Sundale couldn't help whimpering as the grip felt like claws ripping into his whole body. His instincts expected to be eaten alive. His mind could only dream of such a fate.

The admiral grabbed his scruff and tugged until Sundale was forced to look at him. Their eyes locked, and Sundale's shudder grew. The only reason he didn't beg was because he couldn't catch enough breath to speak.

"One last chance, Captain," Admiral Solez said. "The transmission codes for the Marcallan Prefect."

Sundale again closed his eyes. He swallowed, breathed, swallowed again, tried to get his mouth at all wet. When he somehow managed to do so, he threw every shard he had into one last stand.

"Bite me," he said. He shook with fury for a blessed second before the fear retook control.

Admiral Solez sighed, more like growled, in reply. A sun burned behind his eyes. There was nothing but contempt for his captive. Then, a scraping sound. An unmistakable announcement of a metal blade rubbing against the floor. *He's going to do it! I made him mad enough. He's going to kill me. He's going to kill me!*

A fatal blow never came. The dagger flashed across Sundale's face, and a louder scream than ever echoed as it slashed across his right eye. Pain coursed through Sundale's entire body, which grew worse as he again struggled. He continued to whine as he felt his blood seep across his face and down onto his neck and chest. His eyes couldn't open. They couldn't bear to see that fire anymore. They didn't want to know what was coming next.

"Fair is fair, Captain," Admiral Solez said, light pleasure in his voice.

"You cost my soldier his eye. Now I will take far more." He pulled harder on Sundale's scruff, forcing his other eye to open and stare at him. With each pause thereafter, Admiral Solez added another shallow cut to Sundale's arms and body, drawing a sharp yip with each one. "I will have... those codes, Captain. I will learn... what you know. I will get... what I want. Or so help me... I will... dissect you... myself!"

He added a long, shallow swipe across Sundale's chest. Sundale whined and tried to shake free, but the admiral's hand held firm to his scruff. The holdren could barely breathe as he felt shoots of pain up and down his body as if the cuts were still coming. He could feel his skin being further stained by his own blood, the streams blending until they met and dripped onto the floor.

No. I won't. I won't do it. I won't put myself before the pack!

He felt the words, but he didn't believe them. Different words were creeping up his throat instead. Words of contrition. Why not? He didn't feel like a Holdren anymore. He couldn't feel his pack. He didn't even feel. Life required a range of emotions. A wide berth of thoughts and feelings. He had neither. There was but one: *it must end.*

He'd tried everything to provoke his death. His captor had too much control. The one man who might have helped him had proved he wasn't going to offer it. There was no way out of this. No weak link to exploit. No way of escape. No hope of death. He had but one path left. He was dead anyway. Why prolong it further?

For Jason.

It was the only shard Sundale still had. The one thing keeping him going. But he had to hold onto it. He had to merge his being with it for even now, as the blood made its way into the corner of his mouth for him to taste, that last shard was becoming harder and harder to hold.

Admiral Solez eventually threw him face first onto the floor. Another yip echoed as every burn, cut, and bruise repeated the impact. This time, hope never formed.

"You leave me no choice, Captain," Admiral Solez said. "Guards! Hold him down."

The two guards rushed in to hold Sundale on his chest. A few days ago, it took two just to hold his paws. Now it took only one to keep his legs stretched out and planted while another kept him from rolling over. More struggles came, but it only drew more whines and more shudders.

The latter grew worse when Admiral Solez picked up the clippers.

"It seems I must take drastic measures with you, Captain." He knelt in front of his captive, almost looking apologetic through his anger. An element Sundale disregarded as an act or delusion. "I will have what I want. And from here on, I will not be kind about it. This is your last chance, Captain. If you continue to resist, then I will start with your tails. Then it will be your ears. Then I will declaw you myself, right here. If you continue to defy me, I will then remove your paws, one, by, one, until you tell me what I want to know!"

Sundale looked into his eyes. He saw that fire, thought he saw a shadow but disregarded it, and knew he was serious. Sundale shuddered and pulled. He told himself every lie he could hold onto. The bonds and the guards held him in place. The admiral rose, tapped the clippers against the floor, then walked very slowly toward Sundale's tails.

Whimpers and shudders were all Sundale had. *It has to end. I have to end it. But Jason...* His helplessness hurt more than his wounds. He was about to lose the one thing that made him unique as a holdren, and he could do nothing. He couldn't even leave a scratch anymore. He looked for Simon, but found him the same immovable soldier he'd been.

Admiral Solez arrived at Sundale's hips. He knelt down and set the clippers beside him. The sound sent a shudder through Sundale so strong he was pretty sure it pulled several muscles. Sundale felt a strap go around the base of his outside left tail. It was tied tight. So tight his tail was starting to tingle only seconds later. *A tourniquet. He's going to do it. I can't, but I can't... I can't...*

Sundale shook and pulled, whimpering almost as loud as when he was being shocked. Those words, they were crawling up his throat. As he felt the clippers being tested on his tail, felt the sharpness of the blades, that last shard, the one for Jason, his first father, was slipping through his fingers by the second. He had to hold on, but he couldn't hold on, but he refused to not, but he had no choice, but –

All light in the room vanished. Sundale flinched at the change, wondering if this was some extra step in his torture. Instead, he noticed the clippers weren't held tight against his tail anymore. As his fear gave way to a sliver of curiosity, he realized they had actually slipped down to the side of his hip. This wasn't Admiral Solez's doing. Something was happening.

Based on the echo of his voice, Admiral Solez wasn't happy about it either. "Admiral Solez to Command Deck, what happened? Commander deck report!" Silence. Solez sighed another near-growl as barely-there emergency lights kicked on. "You three stay here. I won't be long. Don't let him get up."

He turned to leave, paused, then knelt beside Sundale and grabbed the scruff of his neck again. "Don't think this saves you, Captain. Once I've cleared up this little malfunction, I'll be back to finish our conversation."

Sundale found a way to shudder harder. "I'll be here."

It was meant as defiance, but it came out almost as a promise. As if Sundale were promising... promising to... do something some part him swore he wouldn't allow.

Admiral Solez threw him down in response. Sundale could only add another whine followed by more whimpers. Admiral Solez stormed out of the room without another word. Without an order otherwise, the guards continued to keep Sundale pinned to the floor.

Sundale felt someone remove the tourniquet, and maybe some protests about doing so, but both were a thousand light years away. He couldn't get past the truth *he* was facing.

He had one shard of will left, but not for much longer. He might lose his tails first, maybe even both ears, but it wouldn't last. He knew it. The words of contrition had gotten too far up his throat. Even as he tried to tell himself he wouldn't, that his blood wouldn't allow it, with so much of that blood on the floor, he wasn't so sure. How much more could he take? Even now, he was relaxing, but that would only make it worse when Admiral Solez came back. Sundale couldn't hope to keep control. He didn't see any way he could avoid surrendering.

The internal battle didn't help any.

No individual is worth the pack. You were born into that. You know you can't!

I know I want it to end. I know I'm already dead. I know I can't feel my blood anymore. I know my pack isn't here to help me. There is nothing else I can do.

You cannot, you will not, surrender.

How do you know I haven't already?

"Sir? What are you doing?"

The guard's voice drew Sundale ears up, but fear kept his eyes closed.

That is, until he heard a thump accompanied by grunt from the same man.

Sundale looked up in time to see the guard at his torso collapse on him like a ton of bricks. Felt like twice that as it made the injuries hurt that much worse. The impact knocked too much wind out of him to whine. While he regained his breath, his eyes remained locked on Simon. The young soldier swung the shocker hard and fast across the head of the second guard as he rose and drew his weapon. The swing was adapted into an upper cut, which sent the guard hard onto his back, thankfully away from Sundale. After a moment of looking at both guards, Simon tossed the shocker aside before pulling the first guard off the holdren's back.

"What are you doing?" Sundale asked, his voice a distant whisper.

Simon picked up the dagger, and Sundale's ears fell in fear. *I'm not that lucky.*

"What I should have done days ago," Simon said. He reached down and began cutting the ropes from Sundale's legs. "I'm getting you out of here."

Some part of Sundale refound hope, but it was overridden by the truth of the situation. "We'll never make it. *I'll* never make it."

Simon removed Sundale's cuffs without slowing down. "Oh yes we will. I've messed up the main computer so much, it'll take them hours to get it back up. By then, we'll be long gone."

"How?"

"I managed to secure some help. They'll take you out of here."

"What help? We're surrounded by the enemy."

Simon gently removed Sundale's muzzle, then brought their eyes together again. The man he saw was the man he'd seen only four times before. The one the soldier had forced back each time. "That's why I called Interstar. They're out there, right now. They're here to take you home, *Captain Sundale.*"

While the word home remained hallow, the hope of rescue was anything but. To hear his name spoken with conviction, with respect, filled him with a warmth he never thought he'd feel again.

Yet as he tried to get his arms to not complain at each tiny movement, he had to wonder if he wanted to be rescued. Another few minutes, a few snaps of those clippers, and he would have given them everything. He would have put himself before the pack.

No, you wouldn't.

Yes, I would.

Chapter 19

Cobra

Yarain kept adjusting her gear in an attempt to get used it. She'd worn a field pack before, but never one like this. Charges, breaching tools, a field medical kit, the list went on; all of it reachable without removing the pack. Yet it was laid out so it added very little to her profile.

Unfortunately for her, this came with other annoyances. For one thing, it was strapped tighter to her body than anything ever had been. While this kept it from bouncing when she walked, it felt like she had a slab of rock strapped to her back, and her knife was a little farther back than she was used to. Though admittedly not all that heavy, it was still weight her body wasn't used to carrying tight enough to feel like fur.

To say nothing of the armor. It fit fine, but it was a far cry from her fighter crew armor. It covered her entire body from neck to hips in a thick layer that thinned out over the limbs. Because of the need for stealth, her hands and paws were covered as well, though both were so form fitting she would still have full use of her claws. It also sat tighter than even her standard uniform ever had. The limb and paw coverage also meant she lost a touch of her agility – something she'd spent the entire trip getting accustomed to as best she could. Even her tails had a thin layer of protection that ended at the very tips so she could still use them. All of it was colored a dull grey like most armor without an active pigment shift.

Then the helmet, which covered her head except for her lower jaw right at her mouth line, was tickling her whiskers a bit too much for her liking. Possibly a design or manufacturing flaw, definitely a nuisance. She kept her eye holes open since she found the full overlay negatively affected her own natural vision. It didn't make her see worse per se, it just lessened her ability to see motion and adjust to lowlight. At least her ears were left exposed, though they had stiff retractable pockets she would soon be using. It did help that her jaw was open enough for her to use her fangs, it just didn't help enough since soon, all would need to be covered for the sake of concealment.

She focused on trying to get the pack comfortable because it at least felt like it was getting better. Given time, she might get used to it all. At the moment, however, she was close to going crazy.

"Best to let it settle, ma'am," Harrison said, fighting a smile. "It gets lighter once it does."

Easy for you to say. You're used to it. Much like hers, the team's armor was thick and covered the body, arms, and legs. Their helmets did cover their heads in full, though right now the team had them retracted down to the base of the skull. They all carried packs as well, each tuned to their specialty beyond a few common items. They also had very short retractable blades on their arms, apparently used for a quick kill at close quarters.

Yarain slung her rifle over her shoulder, thankful to have something familiar because the weapons Vespers carried definitly weren't. Unlike her simple, twin-barreled plasmoid weapon, their rifles were a little larger, and they had three barrels in a tight, vertical row. The one in the middle was a plasmoid emitter much like her own rifle with a better cooling system, but the upper barrel was actually a laser/stunner combo, and the lower barrel was a heavily modified coil-gun that technology had rendered absolutely silent. She had tried to use one only to find the other weapons too alien for her to use well in this situation. Even Harrison had agreed that she was better off carrying a weapon she knew.

A fact she felt more than ever with the mission so close to being upon them.

"If you say so, Captain." She stepped forward into the cockpit of the slender and wingless Vesper shuttle so she could get a view of the base.

Little more than a troop transport really, though it traded troop seats for storage and other toys. "Any action yet?"

"No, ma'am," the pilot said. "Still no change."

"Are we sure we sent the right signal?"

"The better question, ma'am, is are we sure the guy's virus is working?"

Lieutenant Sarson, the team computer and technology expert and a man strangely well built for being only five-eight, cleared his throat to get her attention. He sounded like a professor when he spoke, though his face was so smooth it looked as if it was incapable of growing hair.

"It is possible, ma'am, that the virus is simply taking longer to work than he anticipated. Crashing a main computer without being detected is no small feat."

"Tried it have you?" Yarain asked, a grin lacing her words.

Sarson tried to act innocent. "On occasion... perhaps. When the... current entertainment is not sufficient for my intellectual needs, one must find a way to... break up the monotony of the day."

Captain Harrison shook his head with a chuckle. "That's our COB Four. Class geek and voted most likely to release a super virus."

"Excuse me, sir. I was voted most likely to create an army of evil robots."

"I stand corrected."

Yarain ruffed a chuckle of her own while watching the base through the forward window. The whole thing looked more like a top than anything else, though the lights dotting the hull, as well as the towers and arrays filling the center both above and below, more or less ruined that image. As did the Polaris insignia so proudly painted on the side.

A very dangerous toy indeed.

A black woman with long braided hair joined her examination of the base. Lieutenant Shillin Rad, or COB Five, had held Yarain's curiosity from the moment they were introduced. Her longer, tighter rifle announced her position as team sniper, though when Yarain looked at her, she saw a cold confidence that suggested that wasn't her only specialty. She'd seen that look in her best hunters back home. The ones that seemed like they could pluck a choice kill from a herd without the herd noticing the member go missing.

When Rad spoke, her voice was as calm as a spring lake, as if you could bounce a stone off it without leaving a ripple. "We sure we'd know if the computer crashed?"

"Without question," Yarain said.

"How so?" Unlike most humans, she didn't sound annoyed at having to ask.

"Even the smoothest crash will kill the lights and wreak havoc with their power systems."

Rad nodded, then returned to her seat without another word or reaction.

Cool as absolute zero. Captain Harrison had described Lieutenant Rad that way. It fit, yet not in the way it sounded. Yarain watched her check her rifle with cold precision and tight focus. She maintained a careful touch as she did, almost like a painter touching up their work. When Rad noticed Yarain's attention, her face remained business, but Yarain could see the woman within retracting like a cub submitting to an adult, which didn't fit the rest of her.

From a human's perspective, her face was so smooth she looked like she was fresh out of the academy. She was thin too, thinner than Jason, but that only added to the contradictory airs Yarain got from her. On one side, the woman wasn't as young as she seemed nor as docile. Yet at the same time, the phrase 'timid as a field mouse' kept coming up, and the search for why had left Yarain chasing her own tails until she got dizzy. As she looked at the woman, she had to wonder just how violent Rad really was.

Furious beeping drew Yarain's attention forward and into the moment. She looked at the console, then at the base in time to see all lights go dark.

"***THAT'S IT***!" she said, almost losing the words in a ruff. "They're down. Move in pilot, nice and steady, keep the cloak intact."

"Yes, ma'am."

Yarain turned to the team, who were already gathering their rifles. She thought back to the kinds of pre-mission speeches she'd heard and tried to expand on what her Holdren mentality wanted to say. *I don't need it, but they do,* she reminded herself.

"Get set. Move fast and silent until we find Sundale. Any alarm will kill him, so keep your shields off until ordered or engaged. The power spike could give us away. Once we find him, no restrictions, but check your targets before you fire. Our informant will be waiting for us at Sundale, and we've been ordered to extract him as well."

"I wish I knew who the guy was," Yoda said. "I don't like being told to hesitate."

"I know, but he's the one that brought us here. In Human terms, we owe him one."

"I'm not denying that, ma'am. I just wish we had more to go on than, 'I'll be wearing a yellow armband.' That's an awfully small detail, especially in low-light overlays."

Yarain tapped next to her eye. "My eyes are better than yours and your gear. Trust me and trust yourselves. The rest will take care of itself."

The captain nodded confidence in reply.

Yarain returned her focus forward with her tails beginning to wave. The thrill of the hunt was starting to thunder in her chest as they approached the base. More so because, for the first time in years, she was leading it. She felt the weight of those lives as if they were more armor on her back, yet to her surprise, that weight was only intensifying her focus. Her mind was running every possible outcome and planning reactions. Her ears were up and searching for every detail that could be added to those plans.

Jason was right. The first mother is still in me. That pack leader was ready to enjoy the hunt, but years of experience kept her breathing calm, her ears perked, and her mind working. She watched everything, making sure she didn't miss a potential problem or advantage. She'd promised Captain Harrison that she'd keep his team—his pack, safe. For the first time, she had no doubt she could deliver on that promise.

Those heightened senses perked further as enemy fighters started launching from the hangers. From the back side of the base came a pair of Polaris cruisers. The forward third of these ships was long and slender, but the rest turned bulky though the entire ship remained smooth.

A set of massive, forward-sweeping wings thick enough to be landing struts sat on the underside where the ship bulked up, followed by another set at the very end of the ship. These cruisers took up defensive positions on either side of the base while the fighters began a patrol around the perimeter.

"Can you handle that pilot?" Yarain asked.

"Piece of cake, ma'am," he said. "You better sit down, though. These shuttles don't have the inertial dampeners fighters do. Don't want you breaking a tail should you fall."

Yarain patted his shoulder with a soft ruff of amusement. "Not much chance of that, Sergeant."

He shrugged with a hum while Yarain took the suggested seat with the team. She laid her tails around the side of her hips since these chairs didn't have holes for them. She had just clicked the strap into place when the shuttle veered hard. The straps caught her, but she hadn't yet stowed her rifle. It went clamoring across the floor despite her best efforts to catch it.

"Yup, she's destined for greatness," Captain Fickle said. Yarain glared at him with her hackles ruffling, despite them being under her armor, which he met with a smile. "I mean that, ma'am. Every one of us dropped our rifle at least once on our first mission. Those that didn't... didn't last long by one definition or another. Some of us think that's our way of using up all of our bad luck before our careers get going."

"Didn't expect you to be superstitious," Yarain said.

Yoda put his fingertips together in front of his chest as he slipped into his namesake persona. "Not superstition, the force. The force chooses who will and will not succeed. Blessed, you have been. In battle, prove yourself you will. Lead us well, you shall."

Captain Harrison leaned over close to Yarain's ear. "In case you missed it, he just voiced his full confidence in you. And he never speaks for himself."

Great. No pressure.

While bracing against another violent turn, Yarain realized it actually wasn't. If anything, the confidence left her more energized than ever. She'd been with them for less than three days, and she already thought highly of them all. To hear they felt the same way made her gear feel a little bit lighter.

"Thank you," Yarain said. "It's been a long time since I had a good pack behind me."

Harrison glanced down the line, smiled, and then the team tried their best to howl. Some weren't too bad, though others were more wounded hound dog than howls. Still, the gesture left Yarain panting holdren laughter for half a minute.

When Yarain recovered, she risked putting a hand on Harrison's shoulder. "Thank you. Though holdrens don't howl like that."

"Well then," he said, "I guess after the mission you'll have to teach us some barks we can use."

"Miracles happen, I suppose. I'll think about it."

Laughs from the team filled the space.

The shuttle never gave another violent turn, but Yarain didn't move from her seat until she felt a soft thump she knew all too well. The pilot quickly confirmed they'd reached the target airlock. Only then did she retrieve her rifle while the team rose and slung theirs over their shoulders almost in unison.

Yarain's ears turned out in mild embarrassment while her mind tuned to the mission at hand.

"Are we locked down?" she called into the cockpit.

A soft click from the shuttle's airlock answered before the pilot did. "Hard lock established, Ma'am. It's all yours."

"COB Four, you're up," Harrison said. "Pilot, keep the toast warm."

"Always do, Sir."

Lieutenant Sarson stepped up to the airlock with the rest of the team standing a few steps behind. All deployed their full helmets, black spots covering the eyes on what were now smooth sheets of armor over their faces. Markings on their arms, backs, and helmets separated them from one another. Yarain's armor held similar markings, but hers were her name and rank since it wasn't built specifically for commando work.

Her tails waved out her nerves as she watched Sarson work, waiting for clearance to proceed. *The hunt is on. May I lead them well.*

Lieutenant Sarson tapped at the console beside the airlock, then opened the shuttle door. Another few taps at the base airlock drew a hum from him. "Guess the guy didn't think about this," Sarson said. "When he crashed the computer, some of the protocols went with it."

"Can you open it?" Yarain asked.

"No manual override outside. I'll have to jack in, input my own protocols. Not a problem, but it will take a moment. And here I thought I'd find a challenge."

"Be quick, Lieutenant. We're on a dangerous timetable here."

"Understood, ma'am."

Sarson pulled a large clip-com from his bag and plugged it into a port beside the airlock. The team remained behind him, rifles ready in case it opened prematurely. All except Captain Harrison, who stole himself aside while rolling his shoulders with deep breaths. When she noticed his helmet had been retracted, Yarain decided to check on him while she waited. When she got close though, the collected man stank of fear. Worse, it was so over-powering, she half expected him to be cowering in a corner.

"Are you all right, Captain?" she said, keeping her voice low.

Harrison nodded as the smell grew. "Fine, Ma'am. Just nerves."

"I've smelled nerves before, Captain. You smell of near freezing."

Harrison huffed with a shake of his head. "You don't miss much do you, Ma'am? It's not what you think."

Yarain stood in front of him with a hand on his shoulder. She tapped at her wrist comm to retract her helmet so her face and eyes could be easily seen, and to get a reprieve from the whisker tickle. "Then what is it?"

Harrison sighed before looking up at her. "They're my team. My pack, as you might say. Every now and then, the nerves get the better of me, and I start thinking too much."

I know how that feels. Yarain perked her ears forward, then forced an awkward nod, hoping he'd read it as understanding and/or support. "Because they're your responsibility. Even though they know the risk and accept it, you still worry. You still feel like it's your job to keep them safe."

"You've commanded before."

She looked past him at the team still waiting on Sarson, again trying to meld what she wanted to say with the extra details humans often needed. "I was a first mother once. What humans mistakenly call an 'alpha female.' It's similar but different. I've also served with Lieutenant Colonel Harlem for a long time. I've picked up a few things."

Captain Harrison gave another sigh while turning to watch his team as well. "We've been through fifty missions together without losing a single member. None of us have even sustained a serious injury. By the law of averages, we're overdue for a casualty. What have you learned about dealing with *those* thoughts?"

"I never think them," she said. When she didn't see or smell a change, she turned him around to face her. "I don't care if it's your five hundredth mission together, it's my first. I promise you, no matter what it takes, I will not lose a single soldier on my first command."

Captain Harrison sighed with a soft cringe. "Please, Major, don't make promises you can't keep."

"I never do."

Harrison stared into her eyes, and the smell of fear vanished. At the same time, Yarain felt her tails calm behind her, as if somehow her own words had silenced them. Something within him reflected a confidence that wasn't all his.

Maybe Jason is right. Maybe this commanding thing isn't so bad after all.

"That's it, we're in!"

Lieutenant Sarson's announcement shattered the moment. Captain Harrison deployed his helmet and rejoined his team with only a moment's hesitation while Yarain had to take a single shake to reset her mind.

After that, the mission took over.

"Color armor for stealth, activate low-light overlay," she ordered, deploying her own full helmet and ear pockets as she stood next to the door. "Pilot, kill the lights."

"Take a round, Cobras!" the pilot said.

Yarain was glad she'd had that explained before hand. Much as actors feel wishing good luck was actually bad, Vespers had taken to using the phase as a way to trigger one's pride. The idea being something like, 'Take a round? Please. Like I'd allow it.' Artificial though it may be, for Yarain at least, it did remind her of the danger she was about to walk nosefirst into. She also noticed some of the others settle in at the phrase, so perhaps they too gained focus from it. Even so, she still found the practice odd.

The lights within the shuttle went out as the team hit a button on their helmets to activate low-light vision. Yarain's eyes needed only a second to turn the dim lighting into near daylight, at which point she took the lead at the air lock. She and the team tapped at their wrist-coms, shifting the color of their armor from dull grey to a pattern of solid black with slight variations to help them blend into the darkness they were about to enter.

Her pack ready, Yarain settled her rifle into her hands, then dropped her muzzle at Sarson with forward ears despite them being concealed in their pockets. He punched the door of the air lock, and it opened to show a quiet base interior so dark humans would have a hard time avoiding each other.

Whoever this guy is, he did good. Even killed most of the emergency lights. She motioned for the team to advance behind her while the pilot and co-pilot took defensive positions within the ship. Each member hugged the wall so quietly Yarain almost didn't hear them. One by one, they knelt behind a support beam until all were within the base and their insertion point was secure.

Yarain took her position at the first corridor intersection, then went flat behind a beam as a pair of fully armed and armored Polaris soldiers crossed the intersection. She took one look at her rifle and knew she needed more agility for this. She motioned for Harrison to lead the team ahead while she secured her rifle on her back. She checked her eyes and ears to be sure they were alone before she shifted into her primal form. As the team moved fast and quiet down the corridors, Yarain stalked her way back into the lead with her nose working and her ears perked. Specialized speakers allowed them to still pick up the faintest sounds despite being covered by the layer of metal. She led the team in spurts through the base toward the cell block.

Yarain's mind fluttered between predator and prey, at times accessing both sets of instincts at the same time. She'd stalk forward, hunting for something to kill, only to dash around a corner and meld with the terrain to avoid detection. *Good thing Fickle insisted on assigning primal-form signals.* Shifts in her middle tail and some leg shakes had been pre-planned and practiced as much as possible. It proved invaluable, as it allowed Yarain to remain in a more natural form without hampering her ability to direct the team and maintain the proper pace.

Except the pace was hardly proper. They spent more time ducking then moving. Patrols were regular, and most carried flashlights, helmets that certainly had low-light vision, or both. Each time they had to hide, Yarain's legs got tighter. She wanted to sprint down the corridor to her cub, but she knew she couldn't. *There had to be a closer airlock.* She knew there wasn't of course, and she knew cutting through the hull would have carried too much risk of early detection. But the moment of venting helped, even though her concern grew with each passing minute.

At one junction, a steady thudding stopped Yarain cold with her ears and middle tail straight up. The team hugged the walls while sounds from the corridors grew by the second. Heavy footing in unison and the rattle of armor suggested they were about to face something much more than a simple patrol. With the corridor fast approaching normal brightness around the corner, she also knew the near-by cover wouldn't be enough to hide them.

Never ignore your path, for any hole you pass could save your life. The proverb rang in Yarain's head as she shook a hind leg while her middle tail pointed straight behind her. She turned around and stalked her way back the way they came just ahead of the team doing the same. She stopped at the doors of a supply closest she'd noted on their way the first time, then perked her ears to check for sounds inside. Hearing none, she hit the door panel with her paw, then led the team inside to hide among emergency repair kits and medical supplies.

Lieutenant Rad closed the door behind them, then all trained their rifles on the door in case they were followed. Yarain's tails arched over for the same while she kept her ears forward to keep tabs on the enemy outside. The patrol kept marching, not as loud as before, but that could mean they had split up or it was just the door dampening the sound. Even so, the closer they got, the lower Yarain's head got. Her ears never fell, for they were needed to maintain vigil, but more than anything she wanted a den to slip into. Based on the racing hearts she heard from the team, most of them felt much the same.

The team held their position, ready to rip through whatever poor soul opened the door. None ever did. The patrol outside marched up to, and then past, the door without slowing down. Yarain held the team in place until she didn't hear a sound for a full minute.

Only then did she relax her tails and posture. "We're clear. Let's move."

"With respect, Ma'am?" Fickle said. Yarain gave him her full attention to encourage him to speak. "This is taking too long. I fear we'll be caught by the reboot before we could ever make it back to the ship."

Yarain tried to find a critique of her skills within his words but found only an honest appraisal of the situation. She decided to offer the same.

"I agree. Unfortunately, I don't see another option. We have to keep moving."

"If I may, Ma'am, I have one. Let me take part of the team. We'll plant some charges in strategic locations, add some confusion for our escape and/or sabotage once we're gone. Either may buy us the time we need. I assure you we won't be seen."

Yarain glanced at Harrison, who at first breathed hard while adjusting the grip on his rifle. She almost saw pulled back ears he didn't have, though she could find no reason for it. It was a risk certainly but not enough to warrant such hesitation. Was there something else in there?

Before she could search for the answer to that, the stress faded into a confidant, if still hesitant, nod of agreement. It confirmed Yarain's own feelings about the suggestion. Everything else evaporated in the heat of the current situation. *I'll deal with the rest at a better time.*

"Take Rad and Hark," Yarain said. "The rest of you with me."

"Copy that," Fickle said. "Completion of charge placement will be Waypoint Pepper."

"Copy. Good... take a round. COB One, let us out."

Captain Harrison opened the door, and the team split on their assigned paths. Lieutenant Maureen Hark, the team demolitionist and the only other member with a full six tabs, Lieutenant Rad, and Captain Fickle went back the way they had come. Yarain led the rest back along their original path with Harrison, Lieutenant Sarson, and Captain Tai, the team medic, close to her tails.

Her group found the going no less slow. If anything, they had longer periods of waiting for the path to clear before they could move ahead. A clock kept ticking in Yarain's head, but she pressed on. Her first worry was reaching Sundale before the computer was rebooted. At least then they had a better chance of ensuring his survival. Ideally, they'd be gone before the reboot, but the chances of that were dwindling by the second.

Feet of corridors felt like miles at the pace they were taken. Yarain's internal clock had hit two alarms by the time they reached the cell block. The scent of old waste matter greeted them there, suggesting at least someone was inside. She sorted her energy matrix to pulse, only to drop it before it built any charge. Normally used to ping for prey like sonar, the pulse would resonate off Sundale's energy matrix as well. While humans, unless they were very close by, didn't have enough energy in their bodies to resonate, the wiring in the walls did. Beyond the low chance of getting a clear ping, there was that thousand-to-one chance it would be detected. Thus, it was ruled out as not worth the risk.

After waiting for yet another patrol to pass, Yarain risked retracting the pockets over her ears so she could perk them toward the door. As good as the speakers were, her naked ears were better. Hearing nothing, she decided that while the pulse wouldn't be much use, she had grown tired of sneaking around. This close to her target, and with time being a factor, she decided now was the time to, as the humans say, 'take the gloves off.'

Yarain exposed her lower jaw before moving to stand at an angle to the door with her ears up and her body low, ready for a sprint. She glanced at Harrison, who hummed softly before motioning for Lieutenant Sarson to take position on the side of the door. Harrison stood on the other side near the control panel while Captain Tai stood with his weapon aimed at the door without anyone so much as looking at him. *A fine pack they are.*

When they appeared set, Yarain gave a soft growl she hoped Harrison understood. *Should have covered that in our training.* He apparently did though since he opened the door before the sound had faded. Yarain burst through, hitting the gap exactly when she had enough room. She held her sprint all the way to the opposite wall, which she braced against so she could leap and fire at whoever she found inside.

She stopped at the wall when she realized the immediate area was empty, though it was the first space to have working emergency lights. Harrison and Sarson were right on her tails, each taking a different direction down the block, with Captain Tai following a second later. All scanned the room with their rifles while Yarain used her own senses.

Despite the growing stench, she found Sundale's scent immediately. He'd been here, recently, as had several soldiers. *So, it's not a ruse. He's really alive!* Deep down, she hadn't really believed it. But her cub's scent merged with her soul the moment she found it. He was near. He had to be for the scent to be that strong.

She flinched when she realized it wasn't just his fur she was smelling. Fresh holdren blood was also there. *Tell me I'm not too late.* Her mother side wanted to tear the room apart looking for him. Her soldier side kept her focused on the moment. The area may have been quiet, but it was not yet secure. She gave another soft growl at Harrison while waving her tails in a warning to be careful. Harrison nodded, then motioned for the team to proceed once Yarain perked her ears in the direction of Sundale's trail.

She may have been keeping herself controlled, but she stayed just ahead of the team, ears forward and nose working in search of prey and family. Neither were found as they passed empty cell after empty cell. Each one brought them further along a growing scent. The blood grew stronger too, which was actually a good thing. *Blood doesn't smell like that when it's cold.* Her cub was definitely ahead, yet she moved slowly, paw by paw, checking every corner for possible ambush.

When she heard a human voice ahead of them, Yarain had the team hold position so she could get a better idea of what lay ahead. She perked her ears forward, zeroing in on the sounds as she would a mouse beneath the soil.

She found a young voice full of concern. "Stay with me, Captain. Don't die on me now, not when I'm so close to getting you out of here."

Yarain's heart soared and shuddered at the same time. They'd found him, but it sounded like he was in bad shape. She had to almost literally swallow her instincts so she could keep herself under control. *Never rush in, even when you 'know' it's safe.* Easier said than done when one's cub is just around the corner. Even so, Yarain held herself back, at least for now.

She glanced at Harrison with perked ears to silently ask for suggestions. He raised his rife in reply. Yarain swallowed an amused ruff before it escaped while dropping her muzzle with forward ears. *That'll do fine.*

She led the team right up to Sundale's cell. They lined the wall just outside, with Yarain rocking her shoulders beside them. *Not yet, Yarain. Wait for the pack.* She waited for Harrison to lean his ear as close to the edge as he could without going over. After a second of waiting that felt more like a day, he raised his weapon again while counting on one hand.

Three...

Two...

One...

GO!

Yarain launched herself into position on the far side of the entrance where she stopped cold facing inward, tails curved over and a snarl on her lips. Harrison and the others were half a second behind her to fill the void, all of them ready to erase any enemies inside.

They found only a young soldier kneeling beside a motionless Sundale. The poor kid nearly jumped out his skin when he saw them. Parts of a medical kit scattered over the floor as his arms flashed up. This let them get an easy view of the yellow armband covering the Polaris insignia.

"Clear!" Harrison said. A soft yip and a shudder from Sundale drew the team's attention to him. There, even Harrison couldn't contain himself. "My God! What have they done to him?"

Yarain's thoughts held the same question word for word, for the dim lights could hide nothing of the scene she saw before her.

Sundale laid on his chest, his tails limp behind him. The fur he once wore lay strewn across the floor, providing a pale distraction to the clear state of his ribs. He was wet as if someone had poured water over him, which seemed likely given the puddle he lay in. A puddle that also had blood, urine, and dissolved feces in it, despite much of it being pushed to the back in a failed attempt to keep it away from him. The stench was even stronger close up, as it all mixed with his shaved fur along the walls. Somehow worse, to Yarain anyway, was the thick collar tight against his neck, as well as the severe contusions on his wrists and legs. When she saw cuffs and cut rope beside him, she knew where those wounds had come from.

But he had plenty of other wounds for her to worry about. A cut across his right eye held it shut, with dried blood covering the right side of his face and muzzle. More blood seemed to have landed on his sides and arms as well. Every drop his own. Contusions, bruises, and burns ran up and down his sides, his legs were swollen and discolored, he had a number of small lesions on his limbs, and his tails were strings trying to tuck between his legs. A shudder of horror mixed with anger ran through Yarain's body when she saw they'd even trimmed his claws. *Someone is going to pay for this!*

With the others giving similar reactions to his condition and nothing else to focus on, Yarain found she could no longer contain the mother within. She rushed to Sundale's side, retracting her helmet so she could rub her bare muzzle against his cheek. She didn't dare let herself check his scent gland. Captain Tai wasn't far behind. Puddle or not, he fell to his knees beside her. His pack hit the floor before he did, and he pulled out a medical scanner while Harrison and Sarson assumed defensive positions just inside the cell.

Harrison tapped at his headset to take over the one duty Yarain had neglected. "COB One to Belly. Passing Waypoint basil. I say again, passing Waypoint basil. Stand by for Waypoint cumin."

His report forced Yarain's soldier side to reclaim control. As much as she wanted to fall apart over her cub, she still had a mission to run.

Sundale didn't make that choice any easier when his good eye opened and locked onto her with all it had. *"Yarain?"* he said. *"Safe?"*

She wanted to lie. She wanted to tell him anything to put him at ease.

To make him not hurt anymore. She didn't, for she remembered her own rescue far too well. She had been feral, angry, ready to tear apart the first non-holdren she could get to. If Sundale hadn't been standing there when Jason set her free... well, there wouldn't have been much left of Jason. As such, she forced herself back into what Sundale needed most. Everything Yarain felt was rolled into a ball and swallowed, where it vanished into her stomach to be dealt with later. All that remained was the first mother. The firm, confident rock that convinced the pack they were invincible even if they were about to die. She used that confidence to convey a feeling of safety and certainty, as if she could create a bubble no one could penetrate. She did allow another nuzzle though, as well as a gentle lick on Sundale's cheek. As much as he needed the rock, Sundale needed the bond of the pack too.

"Not yet," she said. *"Just a little longer."* Yarain looked up at Captain Tai, slowly reclaiming her control. "Can we transport him?"

Tai began digging through his medical kit while shaking his head. "Not a chance, Ma'am. He's too weak. I'm afraid a trip through the transporter would kill him."

The young soldier on the other side of Sundale had since recovered from the shock of their arrival. He now placed a hand on Sundale's back with a cringe of his own. "It's my fault," the man said. "I didn't act sooner. I didn't... I didn't allow myself to see the truth in time to save him"

"Let's not worry about that now, Son," Tai said. "Let's worry about making sure he survives the here and now. Will you two help me roll him over please?"

The young soldier went to Sundale's legs while Yarain took her finesse form so she could take his shoulders. On a three count, they rolled him onto his back with Tai impressing Yarain by running his hand along Sundale's tails to make sure they stayed straight before he landed on them. *He knows how to care for the wounded and is fully capable of protecting them himself.* Harrison's words again. She looked at the tall, tan-skinned man, his face touched by a thin goatee as brown as his hair, and she knew Harrison was dead on. She had no doubt that if someone came to threaten Sundale, Captain Kelly Tai wouldn't need help protecting him. There was too much confidence there, too much focus, and far too big a rifle, to assume otherwise.

Those thoughts died when Yarain let herself look at Sundale again. The wounds only got worse. In addition to more small lesions, she realized that the blood she'd seen before came from multiple cuts all over his body and arms, many buried under blood clots and wet muck that his bathing had failed to remove. There was also a single slash from neck to belly, thankfully shallow, and severe burns all along his sides, on his chest, and at his neck. The young man had applied bio-gel to the worst of the cuts, but it did little more than stop the bleeding.

Captain Tai was cringing at the same time while working with his med pack. "Evil beasts! No offence, Ma'am."

Yarain raised a hand to ease his concerns. "We don't see ourselves as beasts, Captain."

"I apologize, ma'am."

"No need. How soon can we get him moving?"

Tai chose a medicine, then injected the substance into Sundale's arm. "Another minute. I want to be sure my booster has taken effect. Really, he shouldn't be moved at all, but current circumstance don't allow for that."

"What about his eye?" the young soldier asked. "Can you treat that?"

"No more than you have. The bleeding's stopped; that's all we can do at the moment. We can't afford to take any chances we can avoid. That's why I'm leaving that collar on him. We'll deal with both once he's safely aboard the *Alamo*. Among... other treatment."

The young man nodded solemnly.

Faced with nothing to do but stare at her naked cub, Yarain rose and approached the young soldier. "What's your name, Son?"

The young man rose, though his eyes remained on Sundale. "Simon Solez, Ma'am."

A spark from Yarain's memory sent her ears up and her tails waving. "As in *Admiral* Solez?"

Simon shook his head. "That's my father, Ma'am. I'm just a lieutenant junior grade. If only I were an admiral. Then maybe I could have stopped him from doing this."

Yarain couldn't help a soft growl forming within her throat. "Your father did this?"

Simon nodded. "He called Sundale the enemy. Captain Sundale called himself a Holdren."

"And what did *YOU* call him?"

Simon looked at Yarain for the first time. "A scared, stray fox who had done no wrong. He didn't deserve to be treated like this. No one does."

Yarain stared at the young man with stilling tails. She couldn't understand how he ever got caught in that uniform. When he looked back at Sundale, his eyes grew heavy as if he were about to cry. He sounded so sincere, so innocent. To think his own father was responsible for such brutal acts. *I wonder who his mother is.*

She decided not to ask in case it turned out to be a painful memory they couldn't afford. Instead, she silenced her growl while looking straight at him.

"Son, no matter what happens here, you have earned my respect."

Simon dropped his head with a cringe. "I don't deserve it."

"I don't agree, but now is not the time to argue. Stand ready, Lieutenant. We may yet need you." Yarain knelt across from Captain Tai, who was already repacking his med kit. "Where do we stand?"

"We're as ready as we can be, Ma'am," he said. "There's little more I can do here."

"Let's get ready to move out."

"How?" Simon asked. "I couldn't get to a stretcher, and we can't carry Sundale like this. We'd kill him."

Tai huffed amused pride. "Not to worry, young man. A good field medic is always ready for problem patients."

Tai detached something from the back side of his pack, nearly cutting it in half. He unfolded it into a full-length stretcher complete with straps and thin padding.

"A field medic on a commando team?" Simon said as Tai checked to be sure his stretcher was stable. "How does that work?"

"Quite well from what I'm told," Yarain said.

"How? I mean, why bother?"

"With reinforcements possibly days away, it's not a bad idea to have someone on your team that can do more than apply bio-gel."

"But he can't fight, can he?"

"You bet your ass he can," Harrison said from the entrance. "COB Three is the only man I know who can perform emergency surgery in the middle of a fire fight, pause to shoot a man, then return to work without batting an eyelash. He's saved our necks more than once in more than a few ways."

Captain Tai just huffed at the compliment while lining the stretcher up beside Sundale. "Sir, I'm going to need your help as well. I need you to lift his hips and torso from the opposite side. Major, take his head and shoulders. You know them better than I do. Young man, you're in charge of his legs and his tails. Make sure they don't curl under him at any point."

Simon nodded as Harrison slung his weapon over his shoulder. Yarain moved to Sundale's head while Simon took position at his paws. Once all had a good grip on their charges, they gently lifted Sundale onto the stretcher, with only a deep breath escaping as they set him down.

That breath became a snarl as Tai began putting the straps on. When Tai tried to continue, Sundale snapped at him. Tai recoiled, and Yarain placed her muzzle over Sundale's head with a snarl of her own to silence his.

"He's trying to help you," she said.

"I will not be restrained!" Sundale said.

"As your superior in rank and pack, I am telling you not to resist. Am I clear?"

Sundale tried to resist, but another snarl from Yarain sent his ears falling and a whine escaping from his throat. Yarain held her muzzle in place while allowing her growl to fade.

"Proceed, COB Three. He won't hurt you."

Captain Tai remained tentative at first, particularly around Sundale's head and chest. Sundale did continue to growl, but a soft one from Yarain kept his short and his jaws closed.

Once Sundale was secure, Tai moved to take one end of the stretcher. When Simon went for the other end, Yarain raised a hand to stop him.

"Not you," she said. "We're going to need to move fast and quiet. That's not you right now."

"So, what am I going to do?" Simon said. "You can't just leave me behind."

"I don't plan to. COB One, help COB Three with Sundale. Lieutenant Solez, take my side-arm. You and COB Four can cover our six."

"What about our twelve ma'am?" Harrison asked.

Yarain deployed her full helmet, then made a point of drawing her rifle while perking her ears forward. Her hackles tried to rise but were hidden under her armor. "No one's getting in my way."

Harrison hummed understanding, then slung his rifle over his shoulder so he could prepare to help carry Sundale. Yarain meanwhile held her rifle in one hand while offering her P-mag to Lieutenant Solez. Simon reluctantly accepted the weapon from Harrison, only to hold it against him like it might hurt him.

"If you can't engage Polaris soldiers, we need to know now," Yarain said.

"It's just..." Simon began. He stared at Sundale. "The last time I fired a weapon... I'm not proud of it."

"I have faith in you, Lieutenant. Don't think about anything except what is required to ensure Sundale's survival. Let me deal with the rest."

Simon nodded, though he still stank of fear. Try as she might to find a way, Yarain could do nothing more to help him. He'd have to face his demons on his own. Simon was given a mask, goggles, and gloves, and that was all they could do to preserve their cover. Hardly ideal, but it would have to do.

Though it took some coaxing, Tai and Yarain managed to get Sundale to stay silent despite having a hard sheet covering him like half an egg. Even so, Yarain could smell his fear, to say nothing of the shudder she felt when she put her hand on him just before. *Nothing I can do about that now.*

As Tai and Harrison raised Sundale off the floor, Yarain tapped the side of her helmet. "COB Zero to Belly, passing Waypoint cumin. Heading for Waypoint sage. Come in COB Two, status on Waypoint pepper."

"Passing it now, ma'am," Yoda said. "Proceeding to Waypoint sage."

"Well done. COB Zero out."

Yarain motioned for Sarson to join Simon at the rear, then led the team out of the cell block back toward the shuttle. The team worked their way through the corridors in the same crawling pace they had before. Even slower since managing Sundale made finding cover all the more difficult. By the third dive into a side path, Yarain feared the trip out was going to take longer than the trip in. At least he and Simon were staying quiet. *As Jason would say, small favors.*

Favors that ran out when Yarain heard the approach of several soldiers.

Their un-uniformed gait suggested they weren't marching, and the rattle of gear said they weren't merely traveling across the base. With not enough time to hide, she had the team hold position. She approached the edge of the junction, uncovered her ears, and tried to assess the situation.

Even over the rattle of gear, she could hear radio calls in the enemy's helmets advising "the intruders" were dead ahead.

Cover's blown. Let the hunt begin. Yarain hugged the corner of the junction while motioning for the team to take cover. Stealth no longer a problem, she took a second to uncover her lower jaw as well. Simon, for all his fears, trained his weapon the opposite way to cover their six. *Good cub.*

Yarain allowed a breath of relief before inching as close to the corner as she could without being seen. She took deep breath after deep breath, listening to the enemy approach, waiting for the right moment. *Only go for the kill when the neck is open.* She waited, listened, let her ears fall to keep them safe. Then, when she heard them come within a few feet of her position, she flicked on her shield, and pounced.

Yarain whipped around the corner and landed on one knee. Her armor shimmered at the same time as the shield deployed a layer of particles just like a Scorn. At the exact moment her knee hit the floor, her rifle landed level, and her outside tails curved around her sides. She fired all three a fraction of a second later.

Those in front failed to anticipate properly, and sent their counter high, wide, or both. The rest tried to return fire, but couldn't get their weapons in line through their falling and panicking comrades. Yarain sprayed her fire over them until her barrage found only the walls behind them. Then she rose, all weapons still trained, panting in response to her heavy tail use, waiting to be sure she hadn't missed anyone. Her nose found only the stench of burned skin.

Lieutenant Sarson soon joined her to assist in the assault. Instead, he found rows of bodies at least five soldiers long. He whistled in awe while looking at her. "Remind me to stay off your bad side."

Yarain allowed her tails to relax, though her pant grew heavy as the energy use started to catch up with her. She wasn't far from going light-headed either. *I can't do that again. I won't be able to move, never mind how weak my bones will get.*

"That won't go unnoticed for long," she said. "Let's move!"

Sarson reclaimed his place at the rear as the team moved through the base, no longer being slow or careful. The main lights and alarms came on soon after to further confirm they had been discovered. Yarain's ears remained forward and searching, allowing them to get the jump on several enemy soldiers along the way. Few got the chance to fire. None held that chance for long. Only two landed a hit, and those were absorbed by the team's shields.

That changed when the team headed for the last turn before their shuttle. As they made their way down the corridor, a force of enemy soldiers appeared on the far end. The team had just enough time to dive behind support beams before the enemy opened fire. Sparks showered over them and plasmoids flashed by their heads as Sundale was set down behind beams. He whined at the sparks and firefight, but otherwise stayed calm for now.

Captain Harrison picked his way forward until he was on the opposite side of the corridor from Yarain. There, he joined her as she returned fire. This time, she couldn't get a good enough shot to matter. They were outnumbered at least three to one and without the element of surprise to make the kills easy.

"I'm open to suggestions!" Yarain yelled over the firefight.

"So am I, Ma'am," he said. "We can't move till they're gone, and we both know there's more where they came from."

"Got any ordinance?"

"We've each got a couple of pencils and a handful of grenades. We geared for breaching not frontal assault. Hark has more, she always does, but those guys have pretty thick armor. Not much use until we can make a break for it together."

A thick flurry of fire sent Yarain hugging the wall for every inch of cover she could squeeze out of it. A snarl formed, but she could do nothing more to break a stalemate she knew wouldn't last but a few minutes at most. *I shouldn't have used my tails so early.*

When she heard more footsteps coming behind her, she feared that end was upon them. She aimed her rifle and tails, determined to mow down whoever was coming, as were Simon and Sarson.

Yarain breathed great relief when Sarson told Simon to hold his fire. The footsteps soon became the rest of the team. They dove forward to join the firefight, all except for Lieutenant Hark. While Fickle told Harrison to save his explosives, Hark turned against the wall to open a case of some kind. Yarain glanced back at her often to try and determine what she was up to.

After another thick volley of fire pinned them against the wall, Lieutenant Hark emerged from her position with an SMT on her shoulder.

Yarain's ears were perfectly erect as she forced her stare over at Harrison. "She's not serious."

Harrison looked down, then back at her. Even through his helmet, she could see his eyes grow. "Yes ma'am. She is. OVERKILL!"

The team hugged the wall for all it had in the way of cover. Sarson pulled Simon into doing the same while Tai put himself over Sundale. Yarain followed their lead, flattening her body against the bulkheads.

"Fire in the hall!" Hark called.

The SMT round streaked by them, then rocked the base as it hit its target. Cries from the enemy were drowned out by the explosion itself and the subsequent alarms triggered by extensive internal damage.

Yarain felt a change in the situation and decided to press the advantage.

"***HIT*** Waypoint pepper!"

Right on the heels of her order, the base was again rocked by explosions. The lights flickered, and Yarain could feel the base shudder under her paws as warnings of a hull breach sounded. She looked down at Lieutenant Hark, unable to voice the question.

Hark answered it anyway.

"Shield generator, a corridor near the computer core, and an armory I just couldn't ignore."

A regular pyromaniac Harrison had called her. *I think he's off.* Being six feet tall certainly helped, and she wasn't a small woman either. It's a wonder she could find enough cover, but somehow, she'd gotten her shot off without taking a single hit.

Yarain shook the awe from her mind while checking the corridors. She saw only fire and debris where the enemy had once been.

And they're afraid of my *bad side?*

"MOVE!" she barked.

Harrison returned to carrying Sundale as the team scrambled for the shuttle. They rounded the corner just as weapons fire came from the corridor they'd come from. Grenades were thrown to slow the pursuit, but more shouts were coming from the third direction. Fickle, Rad, Sarson, and Yarain hunkered behind cover and laid down a barrage of fire to cover the retreat of the others.

Along with the plasmoid fire came a volley of Stiletto missiles, often called 'pencils,' from the Vesper's rifles. Though only twelve inches long, three rounds were enough to claim five enemy soldiers outright. Two more soldiers were thrown against the walls with more sound from their impact than from themselves. But before anyone could move, the original pursuers managed to fill both sides of the corridor. All parties had their rifles near smoking since they knew the first to get the chance would start chucking grenades. The one Polaris soldier to try anyway felt the full force of two Vesper rifles.

Though the Vespers had better gear, this stalemate kept the team pinned in the corridor. The enemy numbers grew by the minute, and though some were falling, they were being reinforced just as fast. As good as the Vespers' shields were, they'd never hold back the concentrated barrage they'd face.

As Yarain considered a barrage of grenades anyway, she heard a conversation from inside the shuttle.

"Ready for more mayhem, Lieutenant?" Harrison said.

"Always and forever, sir," Hark said.

Now what? Hark's gleeful tone left her almost afraid of what the woman had planned next. Yarain risked a glance back at the doorway, and went straight eared and wide eyed as both Hark and Harrison stepped just outside the doorway behind a portable combat shield. Harrison planted the shield in the corridor, then Hark slid *two* personal mini-guns into slots on the sides of the shield.

"Kick the tires," Harrison said.

"Light the fires!" Hark said.

This team is nuts!

Furious popping filled the corridors as both weapons were unleashed on the enemy. Near constant streams of fire streaked down range. Sparks poured onto the Polaris soldiers like a rainstorm. The few that managed to return fire only hit the shield Harrison kept firmly in place. Hark always sent them diving by veering her streams their way. Some never got the chance. The rest spent much of their time hugging the wall for their lives.

"Get moving!" Harrison said.

Yarain didn't argue. She and the others made their way inside, careful to not get hit by enemy or friendly fire. As each got inside, they took cover behind the door frame so they could add to the cover fire. By the time Yarain got inside, the enemy was staring down three Vesper rifles, Simon's side-arm, and two white-hot PMG's that had not stopped firing. More Stilettos were fired to further lessen the enemy assault.

We need to move. Those barrels should have melted already. But when she saw Harrison and Hark inching their way inside the shuttle, she knew they had it under control. So instead of joining the line, she slung her rifle over her shoulder while heading toward the cockpit.

Her eyes went straight to the sensor screen. She found one of the enemy cruisers parked by the hole that used to be an armory while the other was on a patrolling orbit. At that moment, both were too far away to get a good lock. While enemy fighters were closer, she knew they didn't need long to make their escape.

Yarain checked back on the team to see Harrison and Hark just entering the shuttle. With their extraction point by now compromised, she decided to make some changes.

"Cut HL and all short-term non-essentials. Divert that power to shields."

The pilot snapped back at her with a face full of question. "Ma'am? That'll heat our generator pretty good, and our cloak won't cover the power spike—"

"That's an **ORDER** pilot! Maintain cloaking field, stand-by decoy drones. Once we're at speed, launch drones but hold a steady course." *And pray they guess wrong.*

He and the co-pilot set about following her orders without so much as a shake of the head. The hyper-light coils, a few small systems they wouldn't be using, and even life support were cut to give the shield generator additional power so it could build the layer faster. While it would spike both heat and energy signature, it would also keep them alive a little bit longer.

Not two seconds later, another round of Stilettos and grenades went out before Sarson closed the door.

"GO!" Harrison said.

The pilot broke the connection with the base that instant. The shuttle shook as it began taking fire from an enemy fighter almost a second later. *That's why.* Yarain swayed on her paws while she heard a yip from Sundale. Unable to do anything for him now, she held her place in the cockpit.

The pilot pushed the engines as hard as he could on a direct line away from the base. The sensor screen announced the arrival of many more fighters to the area, all gunning for their shuttle. Despite the pilot's best efforts, they took a lot of fire. As ordered, three cloaked drones broadcasting fake energy signatures were launched. Two began an erratic course to mimic evasive maneuvers while one held a straight shot course with only minor evasion tactics. The exact same the pilot himself was using.

The fighters chasing them scattered among the drones, though one remained on their tail. The transport pilot managed to dodge much of it, but not all. The shuttle shook with each hit and tested not only Yarain's balance, but her control as each one drew a whine from Sundale.

Stay strong, Sundale. We're almost clear.

Simon made his way to her side so he too could look forward. "We're not gonna make it!"

"We'll be fine," Yarain said through a growl. *He is young, I guess.*

"Fine? How can you say that when we have half the Polaris fleet on our tail?"

"We have all of ours at our nose."

As if on cue, two Interstar destroyers, three battleships, and a cloud of fighters filling the gaps decloaked ahead of them. The shuttle passed through their line as the wall opened fire in one glorious flash. Yarain watched the sensor screen with approval as the enemy blips vanished in bulk.

The *Alamo* carrier group, supported by even more cruisers and frigates, appeared ahead. This included one Scorn fighter flying by their window to show her markings. If only Sundale were able to see Jason's reassurance.

That moment will come soon enough. She looked back as they headed for the *Alamo* to see an uncovered Sundale shuddering beside Captain Tai. With her part of his rescue now over, Yarain allowed the soldier and the first mother to fall away so she could be only his mother again.

Instead of retracting it, she removed her helmet entirely so that it flopped against her back. She knelt beside him so she could rub her full muzzle against his once more. *"Rest. You're safe now."*

His shudders ended, but she could still feel the tension in his body. Tension Yarain remembered all too well.

When she and Harmus were fresh from their own rescue, it didn't matter how much her instincts told her that these new humans weren't going to hurt her. The memory of those that had, the years spent caged and mistreated, left her so uneasy she jumped at sneezes for hours. Her body couldn't believe it was over. That she was free and safe. Her guard didn't fall until her body surrendered to the need for sleep. It wasn't until she had sky above, soil beneath, and nothing on the horizon that she truly relaxed. It was a hard few days, but seeing Sundale healthy, respected, and given every freedom had helped her get past her trauma quicker.

Except her trauma had been relatively minor. One could argue three years versus two weeks made up the difference, but she had actually suffered very little injury in all that time. She'd also had Harmus there. The two of them helped each other when the other lost hope. For Sundale, neither was true. He'd spent his two weeks alone and brutally tortured. The pain from that time would linger for a while, and she knew that until it faded, there was little she could do to calm him.

So, she did all she *could* do. Yarain stayed beside her cub the entire time. She licked his blood from his muzzle, rubbed her head against his chest, and tried all she could to put him at ease. She even pulsed at times, letting them feel each other as only holdrens could. While the collar kept him from pulsing back, Sundale offered a soft whine of affection each time. The only proof of success was the fact that he didn't flinch when the shuttle touched down on the *Alamo,* or when the airlock opened to reveal medics standing ready to take him to sick bay.

As they entered, Captain Tai briefed them on Sundale's status and injures. Yarain meanwhile, offered one last reminder for him. *"You will not harm them. If I hear you did, I will not hesitate to pin you where you lay."*

Sundale's pulled-back ears acknowledged his understanding, though his eyes held more plea than submission. *"You aren't coming with me?"*

Yarain's heart split down the middle. One half went to her cub, who she knew from experience could not be alone now. But the other, the first mother, could not bear to abandon her pack mid-hunt. She couldn't decide which half to follow until Simon knelt beside her. He lifted a hand to offer comfort, but withdrew as if she were too hot to touch. Yarain didn't react but did put her heart back together. Sundale wouldn't be alone. While perhaps not the same, he would have someone there he trusted. It would be enough until her hunt was over.

"No," she said at last. *"But I will return when the hunt is done."*

Sundale offered a lick on her muzzle, which Yarain returned. She stepped back to allow the medics to take him out. As they moved Sundale onto a proper stretcher, Yarain turned to Simon. "You will stay with him until I return or he no longer needs you."

It was more than a command. It was an ultimatum. Sundale needed company, but Yarain's pack needed her too. She could not do both, so Simon was going to be what Sundale needed whether he liked it or not.

Fortunately, Simon nodded with a hard sigh. "You have my word."

"Don't we get a say in that?" a medic asked.

Yarain's ears and hackles rose while her eyes narrowed. "No."

The medic looked ready to protest, except Sundale managed a soft bark. When all eyes turned on him, he simply said, "I need him."

The medics dropped all protests then and there. With Simon at his side, Sundale was taken to sickbay. Yarain followed them outside the shuttle and watched her cub go until the doors of the hanger closed behind them. Then she turned back to the gathered team to find Harrison folding his arms and the entire team with retracted helmets standing behind him.

"With respect, Ma'am, your mission is finished here. I don't think anyone would blame you for being with him right now."

Yarain saw them all standing together, every one of them ready to return to action that very second. Part of her wanted to take the out, to be with her cub as her heart desired. Except they weren't soldiers to her. They were fellow hunters. A pack. As first mother, however temporary, she couldn't abandon them now.

"The mission isn't over yet," she said. "Though command should probably return to you, Captain."

Harrison nodded with a smile. "I think we can suffer your command a while longer."

"Very well. Rearm and stand-by."

Yarain and the team went back inside the shuttle without a word. They replaced missing gear and recharged their weapons in preparation for whatever they may be asked to do next. Hark took one look at the PMG clips, then tossed them aside in favor of fully charged ones. She also winced when she was reminded the hard way how hot the barrels still were. All the while, Yarain kept hearing Jason's vote of confidence ringing in her head, as well as something else he'd said. *"None of us really know what to do with the command chair, until we're given our own to sit in."*

Yarain had been in that chair for a couple of hours now. As much as she tried to ignore it, his words forced her to admit that for the first time in years, she felt completely at home.

Chapter 20

A Few Loose Ends

Jason didn't know if Sundale saw his fly-by, but in truth, he'd done it as much for himself as for Sundale. It was as close to his old friend he was going to get for a while.

The Polaris fleet was putting up a solid fight, but with their cruisers already drifting fireballs, their fighters were doing little more than buying time. Jason took his position behind the Interstar battle line to catch any that got by or to assist as needed.

Since none ever got through, Jason got time he didn't care for. It allowed him to think about the fact that he had two humans behind him instead of holdrens. Well, it didn't actually matter that they were human. It mattered that they weren't Sundale and Yarain. Having anyone else back there just felt wrong. Something he tried not to show them. After all, it was nothing they did. They were good officers who did their jobs exceptionally well. They just weren't the friends and crewmates he'd served with for so long. Ironic really, considering he was the one pushing Yarain so hard to take her own command.

Will it still be wrong then?

Yes, but you got used to it when you thought Sundale was dead. You'll get used to Yarain's replacement too. Then, with time, it won't feel wrong anymore.

Lieutenant Harkson Finnley, a temporary fill-in for Yarain, broke through Jason's thoughts with a battle update. "Enemy ships arriving to starboard. I make two destroyers and a carrier. Additional reinforcements approaching from the back side of the base. I've got two, make that three battleships. All ships are launching fighters and point defense drones."

"How are we doing, Gilnt?" Jason asked.

"Magazine full, Sir," Captain Gilnt said. "Shield generator at 50 C."

Lieutenant Finnley came back, "Admiral Redding wants us to engage the destroyers and carrier. He's sending the *Berlin* and the *Tomahawk* to provide fire support. All ships: weapons free."

It was all too prim and proper. Too exact. It didn't hold the same seamless motion Jason had become so accustomed to. Maybe he'd become too comfortable with Yarain and Sundale. He didn't know for sure, and he was afraid to ask.

He did know he had to find a way to deal with it. With his group and the promised ships behind him, he turned to face the enemy ships as instructed. Jason scanned them more with his eyes than his sensors as he planned exactly how to deal with them.

The destroyer, he was becoming accustomed to. The design started out very pointed but quickly grew to a rounded, bulging fuselage with tiny, curved wings making a line down the side only to thin out again at the rear. The bulge was full of weapon points in no particular pattern, offering a truly three-hundred-and-sixty-degree field of fire, though not as focused as the Interstar design. Interstar troops were already calling them "Hedgehogs," which Jason found more than fitting.

The carrier on the other hand, he'd seen in reports but had yet to encounter himself. Her fuselage was long and very blocky, almost like a transport, without any kind of wings in sight. Yet he knew these irregular hull lines were because of an extensive network of defense turrets and increased armor over sensitive areas of the ship. In addition, the sides were lined with short launch tubes leading to her hangers. Reports said trying to land any shots inside those tubes was suicide. After looking at the group of turrets and thick armor around them, he believed it.

Jason also believed he could handle them anyway. True he couldn't catch anyone mid launch, but that just meant he'd have to wait a little longer before he went for the carrier herself.

The carrier began spewing fighters like some kind of artillery barrage while the other ships released their own fighters to add to the force.

When it stopped, half the fighters went to cover the base, while the other half charged toward the Gold Group in a tight cloud. The ships themselves were protected by a rather thin layer of combat drones either turret operator could handle in their sleep. They looked a lot like the shoe design of the Polaris fighter, but much shorter and without any wings at all. The things were so fragile, Jason wondered if he could take one down with his P-mag, though their cannons did hit hard for a drone. The only reason they gave Jason pause was because they were paired with a sizable force of combat fighters and a much more respectable grid of PDF turrets.

"Numbers!" Jason called.

"Eighty type one fighters, sir," Lieutenant Finnley said. "Thirty defense drones in formation around the group."

Twice our number, but half our firepower.

As the enemy fighters held their formation, Jason noticed they were going to meet just outside the range of the Polaris ships. That meant they'd be without cover fire. Upon that error, a plan of action built itself without effort.

"Barrage line boys!" Jason ordered. "Line up and let em have it. Time on target for first round, full barrage after. Fighters, engage your own once they get close. Finnley, recommend the *Berlin* and *Tomahawk* hold their attack on the enemy ships until my order or they get engaged."

"Recommendation relayed and acknowledged, sir," Lieutenant Finnley said. "*Berlin* wants your reasons."

"We deal with the fighters first. Then we get in close to the capital ships, cut through their ECM, relay accurate target data for long range fire, and help punch a hole in their shields."

"Recommendation endorsed. *Berlin* and *Tomahawk* weapons tight until ordered. Weapons free on enemy fighters. First volley time on target."

Too damn proper.

The group held position, adjusting so they created a spaced-out five-line vertical stack of Scorns. The line waited while the supporting ships matched their range to the group's. They matched up just in time to open fire in one, concentrated wave. The firing of the first volley was spread out so that every shot and missile hit the enemy fighters all at the same time. The result was an initial blast that outright claimed half a dozen fighters and sent the rest scattering in hopes of avoiding the barrage. Their efforts only kept them in the field of fire longer. As stragglers got smart and escaped the field, Jason sent fighters to finish them off. Others tried a direct charge, only to be blown away by the concentrated fire. They added to the fireworks as enemy fighters started going down several at a time. *What they'd do? Send in first day cadets?*

The enemy group as a whole, such as they were, finally wised up and charged at once. The barrage knocked off a few more, but an actual dog-fight was unavoidable. *Fine by me.*

"Engage, engage, all fighters engage. Take them down!"

The capital ships scaled down their fire while the group moved in to intercept with their weapons screaming. The ships stopped their fire just as the two groups entered dog fighting range. Though he didn't have numbers, Jason could see the enemy force had been thinned significantly. *Still a danger*, he reminded himself.

Jason had had his eye on the lead fighter the entire time. He'd been the only one to not panic roll, marking him as the most important target. As the opposing fighter groups engaged, Jason flew straight under and past his target, only to flip on his back to pick up the pursuit. The enemy fighter tried ducking, weaving, even a flip or two, but Gold 1 remained on his six. Jason took shots where he could and let his turret operators take theirs as they came.

The Polaris pilot was good, but not good enough. He weaved through traffic, tried reversing direction into the path of another chase — which Gilnt and Harkson turned the tide of as they passed — even going so far as to come within inches of other fighters. Jason held his lock through it all. The enemy turrets did little more than make Jason weave enough to prolong the chase. And he was dishing out far more than he was taking.

When Jason's rounds started hitting hull, he fired four missiles, all of which landed right between the wings and the fuselage. The wings fell from the ship in pieces, and the rest of the fighter tumbled through space like a wayward asteroid. Jason fired another pair of missiles to finish them, but the *Berlin's* main guns got there first.

Kill thieving deckers.

Jason turned over to pick his next target, but found most were already doubled on. Those that weren't were already taking armor damage. So, he joined the chase on the next closest target with a glance to the enemy ships in the distance.

Time for the next step. "Signal the fleet to engage enemy ships. We'll follow just as soon as..."

He trailed off as he saw the enemy ships were warping away. Not just his targets either. Jason's sensor screen very quickly became void of any and all enemy ships, fighters included, save for a few too damaged to run. Only drones remained, which were self-destructing with their command ships no longer in range. The few fighters that remained were either finished off or joined their drones in self-destruct. One tried to kamikaze into Gold 1, but Gold 2 split her in half as Jason slid under her like skipping off a pond.

Screens now clear, Jason slowed to a near stop, trying to understand what just happened. "Do you two have anything for me?"

"Negative, sir," Lieutenant Finnley said. "My scopes are clear."

"Same here, sir," Captain Gilnt added. "In fact, I have more of a mystery for you. Their base is now empty."

"What do you mean empty?" Jason said.

"I'm not reading a single ship or person aboard. As far as I can tell, they've straight up abandoned it."

The spider's back. Jason stared at the base as if he might find some clue as to their thinking while trying to revive his own. No one, not even your basic pirate, would leave a base that intact. Not unless they had a darn good reason for it.

Yet it seemed they'd done just that. If true, it presented Interstar with a unique opportunity they couldn't ignore. Maybe this time they'd actually get something before they had to abandon the place.

Or we'll lose more than a few soldiers and my best friend in the attempt. The thought was distasteful to say the least, but in his mind, it was a risk they still had to take.Before he could suggest they do so, Admiral Redding came on the fleet-wide. "All ships, form a defensive perimeter around the base. Fighters, provide tight cover and stand by to disarm the base. Everyone, stay sharp. We don't know that it's over."

Guess that settles that.

Jason eased over to get in close to the enemy base. He kept waiting for her turrets to open up. When they never did, he joined the forming orbit around the base. He angled his fighter so his own turrets would have a clear target in case things changed. From there, it was a steady stare on the fighter in front of him with one eye on the sensor screen. He could only hope this wasn't the trap he knew it to be.

Minutes later, he saw the Vesper shuttle appear on his scanners again and smiled as his head tilted in a very holdren manor. "Is that COB team going back in?"

"Yes, sir, it is," Lieutenant Finnley said. "Apparently Admiral Redding wants Major Yarain's team to get whatever they can out of the computer."

Wait, who's team? "Yarain? She's still in command?"

"Apparently so, sir."

Wonder how that happened. Considering Sundale's condition, he figured Yarain would be glued to his bedside for the next decade. That, and her part of the mission was done, so there was no reason for her to retain command. Then again, technically, the mission as a whole was *not* done, which meant she was still assigned to the team. To say nothing of the possibility that she somehow felt it was her duty to retain command.

That's what you wanted isn't it?

Well, yeah, but not if means her walking into a trap on her first day.

Not that he could do much about it now. She was on that ship, and would be on that base, right in the thick of it if things went south. About the only thing that kept him from going crazy was knowing it was Yarain. If anyone could avoid a trap, it was her.

I just hope they live to share what they learn in there, Jason added silently.

Chapter 21

Licking Wounds

Yarain sniffed the air as the rest of the team made another sweep of the room to be sure their sensors weren't lying to them. They and her nose found only a room full of computer stations, with one section of the wall covered in displays relating to the status of the computer core. Other panels held sever ports, access points for the core's hardware, and entry points for technicians to enter the innards of the core itself. Above their heads, a catwalk ran along the walls where more components and access points blinked and hummed, ready to be used as needed. The room didn't need any lighting, for all the displays filled the space with the same, almost-white-blue glow all Human computer systems gave off.

"You wanted a challenge, Mister Sarson?" she said. "I need every bit of information in this core downloaded A-S-A-P."

Lieutenant Sarson cracked his fingers before plugging his personal clip-com into one of the core room stations. "You got it, ma'am. Let's see what I can do."

While he went to work, Yarain glanced outside the room at the charred state of the corridor and counted herself lucky they'd placed a charge nearby. It had severed many connections, including one leading to the self-destruct protocols within the core itself. The base commander could have still set it from the core, but with Interstar pounding at the gates, there wasn't enough time. It had taken COB Team an hour to clear enough rubble to get inside, then another half-hour to reestablish connections to other sectors of the base. Then again, when they finally got inside, they got the "pleasure" of seeing shrapnel littered bodies just inside the door, so there was some question who was the lucky one.

A question Yarain herself couldn't answer. The sight was nothing worse than what she did to her prey. Such carnage rarely affected her at all and never affected her much unless it was someone she knew. Even then, it was more feeling sympathy for an injured packmate, or mourning their loss. The rest of the team had commented on the state of the officers but gave no indication it bothered them. After so many years with Jason, Yarain wondered if they were hiding their true feelings about it, or if they too had become accustomed to it. Only way to know was to ask, and now was not the time for that.

That said, she had plenty of time to consider changing her mind. Tension left the team by the first thirty minutes spent waiting on Lieutenant Sarson. Enough that everyone retracted their helmets for comfort. After another hour on top of that, only training kept them vigilant, though not quite as serious. Captain Tai and Captain Fickle engaged in small talk while keeping a close eye on the remains of the doorway. Harrison stayed with Yarain near the center of the room to keep an eye on things. They tried small talk but the combination of not knowing each other, the setting, and the holdren tendency toward short answers, left the conversation more awkward than silence. As for Lieutenant Hark, she made Yarain nervous by juggling a pair of grenades in one hand near Sarson. Thank goodness the pins were protected against accidental knock-outs, or she'd never be able to take her eyes off her.

Though Yarain did allow a moment to take stock of the team demolitionist during their wait. Even tucked into the helmet, one could tell Second Lieutenant Maureen Hark pushed hair length right up to the regulation limit. Tucked or not, the soft black locks were in a very short ponytail, which went rather well with her hard face and narrow eyes. *Not sure where she'd place in a pack. She looks as hard as a necker, but the personality is something else.*

Yarain abandoned the question in favor of a different curiosity. Her eyes drifted up to Lieutenant Rad, who had spent the entire time walking the catwalk alone. She hadn't said a word, changed her route, or even slowed her pace. Just maintained a constant vigil over the team as if still expecting trouble. To be honest, Yarain expected it too, but that didn't explain why Lieutenant Rad was keeping so distant.

It wasn't just her patrol. Before the mission, during the trip, after Sundale was extracted, she remained separate from the team. An enigma Yarain couldn't get a sense for, which for a human was an amazing accomplishment.

"Problem, ma'am?" Harrison asked, after Yarain had watched Rad for almost half a circle.

"Trying to understand her," Yarain said.

Harrison huffed. "Good luck. It took me five months before she would engage in any kind of personal conversation. She still hasn't opened up completely."

"Why?"

"Don't know. I just know she keeps us at arm's length. She never lets it get in the way of the job though. She'll talk out a mission, express her concerns, offer ideas, all without hesitation or doubt. But once the armor comes off, a different kind replaces it. One I still haven't cracked. For whatever reason, she prefers to be alone."

"No, she doesn't." The words came out before Yarain knew they were there. Yet the moment she said them, the first mother within knew them to be true. As if it knew something her conscious self couldn't identify.

Harrison on the other hand put his free hand on his hip while thumping his rifle onto his shoulder. "Really? With all due respect, ma'am, I'm curious what makes you so sure."

I wish I knew myself. "Instinct, Captain."

"Instincts aren't always right, ma'am. And I speak from experience."

"So do I."

With that, Yarain found herself climbing the steps of the spiral staircase to the catwalk. Despite the fact she wouldn't be first mother for much longer, she couldn't leave without trying to connect with, or at least understand, the enigma that was Lieutenant Shillin Rad. The first mother wouldn't allow it.

Rad headed for attention when she saw Yarain approaching, but Yarain waved her down before she got there. "At ease, Lieutenant. I'm just checking to see how you're doing."

Rad turned to keep watch over the room, though kept Yarain in her peripheral vision. "I'm fine, ma'am. No problems."

"Are you sure? For a human, you haven't spoken much."

"I'm not much of a talker, ma'am. I'm better at staying hidden than I am at 'small talk.'"

"There is plenty of conversation to be had that is far from small."

Lieutenant Rad hummed, yet it held no emotion. It was a sound that merely acknowledged the comment, and it drove Yarain crazy. There was nothing to react to. That armor Harrison spoke of stood between them like a wall. *Why is she so distant? I've never seen a human so withdrawn.*

Yarain wanted to understand. The first mother in her wanted to help what it saw as a wayward member return to the strength of the pack. But to do that, she had to get to know the woman, which was proving more difficult than expected.

Yarain eventually sighed out her frustration and surrender while watching Sarson. When he started muttering, she perked her ears to see if she could catch an update.

"Come on now," Sarson said. "Don't be like that. Work with me. Let me in. No need to alert anything. There. That's it. Let me at them. That's a good girl. No need to be snide now."

Yarain panted a quick laugh. She'd always found amusement in watching humans work, especially when hyper focused like Sarson was. So many had their own ways of passing time or helping them think. How humming a tune, or tapping a foot, or swirling a finger made them work better never made sense, but she couldn't argue with the results. Though it often created a fascinating show that kept her mind busy when she needed it. At times when on leave, she would go out in search of such displays, assuming she wasn't hunting or spending time in the wild.

"Something wrong, ma'am?" Rad asked. An even tone, but still clearly concerned.

I suppose that's progress. Let's see if I can use it. "What makes you ask?"

"The sudden pant, ma'am. If it were warm enough for it, you would have been doing it a long time ago."

So, she's got an eye for detail. Interesting. "For holdrens, a pant is sometimes a laugh, Lieutenant. I was laughing at Sarson's mutterings."

"You can hear him from up here? I can barely hear him standing next to him when he's like that."

"Lieutenant, if I listened, I could hear your heart beating."

Rad's eyebrows raised half a hair, which by her standards so far was an outburst. "I never knew holdren ears were that good. Can you hear through walls?"

"Sometimes."

"So that's how you did it."

Yarain perked her ears toward Rad, curious at the thought and surprised to see the armor starting to weaken. "Did what, Lieutenant?"

If they could, Rad's ears would have fallen the moment the question came. She even took a step back as the armor tried to thicken. "Nothing, ma'am. I'm sorry, I shouldn't have said anything."

You're not getting away that easy. "Rad, it's all right. I don't bite."

Rad looked at her confused, to which Yarain gave a playful swish of her tails. The corners of Rad's lips tried to smile but were stopped before they got more than a millimeter up. "Good one, ma'am."

"Thank you. Now please—that's how I did what?"

Lieutenant Rad leaned on the railing and stared into nothing. For a moment, Yarain worried she'd lost her, but decided to wait it out and see what, if anything, came next. Eventually, Rad answered in her usual, distant, emotionless tone. "Phoenix Perch, ma'am. Only ears that good could have found the enemy that deep that fast."

"No different than hunting mice beneath the snow," Yarain said.

"With respect, ma'am, you're being modest. I don't know anyone who—"

"Uh-oh."

All eyes snapped to Sarson at the comment. Yarain's ears perked fully while her tails tensed in case of trouble. When no one said or did anything, she ran back down the stairs, slowing as she approached the workstation.

"What's wrong, Sarson?" she said.

"Computer trap, ma'am. I think I... oh no. Come on, come on, come on. Don't do this to me girl. Come on. Nononono, blast!"

Seconds later, the lights went out, including all displays within the core room as well as the emergency lights. The team clicked on the lights on their rifles. Yarain did the same as well as a light between her ears that was carefully shielded to keep the light out of her eyes while still glowing forward.

"What happened?" Yarain asked.

Sarson tossed down his gear while falling into his chair. "That's it. We've got all we're going to. A security measure just wiped all data from the base. There's no way we'll salvage it."

Yarain growled, frustrated at once again being denied good intel. "Did you get anything?"

"Not much. A few files that *might* give us something assuming we can decrypt them. I'm sorry, ma'am. I should have known better than to go that deep into the source code when I had a download running."

Yarain's ears ticked forward and held there, what holdrens would take as a sign of support. Knowing humans wouldn't catch it, she offered a hand on Sarson's shoulder instead. "It's all right, Sarson. You did what you could. Pack it up. We'll make a sweep of the command deck, see what we can find before—"

She was cut off by the comm link in her helmet. "Belly to COB Zero. Come in."

Yarain tapped the side of her retracted helmet while silencing another growl. *Now what?* "Go for COB Zero. What's for dinner?"

"We'd like to ask you the same thing. The base just went dark, and now we're reading a massive fluctuation in the power output."

"What do you mean by fluctuation?"

"See for yourself."

A soft beep on her wrist-com announced the arrival of data. Yarain checked it to see a sensor read-out of the station's power output. It was a constant wave except every few seconds, it would jump and scatter like a heartbeat suddenly changing rhythm. Stranger still, the jumps were slowly growing more frequent.

Lieutenant Sarson looked over her arm at the read-out, then shook his head. "That's nothing I did. I can't imagine what might be left to cause that either. As far as I can tell, there is literally *no* data left. Not even operational files."

"How can that be?" Harrison asked. "The grav generators are still active."

"Maybe not," Yarain said. "A sudden shut down could leave a residual gravity field for a short while. I'm more interested in them using the same crystal technology we do."

"What? How can you tell?"

"The energy signature is nearly identical."

Lieutenant Hark stepped forward to join the conversation as Rad made her way to the ground floor. "How can that be?" Hark said. "No one had the technology when Polaris fell, and the tech is so top secret even the jantans haven't reverse engineered it. So how did the Pols get it?"

"I'm more worried about these fluctuations," Harrison said. "Last I knew, resonance in power crystals isn't a good thing."

Yarain flicked an ear in dismissal. "It's not, but there are dozens of safe-guards..."

Yarain's stomach vanished as she saw the pieces fall into place.

No data.

No files.

No safeguards.

"***EMERGENCY*** evac! COB One, ***POP*** the transponder. COB Zero to Belly, the station's going to blow. Prepare for emergency extraction. Do not, repeat, *do not* spin hyper-light drives. ***BRACE*** for impact."

On her first order, the team began to gather in the center of the room. Rifles were trained outward while Harrison removed a large box from Yoda's pack, cutting the pack in half or more. He set it on the floor, punched in a code, and the emergency transit beacon glowed to life. One by one, the team stepped onto it and were instantly taken by the sparkle and flash of the transporter. The only delay was when Harrison motioned for Yarain to go first as the last of the team took their turn.

"Commander goes last, Captain," is all she said.

He didn't argue. There wasn't time. He took his turn, followed by

Yarain the second he was gone. She arrived in the transit room to collision alarms blaring and the team watching to be sure she arrived.

"COB is aboard," Harrison said into his comms.

Yarain stepped up to the control strip in the center of the room so she could activate one of the monitors. The dark station grew smaller on the screen as the fleet moved away as fast as they could without hyperlight. A full minute passed, yet all that changed was the size of the station and the passing of the Vesper shuttle.

"Maybe I was wrong," Yarain said.

As if in answer, the station vanished in a blue fire ball so bright the team shielded their eyes despite the feed auto-dimming the worst of it. The screen flickered as the EM wave hit the ship long before the blast faded.

"EM Wave clear," PAICCA said. "No enemies detected. Set condition three. Stay alert."

The alarms were silenced as were the matching lights. With the danger well and truly over, Yarain allowed herself the comfort of letting her helmet fall against her back again.

"That was close." Harrison said. He looked at Yarain while his rifle went over his shoulder. "How did you know it was going to blow?"

"Those spikes were the resonance you mentioned building up," Yarain said. "If it's allowed to get strong enough... well, you saw what happened."

"But you said there are dozens of safe-guards in place."

Details, Yarain. "Which were eliminated with the core wipe. My guess is there was some kind of mechanism separate from the core that was triggered by the wipe. It started building a resonance within the power crystals with no way to stop it."

Several of the team and the techs in the room nodded, though Sarson put words to their thoughts. "Without any safeguards, that resonance reaches a point where the crystals shatter instead of break, causing all that contained energy to detonate. Stick around, you go up with the base. With a core twice the total size of a carrier, try to warp away, and the EM field blows your hyper coils which takes you with them."

"Unless they're uncharged or you can jump before it hits," Yarain added.

Captain Tai asked, "But ships have had their cores shatter before. I don't remember having to worry about hyper coils. Why worry now?"

"As Sarson said, a station has a much bigger core. Even the largest of starships won't generate an EM wave that will do more than get the coils a little hot. And if you build a resonance first, the EM wave is even stronger."

Sarson nodded with a heavy sigh. "I'm sorry, Ma'am. I should have been more careful. I almost got—"

"Don't go there."

"But—"

"I said don't go there. That's an order, COB four." When he nodded but was still looking at the floor, Yarain tried her best to think what a human might say. *They need it.* "No one's perfect, Lieutenant. Worrying about what almost happened will do you no good. Instead, go back through your hack, find the trap, and make sure everyone knows how to avoid it next time. And Lieutenant... Markus. For all you know, you *couldn't* have avoided it. Don't dwell on what could have been. Do what you can to prevent it from coming that close again."

His eyes rose followed by his shoulders, and she could see the fire light behind his eyes. "Yes, ma'am. Thank you, ma'am."

Yarain only perked her ears forward in reply.

PAICCA came on the line again. "Set condition four. All forces stand down. Fleet is returning to base for further assignment. Unit heads stand-by for further orders."

The rest of the team shed their helmets the moment they heard 'condition four.' *So much for 'you'll get used to it,'* she thought with amused ruffs. If any of them knew she was laughing, or why, no one said anything.

Though Captain Harrison had something else to say. "Guess that means you're off the hook. The mission is well and truly over now, and if I may say so, ma'am, you have a cub you should check on."

Yarain's ears flashed back a second at the thought. *I suppose it is time I return to him.* "Thank you, Captain."

"No, thank you. I'm glad you were with us today, ma'am. You saved a lot of lives, ours included."

This time, Yarain's ears pulled back in a holdren blush. "I just used my training."

"With respect, ma'am, you're being modest." *Why do humans keep saying that?!* "You led us well from beginning to end, in all things." Harrison snapped to attention with salute, which the team echoed, Rad included. "It's been a pleasure to serve with you, ma'am."

Yarain's ears again shifted back. She really didn't see the need for all the praise. That said, she couldn't deny it felt good to hear.

She forced her ears back up, then returned the salute. "Thank you, Captain. The team is yours again. Hunt well."

Harrison nodded, though he couldn't hide a cringe. "Safe journeys, Major. I hope your next unit does well by you."

"Next unit?"

"With respect, ma'am, after command reads my report, you won't be with Gold 1 for much longer. Sooner or later, you'll get the permanent command you deserve."

"And they'll be lucky to have you."

The entire team turned in shock that it was Lieutenant Rad adding the vote of confidence. The woman only held her place, not moving so much as an eyelash. Still, given how quiet she'd been, Yarain shared the team's surprise that she said anything. *Didn't think I made that much of an impression.*

"We'll see," is all Yarain could think to say in reply. "Dismissed."

"Aye, ma'am," the team said.

Yarain's ears gave another backward shift as she left the room. She went to the armory to turn in her heavy armor, grateful to be back down to her uniform and basic weapons, to say nothing of being able to go barepaw again. Her rifle had come from Gold 1, but before she could think about it, the armory officer offered to take it there for her. "Go check on your son, ma'am. I got this," he'd said.

She thanked the man, though as she left, she realized the armor had actually settled quite a bit since she first donned it. In truth, she didn't feel its loss as much as she thought. *Maybe I would get used to it after a while, assuming we could fix the problem with my whiskers.*

Something she *was* missing, however, was the pack. That's how she saw them. Even if only for a few hours, they had been her pack, and she had felt their trust every step of the way. The sense of being at their head, the central part of the whole, left her longing for the days when she was a first mother. As she rode the lift to sickbay, it turned from thoughts of the past to a growing knot in her chest.

Lieutenant Rad—Shillin's outburst hadn't just left her blushing. It left her wondering what could be. What was going to be.

She'd stay with Gold 1 for a while, possibly a long while given the war, but Jason was right. She didn't belong there anymore. Her heart was already yearning to return to what she'd just had. Not very likely given the team had a leader and they were Vespers versus a fighter crew, but it didn't change the desire to go back and stay with them for longer than one mission. If she could find a unit half as good, she'd have little trouble leaving Gold 1.

Assuming Sundale was able to recover. Yarain knew she wasn't going anywhere until Sundale was back on duty. If for no other reason than Jason would need her. He'd try to go it alone, and she'd seen the dangers of that mentality too often to let him. So, for now, she was staying put. But maybe next time Jason talked about her leading, she wouldn't be so hostile to the idea.

Yarain finally turned the corner toward sickbay. She almost went on all fours so she could run to her cub that much faster. Jason was already there outside the door waiting for her. *Probably landed the moment he heard 'condition four.'* When he saw her, he folded his arms with a wry smile.

"Not a commando, huh?" he said.

Yarain's ears again fell, but only for a second. Then her hackles ruffled. "We're not talking about this now. I want to see Sundale."

Jason nodded with a chuckle. "As do I. I just hope you realize how well you did out there."

"More than you know."

"That's all I need then. Come on, we — oh!"

Simon nearly ran into him on his way out. The young man had his head down while his eyes were light-years beyond the hull. Only Jason's hands coming up to brace prevented contact. Though it broke Simon's stare, what replaced it might have been worse. He looked at Jason as if he were afraid of being torn apart. Yet somehow, the look wasn't for him either. *What happened since I left him?*

Jason meanwhile seemed to scan Simon's uniform, then instantly relax. "Sorry, Son. I didn't see you there."

Simon had to swallow before he could reply. "It's okay, sir. I... my mind was elsewhere."

"So I see. Can't say I'm surprised. Defection can't have been an easy choice. Anything I can help with?"

Simon swallowed hard before forming a reply. "Actually sir... you might. I need someone to tell me the truth. Not my truth, or their truth, or anyone else's truth. I need *the* truth, sir."

"The truth about what?"

"What happened between Interstar and Polaris."

Jason recoiled with a cringe while Yarain's ears flicked back in much the same way. The stories of those days were well covered in the academy. Failed negotiations, burned olive branches, and one near-disaster that led to the destruction – or rather, what everyone *thought* was the destruction – of the Polaris Confederacy. Blame was spread like seed over a farm though few knew all the events leading up to the final slaughter. Or during for that matter. It was not a happy tale, and without knowing what version the young man had heard, "the truth" likely would not be heard well. Given that'd he'd just betrayed his father, it may not be the best time for Simon to hear such a story.

Then again, for that same reason, it might be exactly what he needed.

Jason shook his head as if he might shake something loose. "I'm not sure you want to know Mister... what's your name, Son?"

"Lieutenant J.G. Simon Solez, sir," Simon said in perfect solider, which instantly vanished with a sigh. "With all due respect, Colonel, all my life I've been fed what I was told was the truth. That fox in there has left me doubting every word of it, but I can't just search your records because those will hold *your* truth. Sundale said you were an honorable man. Please, sir, I need to know the *real* truth if I expect to ever get a good night's sleep again."

Now it all made sense. The fear Yarain had seen wasn't Jason or even Interstar. It was Simon trying to face his choice. He'd just gone against everything he'd been raised to believe. Now that the adrenaline had faded, some part of him still begged the question, "did I make the right choice?" After going wrong once, Yarain could only imagine how much the idea of picking the wrong side a second time might scare him.

Actually, she knew exactly how it felt. She'd faced the same question when she had been rescued herself. She'd trusted humans for a second, and spent the next three years held captive and experimented on for her mistake. Her rescuers were led by her own cub, so that helped. Still, it took a long time for her to be sure she hadn't put her trust in the wrong people again. In many ways, Simon's choice, if wrong a second time, could be worse. It's no wonder the thought had him terrified.

"You should help him, Jason," Yarain said, her voice as distant as her memories.

At first, Jason flinched as if bitten. Then he sighed great frustration. "Look, Lieutenant, I'd be happy to help, but not now. I have a dear friend in there I thought was dead a few days ago. I'd like to see him first."

Simon nodded with closed eyes. "Aye, sir. I'm sorry to interrupt, sir."

Yarain tried to find the right words, but Jason beat her there. He put his hands on the young man's shoulders. "Tell you what. Ask PAICCA to find an empty briefing or conference room equipped for detailed mapping. Head there, tell him to send me there when I ask, then wait for me. I'll go through the whole story once I'm done here. Deal?"

"Deal, sir!"

"See you in a few minutes then. Dismissed."

Simon snapped to salute, then marched his way off with a hidden spring in his step.

Jason stopped him before he got very far. "Lieutenant Solez. I cannot thank you enough for what you did. For what it's worth, you did the right thing."

Simon stood still for a moment before slowly turning to face him. "For the first time, sir, I think I believe that. Thank you."

Jason nodded, and the young man continued on his way.

"Thank you, Jason," Yarain said, a little surprised at the need.

"He deserves to know," Jason said. "Though let's get inside before something else comes up?"

Yarain ruffed a chuckle as she followed him through the doors at last. Two group mates were right behind them, both with burned uniforms, one hopping on a leg. Nurses got to them first and despite the burns, even Yarain could tell it was minor. All she and Jason would do is get in the way, so she watched them go down the row of beds, looking for her cub. A few other beds were occupied, but like the recent arrivals, all appeared minor based on the lack of energy around them. *Even the best of battles will draw blood.* Yarain thought, remembering words from an instructor.

As the two soldiers were guided to their beds, Yarain found the one she was looking for. With the collar gone, Sundale had retaken his primal form. He was laying with his head on his paws, staring at nothing, bandages dotting what she could see of his body, including a larger patch over his right eye. A blanket had been draped over the rest of him which, oddly enough, Yarain knew would be a comfort given his condition. It was as close to a den as he was going to get. Though the thought of how he'd gotten in that condition, and once again seeing the near-naked state of his shoulders, threatened to relight her rage at those responsible.

She did her best to keep that fire under control while she stepped forward to join his side. However, Doctor Blount saw her first and stopped them before she had taken more than two steps.

"I'm sorry, Major," she said. "No visitors."

Yarain's ears perked forward in anger, though she was able to keep her hackles flat. "I'm his mother, Doctor. You can't keep me from him."

"I'm not. He is."

Yarain's heart skipped a beat as her ears shot up. "What do you mean?"

Doctor Blount breathed out stress with folded her arms. "Captain Sundale has made it clear he doesn't want to see anyone. Not Lieutenant Colonel Harlem, not General Carson and… not you. He wants to be left alone as much as possible."

At first, there was only confusion. Alone? Wounded holdrens never shunned their pack. Not unless they were going to die, which Sundale wasn't. If anything, the wounded would do all they could to go *toward* their pack mates, as much for protection as comfort. Okay, they weren't in the wild, but the mentality remained. Yarain could find no reason that Sundale would turn her away when his instincts would want her most.

A soft whine escaped as her mind and heart tried to make sense of her cub's choice. A gentle hand fell on her shoulder. It was human, but still regarded as the pack, which allowed her nerves to focus on it. On Jason. The building panic stopped, tough not the concern.

"Easy, Yarain," Jason said. "Take a breath. Doc, I don't understand. Didn't Lieutenant Solez just see him?"

The doctor nodded grimly. "Though it's more like Sundale didn't want him to leave. They came in together, and each time I suggested the young man leave, Sundale insisted he stay. I never asked why. One doesn't press a patient in such stress. But when I mention the two of you, all he says is, 'I'm not ready.' He won't say anything else except to repeat his request to be left alone. I'm sorry, but until he changes his mind, I have to honor his request. That means you can't come in."

"What did they do to him?" Yarain said, finally voicing the only question that covered everything.

Doctor Blount dropped a hand to her hip with a scoff. "More like what *didn't* they do. You name it, he's got it. Cuts, bruises, fractures, a torn ligament, burns from being shocked, stunner burns, starvation, several small lesions from being kept immobile, and lots of edema in his legs for good measure. On top of that, his energy matrix is so weak and disrupted, I'm surprised he was able to shift forms. As it is… let's just say I'm trying very hard not to think about what they would have done had we not gotten him out of there."

Not quite how I meant the question.

The hand on Yarain's shoulder clenched, which allowed her shoulders to fall. Knowing Jason was that angry, that he cared that much... Sundale may want to be alone but at least she wasn't.

"What are the chances of him recovering?" Jason asked.

"Physically? Quite good. We won't know if we can repair his eye for a few hours. His body has a lot of wounds to heal without the usual supply of resources. We'll need to build those back up before he can handle any kind of accelerated tissue regeneration, and that means leaving used bio-gel in place longer than I'd like. Despite all that, eye not withstanding, I think he'll make a full recovery. Emotionally..." She looked back at Sundale, whose lips curled at a passing nurse though his ears were flat against his head. "I don't know. He's very feral right now. Basic treatment is hard when he's got the nurses so scared their hands are shaking."

Yarain's hackles rose, this time as Sundale's first mother. "Has he bitten anyone?"

Doctor Blount again scoffed, this time with a shake of her head. "Not yet. I'm worried about when that changes, however. When I say he's feral, I mean he sounded like he was going to tear us apart when we first started working on him. If it weren't for Lieutenant Solez, I'm not so sure he wouldn't have tried. As it is, I'm very worried about when we go in to fix that ligament. I haven't got a clue how we're going to treat his eye without losing fingers."

"He won't hurt you. I'd never tolerate it. Remind him of that, and you'll be fine."

The doctor looked at Yarain with a skeptical tilt, to which Jason nodded. "Trust me, Doc. It's more than enough. All the same, be delicate. Treat him as you might a scared fox. Just don't forget he's sentient. That would be insulting and could trigger the very reaction you hope to avoid."

Doctor Blount sighed while a hand went to her temple. "The things you must have to put up with. I'll keep all that in mind. Now both of you, out. My patients need rest and my attention. I'll let you know when you can see him, and I'll update you on the crew of Gold 12 when I have one."

Jason nodded and turned to leave. Yarain stood watching her cub, still trying to fathom what Simon's father could have done to damage his heart in such a way.

"Major," Jason said. "Come on. There's nothing more we can do here."

Yarain gave one last whine, then followed with sagging tails. Though he was clearly alive and safe, she couldn't help wondering if maybe she'd lost her cub after all.

Chapter 22

The Truth

Admiral Solez could feel his chest vibrate. It only got worse when he stared at the Grand Marshal on his screen. He still wore the same black suit and red tie as he ever did, but his eyes seemed darker today. Hollow like a void that could swallow Solez whole. *I almost wish they would. Would save me from the pain of Simon's betrayal.*

Instead, the admiral could do nothing but allow his gaze to fall on the one happy picture he had on his desk. Him in dusty overalls, his tall wife with long black hair beside him, and their young son with a tiny tree in front of him; which they had just planted as part of a new park. It was a good day.

"Admiral? I asked you a question. How... bad... is it?"

Solez had to swallow a planet-sized lump to even get his head on straight. Then he sighed away the knife in his heart before facing Grand Marshal Goodheart with a stern gaze. "The base is a complete loss, sir. Over half of the station's fighters were destroyed or captured. We lost two, – "

"I don't care about casualties, admiral! I'm asking you; how much damage was done to the operation?"

Solez took a deep breath to keep his anger from boiling up into words that might actually get him killed. "We can compensate for the losses, but we are now missing a vital forward operations base. Supply lines, reinforcements, coordination, it will all suffer. In fact, sir, I must strongly recommend we scale back–"

"NO!"

Admiral Solez couldn't keep the shock from his face. He was too busy trying to keep his stomach from leaping onto the console. "Sir... the plan cannot proceed like this. Not without—"

"Make... it... *work*, admiral! The wheels are in motion now. I won't let anything stand in the way of my ascension. We will carry through with the plan. Nothing, I repeat, noth—*ing*, will stop us. Am I clear, admiral?"

Solez nodded through a sigh. "Clear sir."

Grand Marshal Goodheart closed the channel without another word. The moment the screen flicked off, Solez's head hit his hands. *Make it work? There is no make it work. It can't be done.* Not that Solez could actually do anything about it. If he didn't follow orders, Grand Marshal Goodheart would just replace him with someone who would, which would be even worse. It also meant that Solez knew, beyond a shadow of a doubt, that thousands were going to die that didn't have to.

His eyes finally rose, only to land on the picture once more. "Why?" he asked the empty room. "I had no choice. It was the only way to keep them safe. To keep *you* safe. And now... now I... I..."

Admiral Solez's right hand began to shake as if it might vibrate until it shattered. He held it in his other hand and held it close to his chest, which only made the shudders travel down his arms and into his torso. For a moment, he could hear the whines of Captain Sundale echo off the walls as if the torture were happening right then and there. He breathed like he was about to vomit.

His gaze fell on the picture once more. His mind replayed the promise he'd made at the funeral for his wife. He vowed it would never happen again, no matter the cost. He promised her that he would keep their son, their nation, safe. From there, his gaze went to the bear insignia on the wall with the star of Polaris, and his eyes narrowed. Deep breaths brought the shaking to an end. The pain ignited within his chest and became a fire that warmed every part of his body.

Admiral Solez sat straight in his chair, blew a hard sigh out his nose, and then pressed for his aide.

"What do you need, sir?"

"Contact Captain Gullion. I need to know where we stand on Operation Second Visit."

With Sundale shutting him out and no real way to help Yarain, Jason could do little more than keep his promise to Lieutenant Solez. It was the last thing he wanted to do, but the man deserved his answers, even if he wasn't going to like them.

So, with PAICCA's direction, Jason headed to a briefing room just one deck down. On the way, he asked PAICCA to dig up every data file, map, and report he could think of that might cover it all. Eventually, PAICCA said, "Colonel, I'll prime any and all data even remotely related to the Confederation of Polaris. You won't have to wait for any of it."

Jason again wondered just how much 'I' was in PAICCA's 'AI' before dragging himself inside the briefing room. Lieutenant Solez was sitting in one of the forward seats, his gaze still elsewhere. That is, until he saw Jason. Then he snapped to attention with a salute.

Jason smiled with a half-hearted one of his own. "At ease, Lieutenant. You don't need to fear me like that."

"I'm... sorry sir," Solez said.

"You can stop that too. You did more than most would have in your position."

Lieutenant Solez nodded but with a heavy sigh. "I just wish I'd done it sooner. The moment I realized I could never see him as anything but a scared stray... I should have acted sooner."

Jason recoiled. "Stray? I can understand scared, but stray? I can't imagine Sundale ever looking like that."

"I can't explain it, sir. But when I looked at him... he looked like he had no home to wish for. Most people—foxes, whatever you want to use—most wouldn't be able to help thinking of home, or a safe place, anywhere that's not there. He never did. Or he didn't seem to."

"Was it that bad?"

"It... was. But this came before it even started, sir. I'm sorry, I don't know how else to explain it. He looked like a stray we'd picked up on the side of the road that was afraid of what we were going to do to him. It's like he had nothing else to think of."

Jason folded his arms deep in thought. *Stray? Sundale? A touch homesick maybe, but stray?* Try as he might, Jason couldn't see it. Even when they'd first met, Sundale had appeared simply scared then. Stray was never there, nor had it been since. Had something changed during his capture?

Jason shook his head to reset his mind. This was a rabbit hole he was already falling into. He'd not forget it, but he was there for a very different conversation. One that might be just as hard. A heavy sigh, and he was as prepared as he was going to get.

"Well, maybe it was just the situation. In any event, you came here for answers. I must warn you, though; I'm going to bet big you won't like *the* truth."

"Sir, I have to know," Lieutenant Solez said. "I can't make sense of any of it until I do."

"All right. Here's goes nothing. PAICCA, bring up a territory map, circa... I can't remember... five years before Polaris fell."

"Any highlights, Colonel?" PAICCA asked.

"Polaris, United Systems, and Marcalla."

Jason and Solez stepped closer to the screen as the requested map appeared. On it, five large territories, as well as two smaller ones, carved up a portion of the Milky Way. United Systems was more or less a large bubble surrounding the Sol system, though it touched two galactic arms and nibbled at a third. Polaris territory was a shoe-shaped section toward the galactice core from United Systems territory, or "galactic north", with the "toe" curving toward "galactic east" over parts of the Norma Arm, and the "heel" touching the end of the Crux Arm.

To the northeast of Sol sat Marcalla, which crossed three arms of the galaxy with a small territory marked as "Starfront" occupying a bubble directly east of Sol. Starfront was surrounded by Marcallan territory save for their west side which was United Systems. Another small section marked as "Orion's Arrow" was also north of Sol up on the Sagittarius Arm, with the jantans to their east. The coylins were to United Systems' southeast, claiming the parts of the Orion Arm that United

Systems didn't. The last was the Siltians, covering the south and south-east parts of the Perseus Arm United Systems didn't own. As requested, the United Systems glowed in blue, the jantans were in purple, and Polaris in dark navy.

"This is about when things began," Jason said. "By now, the Untied Systems Republic was fully formed and operating, all-be-it precariously at the time. The Jantan Wars had been going on for some time, and the consortiums you see are the last of those that either had refused to join the Republic or were still surviving."

"I do know that much, sir," Lieutenant Solez said carefully, as if trying to not offend.

"You wanted *the* truth, Son. Without knowing what version you've heard; this is the only truth I have to offer."

"Understood, sir. I... I'm sorry."

"Forget it. Anyway, at this point, the jantans didn't really care about Starfront or Orion's Arrow. Neither would last long and everyone knew it. They wanted the resources Polaris held before Interstar could claim any. Polaris had stopped fighting us long before, satisfied to live in their own corner of the galaxy after the colonies connecting them to Earth split off and joined United Systems. That meant Polaris could focus their entire armada on defending against Marcalla.

"They were actually doing quite well, but a five-year siege is hard to survive. Truth be told, it only took four. Year five was the mop-up portion. But I'm getting ahead of myself. At this point, Polaris was talking with Interstar about joint operations. They wanted help defending their territory. Interstar was willing despite them not offering materials, ships, et cetera to our own war effort. Thing is, there was a bit of a sticking point. PICCA, focus on Betty's Bubble."

As requested, the screen zoomed in on the "heel" of Polaris territory where a small bulge stuck out from the bottom of the "shoe," surrounded by Marcallan territory.

"Polaris forces made it clear; this area was to be defended at all costs," Jason said. "The area had a lot of juicy resources that could feed the war effort for years."

Lieutenant Solez nodded. "It was home to nearly two million colonists too. Workers, ship builders, artists. Some of our cultural treasures were made there. According to what I was told, Interstar outright refused to 'waste their time' defending them."

"Waste is hardly the word I would have used. PAICCA, tactical overlay. Show all Marcallan bases, shipyards, and staging grounds known of at that time."

Up and down the bulge, a full eighteen dots appeared. Six of them were listed as "major staging bases." The weakest of the bases was a stage-two shipyard, with a stage-four being the highest yield.

"Jesus," Solez said.

"Needless to say, Interstar considered these colonies to be a lost cause. In a later review, had the two fleets struck hard and fast enough, the five bases closest to United Systems could have been taken. This would have created a path through which Interstar forces could have helped bolster the lines, probably even led to further incursions into Marcallan territory. The new battle lines could have then been reinforced enough to defend until the *London* and the *Browning* hit the battlefield. But it still would have meant losing as much as forty percent of those colonies. Probably less, but they could not have all been defended. Believe it or not, evacuation *could* have been done, but you still would have lost a lot of treasures and resources."

"So Interstar could have done more," Lieutenant Solez said with hope.

Jason hummed with a rock of his head. "Yes and no. They could have tried to talk about which colonies to defend and how much to let go. But back then, we were in full bunker mode. 'Hold the line, give as little as possible, surrender what we can't hold while preserving our ships and crews.' Not the best of strategies, but that was the thinking back then. Then again, the question has to be asked: would Polaris have tolerated even giving up that much? I'm not so sure."

"Why not? What happened?"

"We're getting there. PAICCA, advance to the beginning of the bulge offensive."

The map changed to show an additional three temporary Marcallan bases around the bulge and a tiny reduction of Polaris control over those colonies.

"This is roughly one year after the last map. As you can see, things only got worse. The Polaris lines were starting to crack. They renewed their requests for Republic assistance and again, we said the colonies had to be abandoned. That said, we did offer ships for evacuation, help in reinforcing their deeper defenses, we even offered to send a fleet to hold the line outside the bulge. Negotiations never got anywhere. It was the bulge or bust, and we refused to die for bust. For a while, it seemed like Polaris was going to be alone forever, then this happened. PAICCA, 'final nail.'"

The map advanced again. The bulge was now half the size, though Interstar's territory had nibbled into Marcalla's by a fraction.

"Five months later, which is three months after the *London* class battleship got her trial by fire. By this point, we had ten of them with fifty more about to hit the stars in the next four months and even more shipyards getting upgraded so they could build the larger starships."

"They invested that heavily on an unproven design?" Simon said.

"They saw the writing on the wall. If the *London* wasn't going to cut it, we weren't going to make it. At worst, we'd still have sixty-one new ships when the walls fell. At best, we'd be able to turn the tides a bit. We landed in the middle, mostly just holding our ground though that did give us time to finish the *Browning* class destroyer, so it *was* worth it.

"Anyway, Polaris still had the means to defend if they had defended correctly, but that bulge was now unsavable and mostly impossible to evacuate. Other points had lost ground too. Facing the *London* and her sisters, the jantans decided to focus on Polaris to remove a thorn in their side. Starfront was gone, and Orion's Arrow had decided they'd rather join us than be eradicated. At this point, Polaris came to us again for help. Interstar missed a chance to strike a blow. That bulge was lost, but... PAICCA, double map. Show the Carnia Shipyard cluster, reference star: NGC 3372. Same time, highlight known Marcallan assets of the time."

The screen split in half to show the first section, and another showing a section of territory to the east where Starfront used to be. That territory was now held by the jantans. Just into Marcallan territory, almost right on the border of where Starfront used to be, were dots highlighting seven stage-four shipyards.

"Interstar could have drawn a massive amount of pressure away with very little risk. No one knows why, but Marcalla had left these shipyards largely under-defended. It would have taken every *London*-class we had, but we could have flattened those bases with almost no losses. We knew about it too, but we were worried about Marcalla's reprisal. They'd been leaving us alone while they focused on Polaris. A blow like this would have ticked them off to say the least. They would have reopened that second front for sure or possibly shifted their focus to us. Either way, it would have bought time for Polaris to bunker up and would have meant a lot fewer Marcallan ships in the coming months. This hub was one of their thickest clusters, and they thought we didn't know about them, which is why they never used them to invade. By the time they realized their error we were too well fortified, but that's another story.

"Then again, help from Polaris would have made it a lot easier. We even offered a joint venture at a different, less high-value target. Polaris agreed to meet with all the ships they could spare to begin the assault. Seemed like, at last, they were willing to work with us."

"And Interstar abandoned them," Lieutenant Solez said. "That's how we were taught. Interstar never showed. Nor was any reason or response given. Vital ships left the line, and we lost too much because of it."

Jason huffed, feeling the pain of the truth the young man was about to hear. "One side didn't show, but it wasn't us. A full assault fleet with eight of our new battleships went to meet the Polaris fleet. Admiral Garmon decided to arrive early in case there were tensions to work through. It's a good thing she did. At the time, long range sensors under cloak weren't that good. They arrived to find empty space and a sinking feeling in Admiral Garmon's gut."

"But you said they arrived early," Solez said. "Why would she be worried that no one was there?"

"Partly instinct. The rest because Polaris said they'd be waiting for them. Further, Polaris doesn't have cloaking technology, yet our ships saw no sign of theirs as they got closer to the appointed hour. Turns out there was a reason for that.

"As the rendezvous time got close, Admiral Garmon had the fleet move out of their planned meeting spot and prepare for immediate action. Fifteen minutes after they were supposed to meet the Polaris fleet, a Marcallan assault force warped in and fired on the exact coordinates where the fleet was supposed to have been. The jantans scanned the area but found nothing until the Interstar fleet got close to their heavies. The fleet decloaked, and before they knew what hit them, one carrier, seven battleships, and six heavy cruisers were down for the count. The rest was easy pickings, though some did get away.

"Thing is, when asked about it, Polaris said nothing. No response at all. Yet every Jantan prisoner captured that day said the same thing: Polaris had given them the time, coordinates, and suggested the arrival time to ensure we were there but not too nervous yet. A sweep of the area also found sensor jammers, *Polaris* sensor jammers, in the area. Our fleet would have never seen the jantans coming until it was too late to react."

Simon put his hand on his chest like he was having a heart attack. He took breath after breath, staring at the screen as if he might will it to change. "Surly they didn't. There's no way he'd... you... you wouldn't... this really is—"

"*The* truth? I'm afraid so, Son. That's not the end of it either. As your fall began, we stationed ships on the border to take in any and all refugees, civilian or military. We were ready to fight to save as many as we could. No one ever came. The one time Polaris accepted our offer, they tried to capture our fleet! After the last time, we were wary and triple checked everything. Thus, when the trap was sprung, we were ready to turn tail and run before they had a chance to fire a shot. After that, we didn't offer anything more. We just sat and watched the fall, wishing we could do more.

"To be fair, we *could* have done more. We waited too long to join the defense, and we missed golden opportunities to deal real blows to the jantans. But, Lieutenant, time after time, it was Polaris that refused our offers. There were two other times they tried to betray us, and they were too proud to let go of that territory. Interstar could have done more, but Polaris dug their own grave."

Lieutenant Solez staggered back to a first-row seat as if he were about to faint. Jason could only guess what was going through the young man's head. Without a doubt, his perception of the enemy, and probably his own nation, had been shattered. What else came with it only Simon knew, and Jason wasn't going to ask.

He could only offer one thing. "I'm sorry, Son. I wish I had a better truth for you."

Lieutenant Solez sounded light-years away when he spoke again. "What would you have done?"

"I don't know," Jason said. "As I am now, I can say I'd have hit the targets I mentioned, but that's after the fact. In the moment... I don't know."

"But... you said they were the right calls. Why would you not?"

"Lieutenant, after the years I've spent on the line, one thing I've learned is you never know what you'll do until you're in the situation. You can look back and say what you *should* have done, but I've made bad calls that I later looked at and saw what the right call was right away. So, I can't be sure what call I would have made... except one. Once Polaris tried their first betrayal... I'm sorry... But I would have done everything we tried to do from then on. Including our search for survivors and/or prisoners *after* Polaris fell. After a stunt like that, the risk would be too great to try anything more."

Lieutenant Solez stared at the screen, and then his face fell into his hands. He never sobbed, but the young man kept breathing like he was trying to huff something out of his lungs. This, Jason had seen before.

Simon's world was falling down around him. *The* truth was as hard as Jason feared it might be for him. Worst of all, Jason knew he could do nothing to help. The best he could do was be there, patient and open, while Simon tried to put his world back together.

The first steps came in words not meant for anyone. "For so many years... for so long, I grew up thinking my nation had been wronged, betrayed by... And my father. I always saw him as this great man. A champion of justice."

"A champion of justice," Jason said, "would not have done that to Sundale."

Lieutenant Solez's eyes locked onto Jason as if he'd just destroyed the last of his home world. In a way, perhaps he had. No doubt *the* truth had just obliterated whatever image the young man had of his nation. After a brief moment, Solez's eyes closed, and the first tears fell with a slow nod.

When the eyes opened again, they were heavier than the ship. Yet within them laid certainty. The kind Jason saw in the mirror when he decided to remain in the service all those years ago. When he realized that Sundale had given him the thing he was missing since his father died: a reason to fight.

"Nor would a force of order," Solez said. Sorrow kept his words quiet, but not the conviction. "I know you said not to, sir, but I need to say it one more time for me. I'm sorry I didn't act sooner. I should have seen what my father was."

Jason didn't hesitate. Here was one last block that Simon needed to get past, and Jason had a sudden sense of what this young man's life had been like. Maybe it was God or just his own instincts, but he suspected he knew why this was so hard for Lieutenant Solez beyond the obvious.

"Was he a good father?" Jason said. "I don't mean the soldier; I mean the parent. When you were growing up, what kind of parent was he?"

Lieutenant Solez brightened. "The best. When I was a kid, he tried so hard to be there for me. He even faced a reprimand because he refused to miss my graduation. He turned down a high-ranking position within an Admiral's command ranks because he didn't want to miss a single game of soccer my senior year."

Jason sat in a seat next to him. He tried to force himself to relax as if they were two old friends talking. "How'd you do?"

Simon laughed softly. "We got first in the colony championship tournament. And he was there for every game. He was sick as a dog, could barely get out of bed, still he came to see us win our way into the finals. Then he threw the entire team a huge party to celebrate our championship. He was always there. No matter what, he was there."

"No wonder you didn't see it. Who could see anything wrong with a father like that? I wouldn't have. In fact, if it weren't for Sundale, I wouldn't believe it if you said he was anything else. He clearly loves you. Even now, crushed as he may be, I bet he still does."

"Then why would he do what he did? Why would he lie?"

"It may not be a lie to him. He may fully believe Interstar is this evil fleet that wronged him. As for why he did it..."

Jason had a hard time with that one. A loving, selfless father like that treating Sundale the way he did? What happened? Was it always there, hidden beneath the parent? When Jason hit on the only answer that made sense, he hesitated to share it. Then he remembered his promise to tell *the* truth. Especially about this, he couldn't shy away from that now.

"Perhaps... perhaps he's simply willing to do things you and I aren't. We got info on that first base by tricking a soldier we captured. Yarain could have easily used her claws and teeth to torture him, but we refused to go that far. To us, it wasn't worth it. To your father, perhaps it is. He may even hate it, but in his mind, this is what he has to do to protect his family... to protect you."

"No," Solez said without a shred of hesitation or sorrow. "No, I saw him in the infirmary after Sundale had taken a man's eye. I don't know where my father was, but he wasn't there. He only cared about the soldier's ability to serve. All he wanted was to get what he needed out of Sundale. The cost didn't matter at all."

"Maybe. Maybe not. In my experience, true evil is almost impossible to find. What you get more often is otherwise good people willing to do what they think is right or necessary."

"Nothing good can come of what he did to Sundale!"

"From our perspective. To him, what he wanted could have ended the war, made sure you were kept safe, prevented another fall, all worthy goals. The difference is how far he was willing to go."

"Then why would the idea of me being a hostage mean nothing to him?"

Okay, that one requires more info. "What? More input please."

Lieutenant Solez stared at the screen a moment, then rose and walked over to the controls. After another stare, this time at the console, he shut the screen off with a sigh before facing Jason again. "Sundale broke free once. His hands were still cuffed, but his muzzle was off. He charged toward me; I don't know why. In the... in... in the heat of the moment, I... "

"You shot him," Jason said as if it were the right choice. More accurately, he couldn't find a reason to blame the man. Jason had seen an angry holdren in charge mode before. Having that come toward you would be enough for any man to fire regardless of what else was going through their mind.

"Yes," Solez said. "Just a stunner, though. Anyway, my father suggested that Sundale wanted a hostage he *thought* would give him a chance. As if to say Sundale would have been wrong. How do you react to that? My father, the award-winning dad, cares more about the mission than his own son? Never mind the soldier who is probably going to lose his eye, but all Dad cares about is whether or not the man can still serve. How can that be the same man I just described to you? How can *that* be my father?!"

For a moment, Jason's mind froze. It didn't even go blank. It just stopped where it sat, unable to operate. *How indeed.* When his mind started working again, it folded his hands into his lap in search of an answer.

The father described was the kind of father Jason prayed he would be given the chance. The soldier described could give Hitler a run for his money. How could both be the same person? What answer could there be for the young man, who was clearly growing to hate the man he thought he knew?

The search felt like years, but it was only a few seconds before Jason tapped his folded hands in his lap.

"I don't know," Jason said. "I have... no words for you, Son. I have no truth to offer there. I only know my side-arm and what I see when I look at Sundale now." When Lieutenant Solez turned around to stare at the blank screen, Jason went to his side and put a hand on his shoulder. "I can't answer all of your questions, Lieutenant. Many of them you're going to have to find for yourself, and you may not like what you find."

"They can't be worse than what I've learned today," Simon said.

Don't be so sure. "You still need to find them. It's the only way you're going to move forward. I'm here to help if I can, but I suspect only you can find the right path for yourself. That said, I will say this: by saving Sundale, you've already proven where your heart is. If you build on that, I suspect you'll find your path."

Lieutenant Solez sighed everything out. His shoulders fell with another nod. Jason couldn't tell if it was agreement or simple acknowledgment, and he again decided to leave it be. He'd said all he could think to say. The rest was up to Simon.

Jason was about to leave when Lieutenant Solez spoke again. "Sir, I need to get in contact with your intelligence division. I don't have much, but maybe I can help you end this war."

Jason moved his hand to his own hip. "You sure? What about your father?"

"My father... my father isn't there anymore. The man who replaced him needs to be stopped before he gets his hands on another holdren. He needs to answer for what he did to Sundale, and Polaris... needs to answer for their own mistakes. We can't hide behind a perverted truth anymore."

I so wish it were that easy. "You do realize what that'll mean for the people of Polaris? It won't be easy for them to accept the truth, and they will almost certainly suffer before this war is over. That's assuming they'll even listen to *the* truth."

"We have to try. Otherwise, sooner or later, the lie they've been living will destroy them. I still love my nation, sir, but I want to see it become something greater than it is. I want to see it become a *true* force of order. But we can't do that until the current order falls, for real this time. All I ask is that you do your best to make sure they stand on their own or are protected by Interstar. I don't want them to fall to anyone else."

"I'm only a pilot, but I'll do my best. You have my word on that at least."

Lieutenant Solez faced Jason, for the first time looking every bit a soldier. He offered a salute, then extended his hand. "Accepted, sir. Thank you. For all of it."

Jason found a firm and confident shake from the man's hand. "My pleasure, Lieutenant."

Chapter 23

Vulpine Medicine

The humans called it treatment. Sundale called it another round of torture.

The IV on his right foreleg itched for starters. They'd done their best, but the nurses hadn't figured out why. The winning theory was something to do with the fact that it was held on against his skin more than usual. He'd had one before, but his fur had been thick back then to act as a barrier. With his fur nothing more than a thin layer of fuzz, the attachment got to partially press against his skin which wasn't accustomed to *any* contact, much less medical adhesive. And that was the easiest of his problems.

He could never sleep unless he was alone. Anyone walking by that carried so much as a pen sent his ears back, his lips curling, and his insides shaking. He couldn't help it. Just someone yelling "clear," even in a sentence, drew a flinch. His body couldn't accept it was safe yet.

Then came the *real* treatment.

They'd operated on him twice. The first time to fix a ligament in his left foreleg. The second time for his eye. Given his emotions, even he agreed that being sedated was the best choice. It didn't make it any easier. Allowing that level of trust, knowing he'd be powerless again... If it hadn't been for Yarain's instructions, he never would have allowed it. Even with it, his ears had merged with his head when they'd put him under both times. Try as he might, he couldn't stop shaking. He feared he'd never wake again or worse, he'd wake up back in his cell, his rescue only a dream.

It helped that his trust had been rewarded. He'd woken up on a bed in the back, as far away from traffic as they could manage, with a leg he could move without it screaming at him. After a few hours, it felt good enough to run on again. He knew better, but it was the first time he'd felt good about anything in days.

The second operation hadn't come with any less fear. That time, he awoke with a thicker bandage on his eye, and a promise that it was the last time he'd be sedated. They wouldn't let him touch the bandage, though. It too itched, probably for the same reason, but the eye itself did feel better. Far less pain that faded by the hour, and no resistance to movement even though it was covered. The only time it was a real problem was when they changed the bandage. He'd been told to keep the eye closed, so he hadn't been able to see how much damage remained. Plus, the removal of the old one hadn't gone as smoothly as they'd hoped.

He tried not to think about the lasting emotional damage. Deep inside, he knew the fear would pass as he recovered. No longer using the pan attached to his bed for waste was a day he longed for as well. As for Gold 1... Could he ever go back? Did he deserve to go back? Knowing how close he'd come; he couldn't be sure. Another few minutes, the loss of his tails, what would he have said? What would he have done?

Nothing, and you know it.

It felt like a lie, yet it wouldn't go away. True, he hadn't let go yet, but he'd also had to focus more and more to make sure he didn't. Holdrens never put themselves before the pack. An individual would be expected to die if it meant saving the whole. Sundale's instincts would have told him to hold on for the pack. His pain would have had him say anything to end it. Who would have won? He feared the answer, and he couldn't get over the shame of there even being a question.

Sundale was lost in that question when familiar voices drew his attention to the doorway. He looked up with perked ears to see Jason and Yarain had returned to check on him again.

Doctor Blount continued to bar their way. "I said I'd inform you when he was ready."

"It's been five days, Doc," Jason said. "You can't blame us for trying anyway."

"All the same, Colonel, you can't go in yet."

Jason tried to get Sundale's status from the doctor, but Sundale was focused on the holdren eyes locked onto him. Yarain watched him as if her stare could be the comfort he wanted but hadn't been able to take. How could he? Her presence would only remind him of how close he'd come. And Jason... What if he *had* cracked? How would Jason feel? What would either of them think? He couldn't bear their emotions anymore than he could handle his own right now.

Except their emotions were just as heavy on his heart. After his first surgery, Sundale learned everyone thought he was dead. After getting the details, he held no blame for the mistake. He'd been in a hole that erupted in a fireball followed by an avalanche that buried it. What reason would anyone have for thinking he'd survived? No, he didn't blame anyone. He almost wished he did. At least then he could be angry at someone. Instead, all he had was his mother's shifting ears and an aching heart.

Despite what he'd done, or almost done, he couldn't do that to them anymore. After all, they didn't have to know how close he'd come. They only needed to be near him again, without armor getting in the way this time.

"Let them in," Sundale said.

Yarain's ears shot up, though Doctor Blount turned around almost as fast. She held a hand up to the others before approaching his bed.

"Are you sure, Captain?" she asked. "You were pretty adamant this morning."

His ears perked forward in dominance for the first time in days. "Let them in."

The doctor shook her head before motioning for Jason and Yarain to approach.

Yarain leaned in to rub her muzzle on his the moment they reached his bedside. Sundale returned the rub as they traded whines of affection. She offered a lick that tried to become a cleaning but stopped before she got going. Instead, she knelt beside him so that her head was next to his, staying off the bed but being with him as she hadn't been able to for some time.

Sundale was just glad to feel her fur against his... well, against him. Her scent didn't come with such a quantifier, nor did her aura. He felt her as only pack mates could. He didn't need to see her, for her soul was there with his once more. Any time he wanted, he could move his head over and allow their whiskers to touch, even though his were only just starting to grow back. Being that close, he could feel her energy matrix like a thin breeze, too weak to move his fur, but there all the same.

Thin fur or not, he was happy to feel her near him again. It was only minorly soured by his efforts to keep her from sniffing his cheek glands. While it was normally the way holdrens would greet one another, it would also allow her to find scents betraying the very feelings he sought to hide. Fortunately, she was too busy being a comfort to notice how he never quite allowed her to find them.

Jason had leaned on an empty bed on the opposite side of the aisle so they could have their moment. Eventually, when both holdrens stopped offering whines, he folded his arms with a smirk. It suggested he was about to tease Sundale about something. A warning that Sundale both appreciated and deeply missed.

"Ya know, I'm getting tired of seeing you in here," Jason said.

Sundale could only manage a single ruff of amusement. "I'm getting tired of *being* in here."

Yarain slowly set herself down on the edge of Sundale's bed. Sundale moved just enough to let her sit beside him, an invitation she instantly accepted.

Jason nodded with a heavier smile. "I'll bet. I hope you'll forgive me for it, but I'll ask the dumb question. How do you feel?"

"About like you'd expect. I am healing, though."

"What about emotionally?"

Sundale's ears fell as the pain came rushing back. The fear came close behind followed by the shame of the question. *I can't. I don't care if I never would have. I can't... He can't know how close...*

For a moment, Sundale wasn't on a bed. He was somewhere else. Not his cell, not a cockpit, but walls pressed in all the same. A shudder shook him as fear, anger, and agony mixed together into a ball of emotion he couldn't untangle. There was a voice, he thought, just on the edge. Was it only one? What was it saying? Where was he? What—

The shudder ended the moment he felt Yarain lean in against him. As quickly as it had started, he was back in the moment. In truth, he'd never left. He'd remained aware, saw his mother's ears shift when the shudder started as well as Jason shaking his head in anger at himself.

Jason had already thrown his hands up by the time Sundale came out of his moment. "It's all right, Sun. It's too soon, I'm sorry. I shouldn't have asked."

Sundale forced his eyes... eye to find Jason's. Some of the panic returned but remained in the background this time. A single shudder ran through him as those last moments flashed before him as if he were reliving it. More than the pain or the fear, there was the struggle. The internal battle to not give in, to not betray his pack. The memory kept his insides quivering, making it harder to breathe easy.

"Give me time," Sundale said. "It's still raw for me."

"But it's over now," Yarain said. "Leave it where it belongs."

"It's not that easy."

"I never said it was. It just is."

Jason huffed with another shake of his head. "What I wouldn't give to live like you do. There's a lot in my past I'd love to leave behind."

Yarain nuzzled her cub before perking her ears at Jason. "The past is done with, Jason. We remember for the lessons, but we don't live there. We live in the now."

"I'm afraid it's not that easy for us humans. We love to dwell on the past."

"I've noticed."

Sundale tried to bark to silence the subject. What came out was a low yip. It accomplished the goal, however. Yarain gave him another nuzzle while Jason offered a comforting smile.

"Well, I'm glad to have you back," Jason said. "Gold 1 hasn't been the same without you."

I missed you too. Sundale leaned his head to rub against his mother's hip. She in turn rubbed her head against his back, and for the first time since his capture, his body relaxed. He felt himself falling but in that soft, soothing way one does as sleep takes hold. Actual sleep wasn't far behind, though doing so would mean losing this moment he didn't want to let go of.

He was safe here, protected. He didn't need to hold tension anywhere or even keep his ears perked. For this single, blessed second, there was nothing beyond the presence of his pack. More so when Jason gave a gentle rub behind his ear, right where he liked it. Something only those closest to him were ever allowed to know. Between the two, Sundale didn't even feel his missing fur anymore.

That is until a cleared throat brought all their eyes to Doctor Blount and a nurse with a tray of tools. "I'm sorry to break this up," Doctor Blount said, "but I want to check that eye of his."

"Can I stay?" Yarain asked. It was almost an order.

"Not there you can't. We may need to work on him. I can't do that with you in the way. I'm sorry, Major. I need you both to step away."

Tension pulled on Sundale's legs. His ears fell not in fear but in preparation for combat. Just as he was starting to heal, pain was coming for him once more. Slight and beneficial as it was, the switch brought all that fear and anger to the surface. It meshed with his instincts to send him straight into fight or flight mode.

When his lips curled up, a sharp ruff from Yarain sent them drawing back instead. *"Be at ease, Sundale. She's here to help. You will not harm her."*

"She cares nothing for how I feel."

"Even so, you need her care. You will not harm her."

Sundale gave a low growl, but it was his only protest. His ears and pulled back lips signaled his surrender to his first mother. Yarain stood and joined Jason as he once more leaned with folded arms against the opposite bed.

"You two aren't going anywhere, are you?" Doctor Blount said.

"Nope," they both said, Yarain barking the word.

"I don't like an audience during treatment. I want you out."

"Bad idea," Jason said. "I don't know what was said, but it's clear Sundale is having a hard time with this. You need us, his pack, here to help him stay calm. Unless you'd rather him break your hand with his bite."

Doctor Blount sighed before signaling the nurse to begin. "Just stay out of my way."

As the nurse attached the tool tray, Doctor Blount put gloves on with another sigh. "All right, Captain. First, we'll need to take that bandage off. It's going to sting, but I need you to hold still."

"It did a lot more than sting last time," Sundale said.

"The wound was raw then. Fresh bio-gel will have helped that. Now please, Captain, try to hold still. Keep your eye closed until I say otherwise."

Sundale shuddered with flat ears as her gloved hands ignited his fur. Every hair she touched still expected pain on top of being so sensitive because they were short. Still, he kept his protest to only the slightest curling of his lips. A steady glare from Yarain made it clear that was all he was allowed.

Doctor Blount moved gently but steadily along the sides of the bandage, removing it in a slow, smooth motion. She paused only once to check for anything clinging to it before finishing the pull. Not that he'd tell her, but the bio-gel did make this round far less painful than before. The last time, it felt like she was ripping his fur out with tweezers. This time, it was only a sharp pull that was more irritating that painful.

At last, the bandage was off. Sundale shook his head gently to shake off the tingle and found the now exposed skin felt cool as air touched it for the first time in a couple of days. It was oddly soothing, which helped him drop his display for good, though his ears couldn't quite come up yet.

Doctor Blount traded the old bandage for a hand-held scanner she hovered over his right eye. As it hummed away, Sundale watched her with his other eye, waiting for news he feared would be bad.

After a minute that felt like an hour, she dropped the scanner against her hip. "Okay, Captain, open up. Let's see what we've got."

Sundale blinked his other eye open. At first, parts of the eye lid felt stiff, but that passed after a few blinks. There was something else there, though. An odd tension... stiffness... he couldn't put a word to it, but it sat right in the middle of his right eye lid, and he couldn't seem to get rid of it. Even when he carefully rubbed a licked paw over it, the feeling seemed to remain. He wondered what it was, though found the sensation already fading into normalcy.

Whatever it was, it couldn't keep him from realizing his fears had been unfounded. Once the eye adjusted to light, his vision changed only in increased range. The quality, depth, movement acuity, it was all still there. Even as he pawed at his eye, he realized nothing had changed from before.

"Well, Captain?" Doctor Blount said. "How's your vision?"

"Seems perfect," Sundale said.

Jason let out a sigh of relief while Yarain's ears ticked forward in approval. The doctor meanwhile gave a grave nod. "Well, one out of two ain't bad. At least we managed the important one. Though watch how much you rub it. We're already pushing the limits of how much we can accelerate your healing right now."

"What do you mean one out of two?" Jason said. "What's two?"

"I had hoped the cut would heal more. Then once his fur grew back it would cover it up. But it was three full days before we could do any real repairs, and we couldn't risk taxing his body any further to accelerate the healing process. The body spent too much of that time panic repairing. I'm afraid it's not going to get much better."

Sundale was actually more confused than worried as shown by the soft tilt of his head while his ears came up. "How much better could it get? Aside from some kind of tension, everything feels fine."

"I suspect that 'tension' is the wound, Captain. But you're right. It's not really a problem. I doubt it'll even affect your insulation once your fur grows back. It just means you have your first battle scar. At least, the first one anyone will be able to see."

"What do you mean the first anyone will see?"

"You'll have some slight scars, but they're so slight even the thinnest part of your fur will cover them completely. Your eye on the other hand..."

Doctor Blount looked around, then flashed a finger up before heading down the row toward her office. Sundale sat up to watch her go with his ears perked as the blanket slid onto his tails. Yarain also had her ears up, though the small state of her lips suggested she wasn't too happy with the doctor's sudden departure.

"Uhhh, nurse?" Jason asked.

"No idea, Colonel," the nurse said.

"Woman could use some lessons in bedside manner," Yarain said.

"She cares, ma'am. She's just not good at showing it sometimes."

"That's an understatement," Sundale said.

Before the conversation could take off, the doctor returned with a small make-up kit. Without a word of explanation, she opened it and turned the mirror toward Sundale.

Sundale's ears fell back at what he saw. The near-naked state of his body he expected, though felt no better about. It was his eye that had his insides turning. Or rather, the roughly three-inch scar that ran in a line vertically across it. It was still red in the middle, which part of him knew would fade some. Thing is, it would only fade *some*. Meaning it would be there as a reminder, *forever*.

"Is there nothing you can do?" Sundale asked.

Doctor Blount pocketed the make-up kit. "Nothing you'd like. More likely any attempt would make it worse at this point. As miraculous as modern medicine can seem sometimes, there are some things we can't quite manage. Ensuring we don't mess with fur follicles makes it that much harder. I'm afraid you'll have to make do with perfect vision at the cost of a small scar. I wish I could do more."

Another soft whine escaped as Sundale thought about that trade. The scar itself really wasn't a problem. If anything, scars suggested an individual was worthy of respect, for experience came with those scars. It was the reminder. One he'd never be able to forget. He'd see it every time he saw himself in a mirror or a window or the calm waters of a river. It would always be there, reminding him of what they did to him. Of how close he'd come. Even if he could move past that, humans loved to ask about scars and birthmarks. They would pressure, press, and demand to know the story, and no amount of refusal would keep the memories from surfacing. For the rest of his life, he would have to live with what happened when he got it. All of it.

Sundale's shudder returned followed by panic. He didn't want to run or fight, he just wanted reality to be something else. He wanted to forget it all, leave it behind, but he couldn't. Humans would never let him. His own face would never let him. He would always be there, as he was now.

Voices echoing in the distance. Air leaving the room as every hair searched for danger. He had to leave, but he knew he couldn't. He had no power, no control, no hope of things changing. He couldn't move. They'd taken that from him too. He couldn't breathe. The quiet voices were getting louder. He could almost hear them now. He could just catch parts of one in particular.

"... being in Interstar... doomed your entire race... I could even let you go home... go home..."

Sundale snapped at a touch that lit his whole body on fire. He tried to find his breath as he realized he'd come a whisker away from biting Jason's hand. Sundale's ears went as flat as they could when they saw the shock on Jason's face, as well as the concerned perk in Yarain's ears.

"I'm sorry," Sundale said.

"That bad, huh?" Jason said, shock turning to concern.

"You have no idea."

"I'll bet. God, Sun, if I'd known. If I'd had any idea—"

"*JASON*, I don't blame you. I never did."

What Sundale wasn't saying was that he held more blame for himself. After the near miss just now, many humans would have looked at him differently, as if he were a stranger. Jason's shock wasn't that. Surprise certainly, for Sundale had never snapped at him like that before, but the stare wasn't "who is that?" Jason's stare had been "they hurt him more than I thought." Jason still saw Sundale the same. Wounded yes, but still the same fox he'd known for eleven years.

Except Sundale wasn't so sure. Having come so close to surrendering, to putting their lives, *Jason's* life, at risk, the support felt more like new wounds forming. What if he had broken? Would he have stopped at the transmission codes? Would he have given up something that would have led to Jason's death? To Yarain's? The fact that he was even asking hurt more than when the blade swept across his eye. Jason's support only made it worse since Sundale did not feel he deserved it.

The doctor and nurse ran one more scan before the nurse left with the tray. Doctor Blount shined a light into Sundale's eye in one last check, to which Sundale gave a soft growl of protest. How many times did she need to be told his eye was fine before she left him alone?

"Well, Captain, the good news is I think you'll be out of here in a day or two," she said. "I want to keep an eye on those cuts before I let you leave my care. I also want to be sure your eye doesn't degrade now that it's open to the air."

"Just tell me when I can leave," Sundale said.

The doctor hummed agreement as she moved to the wall to check his vitals and chart.

Jason sighed with a glance at Yarain. "I think we better go. Let the poor fox rest."

"I agree," Yarain said.

She leaned in for another nuzzle. Sundale returned it with a soft lick, though he still used it to protect his cheek glands. Jason stepped forward to try his rub again, slowing only to make sure Sundale would let him. When Sundale's ears perked forward, Jason rubbed his right cheek as he had tried to do before.

"It's gonna be a long road, Sun," Jason said. "You'll have to find a way to move past it. Which I know sounds a lot easier than it is. On the bright side, the scar adds a bit of character."

Sundale huffed, more like hacked, as he pushed Jason's hand away. "There's nothing good about it, Jason."

This time, Jason didn't react at all. He dropped his hand to his side as if nothing had happened. "Sure there is. It's proof you're stronger than they are. Every time they see it, they'll see the holdren they couldn't break. You'll be a point of fear for them, and inspiration for the group."

Not if they knew the truth. The longer Jason went, the more Sundale's insides shook. If he knew... if *any* of them knew how close he had been, they wouldn't see the scar as inspiration. They, like Sundale, would be reminded of how he'd almost broken. Something that would almost certainly damage or destroy the comradery between them.

Perhaps, if Jason did *know, he'd understand. Maybe even help me through it.* A welcome thought, but Sundale wasn't willing to take that chance. Even if he'd forgive him, once Jason knew, others would eventually find out, and that he could not risk. No matter how small the chance.

"You do not understand what they did to me," Sundale said.

Before Jason could reply, Yarain placed a firm but comforting hand on Sundale's chin. "Sundale, it's the past. It's over. There's no reason to keep it."

"How can I drop it with a reminder branded on my face?"

"By separating the mark from the event. The scar is a testament to your strength. The event is irrelevant now. What matters is the present in which you need only recover so you can rejoin the hunt."

"Doesn't your captive experience still linger?"

"No."

It felt like another knife, this one straight to his heart. He'd only been held captive for a couple of weeks, yet he couldn't get away from it. She'd been held for *three years* with frequent experiments done to her and Harmus over that time. Yet she carried no scars, physical or otherwise. His mother was stronger than he was.

He needed someone to understand, and no one there did. No one there could. He felt more alone than when he was in his cell. The frantic need to hide, to be away, was even worse.

Jason sighed, and Sundale waited for another dagger.

"Yarain, when we rescued you, the first time you saw anything close to a cage, both you and Harmus snarled up a storm. I seem to recall you bit a nurse trying to treat you when that treatment stung a bit."

"I didn't stay there, Jason," Yarain said. "I put it behind me."

"And how long did that take?"

"That's enough!"

It was Doctor Blount's hard voice that stopped everyone in their tracks. Even Yarain was pulling her ears back as Blount stood there glaring at Jason and Yarain, daring them to test her. When neither accepted the challenge, she continued.

"I want you two out, now. Don't say another word, Human or otherwise, just get, *out*. When he's ready, I will let you know. Until then, I don't want you in here. Am I clear?"

Jason couldn't help a sigh, but his nod appeared to keep the doctor's wrath at bay. Yarain's ears went full back in submission before she followed Jason out the door. She slowed only to glance back at Sundale a moment.

Sundale meanwhile felt relief wash over him like a tidal wave. It wasn't until that moment he realized just how tense he'd been. What was left of his hackles had begun to rise, though they were too thin for most holdrens to notice. While he did hate to see his pack leave, he didn't mind the conversation ending.

After he coaxed his hackles down, Sundale laid back down to rest. Doctor Blount carefully slid the blanket on with an eye on him for any indication he objected. He didn't. Until his fur came back, it was as close to a den as he was going to get. She checked his vitals one more time, then turned to leave for her next task.

"Thank you," Sundale said.

She stopped at the head of his bed. "I didn't just do it for you, Captain. I don't like debates in my sickbay. Especially over—"

"I meant the blanket. But... that too."

Doctor Blount nodded with the first smile, however small, he'd seen her give. "You're welcome. I wish I could do more for you."

"You've done enough."

It was an odd phrase he didn't expect, yet he looked back and realized she had. She'd put him on a back bed after his operations. She'd cleared the area that first day when his bandages needed changing. And when sickbay got hit with a flood of injuries, she'd left strict orders to keep the beds around him empty unless they were needed. Despite her tendency to be harsh, she *had* tried to make things easier for him. If he could only understand why his treatment frustrated her so often, maybe he'd find a way to help her interact with him better.

That said, she surprised him by asking a question she very clearly meant as a joke.

"You sure? I could always knit you a sweater."

Sundale panted a laugh that felt better than a fresh kill on an empty stomach. "No, thank you."

"Captain... Sundale, if you don't mind."

"I don't."

"Okay. Sundale, I may have kicked them out, but they are right about one thing. You'll need to find a way to come to terms with what happened to you. That scar isn't going away, but the pain will. Once it's gone, you'll be left with a mark that really does add something to you. I don't know what the best steps are, but you need to take them. It's the only way you're going to heal from this and get back into a Scorn."

For once, it didn't feel like a battle. Okay, it did, but nothing like the one he'd just had with Jason and Yarain. Sundale didn't like so many individuals telling him he had to "get over it." At least Doctor Blount seemed willing to let him find his own way to recover. Yarain wanted him to drop it like shed fur. Jason... Sundale couldn't figure out what Jason had in mind. Neither understood what he'd been through. Nor could they. Not without knowing all of it.

"I don't know if I can ever go back," Sundale said, more to himself than the doctor.

"Of course you can," she said without emotion. "But after everything you've been through, perhaps the question you should be asking is; do you want to?"

Sundale's ears perked at her as the question hit like a mountain. He couldn't form a reply because he was too busy asking the question and then dealing with the many answers that popped up.

After a moment of him staring, Doctor Blount nodded with a huff. "Don't try to answer now. You need to heal your body before you do anything. Gold 1 will always be there when you're ready. Let me know if you need anything."

She left without another word, leaving Sundale alone with the thought. Would anyone blame him? Two "seizures," captured, tortured, scarred for life; it's a wonder he hadn't lost it already. Maybe he'd given Interstar all he had. Maybe it was time he left it behind.

Except Jason needed him. The man loved to take on all the pressure alone. He needed someone there to carry some of the burden. Yarain did her part, but she didn't have the same connection Sundale did. She was a dear friend and comrade. Sundale was a litter mate. Only a sibling who was also a pack mate could get Jason to look at himself and realize he couldn't do it alone.

And yet, Sundale had to ask another question: did he have the strength to do that anymore? He'd snapped at Jason once and was getting closer to doing it again before Doctor Blount put an end to it. He had no way of knowing how many more "seizures" he was going to have, or what was going to come of them. Yes, Jason needed him, but it would be silly to burn Sundale out in the process. Then Jason would be on his own, and Sundale would be worse off than he already was. A pointless sacrifice that would accomplish nothing.

Sundale's thoughts were broken by, of all things, a simple itch. It grew on his paw until he had to surrender and dig in to silence it. When he did, he saw the nearly faded marks left by the cuffs. He paused his biting to let himself stare at them so his mind couldn't ignore them.

You still have fresh wounds, he told himself. *Right now, they need your attention. Your decision will still be there when they're gone.*

Sundale wasn't so sure, but he surrendered all the same. After the itch was silent, he laid his head on his paws and let himself fall into deep sleep for the first time in weeks. As luck would have it, the only dreams he remembered were those of long hunts with his pack. The rest were never recorded.

Chapter 24

The Proverbial Straw

Sundale gave a soft growl, but that was his only protest as he pressed his left paw against Doctor Blount's hand. His ears were flat in response to the growing burn and strain in his leg. He wasn't even pushing that hard, but between the many days bound and the recent injury, there was a lot of strength that needed to be reclaimed. Though right now, it seemed like all Doctor Blount wanted was to cause him pain.

That pain made seconds feel like hours until at last she said, "Okay, let it go."

Sundale pulled his leg tight against his body as pain… never came. He had expected another round of agony, yet it faded into a mild throb instead. As he carefully extended it, he found the leg stiff and sore, but largely without complaint. At the same time, Doctor Blount was scanning the leg with an approving nod.

"Remind me to commend Doctor Gustov," she said. "I think he out did himself this time. Well, Captain, I want you to take it easy for the rest of the day but otherwise, I'm letting you out. You don't have to stay any longer, and I think we can leave all of the bandages off provided you be careful with any scratching. Understood?"

"Understood," Sundale said. "Thank you."

He gave his leg another extension before advancing to stand on it. Again, things were stiff and sore, but there was very little lingering pain. That said, when he went to jump off the bed, the leg tensed as if about to cramp. He stopped cold so he could tuck it against his body before it did so or retore the tendon. This early in his recovery, he refused to risk new injury that would delay his freedom for even a second. Thus, he landed with great care to ensure his left foreleg took no impact at all. He transitioned to the floor without incident, though a lack of practice landing on three legs did mean he was a bit wobbly.

Which of course drew Doctor Blount's attention. "Everything all right, Captain?"

"Yes," Sundale said. He carefully let the leg take its usual weight and found little tension or complaint in it.

"That's it? Just, yes?"

Humans and their details. "It was tense, so I didn't want to risk landing on it. It's fine. It's just stiff."

"Physical therapy will help that. We've repaired the damage, but you'll still need to work it back into shape, so use it gently for a while. I don't want you back here for anything other than a checkup. As for your emotional recovery—"

"I'll handle that on my own," Sundale said.

"Not on my ship you won't. You can't just sleep this off, Captain. You have to see someone about this."

Sundale turned to face her with a growl. "Like who? What human could understand what I went through? You don't think like I do."

Doctor Blount rolled her eyes. "So Colonel Harlem keeps telling me. Since he knows so much about you, maybe *he* might be a good start. Or his wife, or God forbid, *your own mother* maybe? I don't care who it is, hell, talk to PAICCA if you have to, but you *will not* do this alone."

Sundale ears fell in fear. She didn't understand. How could she? Talking about it meant facing them with the truth. His heart couldn't be near them without thinking about how close he'd come to betraying them. He couldn't talk about what really happened without being where he suddenly found himself.

He was trapped in darkness that pressed in on every side, even from within. It was creeping over him, blinding his senses bit by bit. The only clear sense was his hearing as the voices echoed on the edge like before. They kept him bound, helpless. He was caught in their will, ready for them when they came for him. He could do nothing about it. Whenever they so chose, the darkness would take him back without any chance of escape this time. It was swallowing him whole the more he thought about it, until at last he shook his head as if drying off. The action allowed him to clear his mind of everything, including the darkness.

Though the pain remained to lace his words. "I can't be near them now."

Sundale watched Doctor Blount. He expected her to scold, lecture, or out-right order him to speak to someone. Except for a full minute, she didn't say a word or move a muscle except to fold her arms and shift her gaze so she could look him over. When their eyes met, Sundale found no glare there. No fire of anger. If anything, it was more like the stare he'd seen humans give a piece of art, as if her eyes could pick him apart hair by hair. Whatever she was looking for, the search bore into Sundale, seemingly drilling through the darkness and the pain. The longer she held it, the more both faded until even his fear had been burned away. All that remained was her, him, and a stillness within as he waited for her next move. He could do nothing else... because he had nowhere to go.

"So that's what the Polaris officer meant," she finally muttered.

Sundale turned his head, confused at the statement. "Meant about what?"

Not a single hair on Doctor Blount moved. That is until she slid onto one knee in front of him. Sundale took a step back, not out of fear, but out of the same respect given to any first parent claiming a space. It was an act of pure instinct, and one he hadn't expected her to draw from him. Stranger still was the smile that formed on her face. It was so tiny it almost wasn't there, yet it and her eyes carried a crispness he'd only seen twice before. First, when Karol learned his real name and nature, then again after he and Jason had a conversation about Sundale dropping out of the academy.

Both times, they were never the same around him.

"Why can't you be near them, Captain?" Doctor Blount said.

"I can't trust myself."

It was the first thing he could think of. It was also only half of the truth. The other half was that he feared he would put himself before the pack again. That he would be selfish as no proper Holdren should be. Those that are rarely lasted long in the wild, or they got members of their pack killed because of that selfishness, sometimes both. It's the biggest reason such members are driven out if not killed. The risk to the pack is too great.

Even if she knew the truth, Sundale wondered if Doctor Blount would understand it. Jason had a hard enough time with the Holdren mentality, and he understood holdrens better than anyone. Doctor Blount had shown little of that, though that crispness he'd seen in her suggested that was changing. Whether it had changed enough remained to be seen.

For the moment, her eyes remained locked on him as she sat back on her kneeling leg. "Snapping at Colonel Harlem is understandable. As you said, it's still raw. After the last two weeks, I'm not surprised your animal side took over, if you'll forgive the comparison."

Not the risk I'm talking about. "It's more than that. I can't... I can't be sure I'd be a proper packmate. Until that changes... I can't risk being near them."

More half truths, ones missing key parts which compounded his turmoil. Worse than being selfish, now Sundale thought he knew better than a first mother, as evidenced by him with-holding information from her. That was close to being a challenge, for only a first parent could decide what the pack did or did not need to know. Piece by piece, he was losing all the things that made him a Holdren. Worst of all, there appeared to be no sign of it slowing down.

Whatever Doctor Blount thought, she hid perfectly. "You can't be alone either. Holdren or not, you have to be near someone if you're going to recover from this."

Sundale snorted at her, which a Holdren would have pinned him for on the spot. "I'm scheduled for multiple physical therapy sessions and follow up exams. I'll hardly be alone."

In lieu of fangs, Doctor Blount's eyes narrowed as did her lips. The glare was worthy of a first mother, which sent Sundale's ears and tails falling just as quick.

"Sarcasm won't work with me, Captain," she said. "You know damn well what I mean. You can't be near your crew? Fine. Choose someone else. The Polaris officer, what was his name? Simon? He might do. I know a few crew members who admire you. I'm sure you have others elsewhere you could turn to that won't be on the front lines. Or you could spend time with me. I'll be your pack while you recover."

Sundale's insides shook at the idea, more out of fear than anger. "You don't understand. I can't be near *any* pack."

Doctor Blount sat on her foot so she could fold her arms. "Too bad. If I have to put you on a chain – and don't think I won't – you *will not* be allowed to hole away on your own for this. You have to be near someone, and I don't mean proximity, Sundale. Solitude will only make the wounds that much worse. So, I want you to find someone you're willing to be near. It can be me, Simon, someone from the crew, or someone back home. It's *your* choice. I'll accept your decision, but only if it involves being near someone."

Your choice. Those words hung louder than the others. The glare remained, but it was still that of a first parent. She had laid down his boundaries, then left the rest up to him. She had left him with control. The very thing he'd felt missing since his capture.

The only sting was a third word. *Home.* He desperately wanted to *go* home, except there was no home. The place of his birth was no doubt held by another pack by now. Earth, despite a few truly wild forests, still felt alien to him. Gold 1 was where he hunted, but it wasn't the kind of home he needed. He had no where to go, and right now, no one he felt safe allowing to protect him. He'd almost put himself before his pack once. Until... *if,* he could be sure he wouldn't do it again, he didn't dare put another pack at risk.

Except Doctor Blount wasn't going to let him off that easy. That much he knew for a fact. Though he had control, like any first parent, she'd set clear limits to that control. What he did with it was up to him.

Limited as it was, it did allow weight to fall as if a dozen riders were sliding off one by one. Eventually, Sundale felt light enough to fly. It allowed him to consider what a few minutes ago would have been a nightmare.

"If... I choose you," Sundale said, "what would that be like?"

Doctor Blount unfolded her arms so she could half lean on her knee. "We'll spend time together. On my off hours or during your therapy sessions, wherever we can manage it."

That sounds fun. "Holdrens aren't good at small talk."

Doctor Blount laughed lightly. "Neither am I. I just don't want you alone as you rebuild yourself. You need time to heal and at least one additional body to help you do that. We could eat meals together, fail badly at small talk, maybe even find ways for you to help around here. All that matters is that you spend time near someone."

Not getting better. "I can't recover by spending every waking hour with you."

"I'm not asking you to marry me." Doctor Blount rose to her feet. As she did, Sundale could feel her energy change as only animals can. It had gone rigid, forceful, everything one would expect from a first parent. It was a deliberate act that forced Sundale's ears to shift back a moment in submission. Another tiny smile suggested that was exactly the response she was looking for.

"You'll have your private time," Doctor Blount said. "More than I'd care for I suspect given your request for private quarters. But as long as you spend time being social, even if it's only with one other person, I'll be content. Though, Captain, no matter what, you'll have to convince me you're ready before I let you back into the field. If I have any doubts at all, you will remain grounded. Understood?"

It was this forcefulness that made the decision easy. Doctor Blount wasn't trying to force him down a path or make him just get over it. She was setting boundaries, then letting him roam free within them. Few humans would understand why this was actually calming. In an odd way, it grounded him. Made him feel like he need only follow her, and he'd be okay. Strange that in the span of minutes, Doctor Blount had learned something Jason didn't fully understand and Yarain had apparently forgotten. This newfound understanding left no question which of the bad choices Sundale liked the most.

"Understood," he said. "I'd like to be near you."

Doctor Blount nodded with another tiny smile. "Then I'll see you after your first physical therapy session on Thursday. We'll work on other meet up times later. Until then, Captain, you're free to leave."

"Thank you, Doctor Blount."

"Call me Jannet. If we're going to be near each other, I'd rather drop the formalities. And don't worry about regs. A few properly worded medical recommendations will make sure you stay on board for the duration of your recovery."

"Very well. Thank you."

Sundale left without another word. He didn't bother to see if Jannet was insulted by it, but if she was going to spend time with him, she was going to have to get used to how holdrens did things. In his mind, the conversation was over, and he had no reason to remain. If Jannet wanted to say something more, she could have stopped him.

Since she didn't, Sundale made it all the way to the lift without saying another word to anyone. The only conversation he had was with PAICCA, and even that only enough to check on his request for private quarters, and if granted, where it was.

Turns out he had gotten his request, except Sundale couldn't stop a quick cringe when he recognized the deck. It got worse when the lift doors opened, and he was literally nose to nose with the one individual he couldn't face right now.

"Sundale!" Yarain said. *"I'm glad I... what's wrong?"*

Sundale tried and failed three times to form words. He had no answer to give. At least, not one he felt he could inflict on her. So, he went with the next best wound. He walked past her without saying a word in either language. She called after him, first in words, then a set of quick barks like the ones he gave Jason. She barked her call twice, but he kept moving since he no had words, or barks, to offer her.

He had even less for Jason when he came out to check on the barking. Sundale kept walking as if he weren't there. He had to. If he stopped or even slowed for a second, he'd be caught in a conversation, the very idea of which had his gut turning into a pretzel.

However, holdren ears are hard to turn off.

"Oh," Jason said. "So that's... Sun? Hey, Sun, where are you... Sundale? Captain!"

Three corridors down, or the equivalent anyway, Sundale walked into his room along the outer hull. Unlike Jason's group leader accommodations, this room was little more than a double bed, a bathroom, a space in the wall for working with a computer, and just enough table space to squeeze at most four humans close to the window for a meal. Sundale had heard humans compare it to a "budget hotel room" though having never been in one, he couldn't say how accurate it was.

"PAICCA, enact privacy mode," Sundale said. "Block calls that aren't medical or duty related. Add an exception for Doctor Blount."

"Understood, Captain," PAICCA said. "I have a vital message here from operations. Do you want me to bring it up?"

"Read and paraphrase."

"You will need to wear the jump suit and wrist com provided while on board as the *I.C.V. Alamo* will still be entering combat. The quartermaster promises the former is holdren friendly."

"Any idea when the next engagement will be?"

"Baring ambush or sudden order, two days at the earliest. We are currently in space considered to be clear of enemy forces."

"Thank you, PAICCA."

Sundale glanced at the folded jumpsuit and wrist com sitting on the bed. His stomach again churned. It wasn't quite his uniform but being solid blue with his name and rank on it made it close enough. Too close for him to deal with right now. He turned away, feeling like he was walking away from a funeral.

He dragged himself to the loveseat closest to the window, where he laid with his head on his paws looking out. As he often did, he wondered if any of those stars were his. Maybe if he could recognize the shine, he could finally find the home he'd lost. The home he needed.

A Scorn flew by, breaking his thoughts before they could form. For a second, part of him yearned to return. Then it twisted as he remembered how close he'd come to betraying it. How close he'd come to betraying *them*, his pack. The very ones who just a minute ago were barking at him to stay near them. A request more dangerous than they knew.

If holdrens could, he would have shed tears as the silence pressed into his fur. There was no wild. No pack. No one there to lick his wounds or to call for him. There was only a small room and scars beyond the one over his eye. *"A scar is nothing more than pain left behind."* How hollow his own words felt now that there was no one there to comfort him in his pain.

Deep down, he knew it was his own choice, and maybe even for silly reasons. But for that night, until sleep took hold, he could only search for a way to come to terms with the last victory Admiral Solez had achieved.

His choice or not, he was now... alone.

The End... for now.

About the Author

Forest Wells is an author with dysgraphia, but those things don't go together, which is why he did it anyway. He specializes in stories that focus on the emotions and personal journeys characters face regardless of the genre he's writing. All of which is fueled by his deep passions for all things wild canine, sci-fi and fantasy, and really any well told story. When he's not writing, or helping with his parent's Girl Scout troops, you'll find him watching his favorite NFL and NHL teams, watching E-sports, or gaming himself. Assuming he's not caught up in the biggest of all procrastinating tools: Twitter. His first novel "Luna, The lone Wolf" was released in April of 2019, but he had a few short stories and poems published in anthologies before that. He currently lives in his home town of Thermal, California.